The Rossington Inheritance

MARY TANT

Death at the Priory

Threshold Press

First published 2008 by
Threshold Press Ltd, Norfolk House
75 Bartholomew Street, Newbury
Berks RG14 5DU
Phone 01635-230272 and fax 01635-44804
email: publish@threshold-press.co.uk
www.threshold-press.co.uk

British Library Cataloguing in Publication Data
A catalogue record for this book is available from the British Library

ISBN 978-1-903152-17-1

Designed by Jim Weaver Design
Printed in England by Biddles Ltd, Kings Lynn

For dear Sammie
who was with me
when I wrote this book

Rossington manor and priory

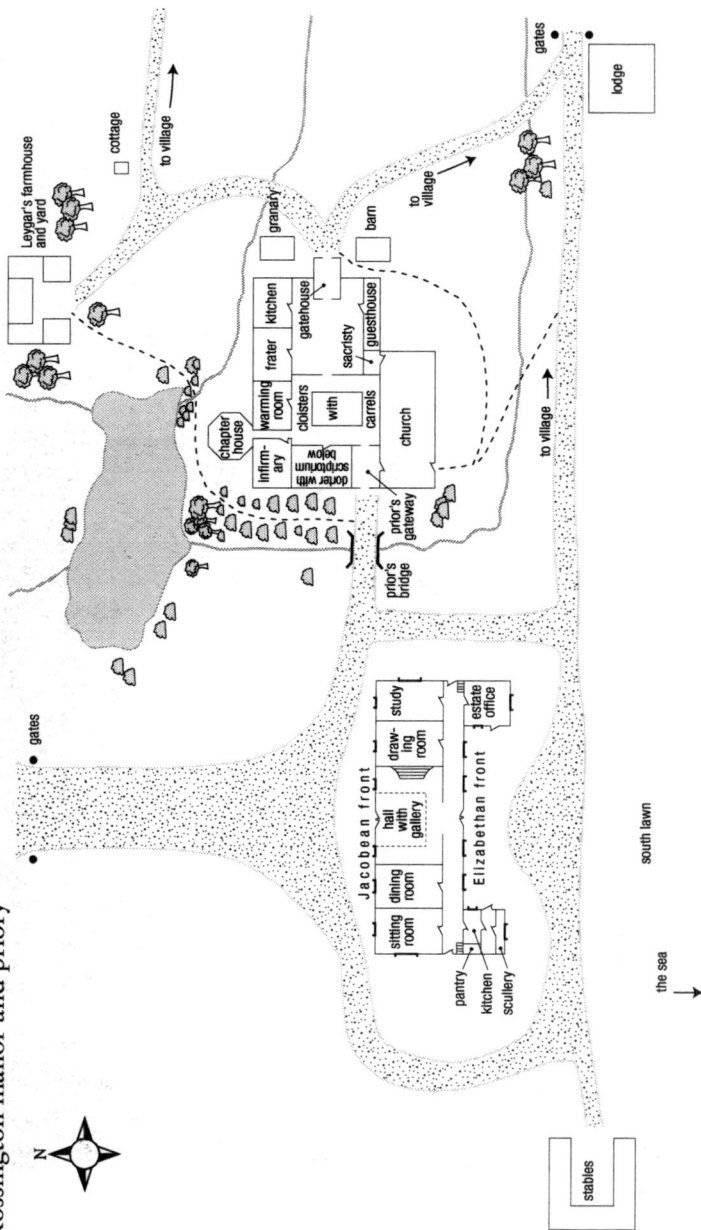

N

Leygar's farmhouse and yard

cottage

to village

granary

kitchen

gatehouse

frater

warming room

cloisters

with

chapter house

infirm-ary

sacristy

carrels

church

guesthouse

barn

to village

dorter with scriptorium below

prior's gateway

prior's bridge

to village

gates

gates

lodge

Jacobean front

study

drawing room

estate office

hall with gallery

dining room

Elizabethan front

sitting room

pantry

kitchen

scullery

south lawn

the sea

stables

Roscombe village

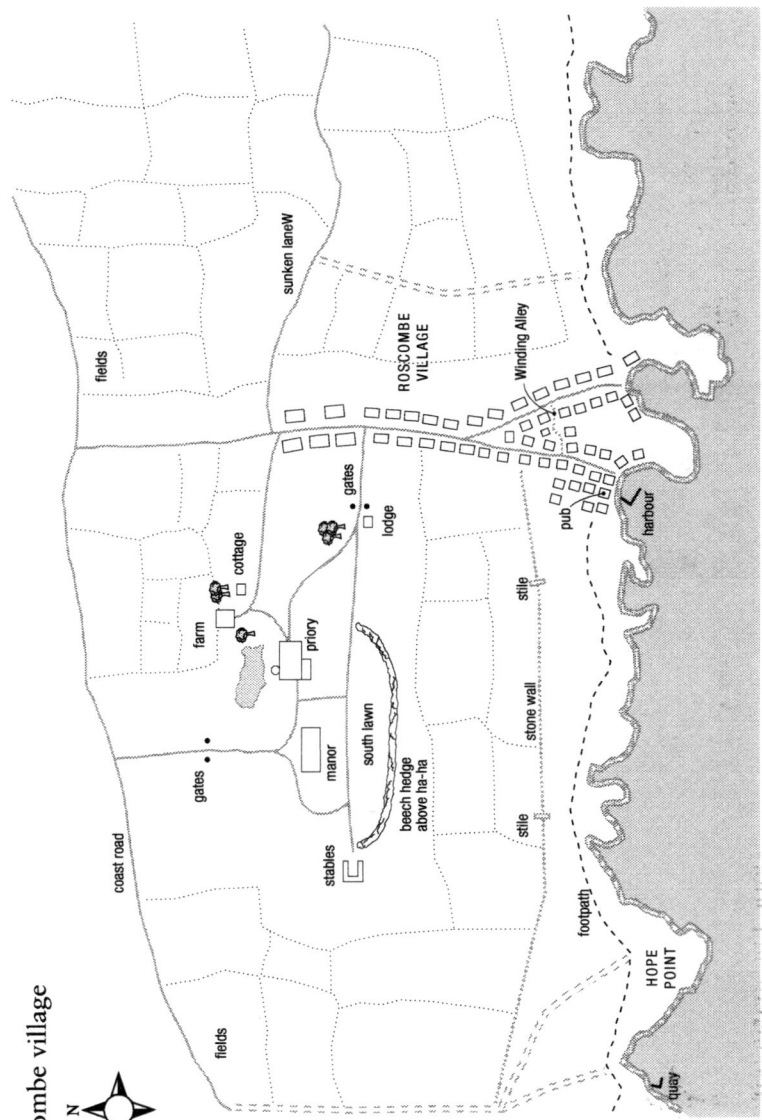

N

coast road

fields

fields

gates

stables

manor

south lawn

beech hedge
above ha-ha

priory

farm

cottage

gates

lodge

stone wall

stile

stile

footpath

HOPE
POINT

quay

ROSCOMBE
VILLAGE

sunken lane

Winding Alley

pub

harbour

ONE

The group of people straggled along the gravel track, their dark clothes in stark contrast to the white Jacobean front of the manor house ahead. Lucy Rossington was already climbing the shallow porch steps and as she reached the top the young man accompanying her pushed the heavy front door open and stood still, looking down at Lucy, whose slender figure barely reached his shoulder. 'This is going to be hard work,' he said grimly.

'Yes, I know,' she murmured ruefully as she entered the hall, which was gloomy in the late afternoon light. 'Leave the door open, David. Would you let Gina know we're back? It might be easier if we ply them quickly with plenty of tea and sandwiches.'

He nodded and strode thankfully along the western corridor to the kitchen wing. Lucy pulled off her velvet hat and tossed it onto a shelf under the gallery stairs, then slipped out of her long coat and hung it carelessly on the crowded rack. She smoothed down the skirt of her black dress and ran her fingers through her chestnut hair, pushing it away from her face. Turning back towards the front door, she glanced in the gilt-framed mirror that hung on the wall, lifting her pointed chin and pinning a resolute smile on her lips.

She stood just inside the doorway, hidden in the shadows of the room, and looked out along the gravel track that led to the old priory buildings. Mike Shannon was almost at the foot of the porch steps and Lucy felt a spurt of amusement as she realised that the archaeologist was subduing his normally exuberant pace with some difficulty. His companion, a stout man in his late thirties, wore an expression of sombre disapproval with the ease of long practice and Lucy's brief sparkle died as her gaze fell on him. Beyond them the remaining mourners advanced singly or in constrained pairs towards the house.

For a moment Lucy felt they were all unreal, just silhouettes against the bare branches of the trees and the polished green of the rhododendron bushes. Sudden harsh cawing shattered the impression, and a flock of rooks appeared over the tower of the small church they had just left. Calling raucously to each other they circled the tall beeches and began to jostle for roosting space in the branches.

She pressed the main light switch, bringing to sudden glowing life the mullioned windows and the half-panelling on the stone walls. Mike, his voice abnormally polite, was encouraging his companion to enter the house, and she stepped forward, squaring her shoulders.

'Yes, do come straight in, Professor. It's rather chilly now the sun is going,' Lucy tried consciously to infuse a note of welcome into her voice.

'Indeed it is,' he responded, stomping across the threshold. 'Weather's on the turn if you ask me. We'll be having snow soon.' She took his hat and overcoat as he removed them and passed them to Mike, who looked at them blankly.

'Come through to the drawing room,' Lucy invited the older man, who was rubbing his hands briskly as he stared crossly at the empty hearth. 'Our housekeeper's lit a fire in there, so it will be warmer. Professor Shannon will bring the others through as they arrive.' She glanced meaningfully at Mike, who nodded vigorously and turned away to the coat rack. Professor Mersett hesitated, and Lucy smiled at him. 'Tea is on the way; I'm sure you could do with a hot drink and something to eat after your long journey.'

'One doesn't care to dwell on such things at a time like this,' he said pompously, 'but there's no denying that a little sustenance would be most welcome. No doubt the students will think so.' He trod firmly beside her towards the drawing room and Mike expelled his breath in a huge sigh, which was probably clearly audible in the passageway.

'Old fool,' he muttered, carelessly throwing the coat and hat he still held onto a carved chest as his attention was caught by the woman entering the hall. 'Liz,' he exclaimed, 'I've emailed Archison about that painting he's working on at Frenham. I only saw it briefly when I was over there, but I'm pretty certain the design is almost identical to what you've uncovered.'

'That will be interesting,' Liz said in her gentle voice, while she hung her coat up neatly. 'How soon do you expect to hear from him?' She pulled Mike's coat off his shoulders as she spoke and he shrugged out of it absently.

'This evening, of course.' He looked down at her, his blue eyes widening in surprise. 'There isn't any reason why he should dither about it. Either there's a strong similarity or there isn't.'

'Mmm,' Liz murmured, her eyes following the line of the shallow stairs up to the gallery that ran around the hall. 'This is what's mentioned in the architectural guides, isn't it?'

Mike grunted, and Liz unwillingly drew her gaze away from the upper floor. 'Where are we supposed to go?' she asked, glancing round the room. 'Do you know?'

'The drawing room,' Mike replied gloomily, gesturing vaguely towards the eastern end of the house. 'Lucy's already there with that fool Mersett.' He turned as the remaining mourners came into the hall, huddling together just inside the doorway. 'Ah, here you are at last. There's no need to hang around. Let's get this over.' He beckoned them to follow him and turned abruptly on his heel.

Liz gave up trying to tidy the soft hair she had tied into a loose chignon, and took Mike by the arm, steering him out of the hall. 'Dr Archison can probably give me some useful tips anyway. He is an expert in the field, after all.'

Mike snorted. 'Him! More like a fussy old woman. Still,' he added grudgingly, 'he does know his stuff, but I wouldn't have thought he could teach you much.'

Professor Mersett broke off his conversation with Lucy as the group entered the drawing room, where golden flames rose from logs burning on the stone hearth, sending flickering shadows over the cream-coloured walls and russet curtains. He called across to a man with a liberally freckled face at the head of the small band of students, 'Ah, here you are, Hamilton. Come and meet Mrs Carey.'

Mike swung round from his animated conversation with Liz. 'Miss Rossington,' he said sharply, and Professor Mersett stared at him blankly. 'She's Miss Rossington,' Mike repeated, enunciating his words with insulting clarity.

The professor's heavy cheeks flushed, and Lucy intervened swiftly, 'Yes, I use my own name, not Hugh's.' She smiled at the men beside her. 'It confuses a lot of people to begin with, but they soon get used to it.'

Professor Mersett stared at her disapprovingly and restrained himself from commenting with a visible effort. 'Yes, well,' he said stiffly, 'I'd like to introduce Dr Hamilton to you. He's kindly agreed to take over the student party for the remaining months, so that Professor Shannon is free to concentrate on the excavation. It's particularly good of Hamilton, as he's in the middle of writing an important paper.' A loud snort from the direction of the window attracted his attention and he tightened his lips, before turning to say, 'Ah, Shannon, I believe you already know Dr Hamilton.'

'Of him, yes,' Mike said, turning to stare at the freckled man who was speaking quietly to Lucy. Mike carried on loudly, 'He wrote that paper about the Alam excavation.' His tone clearly expressed his opinion.

Professor Mersett pressed his lips together so tightly that

they were almost invisible.' Yes, that's so,' he said. 'It put forward some very interesting ideas, and certainly makes him a strong contender for the chair of archaeology.'

Mike's expression was incredulous, but he was prevented from replying as Duncan Hamilton turned towards them. 'If that's so, it will be an interesting contest,' he said calmly, holding out his hand to Mike, who gripped it absently. 'I've looked forward to meeting you, Professor Shannon. I found your comments on my Alam paper interesting. Wrong, of course, but stimulating.'

There was a hushed silence in the room where everyone had been listening, openly or covertly, to the conversation between the three men. The group of students clustered by the long table in front of the window had been gazing with approval at its laden surface and now turned to stare at Dr Hamilton with awed faces. One of the girls beside David had a smile on her lips, but many of the others started visibly when Mike broke the silence with a terrific bellow.

He roared with laughter and slapped Duncan Hamilton's shoulder. 'Well, man,' he said when his laughter subsided, 'if you're wrong in your assumptions, that's certainly the way to carry it off.'

'I imagine it's the way you practise yourself,' Duncan said.

'Naturally,' Mike nodded, 'it would be, but I haven't had to yet. What you failed to grasp at Alam is one of the basic principles of excavation.'

Liz turned to the man who had just slipped into the drawing room and come to stand near her, nervously chewing his thumb nail. 'Well, that seems to be alright. Mike likes nothing better than a good argument about archaeological principles.'

The man stared at her in surprise. 'He likes to be right, that's all. He's incredibly overbearing,' he added resentfully, glaring across the room at Mike, 'and he can't ever let anyone else express an opinion. Do you know what he said to me the other day?' He broke off as Gina appeared, her brightly flowered pinafore fluttering around her as she wheeled in a trolley bearing large pots of tea and coffee. 'At last. I thought we were never going to get a drink.'

He walked quickly over to the table, waiting impatiently while Gina unloaded the trolley. He picked up one of the coffee pots and was about to pour from it when Lucy spoke, making him start and spill some of the coffee onto the white tablecloth. 'That's kind of you, Steven. Would you like coffee, Professor, or would you prefer tea?'

'Tea would be very nice, thank you, Mrs...er...mm. I don't really approve of all this coffee drinking. Not good for the nerves,' he said, glancing at the coffee stain on the tablecloth.

Steven sullenly poured out a cup of tea and handed it to Lucy, who passed it to the professor.

'How is your own work going, M...er....mm?' he asked her as they moved to stand close to the hearth, where he turned his back to toast against the flames. She stared at him in surprise and he smiled smugly. 'I was at a dinner party last week, and one of the other guests was Miles Raden. He was very enthusiastic about the project you're engaged upon. I gather the Trust sponsored you against a lot of competition.'

'I see.' Lucy's face lit up with enthusiasm. 'Miles is very good about it, because it's going to be rather a long-term project. It basically involves recording the types and locations of coastal flora in the south-western peninsula, and identifying the various fauna species connected with each plant. Once we have a clear picture of the whole ecosystem we'll have a better idea of which elements of it are in most danger. Then of course we can work out a viable means of management and conservation for those areas.'

Lucy broke off with a gesture of apology. 'I'm sorry. Once I get started I can talk about it endlessly.'

'Only natural, M...my dear.' Professor Mersett smiled benevolently at her. 'An important project,' he continued. 'I'm sure it will be most useful when you've completed the work.

Are you based here?'

'I have an office upstairs,' Lucy said. 'Hugh, my husband, works in the study next door,' she gestured at the east wall of the drawing room, 'but our work takes us both away quite a bit. I'm glad I was here when the accident happened. David, our estate manager, is very competent but he hasn't been here very long. It would have been rather unfair if he'd had to cope with it all on his own.' She looked towards the young man with the rugby-player's physique, who was deeply engrossed in conversation with a couple of girls from the excavation. Sue, after a second's thought Lucy remembered the name. She's the one with that shock of tow-coloured hair and those ultra-modern narrow spectacles, who's really only listening to David with one ear. And the chubby one next to her must be Josie, the one he knows from home.

Lucy's mind was brought back with a jerk to the professor as he said with deep distaste, 'Yes, indeed. A most unpleasant business all round. I can't understand why John Brett was walking on the cliffs at that time.'

'He was a keen walker, you know,' Lucy said, 'and I think he often liked to get away on his own.'

'I can certainly understand that,' the professor commented, glancing at Mike whose body was taut with energy as he listened to Duncan Hamilton.

'Perhaps,' Lucy said noncommittally, 'but I think he was very worried about his private life.'

'Yes, yes, of course.' Professor Mersett frowned crossly. 'A great pity his widow didn't choose to be present today. I suppose she is his widow, even if they are separated.'

He paused to select with care a turnover from the plate Lucy offered to him. He bit into the crisp pastry and munched away with obvious appreciation, gazing round the room as David came over to put more logs on the fire. The majority of the students were clustered together at the far end of the table, conscientiously working their way through Gina's pies and cakes, and occasionally talking among themselves in subdued voices. They had obviously done their best to subscribe to funereal convention, wearing their better jeans and less bright jumpers. Sue had even donned a dark green dress lightly splashed with white flowers, which only conflicted marginally with the green and blue frames of the narrow rectangular spectacles which perched on her nose. The chubby Josie she was chatting to had matched her spiky black hair with the black lace bow she had tied onto her denim jacket.

David dusted his hands and moved back towards the students, passing Steven who stood morosely nearby, fidgeting with his shirt cuffs. Steven scowled after David and stepped forward. He said something to Sue and put a hand on her arm, obviously attempting to turn her away from her companion. She replied briefly, moving so that his hand dropped as she swung back to Josie, who laughed as Sue said something quietly to her.

Steven retreated to the window, turning his back on the gathering dusk outside to focus his resentful glower on Mike. Professor Mersett observed him for a while before looking at Lucy. 'One of your chaps?' he enquired, nodding slightly at Steven.

'Yes, he's here to catalogue my father's books. Daddy was something of a bibliophile, and Hugh made us aware that he had acquired some rather valuable books.' She added, as the professor seemed to be waiting for more, 'Steven is very efficient.'

'No doubt, no doubt,' the professor agreed. 'But he doesn't appear to feel very friendly towards Shannon. Not,' he added dryly, 'an uncommon situation, of course.'

Lucy glanced at Steven and then back at the professor, who was watching her. 'Mike unwittingly referred to something that occurred in Steven's previous job, and Steven took umbrage.' She sighed in exasperation. 'He's rather over-sensitive about it, because Mike certainly didn't know at the time about any connection with him.'

'Hmm. No, I suppose Shannon wouldn't be subtle. If he has anything to say, he says it straight.'

Lucy's lips twitched and the professor smiled at her with some reserve. He was silent for a while and then he said abruptly, 'Well, I suppose you know your own business best.' He took another turnover and looked round the room again, his eyes coming to rest on the group of students. 'Do you see much of them?'

Lucy followed his gaze. 'The students? A bit, but not a great deal. Enough to tell them apart.'

'They all look much alike to me, except young Sue,' he confessed, looking round for the girl with the tow-coloured hair, who had joined the two archaeologists on the far side of the room. 'She's got quite a flair for her subject. Tell me, has this business disturbed them very much?'

Lucy did not answer immediately. After some careful thought she said, 'Well, yes, I think John Brett's death upset them, especially the way in which it happened.'

'Naturally,' Professor Mersett said impatiently. 'It, er, upset me too. But what I mean, as I think you know, is will they miss him? Will it affect the project?'

Her face clouded. 'No, soon I don't think any of them will notice that he isn't around. Or if they do, it may be with some sort of relief.'

'Ah, thank you, my dear. He could be difficult and I have suspected that students sometimes found him rather overbearing.' The professor frowned. 'And I know he had a lot of problems working with Shannon. He complained about it several times.'

Lucy hesitated, and then said reluctantly, 'I can only speak from a very superficial knowledge, as I really didn't see much of him. But it did sometimes seem to me that his instructions could be inconsistent and that the students rather resented this. And of course Mike doesn't like anything that delays the excavation.'

'Naturally. But we won't have that problem with Hamilton. He's a very sound man, very sound indeed.' The professor glanced over to the far side of the drawing room, where Duncan Hamilton stood listening to Mike with a faint air of amusement. 'He's good with the students, and it even looks as though he may be able to cope with Shannon.'

'You sound as though it's too good to be true, Professor,' Lucy said.

He looked down at her soberly, 'I hope it isn't, my dear Mrs, er, Miss Rossington. Ah, no thank you, no more to eat.' He waved away the cake she offered him, and glanced first at his watch and then at the window where the dusk was merging with a light evening mist into a opaque greyness. 'I really should be going if I want to catch the through train.'

'Of course. David will run you to the station.' She caught the young estate manager's eye, and he came over to her side with barely concealed relief. 'David, the professor has to go now.'

'Fine,' he said cheerfully. 'I left the car in the courtyard so we can get straight off.'

'That's very good of you,' Professor Mersett said. 'I must just make my farewells.' He walked firmly across the room, and David planted himself by the door, peering surreptitiously at his watch. He straightened up as the older man rejoined him and shepherded him diligently out of the room.

The professor's departure was clearly regarded as a signal for most of the archaeological party to leave, and they straggled out in his wake. Steven lurked in the window seat, half-hidden by the thick curtains, as Mike turned to Duncan, obviously ready to carry on their conversation. Duncan shook his head and held out his freckled hand in farewell. He walked over to Lucy, saying briskly, 'I won't stay any longer, but I'm very pleased to have met you. I hope to see some more of you, and to meet your husband soon.'

'We'd like that,' Lucy replied. 'Hugh should be home in the next couple of days.' A thought struck her. 'What would you think about coming up with the students for drinks one evening? Or would that seem too thoughtless in the circumstances?'

'Not at all.' Mike said over Duncan's shoulder as he picked up another pasty from the table. 'Just what they need. Don't you agree, Hamilton?'

'Yes, I think it's a good idea,' Duncan said. 'They do seem a bit strained. And, after all, it is nearly Christmas.'

Mike looked startled as he brushed crumbs from his chin. 'What? Good Lord, so it is.' He made a face at Lucy, who was laughing at him. 'Does this mean Will's coming back on vacation?'

'Of course. He'll be here tomorrow, and Gran some time next week.' She turned to Duncan. 'Will is my brother. You're likely to see quite a lot of him during the holidays.' Mike snorted with laughter. 'He's very interested in the work you're doing.'

'He can be a pest,' Mike said bluntly, running one hand through his unkempt red hair, 'but he has the makings of a decent archaeologist in him. He's worth a bit of trouble. Look, Hamilton, I'll come along with you and show you the cottage. I suppose you're taking over the place that Brett had?'

'I believe so,' Duncan replied, glancing enquiringly at Lucy as Mike strode away from them.

'Yes, we thought that was best,' she said. 'I hope you don't mind. It's on the back lane to the village, between the priory and the farm where the students are lodging. Gina packed up Brett's personal things and sent them to the university, and she arranged for somebody from the village to clean the place.'

'That's just fine,' Duncan said. 'It's very good of you to take so much trouble.' He smiled at her as Mike put his head back round the door, glaring impatiently. 'I'd better catch up with Shannon, before he comes to collect me.'

Later that evening Lucy's face was taut with concentration as she stared at the location chart she was colouring on the computer. The office curtains had not been drawn and the velvety black night sky was visible, with stars glittering above the cliffs.

Completely unaware of the view, Lucy looked round her desk
and then shuffled through the papers piled on its surface. Where
on earth did I put my notebook, she thought crossly, yanking
out one of the drawers. Ah, here it is.

She started to flick through the pages, backwards and forwards, sighing in exasperation. The grandfather clock in the hall
began to chime the hour and she glanced at her watch, realising
with a start of surprise that it was nine o'clock already. Maybe
I'd better not do any more this evening, she pondered, tucking
a stray strand of hair behind her ear. It doesn't seem to be going
very well anyway. Her stomach rumbled loudly in the silence of
the room. Lord, she remembered suddenly, I hope Gina's casserole has survived.

She shut down the program she was working on and began
to sort through her scattered papers, stopping abruptly as she
heard footsteps. That's odd, she thought, frowning, I didn't
expect Mike to leave Duncan Hamilton so soon. The footsteps,
light and even, drew nearer. Lucy clutched a pile of papers as
she turned in her chair and listened to them approach. The
handle turned, the office door opened silently and she stared in
surprise at the man who stood there, his brown corduroy trousers and tweed jacket blending with his own colouring.

She sprang to her feet, dropping the papers she was holding.
'Hugh!' She went quickly forward, both hands outstretched,
and was gathered firmly into his arms as he bent his head to
kiss her.

She leaned her head against his shoulder and he buried his
face in her chestnut hair. 'Mmm, you always smell of honey,
Lucy.'

'Flower shampoo, that's the secret, you know.' She drew
fractionally away from him. 'Hugh, I wasn't expecting you so
soon. Did something go wrong?'

'Not exactly. The chap I was hoping to see about his
Bauhaus thesis couldn't make it, so there wasn't any point in
hanging around.'

She studied him warily. 'You haven't come back because of Brett's death, have you?'

Hugh's mouth twisted sardonically. 'Lucy, I know you're perfectly capable of managing anything. I've come back because I didn't want to waste time in Oxford when I could be here – with you. Is that acceptable?' he asked, an eyebrow raised in query.

Lucy put out a hand and rubbed his cheek apologetically. 'Yes, I think I find that quite acceptable.' She put her head slightly on one side, regarding him quizzically. 'Though I'm surprised you aren't more interested in what's happened here.'

'Well,' he drawled deliberately, 'I confess to feeling left out of things.' He abandoned the affectation and spoke urgently, 'Lord, Lucy, I'm starving. Is there anything to eat in the house or must we go out?'

'As it happens, you're in luck. Gina left a casserole in the Aga, and I haven't started it yet. Mike rang to say that he was eating at the pub with Duncan Hamilton, so there should be plenty for us both.'

'Good.' He glanced at her desk, and bent to pick up the papers she had dropped on the floor. 'Have you finished here?'

'Not really, but I was just clearing up when you came in. It hasn't been going very well.' She sounded irritable as she took some of the papers from him.

He laid the last ones on the desk and took her arm, steering her towards the door. 'That's the lot. I'm glad you weren't carrying plates if that's the effect I have on you.' He considered her slender figure thoughtfully as they went down the west stairs. 'You aren't usually so jumpy. Is this business bothering you?'

She shook her head impatiently and then smiled ruefully. 'Probably,' she admitted, pushing open the door into the large kitchen and bending down to fuss the big black dog who rushed over to greet them. 'But I think it's more today's events.'

'Okay, let's eat and you can fill me in on what's been going on.' Hugh caught the big dog's front paws as he leaped up.

'Down, Hades!' Hades lowered himself reluctantly onto the flagstones near the table while Hugh went to the Aga, opened the oven door and sniffed the air appreciatively. 'Mmm, that smells good.'

Lucy crouched to fondle the little brown and white spaniel who had approached her more sedately. 'Juno will be glad to see Gran again,' she commented, seating herself on one of the benches as the little dog pottered back to curl up on the bean bag under the table. Lucy sat quietly, leaning her elbows on the table with her face propped in her hands as she watched Hugh take the casserole out of the oven and spoon large helpings onto two plates. The kitchen was one of her favourite places and she relaxed slowly, enjoying the glow cast by the lamps dotted around the room. Hades shifted, propping his head heavily across her feet as she looked round at the familiar white walls, lined with gleaming copper pans and moulds. The herbs hanging from the airer rustled as Hugh walked over to the wine rack. A faint dusty smell of thyme and marjoram drifted across to Lucy, conjuring up memories of her grandmother picking the fresh herbs for Lucy's bridal flowers one sunny June morning earlier in the year.

She fingered the well-worn wood of the old pine table, looking up welcomingly as the bench opposite creaked with Hugh's weight as he sat down. They were companionably silent while they ate the first mouthfuls of Gina's casserole, and then Hugh gave a sigh of satisfaction and stretched out a hand for his glass, sipping gratefully at the wine. 'What happened today?'

Lucy swallowed some of her own wine, savouring the flavour as it slid down her throat. 'The funeral was okay, and so was the gathering afterwards. David and I were a bit afraid that was going to be difficult, but it actually went very well. He was a great help, and Mike was on his best behaviour.'

She looked at Hugh, a touch of anxiety darkening her hazel eyes. 'David was going to take Professor Mersett back to the station, but when they went out into the courtyard they found that two of the Land Rover tyres were flat. There were nails in them.'

Hugh raised his eyebrows in surprise. 'And who has David upset?'

'I don't think it was particularly aimed at him,' Lucy said. 'Duncan Hamilton left his estate in the courtyard too, and it had the same problem. We found several more nails scattered across the back drive.' A gamine smile lit her face. 'So Mike had to fetch his own car, and as he was determined that the professor shouldn't miss the through train, I imagine it was some drive.'

Hugh grinned, and then drew his brows together as he considered what she had told him. 'Somebody may have been careless,' he said, 'rather than malicious.'

'Perhaps.' Lucy sounded dubious. 'But two tyres on each car doesn't sound accidental to me. And wouldn't they have said something about dropping the nails, when they realised what had happened?'

'Too embarrassed, probably, or even scared,' Hugh said, passing the bread board over to his wife. 'Who is Duncan Hamilton? And why is Mike pubbing with him?'

Lucy took a piece of crusty bread and wiped up some of the succulent gravy from her plate. 'He's John Brett's successor. And Mike is presumably filling him in on the dig and what they've found.'

'Did Mike know him already?'

Lucy chewed her bread thoughtfully and swallowed it. Hades sighed and got up pointedly, sauntering over to curl up with the little spaniel. 'No,' she said. ' I don't think they'd met before. Professor Mersett seemed amazed that he got on with Mike, but I think they'll work well together, even if they don't always agree.'

'Nobody agrees all the time, especially with Mike.'

'I know,' she said. 'But the rows with Brett made life rather unpleasant for everybody, especially the students. I don't think anyone here is really going to miss him, you know.'

'He was incompetent,' Hugh said bluntly. 'Mike would never tolerate that. And he didn't have a particularly, ah, endearing personality either. But what happened to the man? Did he actually fall off the cliff?'

'It seems that he must have done,' Lucy replied carefully. 'Apparently he received a letter from his wife, finally and absolutely refusing to consider a reconciliation, and he went walking. He used to go up on the cliffs a lot, you know. A sea mist came in quite suddenly that day while he was out, and he must have lost his footing on that particularly narrow bit near Hope Point. I was at the stile myself when the mist came down. I waited for a while as Hades had rushed on ahead, but as it obviously wasn't going to clear quickly I called him back and came home.'

Hugh frowned. 'Did he jump?' he demanded.

'No,' Lucy replied slowly. 'It didn't look like it, and the coroner brought in a verdict of accidental death. They found traces of soil and grass under the nails of both hands, so it looked as though he had tried to catch hold of something to save himself as he fell.'

Hugh's mouth twisted. 'Poor devil.'

'Everyone was a bit shaken at the inquest,' Lucy said. 'Even Mike was subdued.'

Hugh cocked an eyebrow. 'But life goes on?' he asked softly.

'It does.' Lucy sounded sad. 'Especially at the dig, almost as if nothing had happened.'

'Was he buried here?'

'No. The funeral service was here, but his body was taken over to the crematorium. The university arranged it all, as he didn't seem to have any family, or at least any who cared. His wife didn't even come to the service.'

'Poor devil,' Hugh repeated. He glanced at Lucy over his glass. 'Did they all come back here?'

'Not the vicar,' Lucy replied, 'but everybody else. It went quite well, really.' She smiled reminiscently. 'Professor Mersett is actually rather a pet.'

'Oh?' Hugh was interested. 'He didn't strike me like that when I met him.'

'I expect you haven't got the right approach,' Lucy chided him.

'Perhaps,' Hugh conceded. 'I'll evaluate yours next time.'

'Next time!' Lucy exclaimed, horrified. 'I hope there won't be another.'

'He won't come just for funerals. He's bound to come down again, if the dig goes on for as long as Mike expects.' Hugh considered his wife's head, bent studiously over the remains of her meal. 'Lucy,' he said quietly, and she looked up reluctantly to meet his eyes. 'You don't think it was an accident.' He made his words a statement rather than a question.

She stared at him, and then said, 'I don't know it wasn't.'

'But something bothers you about it,' Hugh persisted. 'Come on, what is it?'

'That's just it.' She sounded puzzled. 'Something struck me as being wrong, but I don't know precisely what it was.' She got up and moved the kettle onto the Aga. 'I was probably just picking up on the general atmosphere of strife.'

'Hmm,' Hugh helped himself to a large piece of the apple pie that Gina had left on the table and absently poured cream over it. He looked up at Lucy. 'Have you mentioned this to anyone else?'

'No,' Lucy replied, a trifle shamefaced. 'It seemed silly to discuss it when I can't point to anything specific.'

'Then don't say anything. To anyone, not even Mike.' A thought struck Hugh. 'And especially not to Will. He's due home soon, isn't he?'

'Yes, tomorrow. But Hugh, I don't really know there was something wrong about Brett's death,' Lucy expostulated as she put boiling water into the coffee pot.

'No. It's quite possible that you've been affected by the doom and gloom that seems to have hung over the dig, but you aren't usually fanciful.' Hugh smiled affectionately at her as she put the coffee pot on the table and sat down again. 'Anyway, there's nothing to be gained at the moment by mentioning vague feelings, without any solid facts. And should there be something to find it would be wiser not to alert anyone at all.' He looked at her grimly. 'And safer, Lucy.'

A cold shiver rippled through her body. 'But you surely don't think it could involve Mike?'

'No, of course not. But Mike would certainly think it was a great joke, and can you imagine him keeping it to himself?'

'No,' she admitted, and then stared at him, suddenly appalled. 'Hugh, we're taking this seriously. It's ridiculous! I'm sure nothing's wrong really,' Lucy ended emphatically.

Hugh nodded. 'Fine. Just don't mention it.'

She poured out two mugs of strong black coffee, pushing one across to Hugh. 'Christmas looks as though it's going to be fun,' she said, deliberately changing the subject. 'I met Colonel Evesleigh the other day.' She smiled delightedly, remembering the scene as she added milk to her coffee. 'He was riding Sabre on the cliffs and got the most awful shock when he saw me crouched among the rocks, peering into the crevices for plants. He obviously thought I was quite mad.' Hugh chuckled. 'He said Anna's coming home for Christmas. Won't she be interested in the Dudley letters, even if they aren't authentic?' She blew gently on her coffee and sipped it, then glanced at him curiously. 'Did you show them to anyone?'

'Yes, to a couple of people,' Hugh replied. 'There's a certain amount of subdued excitement, but a great deal of caution, of course. No one's prepared to commit themselves to a definite opinion until they've carried out a lot of tests, which is only to be expected. I've brought the majority of them back, but left four there for authentication. If they are genuine we'll have to leave the rest with them to be examined. But in the meantime I'd like to make transcriptions of them.'

Lucy pulled a face, and he smiled understandingly. 'I'll enjoy it, you know, and it will be easier for Anna to read them from a printed copy. When are we seeing her?'

'Oh, I invited them both over for Christmas day,' she said blithely.

Hugh groaned, and Lucy looked at him in astonishment. 'But Hugh, you like them.'

'I like Mike too, but bickering between him and Anna for the whole day won't improve Christmas.'

'Oh nonsense, Hugh, it isn't that bad,' Lucy protested. 'Anyway, they haven't seen each other since Anna went to Paris, so maybe they'll get on better now.'

Hugh stared at her in disbelief, but before he could say anything the courtyard door banged loudly. The black dog shot to his feet, barking furiously, and raced out of the kitchen and along the corridor to the hall.

The little spaniel lifted her head curiously as they heard Mike restraining the dog's excitement, 'Down, Hades, you great brute, get down.' He stamped along the corridor and threw open the sitting-room door, grunting in disbelief as he saw the empty room. He burst into the kitchen, talking as he came, 'Lucy, I can't believe you're still eating. Has this damned dog been out today? He's…' He broke off with a shout of surprise, 'Hugh! Man, what are you doing here? We weren't expecting you for a couple of days yet.' He strode across the room and thumped Hugh on the back, beaming with delight. 'What a damned good thing you're back. Do you know what that fool Hamilton is planning to do? He wants to give the students time off over Christmas and the New Year! Ten days! Ten whole days! The man's a fool!'

He paused for breath and Lucy said quickly, 'Well, I expect most of them will want to go home and nearly all of them live quite a distance away.'

'Why on earth would they want to go home?' Mike demanded.

'Most people do, Mike,' Hugh assured him. 'I should think

Hamilton is just making the best of it.'

Mike looked unconvinced, but Lucy gave him no chance to continue. 'Well, Anna's coming home for a break, and I was just telling Hugh that I've invited her and her father for Christmas day.'

'Who are they?' he asked, his face blank with incomprehension.

'Mike!' Lucy was outraged, and Hugh began to laugh. 'You can't have forgotten Anna.'

'I don't see...' Mike began haughtily, and then turned indignantly to Hugh. 'What the hell are you laughing like a mad hyena for?'

Hugh struggled to control the laughter that was bubbling up inside him. 'Do you remember the priory chalice, Mike?' he asked.*

'Of course I do,' Mike said crossly, sitting down heavily on the bench beside Hugh. 'A beautiful piece of work. My blood boils whenever I think of how close that rat nearly came to getting away with it.' He scowled until a sudden look of ludicrous dismay crossed his features. 'Oh God!' he exclaimed. 'Not,' he turned to Lucy and spoke almost pleadingly, 'not that god-awful woman. You don't mean her, do you?'

'Mike!' Lucy was torn between indignation and laughter.

'Christ,' he muttered, pouring himself a mug of coffee, 'it's enough to make me visit my family.'

'Well,' Lucy began stiffly, but Hugh spoke over her. 'Come off it, Mike, you enjoyed every minute of every row you had with Anna at Easter. You two were probably the only ones who did.'

Mike was glowering into his mug, and muttered, 'But the woman's impossible. Now, if only she were more like Liz it wouldn't be so bad.' Lucy hid a smile as Mike's head jerked up. 'Hugh, you haven't seen the painting that Liz is uncovering

---

* See *The Rossington Inheritance* (Newbury, Threshold Press 2007)

on the chancel wall. I'm convinced it's of the same period as Archison's find at Frenham.' He brightened and swung round to Lucy. 'That's it, of course. Let's ask Liz for Christmas, too.'

Lucy looked at him in some surprise. 'Is she staying here then?'

'Yes, she mentioned it when she joined us in the pub. That would make the bloody day bearable.'

Hugh looked at Lucy, a query in his eyes, and she shrugged. 'I don't mind, if you don't. We'd better find out what Duncan Hamilton is doing too. Oh,' she suddenly remembered, 'I told him we'd have all of them up for drinks before Christmas. We'd better arrange an evening for that. It'll be when Will's back and he'll enjoy it.'

Hades lifted his head eagerly at the sound of his master's name. 'Yes, he'll be here soon,' Lucy promised him affectionately.

Mike spoke before Hugh had time to say anything. 'Good, I'd like Hamilton to meet your little brother.' His smile was tinged with malice.

'Christmas day is a fortnight tomorrow, isn't it? Well, why don't we ask them for next Thursday? Would that suit you?' Hugh asked Lucy.

'Yes, that would be fine. Gran is likely to be back by then too.'

'Let's hope she isn't bringing anyone for Christmas as well,' he said wryly. 'We aren't missing anybody out, are we?'

'Well,' Lucy began reluctantly, 'I haven't asked Steven what he's doing...'

'God!' Mike exploded. 'We haven't got to have him, have we?' He glared at Lucy. 'What the hell is wrong with him? He came to the pub with Liz, but wouldn't come across and join us. Not that we wanted him,' he added frankly, 'but the fool just sat at the bar, drinking himself into a stupor and gawping at us, when he wasn't trying to paw young Sue. Fortunately, he's chosen the wrong student there. That one won't stand any nonsense.'

Lucy hesitated and then said, choosing her words carefully, 'I think he misunderstood something you said about that business at Kingsley Hall. He thought you were implying that he was involved with the theft there last year.'

Mike snorted. 'The man's a fool. Still,' he added, 'if he's that sensitive about it, I could really think he was involved. Only he's too stupid. It seemed a pretty skilled job to me. The police haven't traced the books, have they?'

'No,' Hugh replied, 'nor the person who stole them, which does make life difficult for Steven. I know he'd been having difficulty getting another job when I came across him.'

'I'm not surprised,' Mike declared, crouching to stroke Juno as the little spaniel rolled appealingly onto her back. 'But I'm not having him staring at me like some malevolent zombie. I'll land him one if he doesn't pack it in.'

'I'll speak to him,' Hugh said, trying hard not to laugh.

'Well,' Mike growled, 'perhaps I should.'

'No, no,' Hugh declared hastily, 'it'll be easier for me to do it. And what's all this about the Walbury Chair of Archaeology? I hear you've applied for it. You've been keeping that quiet, haven't you?'

Mike straightened up and stared at him. 'Of course, I'd forgotten you've been in Oxford.' He shrugged. 'It's a good career step, but,' he frowned, running a hand through his hair, 'I suppose I'm not convinced about it. I've always suspected that you'd be buried knee-deep in bloody papers and committees and never get any real work done.' He grinned. 'I haven't decided whether I really want it, you see.'

'You're sure it's yours, anyway?' Hugh asked, his eyes gleaming with amusement.

'Of course I'm sure,' Mike said. 'As far as I know the other applicants are only Mersett,' he snorted, 'and some woman from York. I gather Hamilton is in the running as well, so that will make it a bit more interesting. Brett,' he added as an afterthought, 'put in for it too, poor sap.'

Hades suddenly whined and placed his paw on Mike's knee. 'Look,' he said abruptly, 'this damned dog needs a walk. I'd better take him down to the lake otherwise we won't get any peace.' He stood up and Hades sprang to his feet, his long tail wagging furiously. 'Come on then, you wretched hound. Let's go.' Hades bounded into the scullery corridor and scratched at the back door while Mike pulled on his boots and coat. Juno pottered over more sedately and the door slammed behind the three of them.

'Hades has been out twice with me today,' Lucy said, 'but Mike persists in thinking he's under-exercised.'

'It gives him the excuse to go out himself,' Hugh explained. 'He enjoys it much better if he feels forced to do it.'

Lucy drained her coffee mug and put it down. 'I'm glad you're back, Hugh. You won't mind having all these people for Christmas, will you?'

'Not really. It does sound as though it's going to be a lively festive season. Lord,' he put his own mug down with a bang, 'I'd almost forgotten.'

Lucy looked at him, her head enquiringly on one side.

'I had an interesting chat with Tom Purchell about the lecture series he's been giving on housing and the environment. He's interested in putting his notes together for a monograph.' Hugh caught himself up. 'I'll tell you more about it later, but he also gave me the name of a chap who's beginning to make a name for himself with his plans for conversions of historic buildings. Talmage, Anthony Talmage.' His mouth twitched. 'A very exquisite Brideshead figure. You'll enjoy him. I had a chat with him, and he's coming to have a look round on Tuesday. I've asked him to stay Monday night.'

'Oh, Hugh, no,' Lucy groaned. 'We haven't even decided what we want to do.'

'I know. But it won't matter; he can get an impression of the place and give us some ideas to think about. He's actually coming down on Monday to look over an old farmhouse near the estuary, so it seemed silly to miss the opportunity to get him here.'

'We are talking about the priory conversions, aren't we?' Lucy asked suspiciously. 'You'd better tell Mike and David too.'

'Of course I will,' Hugh said. 'I want to get Anthony to look at the stables as well, but I don't think they'll be suitable, Lucy.' He leaned across the table. 'We must decide what we're going to do. Now that business is picking up I can't run a publishing company from the study. I need a permanent base and,' he spread his hands 'room to expand.'

'What's wrong with the stables then?' Lucy demanded.

'Lucy, don't be stupid,' Hugh said, rubbing his forehead wearily. 'Will isn't going to want us around in a few years' time, and I don't want the expense and trouble of an upheaval.'

'Will won't want us to go,' she said stubbornly. 'It's my home too.'

'But it's his house,' Hugh pointed out, 'and his property. He may have his own ideas about what he wants to do with it.'

Lucy got up abruptly, pushing her bench back gratingly across the flagstones. 'Look, Hugh, I don't want to talk about it now. Let's think about it another time.' She stalked out of the room, her face set coldly, and left him sitting at the table, staring after her.

Hugh rubbed the back of his neck before getting up and walking out to the hall, where he picked up the bulging briefcase he had left under the stairs and carried it down the far corridor to the study. Switching the lights on, he shut the door behind him, and then walked across the thick rug to lay the briefcase on the desk between the windows. He closed the red brocade curtains before taking a key out of his pocket and opening the briefcase.

From it he withdrew a large manilla envelope stuffed almost to bursting point, and half extracted from this some stiff papers covered with a fine sprawling handwriting. He ran a quick eye over them, and then pushed them carefully back into the envelope and put it in the top right-hand drawer of the desk, locking it and replacing the key in his trouser pocket.

TWO

Lucy leaned on the huge boulder, staring out across the sea that lay beyond the end of Hope Point. Foam-crested waves rose and fell with hypnotic regularity on the blue water, highlighted with turquoise, which gleamed and sparkled in the winter sunshine. Anna Evesleigh stood nearby at the edge of the cliff, her hands tucked into the pockets of her scarlet duffle coat, her black curls blowing in the wind. In the distance a swirling flock of gulls circled in screaming anticipation around a couple of fishing boats that had put out from Roscombe harbour, and birds on the cliff ledges below her took off purposefully to join the noisy throng.

Anna drew a deep breath as she lifted her face full into the wind until her long hair streamed out behind her. 'How I've missed this,' she said. She turned to her friend and smiled at the expression of amazement on Lucy's face. 'I know, but it's quite true. I think I've been homesick for the cliffs, and the sea, and the moors. Oh,' she gestured around her, 'I don't know. Maybe I just need a break.'

Lucy shook off her own thoughts and turned round, pressing her back against the rock as she said sympathetically, 'I should think you do. The show's been running for nearly six months now. It's a great success, isn't it?'

'Yes, it's likely to run for some time,' Anna replied flatly. She displayed none of the euphoria which might have been expected from a relatively unknown actress whose name had been made by the production.

'Your Madame de la Motte Valois has been well reviewed everywhere,' Lucy persevered. 'Your father even subscribes to a cuttings agency, you know.' Anna's face did not lighten at this revelation and Lucy scanned it, trying to read the expression on it. 'Don't you want to carry on with the part?' she asked cautiously.

'I don't know.' Anna looked bleakly at Lucy. 'I've got a number of other offers. Parts I'd have given my eye teeth for a year ago.' She fell silent and Lucy waited, a niggle of concern beginning to make itself felt in her mind.

'And now?' she prompted at last.

'And now I don't want any of them.' Anna's mobile features twisted briefly into a grimace of irritation. 'There's nothing at all wrong with them, but somehow they just don't seem to be enough.' She turned to stare out at the sea again, and there was a long pause. 'Do you remember Edouard?' she asked suddenly.

Lucy nodded as she recalled the gaiety and laughter of the brief summer visit she and Hugh had made to Paris. The Frenchman was not, she reflected, likely to be easily forgotten by any woman. Then, realising that Anna was not looking at her, she said, 'Yes.' Thinking this a little bald, she added, 'He was charming. Hugh liked him too.'

'He wants me to marry him,' Anna said in an expressionless voice.

Lucy glanced at her in surprise. She was puzzled, and the niggle of worry squirmed harder. Anna did not sound at all like her impulsive, vivacious self. 'I see,' she said carefully. 'Are you going to?'

She was startled when Anna swung round and said rather desperately, 'That's just it, Lucy. I don't know, I just don't know.'

'Do you love him?' Lucy asked bluntly.

'I tell you, *I don't know*,' Anna said. She clenched her hands inside the coat pockets. 'I always thought I'd just know when it was the right man,' she tried to explain. 'I always have before. They've been fun and I've liked them very much, but I always knew there was no more than that in it for me.' She shrugged elegantly. 'Edouard is a darling, and he's being very patient. He thinks I'm worried about losing my career just as I'm being recognised as a good actress, and he promises that he would never stand in my way. But it isn't that. I'm very fond of him, but I don't know if that's the same as loving him.' She looked pleadingly at her friend. 'Lucy,' she said tentatively, and then stopped. Lucy met her eyes encouragingly and Anna went on hesitantly, 'Lucy, how did you know about Hugh?'

'Well, I just did.' Lucy saw that Anna clearly thought her answer was unhelpful. She tried again, 'It was as if I recognised him as soon as I saw him.' She glanced round the cliff-top reminiscently. 'It was here, you know, that we met for the first time.'

Anna was, most unusually, frowning and Lucy went on quickly, 'It can't be the same way for everyone. Look, Anna, it sounds to me as if you've been overdoing it, and that's probably why you're feeling so undecided about everything. Why don't you just shelve it all? Enjoy being here for a bit, and see if things sort themselves out.'

Anna regarded her thoughtfully, and then the tension seemed to drain out of her. 'Yes, that's a good idea, Lucy. I'll take it as time out and let nothing bother me for these few weeks.' Her dark blue eyes began to sparkle. 'It will be fun to spend Christmas with you, just like when we were children. Do you remember the year we got stuck in the snow drift down by Leygar's Farm? We got back for lunch dripping wet, and your father didn't even notice.'

Lucy began to laugh. 'Yes, and how worried he was later when he found pools of water in the hall. He thought the roof had started to leak. Mind you, I can see now why he didn't think it was very funny.'

'Is the house still a problem, Lucy?' Anna asked as they turned away from the glittering brightness of the sea and began to walk slowly back across the uneven turf, skirting the clumps of gorse which still bore a scattering of yellow flowers. 'I've been so busy maundering on that you haven't had a chance to tell me what's been happening here.'

'Well, we're surviving, which is the main thing,' Lucy said. 'Will still goes to Gudwal's and not the local sixth-form college, rather to his regret. But if he passes his driving test he'll probably come home for weekends. Hugh is signing up some prestigious authors and I'm working on the Coastland Project. We aren't going to be rich, but we're mostly managing to do what we want. Except for Will!' She added, 'And the roof's been repaired, so we don't have to rush around with buckets and pans every time it rains.' She glanced at her friend. 'You've no idea how nice it is to be able to lie in bed and listen without any qualms to the rain drumming on the slates.'

'A lot's happened to us both this year,' Anna remarked. 'You certainly never thought you'd end up doing this when you left university. Do you ever regret giving up the chance to go to South America?'

'No,' Lucy replied without hesitation. 'The manor was far more important than anything else.'

'Well, Daddy reckons you've done wonders. I gather you've got things marching along pretty well. What happened about the tourist teas?'

'Oh, they've been quite successful,' Lucy said, 'rather to everyone's astonishment.' Including mine, she thought with a flash of humour.

'How on earth do you manage them too?' Anna asked.

'Oh, I don't,' Lucy said. 'I ran them at Easter but when my work with the Wronham Trust expanded I got Gina Bretton to take them over during the summer. She was at a bit of a loose end with both her sons gone, and I think she was glad to have something new to do. Gran worked with her at first, but Gina took to the whole thing like a duck to water. We had to put extra tables on the South Lawn and use the hall too by the end of the holiday season.' She smiled mischievously. 'It was one of the best things I ever did, you know. She's somehow become a housekeeper cum cook for us as well, and we eat like lords all the time. Will swears that he'd starve if he didn't take a hamper of her best goodies back to school, and when he's here he haunts the kitchen more than ever. So does Hugh for that matter.'

'Of course it just goes to show,' Anna said as they reached the top of the cliff path. 'If you hadn't stayed to put the manor on its feet you wouldn't have met Hugh. I suppose it's been difficult for him though.'

Lucy stopped and stared indignantly at her as the wind buffeted them, pulling at their clothes and lifting their hair in floating clouds. Anna gave a gurgle of laughter. 'I don't mean you, stupid, although I know you can be pretty stubborn. But it must be hard to try and run his business from here. Still, I suppose it won't be long before Will takes over for himself.' She glanced at her friend curiously as they moved on. 'What would you do if you had to choose between Hugh and the manor?'

Lucy kept her face expressionless, but anger surged inside her, strangling her voice. Even Anna, she thought, gritting her teeth, why does everyone have to make things so complicated? Why should I have to choose? A coldness invaded her stomach and she bit her lip, realising that Anna was looking at her expectantly. Before Lucy had time to say anything a plump woman came into sight struggling up the crooked path, hampered by the long thick skirt that the sea breeze wound tightly about her legs. 'Oh, hello, Tilly,' she said unenthusiastically. 'We don't often see you up here.'

The woman looked up, startled. 'Heavens, Lucy. What a shock you gave me.' She struggled vainly to control the filmy scarf that surged about her throat, writhing as if it were alive. One hand began to twiddle with the wispy curls that straggled round her red-veined cheeks, while her bloodshot eyes gleamed with hostility as she stared at them.

'I thought I'd come out for some fresh air.' Her light breathless voice faded into a titter. 'I suppose that's what you're doing. I think it's very brave of you to still come here. I do admire you so much.' She looked at Anna brightly. 'Of course, it's so nice to have support, isn't it? Although I'm sure we didn't expect to see you back, Anna, now that you're so famous, and rich as well, I suppose. And the place really doesn't have happy memories for you either, does it?'

She paused to catch her breath, and Anna said sweetly, 'But then, Tilly, I had a wonderful childhood here, so it would take more than one or two unpleasantnesses to spoil it for me.'

The look of hostility deepened in Tilly's eyes as her fingers tightened on her curls. 'How nice for you,' she said, adding pointedly, 'and of course there's so much going on, isn't there? How lucky that I've bumped into you. Edie Shade is staying with me, you know, and she is so interested in what you're doing. She couldn't come out with me because she had some things to do, but she said she'd catch me up. She's a very strong walker.' She looked behind her, but nobody else was in sight. 'I'm going to bring her up to see you, Lucy. She's a famous psychic, you know, and she feels very deeply about the work you're doing at the priory. She can tell you a great deal about it. I believe it's a ley crossroads, or something of that sort, and very important.'

She paused and a figure seemed to materialise behind her, startling Lucy and Anna. 'Tilly,' the woman said sharply, 'you don't understand what you're talking about.'

Anna smothered an urge to laugh, and glanced at the other woman with amusement. This died instantly as she met the stony black eyes set in the narrow white face. She was thickset and taller than any of them, and probably in the same age bracket as Tilly, the mid-to-late thirties. Her dark hair was cut severely short, emphasising the general air of oppression that she exuded.

'I'm Edie Shade,' she said in a harsh voice. Her eyes

narrowed as she regarded Lucy. 'You live at the manor.' It was a statement rather than a question, and she went on without waiting for a reply. 'It's fortunate that I've met you. You don't realise what you're doing at the priory. It's most dangerous.'

'Oh dear,' Lucy murmured lamely, and immediately felt how ludicrous the words sounded. She rallied and said swiftly, 'You must come up and tell us all about it. Sometime after Christmas would probably be best. We can't stop now, though, as we want to get back for lunch.'

She stepped forward as she spoke and Tilly stood aside with obvious reluctance to let them pass, tightly clutching the folds of her thick skirt against her legs. Edie was less easily moved, standing in the centre of the path so that they had to tread through the heather to get round her. She was frowning and they could feel her black eyes fixed on them as they resumed their downward stroll.

'Phew!' Anna let out her breath as soon as they were out of earshot. 'What a poisonous woman! Who on earth is she?'

'I've no idea,' Lucy said. 'Tilly's always having the most peculiar people to stay. Can't you just imagine the conversations they have?'

Anna stared, then a smile curved her lips as she said, 'I hope I'm here when they come to visit. I didn't realise Tilly had stayed in the village. Does she still paint those ghastly plates and cups and things?'

'Yes,' Lucy replied, adding fairly, 'They're actually very popular, you know. She's quite a good artist, even if we don't like what she does.'

They both fell silent, pausing on this part of the cliff path as the manor household usually did. They were dressed in a similar fashion: Anna, a head taller than her friend and nicely rounded, in smart blue jeans and a patterned designer jumper under her bright duffle coat. Lucy was slight and boyishly slender in shabby black jeans and a loose fisherman's jumper whose soft green shade complemented her chestnut hair and lightly tanned skin, and accentuated the emerald flecks in her hazel eyes.

Surrounded by the piercing clamour of an alarmed wren they looked down on the valley where the red brick south front of Rossington Manor glowed warmly in the clear winter sunlight. This façade of the house and the two wings that stretched out from it, flanking the flagged courtyard, were still obviously Tudor in origin, built by Harry Rossington when he acquired the old priory and its lands from Henry VIII. It was only the north front, not visible from where they stood, that had been altered when a later Rossington had added the white Jacobean façade and portico. Fortunately, the current Rossingtons felt, the family tastes had not generally run to architectural improvements, and nor had the family finances.

Beyond the house to the north, scattered clumps of trees stretched their bare branches starkly black against the clear blue sky, and the lake formed from the old priory stews shone like polished steel. When the trees were in leaf it was not possible to see the farm buildings to the north east of the lake, but today faint glimpses of the farmhouse and barns were visible through their protective barrier of gnarled old oaks.

In the east, plumes of smoke were torn from the chimneys and blown across the sky above the uneven tiled roofs of the village. A flock of gulls wheeled in a far field, trailing a diminutive tractor as it valiantly ploughed the rich red earth, and the wild high cries of pied lapwings drifted up to them from the meadows below the cliff path.

Lucy turned suddenly, thinking she had heard a sound behind them, but there was nobody to be seen. Heavens, she thought ruefully, that woman has made me edgy.

Anna was staring towards the mass of buildings that she knew had been the old Cistercian priory, which stood between the manor house, once the home of the prior, and the farmhouse. They lay south of the lake and beyond the brook, whose course was marked by a ragged line of bushes and trees that obscured most of the priory from view. From here she could only see the crenellated tower of the small church, as well as part of the roof of the dorter on the west side of the complex.

'Did you ever get anywhere with the dig?' Anna enquired casually as they started walking again, leaping lightly down the rocky outcrops in the path as they made their way towards the stream at the bottom of the narrow valley.

Lucy turned to look at her in surprise. 'Surely you knew work started on it just after you left in the spring?'

'Oh yes,' Anna agreed. 'But what happened?'

Lucy marshalled her thoughts and attempted a clear explanation of the months of complicated work. 'Well, they've been working on the basic layout of the main buildings around the cloister garth. Now Mike has got two groups working separately, one there on the scriptorium and carrels, and the other in the entrance courtyard around the guest house and what he thinks may have been the sacristy.'

Anna stiffened, her eyes widening as she said sharply, 'Mike! Surely you don't mean that dreadful man who was here at Easter?'

'He's in charge of the dig,' Lucy explained. 'But there are quite a lot of other people involved, so I don't expect you'll see much of him.'

'That will suit me very well,' Anna said emphatically. 'He was the rudest man I've ever met.'

Lucy thought guiltily of Christmas, and then mentally shrugged. 'You'll see him on Christmas day, though. He isn't going away.' Anna stared at her blankly and Lucy said, 'He lives with us, you see, and he's spending Christmas here too.' Her lips twitched. 'He thinks it's a complete waste of time, and really doesn't understand how the others can want to leave the dig at all.'

'Lord, Lucy, how on earth do you manage with him around all the time?' Anna sounded aghast as the two women branched off from the cliff path, picking their way through the stunted willows edging the stream.

'We like him very much, you know, Anna, and anyway,' Lucy added, 'we don't see that much of him. We're both away a fair bit, and even when we're here Mike's at the dig almost every waking moment.'

'Well, let's hope it exerts its fatal fascination on Christmas day,' Anna said grimly, and then unexpectedly her brilliant smile broke out. 'But if you can cope with him all the time, I'm not going to let him get under my skin during these few weeks.'

Lucy showed no sign of the relief she felt as she climbed over the stile at the bottom of the cliff path and began to walk across the meadow towards the manor house, lapwings flying up in a designer flurry of black and white around her. Anna caught up with her and walked silently at her side for a while before asking curiously, 'What have they found?'

'Nothing else that you'd class as treasure,' Lucy replied. 'I think the chalice will have to do us in that respect.'

Anna shivered as she remembered how the priory chalice had been discovered earlier in the year, and Lucy went on, 'But lots of little things: coins, tools, pots, oh, all sorts of things. Anna, there's the loveliest clasp they found in the entrance courtyard. A golden true lovers' knot, with the initials W and A. It looked like nothing on earth when it was uncovered, but now that it's cleaned up it's quite exquisite.'

A hint of laughter appeared in Lucy's eyes as she said, 'You'd be surprised at how good we've all got at cleaning up the finds, and piecing bits of pots back together again. At first Will was a bit disappointed not to find anything more exciting, but he's got well and truly hooked on the whole business now. I sometimes wonder if he'll want to do it professionally.'

'Would it bother you if he does?' Anna asked.

Lucy shook her head, so that her hair swirled around her face. 'No. He must make up his own mind about what he wants to do. This summer he was completely engrossed in the dig, but if something else interesting comes along he'll probably be just as involved.' She looked at her watch and then turned to her friend, as they scrambled up the ha-ha and skirted the beech hedge that crowned it. 'Would you like to go and see what's been going on? There's just time before lunch.'

'Yes, alright,' Anna said, and they cut across the South Lawn. 'Who's that?' she asked quickly, looking towards the gates at the entrance to the back drive.

'Where?' Lucy demanded, stopping and turning her head to follow Anna's gaze. 'I can't see anyone.'

'I thought I saw somebody lurking by the gate piers,' Anna said. 'Never mind, there's no one there now. I must have been imagining it.'

Lucy hesitated and then followed her friend onto the gravel track that led past the estate office in the east wing. Anna peered through the window as they passed, but could see no one inside. 'You did get a new estate manager, didn't you?' she asked.

'Yes,' Lucy said. 'We had to. It wasn't long after Graham was killed that we realised it would be impossible for any of us to do his work indefinitely. We coped for a while, and then we were lucky enough to find David.'*

Anna glanced at her enquiringly, and Lucy said emphatically, 'We were lucky. We can't afford to pay much, you see, and David's very good at his job.'

'Why did he come here then?' Anna asked bluntly.

'Because we've virtually given him carte blanche to put his ideas into practice. Organic farming,' Lucy explained succinctly. 'It isn't as complicated as it seems,' she continued, 'although I think some of the farmers will need a bit of convincing. It's actually quite handy that we haven't been able to afford many improvements in the past. The farms are still generally small, and many of them are virtually run by traditional methods anyway as we've never had enough money to make changes. But David is making it all more competent and bringing it up to date. It's surprising what an interest there is in organic produce.

* See *The Rossington Inheritance* (Newbury, Threshold Press 2007)

Ours is officially only semi-organic until we get our certification, but we're already supplying quite a few outlets locally, and even Mrs Hamble takes some in the village shop.'

'For Tilly and her friends, I expect,' Anna said lightly.

They emerged onto the main track that led across the brook to the gateway whose ruined tower once guarded the prior's private route from his house to the monastic enclosure. Anna stopped abruptly on the bridge and stared at the buildings. Looming masses of dark-leaved rhododendrons screened them, so that she could only see the crenellated tower of the church to the south of the gateway and the dorter above the scriptorium on the north. 'I haven't been here since Graham was killed,' she said slowly. 'It seems much longer ago than the spring.' She stood remembering in silence, and then pushed the memories out of her mind. 'What are you doing about the chalice?' she enquired.

'We haven't decided,' Lucy replied wryly. 'It's worth a stupendous sum, you know, and at first we felt sure we'd have to sell it. We don't really want to as we all feel it belongs here, and I suppose,' she added, 'we feel Graham would have liked us to keep it.' She looked frankly at Anna. 'We may not be able to, but it might be possible if we can find other ways to keep our heads above water. In another year we may be taking paying guests in the priory. That's something else David is keen to organise under his estate manager umbrella. In fact, Hugh is showing an architect around now to discuss possible conversions, and I expect David's got involved in that too. I wouldn't be surprised if they've got it all settled between them.'

An unusual note of resentment sounded in her voice, but Anna, struck by another thought, missed it. 'Heavens, Lucy, isn't it dangerous to keep the chalice here if it's worth so much?'

'It isn't here,' Lucy reassured her. 'It's at the bank in Corrington. The British Museum conservators examined it and found they didn't need to do much to it as it was in fine condition. So we arranged to leave it in a special vault at the bank until we decide what to do with it. We'd really like to have it on permanent display in Corrington museum, although they'd have to look into the security issues. Will would particularly like to bring it back to the manor for special occasions, but we may have a replica made instead. We just haven't thought any more about it.'

They passed under the ruined gateway arch and emerged into the cloister garth where they came to a halt as Anna looked around in disbelief. For as long as she had known it the garth had been littered with carts, bales and obsolete rusting farm equipment. These had rested haphazardly between the broken masonry and truncated stumps which were all that remained of the pillars which had once supported the cloister walk. When they were children it had been an ideal playground for all sorts of games, from the make-believe adventures that Anna invented to the more mundane hide and seek.

Now every piece of farm equipment had disappeared and the top levels of soil had been carefully removed. Neatly aligned trenches had been cut across the garth, and were marked off with ropes. 'Isn't it strange, Lucy?' Anna said in a wondering tone. 'In spite of all the games we played here, I never really thought about what it was like when the monks were about.'

Lucy was staring at the ground in astonishment. 'Why is it so wet?' she demanded, pointing to the puddles that lay in the depressions. 'It hasn't rained for ages.' She picked her way carefully across the muddy soil to peer into the trenches, which had a thin layer of water along their bases.

'Maybe it's a new method of excavation,' Anna said. 'You know, save effort, wash the surface soil away, something like that.' She wandered curiously through the central arch into the western aisle of the cloisters, where the monks had worked in fine weather at the famous illuminated manuscripts which had contributed to the unexpected wealth of this isolated West Country foundation. The flags of the walk had been raised and the top layer of soil had been lifted in marked areas. It looked as though work had been going on here recently as trowels and sieves lay where they seemed to have been dropped. 'That's odd,' Lucy commented. 'I wonder where everyone is.'

'Hmm?' Anna murmured, only half listening as she peered into the scriptorium and then wandered down to look into the infirmary at the north-western end of the cloisters. The last time she had seen these rooms they were still being used as extra storage space for Leygar's Farm, and were cluttered with miscellaneous sacks and boxes. Now they stood scrupulously clean and bare. 'Have they done anything to the chapter house?' she asked, pausing at the entrance to the narrow passageway that led between the infirmary and the warming room to the octagonal room beyond. 'It was my favourite place.'

'No, not yet,' Lucy replied, glancing at her watch. 'Look, come through to the gatehouse and I'll show you quickly what's been found. Mike uses the tower room above the entrance as an office cum finds room.'

They picked their way across the muddy garth into the entrance courtyard, which was perfectly dry. The old frater and kitchen lined the north wall, but work seemed to be concentrated on the guesthouse and sacristy on the south. The gatehouse was in the centre of the eastern wall, a solid stone tower which originally had cart and pedestrian gates at both sides of the entrance porch.

In the middle of the porch's north wall there was a small wooden door, whose bleached oak was heavily studded with nails. This led into the room the porter had used, while stairs led out of its far corner up to the single room which occupied the whole of the first floor. Lucy turned the ring handle and then frowned as the door refused to open. 'That's odd,' she said, twisting the handle again and leaning against the door in case it had stuck. 'I wonder why Mike's locked it.'

As she spoke there was an outburst of barking behind them and Hades rushed towards them, his long tail lashing wildly. He ran excitedly backwards and forwards from Lucy to Anna, licking them indiscriminately. Anna bent down to fuss him and his body squirmed happily as she petted him.

'Lucy! Come and see this!' It was Will's voice, and they turned quickly at the note of excitement in it.

He was just inside the courtyard, beckoning furiously, his thin face flushed. 'Oh, hello, Anna,' he said belatedly, not quite disguising his dismay as he realised she was there.

'Hello, Will,' she replied meekly, noting that his wiry figure had grown taller than his sister's. 'What's all the excitement about?'

'Liz has found part of a another painted figure on the chancel wall, and Mike thinks more of it might have survived,' Will said eagerly.

'Liz?' Anna queried.

'She's the art specialist who's been cleaning the whitewash off the church walls,' Lucy explained briefly as they followed Will's energetic figure back towards the Prior's Gateway. 'It concealed the mediaeval wall paintings underneath and she's already found a tree of life on the nave's south wall, with amazing little figures in the branches. It's in good condition but a bit patchy though and Mike's been hoping she'll find something more complete.'

They entered the cloister garth as she finished speaking, and began picking their way round the trenches towards the church. 'Why is it so wet here?' Lucy asked Will.

'Somebody left the yard tap on overnight. Not much, but enough. We had to bale some of the trenches out.' He grinned over his shoulder at his sister. 'Boy, Mike was mad!'

Lucy was frowning as they passed through the open north-west door of the church, treading lightly over the time-worn stone step into the nave. Narrow windows filled with clear glass lit the plain interior. Winter sunshine cast faint panels of light across the flagstoned floor, and the bare silver-lichened branches of ancient oaks were visible outside, starkly outlined against a high blue sky. The aura of peace and serenity that normally emanated from the ancient building was obscured today by the buzz of noise rising from the tiny chancel bathed in bright artificial light. A cluster of people had gathered here around a narrow scaffolding tower, and at the head of them they saw Mike in his patched moleskin trousers and a baggy red jumper which clashed horribly with his tousled hair. He was examining the north wall closely, while Liz stood at his side, sober in dusty blue denim overalls, her hair slipping unheeded from its chignon.

Mike glanced over the heads of the students who were all peering hopefully round him. 'Lucy! Come and see this! Liz has found the beginnings of a large figure.'

The group of students shuffled to one side to let Will lead the two women up to the patch of wall that Mike was studying. 'See here,' Mike said without looking up again, pointing at a shape that was dimly visible against the ancient plaster. 'There's the outline of a raised hand and the curve of an arm.'

Anna and Lucy peered more closely at the indistinct marks. 'Ye-es,' Lucy said cautiously. 'I think I see what you mean.'

'Do you know who it is?' Anna asked curiously, her head tilted to one side as she tried to make sense of the worn patches of colour.

Mike glanced at her in surprise, registering her presence for the first time. 'Oh, hello, er, er,' he said unenthusiastically. 'Not yet,' he returned to her question, 'but almost definitely one of the saints. Do you know which saint the priory church was dedicated to?' he shot at Lucy.

'It's Saint Ronan now, but I don't know if it always was. I suppose we can find out.' Lucy looked at him enquiringly.

Mike nodded vigorously. 'Of course. Set that book chap, whatshisname, onto it. He might as well make himself useful.'

A flash of pure amusement crossed Anna's face, and Mike noticed it as he turned to Liz, who was waiting patiently at his side. 'Are you going to concentrate on this section?' he demanded.

'Yes,' Liz replied. 'I'll sample some more pieces of wall later, but I'd like to uncover all there is of this first.'

He nodded approvingly. 'Will it help if I assign one of the students to work with you?'

'Yes, it certainly would,' Liz said with sudden pleasure. 'If Duncan doesn't mind,' she added.

'Oh, that won't be a problem.' Mike waved the possibility away impatiently. 'I'll have a word with him, of course, but he'll appreciate the necessity.'

He glanced round at the crowd of students and then beckoned to one of the girls. 'Sue, you'll do. It'll be good experience for you.' He gestured largely at the remainder of them. 'No need for the rest of you to hang around now you've seen it. You've all got your own jobs to do.'

The students straggled slowly away, talking agitatedly amongst themselves, leaving Sue standing irresolutely on her own. Anna had been studying the painting on the south wall and she turned to Sue. 'Do you know anything about it?' she asked.

'A little,' the girl answered warily, pushing her spectacles up her nose as she considered Anna. 'What do you want to know?'

'Well, for a start, who painted it and who are the little figures?' Anna said, smiling brilliantly at Sue. 'I don't know anything at all, you see.'

Sue suddenly smiled back. 'You really need to talk to Liz or Professor Shannon, because they know all about it,' she said deprecatingly, nodding towards the couple who were engrossed in a discussion of their own. 'But it was painted in red ochre, probably by one of the monks of the priory. He may have done that one too.' She gestured towards the north wall of the chancel.

'It's a format that's more generally seen in windows, with the tree growing out of Jesse's body. Look,' Sue pointed to a blurred outline at the base of the picture, 'on the branches you see figures of prophets and biblical kings, with Christ and the

Virgin at the top. We don't really know yet who all the figures represent, but Professor Shannon is trying to get Dr Archison down from Frenham. He's found something like this on his site and he may be able to give us some ideas, as he uncovered his tree last year and has been working on it since then.'

A sarcastic snort from behind made them both jump. 'I wouldn't count on it, Sue. He's more likely to be hoping that there aren't any similarities. Especially if you and Liz uncover a complete saint's figure on this wall. He hasn't got one of those.' Mike grinned maliciously.

'Is it such a competitive profession?' Anna asked in surprise.

Mike glanced at her. 'Cut-throat,' he declared wickedly. He roared with laughter at the look on her face. 'I'd forgotten you were so gullible,' he remarked, noticing with pleasure her expression of fury, and carried on quickly before she could retaliate. 'Seriously, no, although we'd all like to find something unique, we're a reasonably co-operative lot.'

'Anyway,' Sue interposed loyally, 'the priory chalice is unique.'

Mike turned an approving glance on her. 'So it is. Ah, that reminds me,' he swung round. 'Lucy!' She glanced up from her conversation with Liz and Will and he beckoned imperiously to her. 'Lucy, most of the people working on the dig now haven't seen the chalice. It would be useful for them to appreciate the quality of the workmanship, so can you arrange for them to have a look at it?'

It was an instruction rather than a request and Lucy's lips tightened, but before she could answer Will said, 'Yes, do, Lucy. I'd like to see it again.'

'I'll have to see what the bank advises,' she said noncommittally.

'Oh, come off it, Lucy. You know damn well the bank won't want to let it out of their clutches,' Mike declared, tugging angrily at the neck of his baggy jumper. 'It's doing no good just sitting there in a vault. The workmanship is exquisite, and I'd

like to show it to old Archison when he comes too,' he finished
ingenuously.

'I suppose we could bring it out,' Lucy conceded reluctantly.
'Perhaps it's time we decided what we're going to do with it
anyway. Let's see what Hugh thinks.'

Mike glanced at his watch. 'Is he home for lunch?'

'Yes,' Lucy said shortly, adding a caveat, 'but he's bringing
Anthony Talmage, remember.' He stared at her blankly and she
said in exasperation, 'Really, Mike, you met him at breakfast.'

'Oh, him. The architect,' Mike dismissed the visitor without
a qualm. 'Hugh's been about the place with him all the morning.
I'll come back with you and we'll sort it out now. No time like
the present.'

From behind his back Anna met Lucy's eyes and pulled
a face. Mike swung round but Anna met his suspicious eyes
blandly, although she was aware that Liz had observed the
interchange. 'It will be just like old times,' Anna observed
sweetly, and saw Liz's placid face marked briefly with a tremor
of uncertainty.

'Hmmph!' Mike began to stalk down the nave between the
simple wooden benches.

He was stopped by Sue's uncertain voice. 'Professor
Shannon, should I start work with Liz immediately?'

He stared at her in astonishment and she hurried on, 'It's
just that Dr Hamilton wanted me to finish cleaning the brooch
we found yesterday.'

Mike scowled. 'Leave it. No,' he sighed, 'I suppose you'd
better carry on with it until Hamilton gets back. I'll have a
word with him then.' He stamped crossly over the worn stone
flags to the door and Lucy cast a look of relief at Anna and Will
as they followed him.

'Why the devil did the man want to go to London when he's
needed here?' Mike demanded unreasonably as they emerged in
the ruins of the Prior's Gateway.

'You know very well that he had to see his publisher, Mike,'

Lucy said patiently. 'He's taken on the dig at short notice, so there are bound to be some earlier appointments that he wants to keep.'

Anna fell behind with Will as Hades frisked around them, hopefully dropping sticks in front of them. Anna looked back at the priory and almost stumbled over one of Hades' larger offerings. 'Hades! You bad dog,' she scolded. 'I couldn't throw that even if I wanted to, and I don't.' She stepped over it but the big dog was undeterred. He picked up the stick and trotted past them, making Anna dodge to avoid being caught behind the knees by his toy. Hades ignored them and raced after Mike and Lucy. 'Your dog hasn't changed in the slightest, has he?' Anna said happily.

'No, he's just the same as ever. Watch!' Will commanded. Anna looked ahead to see Hades repeat his trick, dropping the large stick in front of Mike, who was so busy talking to Lucy that he did not notice the dog's actions. A second later he roared with rage as he tripped heavily over the obstacle, and Hades' wide mouth split in a hairy grin, his tail lashing furiously with delight. Mike picked up the stick and threw it mightily into the bushes and Hades bounded after it.

'It never fails,' Will said. 'Hades knows Mike always throws a stick for him.'

'Who is Hamilton?' Anna asked curiously. 'Mike seems to have an unusually healthy respect for him.'

'He's the chap in charge of the students,' Will explained. 'I've only just met him myself, but he seems to be alright. Better than the other one at any rate.'

'The other one?' Anna queried. 'There seem to be loads of people here that Lucy hasn't mentioned.'

'The chap before him, John Brett. He died, you know. Fell over the cliff just beyond Hope Point, where that stretch of shale is.' Will added regretfully, 'I wasn't here then.'

'When was it?' Anna asked, horrified.

'Oh, a couple of weeks ago, just before the end of term. I

wanted to come back early, but Lucy wouldn't let me,' he added crossly.

'Heavens, Will, how awful,' Anna exclaimed.

'Yes, I suppose so,' he replied. 'But Brett was a bit of a pain, you know, and always arguing with Mike. You should have heard them,' he said with relish.

'Who is actually in charge of the dig?' Anna asked, puzzled. 'I thought it was Mike.'

'He is,' Will assured her. 'But the students are here as a party from the university. Different ones come each term, but they have an archaeologist in charge of them to supervise their training or something. He's supposed to liaise with Mike about what they do.'

'I see,' Anna said. 'It sounds as though it could be a bit fraught.'

'It was,' Will assured her fervently. 'But Sue says that it's better with Duncan Hamilton.'

'How does Liz fit in?' Anna was still curious.

'Mike fetched her down to look at the church walls. I think he was already hoping to find paintings. She's okay, I suppose.' He glanced ahead. 'Come on, Anna. Gina's made chicken pies for lunch, but if we don't get a move on there won't be much left. You should see what Mike eats,' he said admiringly.

'Look!' Anna pointed to the big black dog peering round the oak door that led into the manor's hall from the back courtyard. 'There's Hades waiting for us. I haven't seen Juno yet. Is she still around?' she asked anxiously.

'Yes, but Gran only got home yesterday afternoon. Juno's ecstatically happy to have her back and hasn't left her side since.'

Hades squeezed past the door which Mike and Lucy had left ajar. He galloped to meet Anna and Will, then turned and led them purposefully back into the house. Will ran upstairs to quickly wash his hands, while Anna hung her coat up under the stairs and tidied herself in the cloakroom.

Hades waited impatiently for them in the hall and then dashed ahead of them along the western corridor to the dining room. A babble of voices came through its open door, Mike's clearly distinguishable above the rest as he described Liz's latest find. Will went straight into the room to his place at the table but Anna paused in the doorway, taking in the scene in front of her.

The dining room, half-panelled in oak, was one of the original rooms of the priory. Johanna, Lucy and Will's mother, had redecorated all of the rooms when she first came to live at the priory, and the colour schemes had not been altered since her death just after Will was born. The cream walls and soft green curtains reflected the shades of the worn rugs scattered over the polished wooden floor. Hades lay comfortably across one of these rugs in the mullioned bay window, the sunlight warming his body as his bright eyes watched Will.

The carved stone fireplace in the east wall dominated the room, in spite of the wide table in the centre at which six people were now sitting. Only one of them was unknown to Anna, a man glowering resentfully across the table from his seat between Lucy and her grandmother. Anna wondered idly if this was the new estate manager Lucy had praised so fully, sitting so appropriately beneath the portrait of the prize ram beloved of one of the eighteenth century Rossingtons. As she identified the focus of the man's glower, Mike's passing reference to the 'book chap' popped into her mind.

Hugh rose as Anna entered, interrupting Mike's monologue without compunction. He held out his arms and drew her close to kiss her soundly. 'Anna, it's good to see you. It's been far too long since you were here.'

Mike choked on the sip of wine he had just taken, and Will had to thump him hard on the back, grinning broadly all the time. Hugh raised an eyebrow in mock surprise and Anna ignored the fuss, walking gracefully in a cloud of scented air down the table to the slight woman who sat at the end of it, with the dainty brown and white spaniel at her feet. 'Hello, Gran Rossington,' she said softly, bending over to kiss the sallow cheek warmly.

The elderly woman looked up at her, her dark eyes bright with affection in the small pointed face which was so like her granddaughter's, apart from its frame of iron-grey hair. 'It is good to see you home, Anna,' Isobel said. 'Have you met Steven yet?' She indicated the man sitting to her right, who promptly rose to his feet. He leaned across the table to shake hands with Anna, eyeing her appreciatively, and revealing his own carefully co-ordinated trousers and jumper. 'He's helping us to catalogue William's collection of books. Now,' she continued, as Steven released Anna's hand reluctantly and resumed his seat, 'go and sit between those two and keep them amused.'

Anna smiled at her mischievously, subduing the urge to wipe her hand down her jeans, and moved round to her place between Hugh and Mike. Lucy sat on the other side of the table beside Steven and met Anna's eyes with complete understanding. She pointed at the sideboard, where Mike was helping himself from a variety of dishes. 'Help yourself, Anna, before you sit down. Gina has done us proud.'

'She always does,' Will said happily from his place next to his grandmother. He scowled at his sister. 'And you eat here every day, nearly,' he amended hastily, 'while I starve at Gudwal's.' He glared round the table.

Hugh said blandly, 'Doesn't your hamper last long? Judging from its weight last time you went back I thought you had more in there than we've eaten since you left.'

'Huh!' Will tried to look indignant, but could not maintain it. 'Everyone comes to share it, and it lasts no time at all,' he said regretfully.

'Look, Hugh,' Mike sat down next to Will with a plate piled high with pie, potatoes and vegetables, and returned immediately to his point. 'I know the chalice is safe in the bank, but it should be much more widely known. It's about time you decided what to do about it.'

Hugh looked quizzically at Lucy. 'What's brought this up now?'

'Mike wants to show the chalice to the students,' she said, adding with a straight face, 'and to Dr Archison.'

Mike looked slightly abashed and then belligerent. 'I do. A piece of workmanship like that should be available to scholars, and you should be making sure that it is.'

'I can't disagree,' Hugh said, 'but what do you have in mind?'

'Well,' Mike hesitated, nonplussed, running his fingers through his tousled hair.

'Lucy said you don't want to sell it unless you have to,' Anna said, a querying note in her voice.

'No,' Will said emphatically, but a trifle thickly, masticating a large mouthful of pie, 'we don't.'

'Then,' Anna suggested tentatively, 'couldn't you decide which is the most appropriate museum for it, and let them put it on show as an indefinite loan, or something like that?'

Mike regarded her with unflattering awe. 'That's an amazingly good idea.' He turned to Hugh. 'That would give people the opportunity to see it, without committing yourselves in any way yet.'

Hugh looked interrogatively at the Rossingtons, who all nodded in agreement.

'I'd prefer it to be in Corrington museum if they can upgrade their security sufficiently,' Lucy said.

'Yes, and couldn't we bring it here first so that the students can see it?' Will asked eagerly. 'Lots of them have asked me about it.'

'And Liz ought to see it,' Mike interposed. 'She'll appreciate how unique it is.'

'I know. What about when we have Christmas drinks with them all?' Will suggested.

Hugh's eyebrows drew together. 'It's a nice idea,' he said,

'but I'm not sure it would be wise.'

Will and Mike stared at him in astonishment. 'Wise?' Will asked in surprise. 'You can't think anyone here would damage it or,' he hesitated, 'steal it?'

Steven glanced up from his seat by Lucy, his face reddening and his hands clenching his knife and fork as they clattered loudly on his plate.

Anna silenced the words that had sprung to Mike's lips as she said quietly, 'After this spring, could you afford to take the risk?'

Isobel Rossington spoke firmly from the end of the table. 'I think it would be best to see what the bank advises before we make a decision. I have to go into Corrington tomorrow, so would you like me to speak to the manager then?'

Her family assented gratefully and she forestalled further discussion by turning to Anna. 'Now tell me about Paris, dear. I haven't had a chance to catch up on your news yet.'

Lucy glanced at her friend anxiously but Anna was perfectly composed. She soon had the whole table, even Steven and Mike, laughing over her parodies of some of the show's more bizarre patrons.

'I beg your pardon.' A composed masculine voice broke apologetically into the hubbub, which ceased abruptly.

The tall loose-limbed man who stood just inside the doorway was looking round with complete ease at the staring eyes. He wore his shabby tweeds with an air of distinction and Steven scowled resentfully down the table, fiddling nervously with his shirt cuff. A faint smile touched the man's mouth as he addressed Lucy and Hugh, 'I'm afraid David and I got rather engrossed in plans and I'm disgustingly late. He's bolted off to meet a farmer and I've come to see if I've fallen totally from grace.'

Hugh got to his feet without haste. 'Don't worry, Anthony, meals are generally casual here. You've met most people so I'll introduce you quickly to the others, then you can help yourself to something to eat.' He gestured to his neighbour. 'This is Anna Evesleigh, an old friend of the family.' Anthony Talmage acknowledged the introduction gracefully, moving lithely to bend over her hand. Mike's lip curled and Anthony smiled smoothly at him. Hugh continued quickly, 'You haven't met Steven Poole either.'

'Not here,' Anthony agreed, 'but we met at Kingsley Hall early last year, before that disastrous theft.' He nodded to the scowling man on the other side of the table.

Lucy intervened. 'Do just help yourself to food, Anthony.' She indicated the laden sideboard and then, as a thought struck her, she asked, 'Mike, why have you locked the gatehouse door?'

'What?' He stared at her. 'I haven't. It's never locked.'

'Well, it was just before lunch when I took Anna there,' Lucy retorted.

'It must have got stuck,' Mike said without much interest. 'I'll check it when I go down. Or maybe Sue locked it. She's been working on a brooch in there. But I can't see why she should.'

'That reminds me,' Hugh said. 'Mike, the students work on digs all over the place, don't they?'

'Of course,' Mike replied impatiently. 'Why?'

'Anthony wondered where he'd seen some of them before. Was it one in particular?' he asked the architect as he took his seat between Lucy and Hugh.

Anthony glanced at him with a wry smile. 'Yes. But she didn't seem to remember me, so I must be mistaken.'

Mike snorted and Anthony smiled agreeably at him as he began to eat quickly but neatly. After a short while Anthony leaned forward. 'It's a very interesting site, Professor. Surely the guesthouse is unusually large for a foundation of this size?'

Mike held a forkful of food suspended in surprise, before recovering and putting it into his mouth. He chewed and swallowed, regarding the other man thoughtfully. 'Yes, it is indeed. In my opinion…'

Lucy admired the architect's aplomb. Now I wonder if he noticed that himself or if Hugh mentioned it, she thought. It will certainly help him to have Mike's support for his proposals.

She turned to her left and saw that Steven was listening with a scant pretence of interest to her grandmother's descriptions of the libraries she had visited in Florence. 'How were Veronica and Martin?' she asked.

Isobel turned her bright eyes on her granddaughter. 'Very happy, and well settled in their little villa. It's really a charming place, three floors high, eighteenth century, set in an acre of ground on a hillside. There are olive trees on the slopes, they press their own olives, you know, and vines round a central pergola where they celebrate the harvest. Veronica says that in spring and summer the hillside is carpeted with wild herbs. And they're within walking distance of a small village which has the most amazing coffee shop. Everyone was so friendly I can't wait to go back.'

Lucy looked at her in surprise. 'Oh, are you going again, then?'

'Yes, in the spring,' Isobel said quietly.

Lucy was about to ask more when her attention was caught by Steven, who was fidgeting irritably in his seat. 'Do you know who the priory church was dedicated to, Steven?' she asked, searching for a topic that might hold his attention.

'No. Why should I?' he replied rudely, and her lips tightened.

Before she could speak Mike leaned across the table. 'Well, surely you can find out in one of the books. It should be easy enough.'

'I'm not a researcher,' Steven said sulkily.

Isobel thoughtfully twisted her wine glass in her fingers. 'I believe, Mike, that William once told me that it was always St Ronan. He used to tell stories about him to Lucy when she was a little girl.' She smiled reminiscently. 'But surely the diocesan library would know, wouldn't they?'

'I expect so,' Mike said.

'Well,' Isobel said to Anna, 'your father is very friendly with one of the canons at the cathedral. Perhaps he would ask how we could make sure.'

'I'm sure he'd be glad to,' Anna agreed warmly, before saying eagerly across the table, 'Lucy, listen. Anthony's been to that old farmhouse near the estuary. You know, the one set back from the Coombhaven road down a long lane, the one we always found so intriguing when we were riding over there.'

'Yes, of course, I know.' Lucy's face lit up with pleasure as she turned to Anthony. 'I didn't realise that's where you were going. Withern, that's what it's called, isn't it? Or at least,' she amended quickly, 'it was.'

'It still is,' he assured her. 'I can understand why you were fascinated by it. It's very unusual. The main house is eighteenth century, but it has a sixteenth century annexe. It's in a grim state at the moment, but that's probably rather a good thing in the long run as a lot of the original features are still there.' He glanced at Hugh. 'Large Georgian windows, for instance.'

He put his knife and fork down in his enthusiasm and began to demonstrate the layout to Lucy with his well-shaped hands. 'See, this is where the two main blocks of the house are.' He looked round in exasperation and then picked up two spoons. 'Like this.' He laid them in position as he spoke. 'There's a forti-fied farmyard with extremely high walls and a pond fed by a deep spring, so water must always have been readily available.' He arranged more cutlery as he spoke, and planted his wine-glass beside them. Then he turned suddenly to Hugh. 'It would really be much better for your purposes than the stables here, you know.'

Lucy drew in her breath sharply and the colour ran up into her cheeks.

'Why, Hugh, are you thinking of moving?' Anna asked gaily.

'I'm only considering premises at the moment, Anna,' Hugh replied. 'I'll need to establish a permanent base to operate from pretty soon.'

Will leaned forward, his eyes bright with enthusiasm. 'Well, that sounds rather fun. Just imagine what we might find there. Mike, don't you think it could be interesting?' he appealed.

'Yes, possibly,' Mike said. 'Are you going again, Hugh? I wouldn't mind coming with you to have a look round.'

Lucy got up abruptly and went to the sideboard to help herself to a baked apple. As she returned, her face set coldly, she caught her grandmother's eyes on her, puzzled and disapproving.

'Mike,' Lucy said as she sat down, and out of the corner of her eye saw Anthony Talmage glance curiously at her. Well, he needn't think it's all cut and dried, she thought crossly, I've still got something to say about it. She marshalled her thoughts as Mike stared at her impatiently. 'Mike, what happened at the dig?'

'What do you mean?' he demanded. 'Oh, the water. Some idiot left the tap outside the church on, but nobody's been prepared to admit to it. It hasn't done any damage, it's just a flaming nuisance.'

'When?' Steven sounded curious as he shifted in his chair.

Mike glared at him. 'Yesterday evening, I expect,' he said curtly. 'When we left.'

'Why don't you ask David then?' Steven asked, not quite disguising the venom in his voice. 'He may have seen somebody when he was down there last night.'

THREE

Anna leaned forward to put her coffee cup down on the table and said, 'I really must be going. Daddy will have been expecting me for the last couple of hours and I don't want him to get too grumpy.'

'Would you like to see the clasp I told you about before you go?' Lucy enquired from where she sat with her feet tucked under her. 'Or would you rather see it another time?'

'I'd like to see it now, if it won't take long,' Anna replied, stretching lazily. 'Is it down in the gatehouse?'

'No, we keep it up here. It won't take me a couple of minutes to fetch it,' Hugh said, standing up and leaving the room.

Anna sat back and looked round the sitting room at the scattered chintz armchairs, the tapestry-seated uprights favoured by Isobel Rossington and the casual jumble of books and magazines on the tables and shelves. Her eyes moved to the long sofa near the mullioned north window, which was heaped with embroidered cushions that were mostly Isobel's own work. The muted yellow walls had a warm gloss from the burning logs on the stone hearth, and the late afternoon light showed beyond the thick blue curtains at the French windows. She sighed with satisfaction. 'Nothing has changed since I was last here.'

'Well, we all like it as it is,' Lucy said idly, her face half hidden by the curtain of chestnut hair that fell over it, red highlights picked out by the light from the fire.

'Where did your grandmother go off to?' Anna asked. 'I was hoping to hear more about Florence. It sounds as though she had a marvellous time.'

'She said something about going down to the farm to see Molly Leygar. I can't imagine why she needs to see her as soon as she gets back,' Lucy replied, brushing back her hair with a wide sweep of her arm. 'She hasn't seen the clasp yet either. Oh, I've just remembered,' she uncurled her legs and stood up, 'Steven came across one of Daddy's books with pictures of jewellery like our find. I'll see if he can lay his hands on it and then you can see just how lovely our clasp is.'

Anna stared into the fire, so mesmerised by the glowing ember caverns and the flickering flames that she did not hear Steven enter the room and only noticed his presence with a start as he appeared by her chair. She smiled up at him. 'I'm sorry, I was miles away. I didn't hear you come in.'

He gave her a knowing look and offered her the large book he was carrying. 'Lucy said you'd be interested in pictures of jewellery like their clasp.'

He sounded amused and Anna felt an unexpected stab of annoyance. 'Thank you,' she said shortly, taking the book from him and laying it across her knees.

She began to turn the pages, ignoring his presence until he leaned across the arm of her chair, brushing against her shoulder. 'The pages are marked,' he said, indicating slips of paper protruding from the top of the book. He turned to a double spread which was covered with illustrations of mediaeval jewellery and pointed to one of them. 'That, apparently, is very like the clasp they've found here.'

Anna was irritably conscious of the pressure of his shoulder against hers and was about to comment on it, when Steven said suddenly, 'Look, you won't find anything more interesting to do here than this. It must be pretty dull for someone like you. Why don't you come out with me somewhere lively one evening?'

Anna shifted in her chair and said with disarming sweetness, 'That would certainly be different. But luckily I'm not as stupid as I must appear. I find all this fascinating, so I expect I'll be fully engrossed in catching up with what's going on.' She was unable to resist adding, 'Have you actually found somewhere lively to go?'

As she stopped speaking she became aware of a lowering presence in the doorway and glanced round to find Mike glaring at them, his red hair bright in the light from the corridor. Steven followed her gaze and drew guiltily back from her side, his face flushing patchily.

Before any of them could speak Hugh returned, holding a small wooden box. 'Hello, Steven,' he said, as he followed Mike into the room. 'That was clever. I'd just thought of the book myself.'

Steven muttered inaudibly and left the room, watched by Mike's sardonic eyes. Anna felt unaccountably flustered and was glad to take the box Hugh proffered. She bent her head over it to undo the catch and caught her breath as she saw the daintiness of the clasp inside.

The intricate knot was made up of several delicate strands set in a little square of gold filigree, and as Anna looked at it closely she realised that the strands made up two initials. She tried to remember what Lucy had told her they were as she traced above them carefully. 'A, and I can't quite make it out. What's the other letter?' she asked Hugh as he sat down nearby.

'We think it's W.'

'It looks more like M to me,' Anna said, bending more closely over it. 'Whichever, it's quite beautiful,' she added softly, and glanced back at the book. 'You don't really get any idea of how lovely these pieces are until you see them for real.' She was silent for a moment, looking at the clasp, and then she asked, 'Do you know who owned it?'

'No,' Hugh said regretfully, watching Mike put a large log onto the fire. 'It's a woman's girdle clasp, but we don't know any more than that.'

'But what was she doing here if it was a priory? Surely that was for monks?' Anna was puzzled, and then aggravated as Mike gave a snort of contempt.

'They had a guest house,' he said shortly, throwing himself into one of the armchairs, which creaked protestingly. 'She could have been a visitor staying there, or she may have been a local coming to a special ceremony in the church.'

'Maybe even to her wedding?' Anna asked, ignoring his tone with some difficulty.

'Possibly.' Mike said impatiently. 'Bearing in mind the design of the clasp, it's probable that it was a gift. But if she'd lost it on her wedding day she'd certainly have created a terrible fuss until it was found. It's more likely that she lost it later on, when it didn't have so much importance to her. She may have had better jewels by then, or the poor sap who gave it to her may not have mattered any more.'

Anna stared at him, her dark blue eyes wide and reproachful, and then she looked again at the delicate clasp, picturing in her vivid imagination the woman who had worn it and the man who had given it to her. She shook her head. 'I'm sure she would have minded losing it. Why would she come here if she wasn't local?'

'Well,' Mike considered reluctantly, 'we can only speculate, but the priory would almost certainly have been visited by its patrons, perhaps to discuss manuscripts they were ordering. And then the position of the priory near the coast may have meant that people stayed here while waiting for a ship to France.'

Anna digested this in a silence that was only broken by the crackle and hiss of burning wood. 'There were a lot of rebellions and uprisings in the Middle Ages, weren't there?' she enquired vaguely of Hugh at last.

'Yes, lots,' he answered, lifting an eyebrow enquiringly.

'Then don't you see how she could have lost it?' Anna looked at them both, spreading her hands wide. 'Her husband could have been one of the patrons of the house. After all he seemed to have some artistic tastes.' She gestured at the clasp in her lap. 'Then he got caught up in one of the rebellions and found himself on the losing side. He remembered the little priory so conveniently close to the coast, and came down in haste with his wife. They waited here anxiously for a boat, leaving hurriedly when one was ready to sail for France, or Brittany, I suppose.' Anna glanced briefly at Mike, who was watching her, unwillingly absorbed in the story she was constructing. 'She remembered to bring the girdle with her precious clasp, but then they left the priory so quickly, in fear, that she either forgot it or fastened it too loosely. By the time she noticed its loss it was too late to return for it, even if she could.'

The room was silent when Anna finished. She saw with surprise that Lucy had come in unnoticed while she was talking and was now perched in her favourite seat at the north window.

'I can see why you're on the stage,' Mike said, shaking his head as he surfaced from the web of fantasy that had been woven by Anna's imagination. 'There isn't an element of fact in that rigmarole.'

'Except the clasp,' said Lucy quietly, her pointed face still absorbed with the tale.

'And all the rest could be possible, couldn't it?' Anna asked Mike directly.

'It could be, of course, but we can't ever know,' he replied flatly.

Anna smiled at him brilliantly and he blinked. 'But that doesn't matter,' she said, and with unusual forbearance Mike restrained his urge to contradict her.

Hades suddenly bounded into the room and trotted round to greet each of them individually. He was followed more sedately by his master. 'Hello,' Will said. 'What are you all doing, sitting here like dummies?' He turned to Mike. 'Bert has got the door open. He said it was the most difficult lock he's had to pick,' Will grinned broadly, 'and he was glad he was doing it officially.'

'He's an old rogue,' Mike said, 'but he has his uses. It's one of the original doors and it's still pretty solid, so it would have been awkward if he hadn't been able to deal with it.' He looked across at Lucy. 'You were right about the gatehouse. The door was locked and the key seems to be missing. Do you know what time you were there?'

'It must have been about half past twelve,' Lucy said, glancing at Anna, who nodded in agreement.

'Hmm. We think Josie must have left the finds room about twelveish, when she came to see Liz's discovery,' Mike said, 'and she didn't lock the door then. None of us generally do.'

'Did anyone else this time?' Hugh asked quietly.

'No one says so, and I can't see why they should have.' Mike ran a hand irritably through his tousled hair. 'I had a chance to check out the poisonous comment that god-awful man dropped at lunch time about David being in the priory yesterday evening. David was driving down the farm track when I was trying to open the gatehouse door, so I stopped him and asked if he knew anything about the flood. He was taking the Leygar's daughter, whatshername, Philly, back to the farm last night and didn't come in to the priory at all. Of course he didn't hear or see anything relevant.' Mike was distracted momentarily. 'David certainly gets around. Last time I saw him he was leaving the pub with Josie, that chubby student with the spiky black hair.'

'They've known each other since they were children,' Lucy said. 'In fact, I think they pretty much grew up together.' She asked anxiously, 'Did you mention Steven to David?'

'I didn't have to,' Mike said shortly. 'The only person David saw was Steven, lurking under the trees. Suffering from sour grapes, I should think. He probably makes a habit of skulking around spying on other people. Although,' his eyes narrowed, 'if he weren't such a spineless lump I would wonder if that was all he was up to.'

'Oh Lord,' Lucy muttered.

Mike ignored her as he said heavily, 'And now we have Sue trying to break her neck. I'm beginning to feel we're jinxed.'

'What?' Lucy exclaimed. 'Has Sue hurt herself?'

'Oh, she's alright. More worried in case she'd broken her glasses,' Mike said. 'But they're okay, and she only jarred her arm a bit, no more than that. But it could have been worse.'

'What happened?' Hugh demanded.

Mike frowned blackly. 'Somebody moved one of the trench ropes in the north aisle of the cloisters. It's gloomy in that particular stretch and Sue didn't see it, so she tripped over it. Liz has had a good look at her arm. She's a competent woman,' he said approvingly. 'There's no real damage other than a bit of bruising, but she strapped it up and improvised a sling. I arranged for Josie to take Sue back to the farmhouse to rest for a while.'

'She's okay,' Will interrupted, turning away from the table where he had been flicking through the papers. 'She didn't want to go, so they've left her working in the finds room. It's her right arm that she hurt and she's left-handed, so she's managing fine.' As Will's eyes slid quickly away from Mike's annoyed glare he caught sight of the clasp on Anna's lap. 'It's alright, isn't it?' he asked her, walking over to look down at the piece. 'A lot nicer than the brooch Sue is cleaning up now.'

Hades followed his master and leaned his head against Mike's knee. 'How is she getting on with it?' Mike demanded, absently patting the big dog.

'Pretty well, I think,' Will said guardedly. 'Duncan had just got back and was having a look at it when I left. He's going to come up to talk to you, I think.'

Lucy noticed an odd tone in Will's voice and glanced sharply at him. Mike nodded imperviously as he looked down at Hades, who was now pawing his knee. 'Good. I'm glad he's back at last. The sooner Sue begins to help Liz the better.'

Anna took a final look at the clasp, then shut the lid of the box carefully and handed it to Hugh. 'I really must go,' she said regretfully. 'May I see the brooch Sue's working on when it's clean?'

'Of course,' Hugh replied. 'And Mike's putting together quite a collection of other finds down in the gatehouse. They're mainly pottery, but you might like to see them too.'

'Yes, I would,' she said, rather to her own surprise. 'I'll see if I can get over tomorrow.'

Lucy got up from the window seat. 'I'll see you out, Anna. There are a couple of bottles of Gina's rosehip syrup on the mule chest which she'd like you to take home for your father.'

They left the room together and walked down the corridor to the hall. Anna was taking her coat from the rack when there was a thunderous knocking on the courtyard door. She glanced enquiringly at Lucy as Hades came racing from the sitting room, barking furiously. 'Are you expecting somebody?'

Lucy said glumly, 'Only Duncan.'

'Oh, I see.' Illumination spread over Anna's mobile features. 'Trouble?'

Lucy pulled a wry face. 'I think so.' She went to the door and opened it wide to show Duncan planted squarely on the steps, his mouth set tightly in his freckled face.

'Duncan,' Lucy said warmly as Hades sniffed around his ankles. 'Come in. Never bother to knock, the door's always unlocked. How fortunate that you've come now, because I'd like you to meet a very old friend of mine. Anna, this is Duncan Hamilton, who's in charge of the students on the dig. Duncan, Anna Evesleigh is back from France for a short stay with her father, over at Moreton House.'

Anna came forward, prepared to back Lucy to the best of her considerable ability. She held out her hand and bestowed her brilliant smile on the angry man before her.

Very few men could resist Anna's charm, and Duncan Hamilton was certainly not one of them. He gripped her hand enthusiastically. 'How do you do?' he said pleasantly, his mouth softening. 'I'm glad myself that I got here in time to meet you.'

'I've just been catching up on the news about the dig,' Anna said as Hades turned away and mooched back towards the sitting room. 'It's all so much more interesting than I'd expected.'

'You must come and look round,' Duncan invited. 'It helps to see what's being done in the place.'

'Yes, I'd like that. I only had time for a quick look today. I've got to go now, but I'm hoping to come over again tomorrow.'

She kissed Lucy lightly on the cheeks, and smiled again at Duncan, whose expression had brightened noticeably. 'Perhaps I'll see you again tomorrow if you're around.'

'I will be,' Duncan promised, and it was clear that wild horses would not drag him away from the priory if Anna was going to visit it.

She pulled on her scarlet duffle coat, picked up the bottles and tucked them carefully into her deep pockets. Tossing back her long dark curls, she stepped outside and walked lightly across the courtyard to her Land Rover, which she had left by the end of the estate office. Lucy and Duncan stood in the doorway watching her departure, and returned her wave as she swung the Land Rover onto the back drive.

Duncan turned to Lucy as she shut the courtyard door. 'A very nice woman. An old friend of yours, you said?' She nodded and he asked casually, 'How long is she staying with her father?'

Lucy concealed a smile. 'Until the New Year, I think. She has a leading role in *The Queen's Necklace*, which is running very successfully in Paris, so she finds it difficult to have much time off.'

Duncan was clearly interested. 'Surely she's English, though?'

'Oh yes. But her mother is French and Anna is fluent in the language,' Lucy explained. She hesitated fractionally, then went on, 'She and her father are spending Christmas with us. We used to alternate between each other's houses every year when we were children, so it will be rather like the old days for us. If you aren't going away we wondered if you'd like to join us.'

'That would be very nice,' Duncan said at once. 'I'm grateful to you. I was planning to go to my sister in Melrose, but it would be good not to travel all that way.'

'We'll be having quite a party,' Lucy commented deliberately. 'I haven't asked Liz yet, but I know Mike is staying.'

Duncan's face clouded. 'Ah yes, Mike. It was him I wanted to see. Will thought he would be about up here,' he finished interrogatively.

'Yes, he's in the sitting room,' Lucy said. 'Come and see him.' Now, should I say something about this business and try and soothe him down a bit, she wondered as they walked along the corridor. No, it's probably better to leave them to sort it out themselves. 'Would you like some tea?' she asked instead. 'Gina will be bringing it through shortly.'

'That would be nice,' he replied absently.

Lucy opened the sitting-room door and ushered him in. 'Mike, here's Duncan to see you. Duncan, this is Hugh, my husband,' she said.

'Ah, Hamilton,' Mike said, sitting up straight in his armchair as Hugh got to his feet to shake hands with Duncan. 'I wanted to see you.'

Will stood toasting his rump in front of the fire and met his sister's eyes meaningfully, ignoring Hades as the big dog turned round and round on the hearthrug, scratching it up into a heap that he settled heavily onto with a sigh. Lucy grimaced, then basely left the room, murmuring about tea.

'Have you seen what Liz has found on the north wall of the chancel?' Mike demanded.

'I haven't seen it yet,' Duncan replied, planting himself four-square in front of Mike, 'but I've been hearing plenty about it.' He looked grimly at Mike. 'I understand that you've assigned Sue to help Liz. Is that right?'

Mike was totally unaware of impending difficulties as he nodded and said blithely, 'Quite right. Liz will get on much better with some help, and I think she may have found some-thing important.'

'No doubt,' Duncan responded stiffly. 'But the work the stu-dents do is my responsibility.'

Mike stared at him in astonishment. 'I know that, man. I left the girl to fiddle around with the brooch you'd set her to clean. Surely you've no objection to her working with Liz. It'll be valuable experience.'

In spite of himself, Duncan's mouth twitched as he recog-nised Mike's patent surprise. 'Yes, it will be, but not just for her. You can't pick out one of the students. They must all have a chance to gain this valuable experience you're offering.' His tone was blunt.

Mike frowned blackly as his hands clenched on the arms of his chair. 'You don't seem to understand, Hamilton. This could be an extremely valuable find. As far as I'm aware, Archison hasn't found a large single figure yet at Frenham. I'm not letting just any of those students loose on it in case they damage it. Sue is the only one I deem to be capable of helping.'

'There's no doubt Sue is the most able,' Duncan conceded frankly. 'But Josie is nearly as good. And none of the rest are incompetent, maybe just a bit slower,' he said. 'Apart from any-thing else, you'll put the girl in a difficult situation if you pick her out from her fellows.'

Mike got abruptly to his feet, scowling, and Hades lifted his head alertly. 'I'm not having them all messing around with that painting,' he said. 'If you're saying it's all or none, then it's none.'

'Fine.' Duncan was frowning too. 'If that's the way you want it, that's the way it shall be.'

Mike stamped out of the room without another word and they heard the courtyard door slam as Hades' head dropped resignedly back onto his paws.

The short silence in the sitting room was broken as Lucy entered with the tea tray. Hugh got to his feet and swept the magazines and books on the main table into a pile so that she could put it down.

'Was he very cross?' she asked as Will scanned the tray approvingly.

'No more than usual,' Hugh said as he glanced at Duncan Hamilton. 'You managed that very well.'

'He's an able man, I'll not deny that, but he can't always have his own way.' Duncan accepted a cup of tea gratefully, sinking down into the armchair Mike had vacated. 'Does he always take on like that?'

'Generally,' Hugh said, cutting a large piece of sponge cake and handing it to Duncan. 'But he does think about what's been said too, so you'll find he can be more reasonable than he sometimes appears.'

'Aye,' Duncan bit off a piece of cake and ate it appreciatively. 'Mersett gave me the impression that he was impossible.' He looked up with a twinkle in his eyes. 'Not in so many words, you understand, but quite clearly. I haven't found him more than a bit hasty myself.' The twinkle deepened. 'I got the impression that Mersett felt he'd be seeing a lot more of him if either of them gets the Walbury Chair of Archaeology.'

'Are you in for it yourself?' Will asked as he helped himself to a generous portion of cake and took a seat near the table, where Hades came to join him.

'Yes. I think it will be an interesting contest,' Duncan replied.

Hugh sat down opposite him. 'Who else is trying for it? We know Mike is, of course. He's mentioned a few other names, but he doesn't really talk much about it.'

'Well,' Duncan said meditatively, 'you could say that it's becoming a shade incestuous. Dr Archison is being considered, and Mersett himself. And I believe Amelie Carter from York is in the running too.' He finished his cake and licked his fingers before adding, 'Of course, John Brett's death didn't just create a vacancy here on the dig. It also removed one of the contenders

for the chair. Still, we'll all know who's got it by early in the
New Year.'

The talk became more general until eventually Duncan rose
reluctantly to his feet. 'I'm afraid I must be going. I want to
check on the work the students have done while I've been away.
They've been held up enough as it is.' Hades opened his eyes,
then closed them again and shifted heavily in his position across
Will's feet. Duncan glanced around at them all curiously. 'There
seem to be an unusual number of petty problems cropping up at
the excavation,' he said cautiously. 'Have you noticed?'

Before anyone could answer the courtyard door banged and
Hades leaped up and shot out into the corridor, barking furiously. 'Down, you daft dog!' Mike roared, and they heard him
striding towards them. 'Ah,' he said with satisfaction, stopping
in the sitting-room doorway as he caught sight of Duncan. 'I'm
glad I've caught you. I was a bit hasty over this question of the
students,' he said frankly. 'You've got a point, and I've talked it
over with Liz. She's happy to supervise any individual students,
as long as she can decide on what she assigns them. Would that
satisfy you?' he demanded.

'That seems reasonable to me,' Duncan conceded. 'And,' he
added, forestalling Mike, 'it gives you the chance to assess the
level of work you set each individual. I'd not mind that. Sue's
got the makings of a really decent archaeologist in her, but Josie
could be just as good with sufficient encouragement.'

'Fair enough.' Mike met his eyes and grinned. 'I'm meeting
Liz later down at the Lobster Pot to discuss this some more. It's
the only pub in the place, down on the quay, and they have a
decent menu. Why don't you join us for something to eat?'

'I'd like that,' Duncan said. 'I want to take a quick look
round the work and then I've got a couple of things to sort out.
I could be with you about eightish. Would that suit you?'

'That'll be fine. If you're going down to the priory now
I'll come with you.' He glanced towards the French windows, where the curtains were still open. Light from the room

streamed across the terrace and lawn, making the blackness of the winter night beyond its reach even more impenetrable. 'It's really too dark but I'll show you what Liz has uncovered. We've got lights set up, but you'll see it better in daylight, of course.'

Duncan turned to Lucy and Hugh. 'Thank you for the tea.' He looked at Lucy. 'I'll maybe see you tomorrow with your friend.'

'Yes, I'm sure you will,' she replied, aware of the outraged expression on Mike's face.

After they had gone Hugh commented, 'Anna never fails.'

'She certainly helped with Duncan,' Lucy said, her hazel eyes filling with laughter. 'He looked absolutely furious when he arrived here.'

'She's a lot better than she used to be,' Will conceded generously. 'She's quite interested in the dig.' He looked at his watch and pushed Hades off his feet. 'David should be back now. He was going to meet Jack in Leygar's far meadow on his way back from Bremor's. They want to see how easy it would be to cut it traditionally.' Will stood up and Hades moved hopefully to his side.

'Is Jack Leygar interested in David's ideas?' Hugh asked curiously.

'Yes, I think so,' Will replied. 'He's cautious, of course, but a lot of his methods are still fairly traditional, so he probably won't find David's plans so strange.' He glanced across at his sister, his thin face uncannily like hers as it lit with enthusiasm. 'Lucy, do you know what we'll get eventually? I bet they'll bring Jack round if nothing else does.'

She studied him thoughtfully. 'Something in the animal line, I should say.'

'Yes,' Will said eagerly. 'Shire horses for ploughing in the smaller fields and on the difficult slopes, especially towards the sea.'

Hugh raised an eyebrow. 'Is that going to be cost-effective?' he asked.

Will fell indignantly into the trap. 'Of course it is. They cost less to feed and keep than maintaining machinery, and they do less damage when they work in woodland. Besides...' he broke off and grinned ruefully as he became aware of Hugh's amusement.

The telephone in the hall rang as he was about to retaliate. 'I wonder who that is,' Will said generally. 'I'll go.' He started for the door, but the ringing had stopped by the time he got there. As he opened it they heard Gina's voice. He cocked his head, listening as he tried to work out who was calling.

Gina appeared at the end of the corridor, her colourful pinafore floating around her, creating a splash of brightness against the oak panelling. 'Will,' she said, 'it's Anna on the phone for your sister.'

'Thanks, Gina.' He looked over his shoulder to see Lucy getting to her feet. 'She's just coming.'

Lucy walked quickly down to the hall and picked up the receiver. 'Hello, Anna,' she began.

Before she could say any more Anna's excited voice overwhelmed hers. 'Lucy, I've had an idea.' Lucy saw Will pull a face, and waved as he and Hades went out into the courtyard. 'About the priory and the clasp and everything. I don't know whether it's any good, but I'm bursting to talk to you about it. It's so frustrating not to be able to get mobile reception in the valley. I had to wait until I got home. Anyway, are you and Hugh doing anything this evening?'

'No,' Lucy said. 'Would you like to come over to dinner?'

'I'd love to, but I'd better keep Daddy company for a bit. Could I pop over later on?' She laughed deprecatingly. 'It's probably all quite silly, but I'd like to see what you think.'

'Why don't we go down to the pub for a drink?' Lucy suggested. 'There's likely to be a vigorous archaeological debate in progress, but we don't need to get caught up in it.'

'Oh yes, I'd almost forgotten.' Anna's curiosity was aroused. 'Did they come to blows, or was it alright?'

'It blew over quite easily. Your soothing influence on Duncan was a great help.'

'He's rather sweet, isn't he?' She returned to the original subject. 'I'll see you at the Lobster Pot then. I should think I'll be there about eight-thirty to nine.'

Lucy replaced the receiver and turned away, pausing as her eyes fell on her own wedding photograph, standing on the nearby cabinet. Her glowing face smiled out at her as she sat on the arm of a chair, while Hugh leaned over the back, one arm lightly around her, his tanned face alight with happiness.

She bit her lip, conscious of the reflection she had seen in her mirror that morning, a pale face with strained eyes. And Hugh, she thought sadly, looks tired and drawn most of the time. We've lost something, or is it just the strain of trying to combine two lives and two lots of plans? But, she mused as she stared fixedly at the picture, that's us only eight months ago, so how have things gone wrong so quickly?

She was torn from her reverie as the courtyard door opened, and she turned swiftly. 'Gran,' she exclaimed, bending to stroke Juno, who pranced happily up to her. 'We wondered where you'd got to. We've hardly seen you since you got back.'

Isobel Rossington hung her coat and hat up under the stairs. 'I'm here now. I said I'd get dinner as Gina wanted to leave early. Come and give me a hand with a casserole and we'll catch up on each other's news.'

When they opened the kitchen door the herbs on the airer rustled softly and a faint whiff of thyme and marjoram drifted across to them. As she bent over a large yellow tub on the flag-stoned floor Isobel turned to her granddaughter and asked, 'Do you know if something has upset David? I saw him at Leygar's Farm and he was looking like thunder.'

'Oh dear,' Lucy sighed, tying an apron round her waist. 'I'm afraid Mike spoke to him about the flood in the priory, and David may have felt Steven was setting him up. They don't get on very well as it is.'

'Unfortunate,' Isobel commented, filling Juno's food bowl. 'Steven doesn't seem all that likeable, I'm afraid.'

'No,' Lucy agreed with feeling, 'he doesn't. But he wouldn't have come here for the salary we're paying if things hadn't been difficult for him because of the trouble at Kingsley Hall. Hugh thinks he's good at his job and that we should give him a chance.' She sounded resigned as she pulled a board out and began to chop onions on it.

'Hugh's quite right,' Isobel said, watching Juno as she ate daintily. 'But I'm glad he's staying in the village. He would be an awkward house guest.' She opened the fridge and took out a bowl of meat, then turned with it in her hands to face her granddaughter. 'Lucy, what is the problem about the stables?'

Lucy looked up, startled, onion-induced tears running down her cheeks. 'What do you mean?'

'You weren't very happy with the architect's views at lunch time.'

'No, I wasn't, but it's nothing to worry about,' Lucy said unconvincingly. Isobel glanced at her quizzically as she put the meat down near the Aga and reached for a large casserole dish.

'Oh, alright,' Lucy said crossly, dabbing at her eyes with a piece of paper towel. She seized the carrots and started cutting them up. 'I think the stables would be ideal for Hugh's publishing base, but he doesn't agree. He thinks we'd have to leave here when Will takes over the estate. It's nonsense, but he just won't see that.'

Isobel stirred the beef chunks in the cast-iron dish in silence for a while. Juno finished licking her emptied bowl and wandered over to the table, settling herself comfortably on the bean bag underneath it.

'Well,' Lucy demanded, 'don't you agree?'

'Since you ask, Lucy,' the older woman said, putting down the spoon and turning to look at her granddaughter, 'no, I don't. At least,' she amended meticulously, 'I don't think Will would dream of turning any of us out, but I do think he should be left to run the property in his own way.'

'But we wouldn't interfere,' Lucy protested indignantly. 'You know that.'

'Lucy, if your father hadn't died when he did, you'd already be established in your own life somewhere else. That's how it should be. You've done a brilliant rescue job here, but it won't be your concern for ever.'

Lucy brought the prepared vegetables silently up to the Aga and added them carefully to the casserole, stirring them in slowly. Isobel studied her bent head with its stubbornly set lips and sighed faintly. 'Well, it's between you and Hugh. But don't forget that you've got your own lives to make outside the manor. Don't let it absorb you to the exclusion of everything else. It can, very easily. I know that only too well.'

Lucy put down the board and stared at her in astonishment. 'You love it too,' she declared accusingly.

'Of course I do.' Isobel sounded exasperated as she poured stock into the dish. 'But it hasn't been the main concern of my life.' She paused and seemed about to say more when a loud knocking on the back door startled them both and brought Juno out from under the table, barking shrilly. Lucy got up and went into the scullery passage to open the door upon David, his hand raised to hammer on the wood again.

'Lucy,' the young estate manager said with determination, 'I wondered if I could have a word with you and Hugh.' He followed her into the kitchen where Isobel greeted him briefly over her shoulder as she added a generous amount of red wine to the casserole. She put down the bottle and placed a lid on the dish as David's nostrils twitched. 'Mmm, that smells very good.'

'I'll fetch Hugh, unless you'd rather come into the sitting room,' Lucy offered.

'No, I'd better stay here.' David indicated his work trousers, and smiled as Juno came to sniff them curiously. 'I haven't been home to change yet.'

Lucy left him with her grandmother, whose dark eyes considered him thoughtfully. David became aware of her regard and looked up at her as he stroked the little spaniel. 'You and Philly seemed to be very interested in that building in the farmyard this afternoon,' Isobel commented. 'I was down there talking to her mother and I saw you both walking round it. Is there something special about it?'

A tinge of colour crept into his cheeks but he answered readily enough as he straightened up until he towered over her. 'We don't know. Josie noticed it first because it's like an old dovecote near where we both lived in Herefordshire. Philly thought that's what this building used to be too, so we were checking it out. I think ours was unusual so I wondered if that architect chap would be interested in the Leygar's one.'

Juno had wandered back under the table and laid down on the bean bag, ears pricked and eyes watchful through half-closed lids. Her tail lashed gently as the door opened but she did not get up.

'Almost certainly,' Hugh replied, overhearing David's remarks as he came into the room. 'We must show it to him next time he's down.' He was aware that Lucy looked at him sharply, but went on in an unperturbed voice, 'What's the trouble, David?'

'No trouble, exactly,' David said awkwardly. 'But I thought I should let you know.' He thrust his hands into his pockets, bunching his fists. 'I had a bit of a row with Dollery on my way back from Bremor's. The old fool was cutting his hedges, and I had particularly asked him to leave them until later. Cut, he's butchered them,' he said angrily. 'It's as if he's done it deliberately.'

'He may well have done,' Lucy said. 'He's an awkward old man and he likes to annoy people. Did you get very angry with him?'

A deep flush ran up David's face. 'I'm afraid I did,' he admitted. 'I know it's stupid, but I blew up and said quite a lot I shouldn't have done. That's really why I'm bothering you with this.' He sighed heavily. 'I expect he'll complain when he sees you and I wanted you to know what had happened.' He looked at them enquiringly. 'Should I go and apologise?'

'No, I don't think so,' Lucy replied slowly. 'Normally it would be different, of course, but with Richard Dollery it's quite possible you've done yourself no harm. Mind you, David,' she added warningly, 'he'll tell all and sundry about it so you can expect a fair bit of ribbing.'

David looked relieved and his shoulders relaxed. 'Oh, I can manage that. And I'll take care it doesn't happen again.'

'Will said you were seeing Jack Leygar,' Lucy changed the subject. 'How did you get on?'

'Fine. He's very keen to manage his meadows organically. That's pretty much what he does anyway, but we were looking at how he can improve his practice – and qualify for grants.' David grinned. 'And of course he likes the idea of working horses.' His grin faded as he glanced at Lucy. 'Did Will tell you about them?'

'Yes,' Lucy said. 'He's very keen too.'

'Have you got time for a drink, David?' Hugh asked quietly.

'Thanks,' David said, 'but I won't stop. I'd like to get back and change now that this Dollery business is sorted out.'

Lights created small pools of brightness as they shone out into the night from the windows of the low crooked cottages on the main street of the village. The rushing tumbling sound of the brook that ran past the buildings in its stone channel was in their ears as Lucy and Hugh approached the pub perched on Roscombe quay. It was an unevenly shaped building with a top-heavy upper storey looming over the lower rooms. A wooden sign swung creaking from a projecting beam, its faded picture depicting a lobster pot similar in appearance to those that lay in heaps around the quay, jumbled among nets and marker buoys.

There was a constant hum of noise from the interior even

though the wooden door and tiny windows were tightly shut, but as Lucy and Hugh strolled further along the stone quay other sounds faded away until there was only the murmur of waves lapping gently against the harbour wall. A thin slice of new moon shone through a faint haze, luminous among the scattered brilliance of the stars. In spite of the chill in the air they stood in silence for a while, looking out across the sea which gleamed and sparkled enticingly.

Lucy felt a sense of wellbeing surge through her. She glanced sideways at Hugh's remote profile as he gazed over the water. An image of him in their wedding photograph flashed into her mind and she saw, with a stab of contrition, how tired and withdrawn he looked now in the moonlight.

I'm a beast, she thought remorsefully, recalling how she had snubbed all Hugh's efforts to talk to her as they walked down the narrow village street beside the brook. Hugh's really trying to be reasonable about it, Lucy admitted to herself with difficulty, so I suppose he does realise a bit what I feel about the manor. Maybe I should think about it some more. But not now, she decided suddenly. I'll follow the advice I gave Anna and I won't think about it any more until after Christmas. She tucked her hand into Hugh's arm and he glanced down at her, quirking an eyebrow before pressing her hand affectionately.

They turned reluctantly away from the serenity of the night and the sea towards the pub. As they reached it the door opened to reveal the smoky, brightly-lit interior. A man and woman came out together, dark shapes against the lighted room, and the man held the door for Lucy, smiling at her. She smiled back and thanked him, only recognising him when he had moved away. 'That was Tom Peters,' she said to Hugh over her shoulder. 'You remember, he was the sergeant in the investigation into Graham's murder in the spring. I didn't know he lived locally.'

The Lobster Pot was the sole pub in the village and dated largely from the sixteenth century. It retained a traditional stone floor and roughly plastered walls with low uneven ceilings. A narrow bar counter stretched across the back of the single room, curving round out of sight on both sides. Rickety stairs led from one side to the upper floor, where two small bedrooms had recently been renovated for letting to tourists in the holiday season.

The bar was already crammed with people, mainly local fishermen and farmers. Most of the plain wooden settles were occupied but Lucy spotted a vacant pair by a table on the right beyond the fireplace. As she squeezed her way through the packed room the surge of sound ebbed and flowed around her. A loud voice nearby attracted her attention and she caught sight of Richard Dollery. The elderly man was the centre of a group of fellow farmers, who patronised the pub regularly. His face was suffused with colour and he was clearly telling a story that affected him deeply. She glanced at Hugh who was right behind her, and then smiled as she heard Mike's voice penetrating clearly through the general buzz of noise, 'And of course Archison should…'

She peered into the area beyond the counter and caught sight of Mike's red hair and his arms sweeping across the table in a telling gesture. Duncan sat beside him, listening intently, one hand wisely grasping his tankard firmly, and Liz sat opposite, a faint smile on her placid face as she watched Mike.

Lucy squeezed herself past the last human barrier and sank down thankfully onto one of the benches. 'I haven't seen Anna,' she remarked. 'Have you?'

'No,' Hugh said, 'but I'll ask Bill. He'll know if she's come in. She's a favourite of his.'

Lucy settled herself more comfortably, leaning forward over the table with her chin in her hands as Hugh made his way towards the bar. This was a good spot to sit in as she could see across the room to the door. She scanned the crowd, nodding occasionally to people she knew when they caught her eye. Her gaze rested briefly on the group of farmers, who were beginning to look bored with Richard Dollery's long-winded story, and then drifted past them.

Her heart sank as she saw Steven perched on a stool at the far end of the bar, hunched moodily over his beer. None of the regulars spoke to him and he certainly took no notice of them. She shrugged mentally and sat back to enjoy the snippets of Mike's conversation that soared from time to time across the general babble. 'It's inconceivable that they don't... What we must do next... He was a fool, of course... The most important thing...'

She was so engrossed in this that she started when Anna slid gracefully down onto the settle opposite her. 'Bill's doing his mulled wine again. I always know it's winter when I smell that.' She sniffed the air appreciatively.

'I know,' Lucy agreed. 'I'm having a glass. Would you like one too?'

Anna nodded and Lucy waved her arm vigorously, catching Bill's attention at the counter as he was pouring Hugh's drinks. He took in the situation immediately and brought down another glass, speaking to Hugh as he did so. Hugh glanced over his shoulder and saw the two women already engrossed in talk, Lucy's chestnut head bent towards Anna's dark curls to hear more clearly what she was saying.

As he approached the table, balancing the three glasses carefully, he heard Anna saying earnestly, 'And you could alter it for different audiences too.' Lucy saw him coming and moved back so that he could safely put the glasses down on the table.

'Hugh, thank you.' Anna picked up her glass and breathed in the heady aroma of wine and spices. 'Mmm, I do love this.'

Hugh lowered himself leisurely onto the bench next to his wife. 'Well,' he drawled, 'what's all the excitement about?'

Anna's eyes sparkled with enthusiasm and, glancing at Lucy, Hugh saw that her face was alight with interest. 'I don't know if it's going to be possible, or even if you'd want to do it,' Anna began, unusually anxious, 'but I think it's a good scheme.'

'What is it?' Hugh asked patiently.

'A series of plays illustrating scenes from the history of the priory, like my lady losing her precious clasp.' She kept her eyes on Hugh, who was watching her curiously. 'You could do it in all sorts of ways. Professional players might be interested in the summer season, or you could get local people involved on an amateur basis. And another big area is schools, of course. It might be possible to develop scenes of everyday life in the priory that would reflect the curriculum. And perhaps that side of things might evolve into a way of occupying children during the holidays. It could be a sort of amusing cultural activity for them.' Anna spoke faster and faster in her eagerness to express her thoughts.

'The whole thing could go on indefinitely, with a different period or theme each year. And if the weather's bad you could perhaps use the old granary and barn, or parts of the priory, depending on how many people come.' She paused for breath and glanced from one to the other of them hopefully. 'What do you think?'

'I think it's a very interesting idea indeed,' a voice said from behind them. They looked up in surprise to see Duncan smiling down at Anna's glowing face. 'I've heard of similar things being done at other places, but I've never seen them in action, as it were.'

'Yes,' Hugh commented, 'I believe it's a popular idea. Have you seen anything along those lines, Anna?'

She shook her head, deflated to find that her brainchild was not original. 'No, I just thought it could be a clever way of showing people what life may have been like in different centuries. It's sometimes difficult to get an idea from a bare structure and written words.'

'Yes,' Duncan agreed, 'it's often easier to get ideas across in some form of play.' He glanced down at the empty tankards he was holding. 'Look, I must get these, but would you mind if I come to join you? I'd be interested to hear more about this.'

'Do,' Hugh invited cordially.

Anna got gracefully to her feet. 'I'll come to the bar with you,' she said to Duncan. 'It's my turn. Same again?' She looked enquiringly at Lucy and Hugh, who both nodded.

'What do you think?' Hugh asked, watching the pair pick their way through to the bar. He looked at Lucy, his eyes brimming with amusement. 'About Anna's idea, that is.'

Lucy met his gaze reprovingly, but could not prevent laughter from sounding in her voice. 'It sounds fascinating,' she admitted, 'but wouldn't it involve a huge amount of work?'

'Yes, I should think it would,' Hugh agreed, adding dryly, 'but that doesn't usually stop you.'

'Or you,' Lucy said quickly.

'Mmm,' he said. 'But it may well be something we could get some of the locals involved with.'

Lucy glanced around at the people filling the room. Apart from the archaeological coterie they were mainly middle-aged men who worked locally, with a scattering of elders clustered round the blazing fire in the inglenook and a noisy group of youths playing bar quoits on the far side of the parlour. 'Do you really think they would be interested?' she asked dubiously. 'I gather from things I've overheard in the shop that some of our plans are none too popular anyway.'

Hugh shrugged. 'We can't please everyone,' he said indifferently. 'Some people will see a means of making a living, others will see an intrusion by the tourist masses.'

'Yes, exactly,' Lucy agreed emphatically. 'And Anna's idea is likely to bring in much larger numbers than anything else we've discussed.'

'So the arguments on each side will deepen,' Hugh said. 'But don't forget that a lot of them have children, which may be an important factor. And anyway,' he drawled as a sardonic look crossed his face, 'scenes of debauchery at the priory are likely to remind many of them of the Christmas mummery. That's popular enough.' His gaze strayed to a group of students near the quoits table. 'Hmm, that's Philly Leygar over there, isn't it? With the girls from the dig. The ones Will gets on with so well.'

Lucy looked across the room. 'Yes. That's Sue sitting next to her, the one with the glasses who had the accident this afternoon. Josie's the pretty chubby one with spiky black hair. She comes from David's part of Herefordshire. I don't really know the others but it looks as though Philly's getting on pretty well with them all. And here is David. I wondered if he'd be coming down.'

Lucy fell silent, observing how the girls greeted David with pleasure when he joined them. Several of the farmers called humorously across to him and he acknowledged the greetings pleasantly. She glanced round quickly, anticipating a more obstreperous comment from Richard Dollery, but relaxed when she could not spot the elderly farmer and hoped that he had already gone home.

'Philly would be an ideal person to get involved in something like this,' Lucy said thoughtfully. 'I know she helps on the farm, but I think her mother would be glad if she could find something interesting to do locally.'

'Who?' Anna asked, setting the glasses of gently steaming mulled wine down on the table and resuming her seat opposite Lucy. 'Heavens, have you seen Steven?' she continued without a pause. 'Talk about sulking.'

Lucy looked anxiously at the bar counter and saw that Steven had shifted on his stool. One of his hands clutched the handle of his tankard while the other tapped an irritable tattoo on the wooden counter as he watched the table where David was participating cheerfully in the exhilarated student chatter.

'I didn't think you'd want him to join us,' Anna said, adding frankly, 'and I certainly don't want him to.' She shuddered ostentatiously. 'Wandering hands,' she explained as Hugh looked at her in amused reproof. 'And before you ask, they haven't wandered over me but I can recognise the type instantly.'

'Hell!' Hugh exclaimed, looking over her shoulder into the

room. 'No,' he added quickly, 'don't turn round. Tilly has just come in with that woman who's staying with her. I thought she didn't come to the pub.' He looked almost accusingly at Lucy.

'I expect she saw us coming down the street,' Lucy said crossly. 'I thought I saw her in Winding Alley. She's probably brought this woman in to meet you. Anna and I have already come across her.' She met her friend's eyes with fleeting humour.

'Oh no,' Hugh groaned, dropping his head into his hands. 'I can't stand it.'

'Keep talking,' Lucy commanded. 'If we don't take any notice of her maybe she won't interrupt us.'

Hugh raised his head to stare at her in disbelief and Anna gurgled with laughter at the expression on his face. 'Never mind, Hugh. We'll tell her the seats are taken and maybe she'll plant herself on Mike instead.' She turned to Lucy. 'Who were you talking about when I came back?'

'Philly Leygar,' Lucy said. 'I think she could be a useful person to involve in your idea, if it gets beyond the discussion stage.'

'Do you think it's worth pursuing then?' Anna asked anxiously.

'Definitely,' Duncan said firmly, putting down his tankard and sliding onto the settle beside Anna. 'It has two main advantages that I can see. One, it will educate people who might not otherwise have been interested in the subject. Two, it could bring in a reasonable amount of income, which I imagine has to be good news.' He looked enquiringly across at Hugh, whose mouth twisted wryly as he nodded.

'And the third advantage,' Lucy said, 'is that Will is going to love the idea.'

'Do you think so?' Anna asked doubtfully as she raised her glass. 'I should have thought he'd hate it.'

'What about the rest of us?' Mike demanded, banging down his pewter tankard on the table and making Anna start so much that she spilt some of her wine.

'Don't creep up on us like that,' she said crossly, putting the glass back on the table and opening her bag.

'It's guilt making you jumpy,' Mike retorted as Anna found a tissue and dried the outside of her glass. He pointed an accusing finger at all of them. 'You have the look of conspirators, the whole lot of you. Come on, Liz, squeeze in next to Duncan. I'll have this stool.' He dragged one over from a neighbouring table and sat down. 'We'd better find out what they're up to.'

Liz smiled apologetically at Anna and Duncan as they moved up their bench to make room for her. 'He thinks we're missing something,' she said as squeezed herself in. As they resettled themselves Lucy glanced quickly across the room and saw Tilly standing irresolutely by the bar, her bloodshot eyes fixed on Mike as she moistened her thin lips with the tip of her tongue. She looked like a brightly-coloured bird in her thick red Indian cotton skirt and rainbow-striped blouse, but Edie was a more ominous presence beside her. She stared straight at them, a thunderous frown on her narrow white face as Tilly twittered nervously at her.

Lucy thought, Lord, she does look grim. Still, I don't think Tilly will bother us now that Mike is here. She smiled to herself as she remembered Mike's ruthless habit of dismissing Tilly in a few apt words.

She turned her attention back to her own table, noticing how different Liz looked out of her working denims. The clinging terracotta-coloured dress warmed her matt skin and brown hair, which she had left waving loosely down her back.

Liz felt Lucy's regard and looked across the table. 'I hope this really does concern the excavation,' she murmured.

'Of course it does.' Mike said, putting his arms on the table and leaning forward. 'Why else would Hamilton be so keen to get in on it?'

Liz held Lucy's gaze for a moment as a smile hovered on her lips, and Mike said impatiently, 'Well, what's it all about?'

'I suppose,' Anna said sarcastically, 'it didn't occur to you that it might not concern you?'

'Anything to do with the priory concerns me,' Mike replied simply. 'And the more you procrastinate the more you convince me I should have been here earlier.'

She sighed with exasperation. 'Look,' she began, her fingers tightening on the stem of her glass.

Hugh interrupted. 'Just tell him, Anna, or we'll never get any peace.'

Anna's eyes flashed with indignation but Mike was completely impervious, although not oblivious, to this. 'Alright,' she said unwillingly. 'But it doesn't directly concern the dig, and you won't like it any way.'

'I don't expect to,' Mike said, running his fingers through his tousled hair. 'Get on with it.'

'I was thinking of my lady with her clasp. You remember?' She raised a delicately arched eyebrow and he nodded, while Liz and Duncan watched them, puzzled. 'Then it occurred to me what a marvellous scene it would make set in the priory, and how well it could demonstrate a story from the past.' She admitted ruefully, 'I always found history difficult to follow, but I'm positive short plays would easily create images for people to understand.'

'Have you found that in Paris?' Duncan interposed.

'Yes, we have.' Anna turned to him eagerly. 'The story of Madame de la Motte Valois and the Queen's necklace is much more widely known now than it was a year ago.'

Hugh was lounging sideways against the wall watching Mike. 'What do you think?' he asked.

Mike grunted. 'A layman's approach, of course,' he said, adding reluctantly, 'but there's something in it. It would probably appeal to other laymen.' He sounded disparaging and Anna flushed.

'It's the laymen we need to get across to,' Duncan said, 'in this sort of case, at least. Those who have a professional interest wouldn't need to be, ah, enticed.'

Mike snorted disbelievingly but his face was thoughtful. 'How would you organise it?' he demanded, looking at Anna.

'Me?' Anna was startled. 'I wouldn't be doing it. It's just an idea.'

He glared at her, his bright blue eyes glittering with anger. 'You've no business putting forward an idea and then washing your hands of it. It's your profession after all.'

Anna glared back at him as she declared angrily, 'I'm an actress. What you'd need for this is a director, a producer, a researcher, oh, the whole team.'

'And where do you think they're going to come from?' he asked. 'Money doesn't grow on trees round here, you know.'

'I could probably find people who might be interested,' she said crossly.

'Huh! The way you're interested,' Mike retorted. 'Why can't you follow it through yourself if you believe it's such a good idea?'

'Don't be so stupid!' Anna clenched her hands furiously. 'How can I give up what I'm doing just like that. And besides, I haven't any experience in other parts of the theatre...' Her voice died away under Mike's withering look.

'What about Steven?' Lucy interposed. 'Could he do some of the research?'

Mike stared at her in disbelief. 'Him? He wouldn't know relevant facts if they jumped up and shouted at him.'

'Nonsense,' Duncan said briskly. 'You're talking about the chap indexing your books?' he asked Lucy, who nodded. 'Well, I haven't met him, but he must know the sources, which is surely the main thing. He only has to provide a précis of local and national facts and incidents for a given period. Then we can decide which would be worth investigating in more detail.'

'And we've already got some incidents to start with' Liz broke in, leaning forward so that her hair rippled over her shoulders.

They looked at her enquiringly, and she glanced at Anna. 'I

take it you were referring to the clasp that was found on the site.' Anna nodded, and Liz continued, 'Well, you've also got the expulsion of the monks. That ought to make a good scene, especially if you include the riotous living the monks enjoyed before the closure.' She gazed round the table and saw they were all listening intently. 'And you've got the chalice. Surely you could build up a scene that involved its presentation to the priory?' She stopped and laughed uncertainly. 'I'm getting quite carried away with it all myself.'

'That isn't surprising,' Hugh said, amused. 'The idea seems to have caught your imagination, and there's certainly plenty of material to be worked up.'

'That's quite true,' Mike agreed readily, 'but who's going to organise it? I don't imagine either of you will have the time.'

'Well,' Lucy looked at Hugh, 'no, we wouldn't have. But perhaps we can find someone to do it.'

'And how would you pay them?' Mike demanded.

Lucy shrugged a little helplessly, but Hugh was unconcerned. 'You're jumping ahead rather rapidly in the game plan,' he drawled.

'You'd have to get in an amateur,' Mike continued inexorably, 'and what are the chances of getting somebody decent?'

Anna frowned at this. 'Many amateurs are very good,' she said quickly, 'but I think to do this properly you'd have to be very careful about who starts it.'

Mike snorted meaningfully and she stared angrily at him before turning back to Hugh and Lucy. 'Look,' she said hesitantly, 'perhaps I can sort something out.'

'Don't worry, Anna,' Hugh reassured her, unperturbed. 'After all, we're only knocking ideas about at the moment. We don't need to make any decisions immediately.'

'And when you do,' Mike said as he picked up his tankard, 'remember we're all involved in this.'

'Oh?' Anna enquired sweetly. 'Are you planning to play a part in some of the scenes? I can think of several that would suit you perfectly.'

Mike met her limpid stare over the rim of his tankard. 'I'll play myself in every scene. I think you'll find that quite sufficient.'

'I usually find it more than sufficient,' Anna said blandly and Duncan broke into an explosive cough.

Liz got to her feet, edging out from the bench. 'It sounds as though you need another drink. I'll get them.'

Lucy rose too. 'I'll come and give you a hand, Liz.'

FOUR

Will shook the wooden sieve backwards and forwards, watching the sifted soil drift down to the ground. He rested the sieve on the ruined outer wall of the cloister walk and sighed as he bent over it to pick through the stones left in its bottom. I haven't found anything for ages and I wouldn't even mind a shard of pottery, he realised, grinning ruefully as he straightened up. He drew off his gloves to blow on his cold hands and looked around the garth.

The cloister walk had probably never been such a hive of activity since the monastic artists created their masterpieces. Today work was again concentrated inside the remains of the carrels where the individual monks had sat with their paints and parchment. The students were working in pairs to move the soil with trowels and search painstakingly through it for fragmentary pieces, evidence of those former occupants. Terry, a raw-boned Geordie working near Will, kept up a constant flow of stories, which Gavin, his West Indian companion, ignored as he rattled his sieve strenuously backwards and forwards. Otherwise the students worked in silence, even Josie who was normally a cheerful conversationalist. Will had attached himself to her as Sue, her usual working partner, had not arrived yet, and Josie had kept her spiky black head bent over her trowel as she shifted soil diligently, keeping Will busy at his sieve.

Although it was almost ten o'clock the sun had been slow to come through the thick morning mist, and the air was still icy from the heavy frost the previous night. Jack Leygar told David that snow was on the way, Will remembered, as he stretched his aching back. Maybe we'll have it in time for Christmas.

Hades had accompanied his master to the priory and sniffed through the trenches thoroughly to see who had visited them in the night. His investigations completed, the big dog was now lying in the tiny patch of watery sunlight that had reached the far side of the courtyard. His ears pricked up suddenly and Will turned to see what he had noticed.

Liz's dungareed figure was standing just in front of the ruined arch of the Prior's Gateway, surveying the group with an unusually agitated expression. She did not speak to any of them, but turned sharply and went back through the gateway. Will heard the soft crunch of gravel as she set off, almost running, up the track.

I wonder what's biting her, he thought idly. She doesn't usually leave the church once she's started work. I don't think she's even stopped for lunch since she found the first wall painting. Will shrugged and then looked at his watch impatiently. I wish Sue would hurry up. She would have to be late this morning, he thought exasperatedly, when I want to tell her about Anna's theatre idea. Josie hardly seemed to listen when I mentioned it to her, but I'm sure Sue will be keen to hear about it.

Lucy and Hugh had discussed it at breakfast and Will had been scathing at first. But not nearly as scathing as Steven, he thought critically. What a jerk. He recalled with satisfaction the bruising around Steven's left eye. Probably walked into a door, he thought contemptuously. He's not the sort to get into a fight, although he's always whining that people are picking on him. I bet he's messing up the books. We don't want him mucking up the play research too. There is something in the idea after all, Will admitted to himself as he stared across the garth, absently watching Hades' legs twitching as the big dog dreamed. It'll be fun to watch the actors and I may get a decent part as well, he decided gleefully. There's loads of stuff in the attics which might be useful. I'll have to look and see what's there.

Maybe Sue will help, Will speculated happily. She's interested in everything, it's one of the things I like about her. And Josie too, she's normally always ready for a laugh. I thought she'd have a very definite opinion about it. Lucy said none of the students joined them last night so they wouldn't have heard anything at the pub. And I don't see why Duncan would mention it to any of them.

Will heard more footsteps on the gravel path and stared hopefully towards the Prior's Gateway, but nobody appeared in the garth. It must have been Liz coming back, he thought irritably. He glanced impatiently at his watch again and then turned towards the students who were working beside him in the cloisters. He knew them all by now and a couple of them looked up from what they were doing and smiled at him. 'Had enough already, Will?' Josie said, pulling her felted poncho tightly around her body. She sounded more cheerful and certainly looked it, with chubby cheeks made scarlet by exertion and the cold air.

Will shook his head. 'Not yet. Just checking to see if I've got frost bite. Has Sue turned up?'

Terry straightened his back, rising to his full lanky height and rubbing his hand across his forehead, leaving a grubby mark. 'I haven't noticed her,' he said.

Josie chipped in, 'She'll probably go straight into the church when she gets here. She's supposed to be helping Liz this morning, then I get my turn in the church this afternoon. I just hope I don't have to miss any of my time there because Sue's late.'

'Yeh, our Liz wasn't best pleased that Duncan arranged for Sue to go into town to pick up that parcel,' Gavin added, his voice almost muffled by the scarf that was wound round his throat and lower face.

'Bet it'd be different if Mike had set it up,' Josie said bitingly.

'Sssh.' The others glanced round nervously.

'Why should I?' she demanded, looking defiantly at them. 'He isn't here either this morning. Oooh...' Her voice tailed off and she clutched her trowel tightly as she bent swiftly over her work in the carrel, imitated immediately by the others.

Mike's face was grim as he stalked up the cloister aisle towards the student group in its middle. Liz trailed along behind him, her brown hair straggling out of its chignon and hanging unevenly over her shoulders. 'Have any of you been in the church since yesterday evening?' Mike asked abruptly.

The excavators stopped the activities they had hurriedly recommenced and gaped at him in surprise. Seeing the expression on his face, they universally made haste to shake their heads or mumble denials.

He looked piercingly at each of them in turn, leaving them flushed and anxious. 'Where's Sue?' he demanded curtly.

'Duncan asked her to go into Coombhaven to collect a parcel,' Terry, the most loquacious of the student group, answered. He debated within himself whether he should mention that it was Duncan's manuscript and quickly decided not to.

'When?'

Terry stared at him, puzzlement etched across his face.

'When,' said Mike, enunciating his words clearly so that Terry flushed with embarrassment, 'did Duncan arrange this with Sue?'

'Last night,' Terry almost stammered. 'He came up to the farm before we had dinner.'

'What time did she set out for town this morning?'

'Straight after breakfast,' Josie said. 'I saw her drive off. Duncan left her his car yesterday evening.'

'Where the hell is she then? It shouldn't have taken her this long to get into Coombhaven and back.' Mike looked round the garth as if he expected her to materialise out of the worn stones. 'Where's Hamilton?' he asked. 'Is he working in the sacristy?'

The students glanced at each other nervously and Will, standing apart from the others, watched them curiously as he held on firmly to Hades' collar. The big dog had leaped to his feet and bounded over hopefully at the sound of Mike's voice, but his master judged it to be an inauspicious moment for the dog to be gambolling around.

'Well?' Mike demanded irascibly. 'It's a simple enough question, for God's sake.'

'Umm, we don't really know,' Terry muttered, avoiding Mike's angry eyes.

'You don't know,' Mike repeated. 'Well, let's approach this differently. Which way did he go when he came down this morning?'

The silence this time was more pronounced and Mike's blue eyes narrowed. 'Have you seen him this morning?' he asked.

'No,' Terry said reluctantly, while the others kept very quiet.

'Then why the hell couldn't you say so at once?' Mike glared at him. 'Hamilton must have come down early.' He assessed the students again in one swift glance. 'I don't suppose any of you know what he might have had in mind?'

They shook their heads and Mike let out his breath heavily. Will was standing at his elbow, close to the ruined wall, and Mike turned towards him, but just as he opened his mouth to speak they all heard gravel crunching underfoot beyond the Prior's Gateway. Mike spun on his heel and stalked towards the arch, stopping abruptly as Lucy and Anna emerged. 'Oh,' he said, obviously disappointed. 'It's you.'

'So it is,' Anna agreed, making a vivid splash of colour against the ancient stones as her long black hair tumbled over her scarlet duffle coat.

Lucy looked at Mike sharply. 'What's wrong?' she asked.

'Have either of you seen Hamilton this morning?' he demanded.

'No,' Lucy answered, startled, and Mike glanced at Anna.

She shook her head. 'We were expecting him to be here. He was going to show us around this morning.'

A frown etched itself onto Mike's forehead. 'When did he arrange this?'

'Yesterday afternoon. I met him just as I was leaving the house and he suggested it then.'

'Could he have been called away?' Lucy asked.

Mike turned back to the silent group of students, who had gathered behind him. 'Well, do any of you know if he got a letter or perhaps a phone call?'

'He might have done when he went back to the cottage last night,' Josie said. 'But surely he would have left a message if he had to go away.'

They were all startled when Will moved suddenly, releasing Hades who whined as he bounded forward. 'Sue,' Will said urgently. 'Sue, what is it? What's wrong?' He ran across the cloister garth and took her by the arm, shaking her gently, while Hades pawed at her legs anxiously. 'You're soaking wet,' Will exclaimed, letting go of her arm in surprise.

Sue stood quite immobile on the far side of the courtyard, staring at the group in the aisle who had turned to look over the ruined cloister wall. Her face was drained of any vestige of colour and her spectacles were balanced precariously on her nose, while her jeans and jumper clung wetly to her thin figure.

Will put his hand gingerly back on her arm. 'Sue, what is it?'

Mike strode over to them and took the girl by the shoulders, flinching as his hands touched her wet jumper. 'Sue. What on earth's happened?' he demanded.

She shivered and turned a blank stare on him. 'Duncan,' she said with difficulty. 'I can't get him out. He's in the lake.' She stopped, swallowing hard. 'He's dead,' she said bleakly and began to shake.

The others stood motionless until Mike took his hands away

from her and directed a fierce glare at them. 'Have any of you got something to wrap her in?' he asked sharply.

'Here.' Josie pulled off the poncho she was wearing and walked quickly across the open garth, neatly avoiding the trenches. Mike took it from her with a word of thanks and pulled it over Sue's head, knocking her spectacles even further askew.

'No,' Sue's voice was muffled until her head emerged from the folds of cloth. 'Don't bother. There's no time. He's still in the water. I can't get him out. I can't...' Her voice began to rise as she retrieved her spectacles, unwittingly smearing the lenses, which were already badly marked.

Mike shook her hard. 'Alright, Sue. We'll go. Where is he?' he demanded.

Sue gulped and replied through chattering teeth, 'I'll show you.'

Lucy was at Mike's side, touching his arm gently to get his attention. 'She'll catch her death of cold if we don't get her back to the house quickly,' she said.

Mike nodded. 'Sue, just tell us where to go and we'll get him out.'

'I tried to get him out,' Sue replied in a monotonous tone, 'but he's too heavy. He's dead,' she repeated and pulled herself together with an effort. 'I was late so I took the short-cut from the farmhouse down by the lake and across the stream. There was something odd in the water near the bridge and I went to look. It was him. I didn't want to go on through the bushes to the Prior's Gateway so I came past the granary to get here.' She stopped, shuddering uncontrollably. Lucy put an arm round the younger woman, her nose wrinkling slightly at the all-pervading smell of pond water as she pulled Sue close, trying to comfort and warm her.

Mike absently wiped his wet hands on his misshapen jumper as he looked at Will. 'Do you know where she means?'

'Yes, I think so,' Will said promptly, his dark eyes alert in his thin face.

'We'd better go the way she came, by the granary,' Mike said. He turned to the others. 'Right, you two, come with me.' Terry and Gavin stepped forward eagerly. 'The rest of you stay here. Liz, keep them busy.'

Josie stepped forward too, her round chin jutting out. 'I know some first aid. I might be able to help if...' She broke off.

'Okay, you might be useful,' Mike agreed. 'Lucy, you ring up from the house...'

'No,' Anna interrupted. 'I'll run to the house and do that. Lucy can bring Sue back more slowly.'

Mike did not even look at her as he said, 'Fine. You sort it out.'

Anna turned to Will. 'Hades might get in your way. Shall I take him with me?' she asked.

Will agreed gratefully and caught the big dog's collar, hauling him over to Anna. She took hold of him firmly, ignoring his pitiful whines as she pulled the narrow leather belt off her jeans and attached it to his collar.

Mike left them without another word and strode towards the entrance courtyard with Will at his side and the two men at his heels. Josie was considerably shorter than her companions and jogged alongside them to keep up with the pace they set. The remainder of the students stood in a stunned huddle in the cloister aisle, trowels and sieves lying forgotten around their feet.

Lucy urged Sue towards the gateway and the track that led to the house, looking anxiously at the girl as she moved dumbly at her side. Sue was still shaking but she put one foot automatically in front of the other, walking like an automaton, with water still dripping from her soaked clothes. Anna glanced back at them before she passed through the ruined archway and ran towards the house with Hades bounding along beside her, his reluctance to leave his master overcome by the prospect of activity.

The frosted grass crackled underfoot as Will led the way rapidly across the swathe of ground between the outer wall of the priory enclave and the stone granary standing nearby on squat columns. As they emerged from the shelter of the buildings and approached the brook the cold became more noticeable. Will led his party along the bank and the still air was suddenly filled with the sound of rooks cawing and scolding as they flew over from their roost in the beeches beside the village street. The birds swirled through the drifting strands of morning mist, just visible as black crosses to the people below as they pushed their way through rhododendrons still white with rime and reached a rickety plank bridge.

Will stopped and pointed beyond it. 'Sue must have come down from the farm and crossed here. I wonder which side she was on when she saw him.'

'The far side,' Mike said. 'You can't see the lake from here, and anyway, look, she'd leave marks.' He gestured behind them at the straggling line of footprints they had left on the whitened ground. Here and there among them were the wet tracks that Sue had left on her way to the priory.

'Okay,' Will said and stepped cautiously onto the bridge. 'Be careful,' he warned. 'It's slippery.'

They trod circumspectly over the planks and Gavin, the last of them, was just stepping off on the far side when Mike said sharply, 'There.' He pointed through a narrow gap in the bulky bushes to where a slender rowan tree stood in a small glade. Beyond it water glimmered dully in the winter sunshine that was gradually vanquishing the mist. A dark bulk rose, ominously still, out of the shallows near the bank.

Will turned to the bushes and paused, pointing at the marks in the frost that still lay on the grass there, just beyond reach of the weak sunlight. 'This is the way Sue went.'

'Will,' Mike called him back. 'Watch where you tread, all of you. Keep as far as you can to the marks that Sue has already made.'

Will stared at him, his dark eyes widening. Beyond Mike the students exchanged startled glances in the silence that had fallen over the scene since the rooks had faded away. Mike pushed past Will and moved carefully forward between the bushes into the glade, following in Sue's footsteps along a narrow path until he stood on the edge of the lake.

His lips tightened into a straight line as he stared at the floating mass in front of him. Duncan Hamilton lay face down in the turgid water, his coat drifting gently about him in the muddy streaks that Sue had stirred up when she struggled to pull him onto the bank. Looking carefully along the edge Mike noticed at once the wet and scuffed area where Sue had pulled herself out, and saw the blue donkey jacket she had dropped nearby when she went into the water.

'Josie, Will, stay out of the way. Terry, Gavin, you stand on the side here,' Mike said abruptly. 'I'll go in and bring him over to the bank. He'll be a dead weight.' His mouth clamped shut, then he shook his tousled head. 'You'll need to take his shoulders and pull while I lift him.' He lowered himself into the uninviting water, flinching involuntarily as the cold penetrated his trousers and thick jumper. Coils of mud rose from the bottom and unravelled slowly and casually like tentacles around him as he moved cautiously forward in a rising miasma of stagnant water.

Three paces brought him close enough to the body to grip it and put his arm firmly across Duncan's back. The body was heavy, weighted with water-logged clothes, but air trapped within the coat gave it some buoyancy. With an effort Mike moved it closer to the shore where the men crouched on the bank, leaning precariously over the edge to get a hold on Duncan's shoulders. As they tightened their grasp Mike made a tremendous effort to lift the body, and between them they pulled and pushed until they had heaved it awkwardly up onto the bank.

Will's thin face was pale as he watched from his position on the far side of the glade under the rowan, whose orange berries provided the only colour in a monochrome landscape. Josie brushed past him, hurrying to the knot of men as Mike crawled out of the lake and lay panting on the ground. Gavin and Terry turned Duncan's body over and she knelt down to hold his wrist, feeling vainly for a pulse.

The bushes behind them stirred and Anna emerged, creating another point of unexpected brightness in her red duffle coat. She looked quickly at Will standing under the tree, touched with the horror of the scene he was witnessing, and beyond him she saw the group around the body, which lay on the ground streaming with water.

Anna's heart missed a beat as she saw Mike lying prone nearby, but quickly recovered its pace as he pushed himself slowly onto his knees. She crossed the glade, faltering at the sight of Duncan's open eyes staring sightlessly up at her through the strands of green weed draping his face in the grotesque impression of a mask. She turned away resolutely and said bluntly, 'It's obviously too late to do anything.'

Mike raised his bowed head quickly. 'What the hell are you doing here?' he demanded angrily.

'Someone has to meet the police and the doctor on the farm lane and bring them to the right place,' Anna replied equably. She looked down on the body, her face tightening. 'I brought this, in case it helped.' She held out a flask of brandy in a gloved hand that shook.

Josie looked up, her face very white under her spiky black hair. 'Not him,' she said starkly. 'He's dead.' She stood up, rubbing her hands compulsively on her jeans as Gavin turned away and ran into the nearby rhododendrons.

There were sounds of violent retching and Mike looked towards the heaving form that was just visible in the bushes. 'Give him some of the brandy,' he said briefly.

Anna turned reluctantly towards Gavin and felt immensely grateful when Josie came to join her. 'I'll do it,' she said. 'Come and give me a hand.' Anna gave her the flask, deliberately keeping her eyes away from the silent shape on the ground, and followed the girl as she moved purposefully over to Gavin's convulsed figure.

Terry stood irresolutely beside Duncan's body, gesturing towards it as he looked at Mike. 'What should we do with him? Can we at least cover him up?' He glanced towards the blue donkey jacket Sue had left behind in her flight to the priory.

Mike was breathing more easily now, although he stood in a growing pool of water that oozed out of his sodden trousers. He hesitated, seemingly unaware of the wet cloth clinging to his legs. 'I don't like to leave him like this,' he admitted. 'But there's nothing we can do for him. I think it may be better if we move him as little as possible until the police come.'

Will had left the shelter of the rowan tree and drawn closer to the group. He drew in his breath with a sharp hiss as he stared at Mike.

'Do you think it's,' Terry baulked at the thought, but said with an effort, 'foul play?'

Mike stared at him bleakly for a while until the young man began to fidget. 'Your guess is as good as mine,' Mike said at last. 'But in the first place I find it difficult to imagine why he should come here on his way to the dig. From his cottage it's simpler to come through the priory. And, secondly, I can't see why he couldn't get himself out if he fell in accidentally.' He gestured to his own wet and muddy figure. 'The water only comes to just above my waist. He shouldn't have had any problem.'

Anna came hurrying back to them. 'I should have told you earlier,' she said contritely. 'The police said that it would help if you moved around as little as possible. And,' she carefully avoided looking down as she spoke, 'could you move him only as much as you had to if,' she faltered, but recovered herself quickly, 'if there's nothing you can do for him.'

Mike glanced at Terry. 'That settles it then.' He looked sharply at Anna. 'You'd better get to the lane to meet them. Will, go with her.'

They set off silently back through the rhododendron thicket, the sound of dripping water in their ears as the sunlight strengthened and melted the frost on the bushes. Will hesitated when they reached the path that wound round the lake and led to Leygar's Farm. 'Where did you tell them to come?' he asked Anna.

'Along the farm lane to the cottage junction,' she said. 'I thought that was the fastest approach. Should we cut across the park, do you think?'

Will pondered briefly and then nodded. 'It's faster, and we won't mess up Sue's tracks from the farm.' Or anything else, he added to himself.

'I left Hades shut in the kitchen,' Anna told him as they strode across the rough uneven turf, which felt mushy underfoot as it thawed. 'I was afraid he might get out otherwise and come to find you.'

'Thanks. How's Sue?' he demanded anxiously.

'Lucy had just got her to the house when I finished on the phone,' Anna replied. 'She was looking pretty ghastly, and of course she was very cold. Gina had run a hot bath for her, so she and Lucy got her straight into it. I left them dosing her with brandy in warm milk.'

Anna glanced at the youth's set face. 'She did awfully well, Will. She'll be alright when she gets over the shock and the cold. Lucy wants me to ask Dr Bishop to go up to check her over when he finishes here.'

'Did you ring him too?' Will asked.

'Of course,' Anna said. 'Him first, then the police. I was going to ring for an ambulance as well, but the police said they'd see to that.' Her voice wavered, and she paused to control it before continuing, 'Dr Bishop was just leaving his surgery, so he's coming here straight away. I thought there was just a chance that Sue might be wrong, you see. That Duncan might still be alive...'

'Look!' Will interrupted her, pointing ahead to where a silver Volvo estate was visible, coming at speed along the lane past the farm cottage. 'That's Dr Bishop's car.'

'Come on then,' Anna said, and they began to run, stumbling awkwardly in places over unkempt clumps of grass.

Dr Bishop had just turned into the lane leading to the manor and was hovering at the junction, obviously looking for some sign of them. He spotted their figures racing towards him and accelerated rapidly in a shower of gravel, bring the Volvo to an abrupt halt as he drew closer to them.

He was just getting out of the car as they reached him, panting heavily. 'You don't seem that fit,' he greeted them, glaring fiercely from beneath his bushy eyebrows. 'Where's this body then, Anna? I suppose it is a body?' he queried brusquely.

'Yes, I'm afraid so,' she said breathlessly, pushing away the long black curls that had tumbled over her flushed face. 'They've got him out of the lake but he's definitely dead.'

He stared over her head. 'Down by the lake? Well, let's get going.'

They turned back with him, but after taking a few steps Anna stopped. 'I'd better stay here,' she said. 'Otherwise the police won't know where to go.'

The doctor paused and glanced over his shoulder at her. 'Quite right. No need for us to hang around too, Will. Let's get on.'

They had just disappeared from sight into the undergrowth around the lake when Anna heard another vehicle approaching along the farm lane. She turned her head in time to see a police car with two occupants arrive at the junction, and waved her arm vigorously to attract their attention.

As it approached and drew up beside her Anna recognised the passenger. He got ponderously out of the car, a square man of middling height and middling girth. Shrewd blue eyes surveyed her from a rubicund face. 'Miss Evesleigh, isn't it? It's not all that long since I last saw you, Miss.'

Anna searched her memory frantically and suddenly remembered. 'You're Sergeant Peters, of course. How nice to see you again. At least...' she floundered.

He smiled slowly. 'That's alright, Miss. Now what's this all about? Somebody in the lake, you said on the phone.'

'Yes, that's right. Shall I tell you about it on the way? Will Rossington's just taken Dr Bishop there.'

'Just a minute, Miss.' The sergeant turned to the young constable who had climbed out of the car and was standing silently beside it, his eyes fixed on Anna in open admiration. 'Now then, Cranley, you'd better come with us and see where we are. Then you can come back here and wait for the inspector.'

'Yessir,' the constable said, his pimply face colouring as Anna looked across at him.

'The inspector?' she queried as she led Sergeant Peters across the turf towards the lake with the young constable at their heels.

'Inspector Elliot, Miss. You'll remember him too, I expect,' he said comfortably.

Just as if, Anna thought, biting her lip to prevent herself from laughing hysterically, they had all taken part in a jolly outing earlier in the year rather than a dramatic rescue.

'Now then,' Sergeant Peters continued, 'who found this chap in the lake?'

'Sue,' Anna hesitated, realising that she did not know Sue's surname. 'One of the students on the dig. She was coming down from the farm to the cloisters by the short cut and saw something unusual in the water. When she went to investigate she found it was Duncan Hamilton and she did her best to drag him out. Of course he was far too heavy for her and she came up to the priory for help. Mike Shannon, you'll remember him,' she couldn't resist saying, 'took a couple of men down to the lake with Will and they've just got his body out.'

'Professor Shannon.' The sergeant smiled slowly. 'Yes, indeed I remember him, but then, of course, I see quite a lot of him. Leastways I hear him quite a lot.' He chuckled.

'Oh?' Anna was intrigued, glad to have her mind taken away from what awaited them by the lake.

'Yes Miss, down in the Lobster Pot. I often come with the missus now they've started doing meals. Mavis Marling's doing the cooking, and she does a good seafood platter. You can't help hearing the professor if he's there. He's as good as a show sometimes.'

Anna stored these comments up gleefully as the sergeant returned to the current situation. 'And just who is the unfortunate man they've brought out of the lake?' he enquired. 'Duncan Hamilton, you said?'

'Yes, he's an archaeologist too. He's, at least he was,' Anna corrected herself carefully, 'in charge of the students at the dig.'

'Ah, do you say so? Not a lucky job that, it would seem,' he commented, watching her with his shrewd eyes.

'Why?' she asked, puzzled.

'Or maybe archaeology is a dangerous business,' he continued thoughtfully.

'What on earth do you mean?' Anna demanded as they approached the plank bridge. 'Oh,' she caught her breath. 'Of course, I'd forgotten. There was another one, wasn't there?'

'That's right, Miss. Went over the cliff, that one did. Just here, is it? Ah yes, I see.' His eyes scanned the ground and he suppressed a sigh at the sight of all the footsteps. 'Well, I don't think there's any need for you to stay now. I expect you'll be wanting to get back to the house. It would help if you went back the way you came. We'll be up to have a word with everyone later, if you'll ask them to stay put. We don't want any more people coming down here now.' He came to a sudden stop and gave her an enquiring glance. 'I suppose this student that found the body is up at the house?'

Anna nodded, tearing her eyes away from the group that

was just visible through the gap in the massed rhododendrons. 'That's right,' the sergeant said, satisfied. 'You take care of her there then.'

'Thank goodness,' Anna exclaimed, and saw Mike lift his head at the sound of her voice. 'You've just reminded me. Would you ask Dr Bishop to come up to the house when he can? Sue got terribly wet and of course she's very shocked, so Miss Rossington would like him to have a look at her.'

'I'll do that,' he said. 'And I won't keep anyone here any longer than necessary. I expect the men are wet too. We don't want them getting colds.' He watched her set off over the plank bridge and then turned to the young constable, who was waiting patiently beside him. 'You'd better get back to the car, Cranley, and bring the inspector down here when he arrives. Try to watch where you're putting your feet.' The constable set off and Sergeant Peters pushed his way through the bushes as Mike came forward from the lakeside to meet him.

Lucy stood at the French windows staring blindly from the sitting room onto the western terrace, totally oblivious of the sweep of green grass gleaming wetly in the midday sunshine. Her chestnut hair fell around her face, concealing her expression from the rest of the room. Don't be stupid, she castigated herself fiercely. Stop feeling guilty. Just concentrate on the facts and see where they lead. So I was edgy about John Brett's death. Why? There must be a reason. She set her lips firmly as she considered. Well, the police will probably look at it again now, she realised, so maybe they'll find something that will connect up.

Her train of thought was broken as Will said, 'Mike's been in there for ages. I wonder what they're asking him?'

Lucy turned slowly to face the room. She felt insensibly comforted as she saw the familiar jumble of armchairs, the faded colours of chintz and tapestry given new life in the pools of brightness cast by the table lamps. 'I expect he knows a bit more about Duncan than we do,' she said.

Her brother's face lightened. He turned from his stance on the hearth-rug, avoiding the black dog lying alertly beside him, and picked up another log to put on the fire.

'Lucy,' Anna spoke from the depths of the wing chair beside the fireplace, where she had been sitting silently watching the flames, 'surely it's odd that both the men doing that job have died in such a short time?'

'It does seem strange,' Lucy agreed. 'But why on earth should...' she broke off.

Will quickly picked up her words. 'Why on earth should anybody kill them?' He looked at her challengingly. 'That's what you were going to say, isn't it?'

'Yes,' Lucy answered bluntly. 'Why should Duncan have fallen into the lake? And if somebody bumped him off, then Brett's death must seem suspicious too.'

A hissing gasp made them turn round quickly, and Hades leaped to his feet. Liz stood in the doorway, a coat covering her dungarees and a look of horror on her normally placid face. She broke the stunned silence as they all stared at her. 'Lucy, I'm sorry. I couldn't help hearing. Surely they must be accidents. Why on earth should they be anything else?' She stopped abruptly. 'I'm sorry. Of course, I don't even know what's happened. Just a garbled story from Terry.'

Liz sighed in exasperation as she watched Hades resettle himself on the hearth-rug. She pushed back the patterned shawl she had loosely wrapped around her head and shoulders, revealing long brown hair that had almost entirely escaped from its chignon. 'After you all left I took the students into the church. I wanted to keep an eye on the paintings,' she said frankly. 'I'm not risking anything else happening to either of them. Anyway, it's marginally warmer in there. Then a girl had hysterics and began to make some of the others edgy, so I had to deal with her. By then one of the chaps was looking pretty sick, so I had to see to him as well.'

She shook her head in disbelief as she unbuttoned her heavy coat. 'It was some time before I got them sorted out. I thought it was better to keep them working, though God knows what damage they'll do. Most of them are back in the cloister walk, but I've left a couple in the church doing basic tidying. There's no way,' she added sternly, 'any of them are touching those paintings. Anyway, Terry came back at last. He had got very wet,' she bit her lip as she realised how this had happened, 'and had been back to the farmhouse to change his clothes. I gather Gavin was taken ill so Josie is staying there with him. Terry's being very stern and reticent, so I've left him in charge of the excavation while I came here. All he would say was that Duncan was dead and the police were here and that we had to wait for them.' She looked round appealingly. 'For heaven's sake, what is going on?'

'It's quite true, I'm afraid,' Lucy said, leading Liz to the armchair opposite Anna and pushing her firmly into it. 'They did find Duncan in the lake and I'm afraid he was dead before they got there.'

Liz raised her hands to her face, which had gone a muddy grey colour. 'I didn't really believe it, even when Terry said,' she whispered through her fingers. She stared round at them. 'How on earth did he fall in?'

Lucy rapidly reviewed what she had been saying when Liz appeared. 'We don't know yet,' she said noncommittally. 'The police haven't told us anything. They're just hearing our accounts at the moment.' Alibis? she queried mentally.

'But,' Liz's hands fell into her lap and her eyes were fixed on Lucy's face, 'you were saying... I heard you...'

Lucy's lips set firmly. 'One can't help wondering when John Brett and Duncan have both died in such a short space of time.'

'But is there any reason to suppose there's something wrong about their deaths?' Liz persisted, leaning forward. 'Surely not. I can't believe it.'

'No,' Lucy said, 'there isn't.' Her tone became wry. 'It's easy to be suspicious about nothing.'

Anna glanced at her sharply and spoke before Will could open his mouth. 'Lucy has a suspicious nature,' she said as Will glared at her indignantly. 'She always had, even as a child, and of course that business earlier this year just made her worse.'

Liz stared at her, puzzled, and then her expression lightened. 'Oh, do you mean the trouble you had over the chalice?'

'Yes, you must have heard all about it from Mike,' Anna said, stretching out her long legs in front of her and considering her snugly-fitting jeans thoughtfully. Will muffled a spurt of laughter as he turned towards the fireplace, resting his arm against the mantelpiece and leaning his head on it to stare into the flames.

'No,' Liz said doubtfully, 'I don't think Mike mentioned it. I expect I heard about it down at the pub. The locals do talk about it a lot.' She looked round at Lucy and asked, 'Where is Mike? I thought he'd be here.'

'He is. He's in with the police at the moment.'

'Oh, I see.' Liz sounded startled. 'I didn't realise they were in the house.'

'Yes. I expect they'll be glad you're here,' Lucy added. 'They'll probably want to speak to you before they get on to the students.'

'Me?' Liz's voice rose in surprise as her hands clutched the arms of her chair. 'What for?'

Anna regarded her curiously. 'They'll need to talk to everyone to find out when Duncan was last seen.'

'Yes, of course,' Liz relaxed her grip and sank back against the cushions. 'Lucy's beginning to infect me with her alarms. I haven't had anything to do with the police before but you must all be veterans.'

Anna's dark blue eyes sparkled mischievously. 'Oh yes. The sergeant is a pet. He greeted me like an old friend.'

Liz looked taken aback but Lucy said suddenly, 'I am stupid. I wonder if David knows anything about this yet.' She glanced over at Will. 'Do you know what he's doing today?'

Her brother turned away from the fireplace, saying, 'He was going over to Pethick's this morning to discuss their flock. He wants to introduce some older breeds.' Will flushed, catching himself up before his enthusiasm ran away with him. He looked hurriedly at his watch. 'He's coming home for lunch so he may be back by now. Shall I go and see if he is?' He moved forward as he spoke and Hades stirred hopefully on the rug.

Lucy put out a slender hand. 'No, I'd better go. He's often about early so he might have seen Duncan this morning. If the police want me I'll be in the estate office. I'll wait for David there if he isn't back yet.'

The crackle of burning wood was the only sound in the room after Lucy had left it. The occupants were absorbed in their own thoughts and only Anna noticed the gentle aroma of apple arising from the logs on the fire, mingling with the pine scent from the fir cones that filled a bowl on the nearby side table. The silence was eventually broken by Liz. 'Where's everyone else?' she asked.

'Gran went into town this morning, and Steven went with her,' Will replied, moving away from the hearth to sit down on a wide footstool and lean back against a chair beside the coffee table. 'Hugh went down to the quay. They'll all be back for lunch. Aren't they going to get a surprise?' he ended irrepressibly.

They heard footsteps approaching along the corridor and turned to stare expectantly at the sitting-room door. Sergeant Peters appeared in the doorway where his square figure solidly filled the space. He stood still, deliberately looking round at the occupants of the room before he stepped aside to allow Mike to pass him.

The sergeant followed him with heavy steps into the room, his shrewd eyes fixed on Liz. 'And who, Miss, are you?' he asked.

Mike said in a subdued voice, 'Liz, this is Sergeant Peters.

This is Liz Bexington, Sergeant. The art specialist I mentioned.'

'Ah yes, thank you, Professor. Well, Miss,' the sergeant turned to her, 'if it's convenient, I'm sure the inspector would like a word with you.'

In spite of herself Liz smiled at the sound of this stereotyped formula as she got to her feet. 'Of course, Sergeant. Shall I come with you now?' She became aware of the coat she was still wearing, and shrugged out of it, flinging it onto the chair.

'If you'd be so good.' Sergeant Peters gestured towards the doorway.

Mike was standing unusually still, and as Liz passed him she put out her hand and squeezed his arm sympathetically. Mike did not seem to notice her touch, but threw himself into the armchair she had vacated, narrowly missing her coat as Lucy whipped it out of his way. He hunched forward for a few minutes, absently stroking Hades who had crept up to be comforted and comforting in this strained atmosphere.

Mike's face was set sternly as he sat back and passed a hand over his face. 'This is a hell of a business,' he said wearily. 'Where the devil is Hugh?'

'Apparently he went down to the quay,' Anna replied, raising her eyes from a deliberate contemplation of the fire.

'The quay?' Mike sounded exasperated, but still unnaturally quiet. 'What the hell is he doing down there?' he demanded.

'He's gone down to talk to old Bob about hiring a boat to do some fishing next year,' Will said as Hades went back to the hearth-rug, scratching it up around him before lying down on it with his head resting alertly on his paws. 'We thought it would be fun to go out by ourselves sometimes.'

'Fishing?' Mike sounded as if he had never heard of it and did not know what it was. 'Fun?'

'Mike,' Anna drew his attention. 'Do they know what happened?'

He studied her for a few seconds, noticing how pale her cheeks were in spite of the heat from the fire. 'They haven't told me if they do, but,' he yanked at the collar of his thick shirt, 'judging from the tenor of their questions, they think it wasn't a straightforward accident.' He looked round the room. 'Where's Sue?' he demanded, sitting up straight. 'Is she alright?'

'She's fine,' Anna reassured him. 'Dr Bishop gave her a sedative and she's asleep upstairs. Gina's keeping an eye on her.'

'What's happening at the dig?' he asked, almost as an afterthought. 'Did Liz say?'

'She's got it under control,' Anna told him. 'She left the students doing some work in the cloisters with umm, Terry, I think she said, in charge.' She glanced at Will, who nodded in agreement.

'Hell,' Mike said with more of his usual vigour. 'I hope they keep their minds on what they're doing.'

Anna did not answer this, but he met her eyes almost apologetically. 'I know, I know,' he said roughly. 'They can't possibly, but I can't help worrying about what they might miss or damage, even now. It's the most damnable business.'

He relapsed into sombre silence, staring at his bunched hands as they rested on his knees, until Will asked bluntly, 'Do you know if Duncan drowned, Mike?'

Mike looked up and hesitated fractionally before replying. 'I haven't got much medical knowledge, so I don't really know. But,' he looked from Will to Anna, 'you both saw that the lake isn't particularly deep there. Why should he have drowned in such shallow water? That's what strikes me as particularly odd. And,' he added to Anna, 'I don't know if you noticed, but I reckon that he was in the same clothes he wore at the pub last night.'

'You mean,' she blurted out, 'that he may have been there since last night?'

'I don't know.' Mike's mouth tightened. 'But the police must by now. What times did they ask you about?'

'Well,' Anna pondered, 'they didn't specifically.' She explained hastily as a frown began to form on his face, 'They just asked me when I last saw Duncan and what I've been doing since.'

Mike nodded approvingly. 'Elliot knows his stuff alright. That was when you left the pub, was it?' he asked suddenly.

'Yes,' Anna said equably. 'I went straight home and didn't leave the house again until this morning when I came over here.' She stopped speaking and her mouth fell slightly open. She continued with mounting amazement, 'They asked me who I saw on the road. I thought they wanted to know if I'd seen Duncan, but I bet they're going to check up on me.'

Mike's eyes brightened with amusement at her indignation. 'Probably. After all, they do know about your martial arts skills.' He went on hastily as her delicately arched eyebrows began to draw together, 'Did you see anyone? Or, more to the point, did anyone see you?'

'I did pass a couple of cars, but that's no use. It was dark, of course, so I couldn't see whose they were and they couldn't possibly have recognised me either. Still, at least Daddy was up when I got home this time. So I'm better off than when poor Graham died in the spring.' Her expression cleared. 'And this morning I passed all and sundry, so that shouldn't be a problem.'

'It depends on what the crucial times are,' Mike said deflatingly.

Anna considered this, studying his face thoughtfully. 'You do think he was killed, don't you?'

He looked at her and reiterated stubbornly, 'I just don't see how it could have been an accident.' He glanced irritably at his watch. 'I wish Hugh was here. Elliot will want to talk to him too.'

As Mike finished speaking they heard movements in the corridor and looked up hopefully. Anna had to suppress a giggle as she saw how Mike's face clouded with disappointment when Liz appeared.

Liz, though, was in such a perturbed state that she did not

seem to notice this. 'Mike, why on earth didn't you mention the painting?' she demanded as she came into the sitting room and stood on the far side of the coffee table, gripping the back of one of the upright chairs.

He looked at her blankly. 'The painting? I didn't think of it. I suppose it didn't seem relevant.'

They had not heard Inspector Elliot approach. He stood quietly just inside the doorway, a tall man with cool grey eyes, and they were startled when he said levelly, 'And yet I asked you if anything strange or out-of-the way had happened.'

'Yes,' Mike agreed, running a hand distractedly through his hair, 'but I was thinking of things to do with Hamilton. The painting didn't cross my mind.' His voice sharpened. 'Do you think there's some link?'

The inspector was noncommittal. 'We'll have to consider it, of course. Do you have any ideas about how the damage could have been done?'

Will sat up quickly. 'Damage? What damage?' he demanded, looking from Mike to the inspector.

'I understand from Miss Bexington,' the inspector said, watching Will, 'that she uncovered part of an important wall painting in the church yesterday. This morning she found that a further part of the surface had been freshly removed, damaging the work underneath. She thinks this was done deliberately,' he concluded. 'Didn't you know about it?'

Will shook his head and Inspector Elliot came further into the room, revealing his well-tailored grey suit as he stopped in the pool of light cast by a nearby lamp. He glanced enquiringly at Anna, who silently shook her head too. 'You appear to have kept rather quiet about it,' he said to Mike.

'Good God, man!' Mike replied explosively. 'Hasn't enough happened to put it out of my mind? Do you expect me to be worrying about the damned painting when I've just pulled Hamilton's body out of the lake?'

Liz stared at him in amazement but the inspector continued

calmly, 'So have you considered how the damage may have been done?'

'No, I haven't,' Mike replied shortly, glancing at Liz. 'I couldn't agree with Liz's idea at all, as I expect she's told you.'

Liz spread her hands apologetically as the inspector watched them both. 'I'm sorry, Mike. I was very upset at the time and it seemed the most likely way for it to have happened. But now I quite see that Sue couldn't have done it.'

'Sue!' Will exclaimed indignantly. 'She wouldn't have damaged the painting. That's stupid,' he said, glaring at Liz.

'I know, I know.' Liz was flustered. 'I didn't think she'd done it on purpose. I just thought she was so eager that she'd started before I got there, and then got alarmed at the damage.'

'And run away?' Will asked scornfully. 'Sue wouldn't do that. She's got guts.'

'So she's shown,' Inspector Elliot agreed. 'Do any of you have any idea how the damage could have been caused?'

He looked round the room, noting the head shaking and murmured negatives. Only Anna hesitated and the inspector's gaze settled on her, his grey eyes watching as her mobile features reflected her uncertain thoughts.

The colour ran back into Anna's pale face. 'It's probably nonsense,' she said, looking apologetically at Mike, 'but there seem to have been a lot of petty accidents at the priory just lately.'

'Oh?' Inspector Elliot queried encouragingly.

'Yes, I suppose that's true,' Mike agreed morosely. 'More than usual, anyway.'

'What sort of things?'

Anna glanced at Mike and then replied, 'Well, yesterday the trenches were flooded because somebody had left the tap on by the church. And the tower door was locked and the key went missing.'

'It was a morning of stupidities,' Mike said. 'When she arrived Sue tripped over a rope that had been moved in one of the cloister walks. She jarred her wrist, but didn't suffer any serious harm. But,' he added slowly, 'it was odd. There was no reason to move the rope, and no one admitted to doing it.'

'And Mike,' Liz said quickly, 'do you remember John Brett's funeral? Afterwards, you know, when you had to drive Professor Mersett to the station because there were nails in the tyres of both the cars left in the courtyard.'

'Interesting,' the inspector commented. He considered them all thoughtfully. 'Do you have any idea what's behind these incidents?'

Heads were again shaken in concert and the inspector asked Mike, 'Did you associate the damage done to the painting with these other incidents?'

'I haven't really had time to think about it,' he said. 'It seems to me, though, that the other things were irritating, but didn't actually do much harm.'

'But they could have done,' the inspector said softly, and after a second Mike grunted reluctant agreement.

'Well, I'd better go down with Sergeant Peters and talk to the students. Is there a room in the priory we can use for interviews, Professor?'

Mike collected his thoughts with an obvious effort. 'Yes. We use the tower room as a finds repository cum site office. You could base yourself there, although,' he added, 'you won't find it as comfortable as the study here.'

'I'm sure we'll manage,' Inspector Elliot said blandly. 'Sergeant Peters is a dab hand at civilising primitive accommodation, aren't you, Sergeant?' The sergeant, standing behind him, grinned amiably.

Mike pushed himself to his feet. 'I'll come down and show you where it is. I should explain to the students what's going on,' he said. Liz stepped uncertainly towards him, hesitating as he walked straight past her.

'Yes, that would be helpful, Professor. Thank you all for your time. I know you'll tell me if you remember anything else. Anything at all.' The inspector's cool gaze settled momentarily on Will, whose thin face flushed as he grinned. Mike was already standing near the sitting-room doorway, shuffling his feet impatiently, and the inspector moved towards him with an imperturbable countenance. 'Let's get down to the priory, Professor. I'm sure you're anxious to be there.'

Will muffled a laugh, calling Hades over to him as the big dog got hopefully to his feet, his gleaming eyes fixed on Mike. 'Stay, Hades. Mike's going to be busy.' The big dog sat down unwillingly by his master's feet, alertly watching the departing men.

FIVE

The courtyard door slammed and Hades sprang up, barking loudly. He pushed past Mike and the policemen, who had all paused near the sitting-room doorway, and his long tail began to lash furiously as he vanished from sight along the corridor towards the hall.

Hasty footsteps came towards them, drumming on the oak floorboards. A grim-faced Hugh was still wearing his waxed jacket, with a thick scarf wound round his neck, as he entered the room with Hades at his heels. He stopped just inside the doorway, looking quickly round at the silent group of people waiting there, frozen into a tableau in the pools of light cast by the lamps. Mike stood near the door between the two policemen, his tousled red hair vivid above his strained face. Hugh's gaze passed over him and noted Liz standing alone, her eyes wide and startled. Will raised his head to stare at his brother-in-law, and from the fire Anna met his regard unhappily. Hugh paled under his tan. 'Lucy?' he demanded abruptly. 'Where is she?'

His eyes met Mike's in urgent enquiry and his friend responded instantly, shocked at the fear he saw in Hugh's face. 'She's fine, Hugh. She's fine.'

Will sat up straight and chipped in quickly, 'She's in the estate office waiting for David.'

The tension drained out of Hugh's rigid figure and the

colour ran back into his face as animation returned to the scene in the room. He studied the others while he pulled off his scarf and unzipped his jacket. 'So what have you been up to while I've been out?'

Will spluttered indignantly but had no time to answer as Hugh turned to the policemen who were standing quietly next to Mike. He held out his hand. 'How are you, Elliot? And you, Sergeant? It seems just like old times to see you both here again.'

The inspector's eyes held a hint of warmth as he shook Hugh's hand. 'I'm afraid it always seems to be bad news that brings us, but fortunately not as bad as you feared,' he commented.

Hugh casually lifted a shoulder. 'You must blame your man on the door for that.'

'Oh?'

'When I expressed surprise at finding him standing sentry duty in the courtyard, he stolidly informed me that there had been an incident, 'as you might say, sir,' and the inspector would tell me more about it.'

'I see. Certainly that must have been worrying, but, as you know, it is normal practice,' Inspector Elliot replied, watching as Hugh threw his jacket over a chair in the corner of the room.

Mike broke in impatiently. 'The most damnable thing, Hugh. Hamilton is dead.'

'Hamilton?' Hugh ejaculated, swinging round to stare at him. 'For God's sake, he was fine last night.' His eyes narrowed as he turned back to the inspector. 'Murdered?' he demanded without preamble.

The inspector considered him thoughtfully. 'He was found in the lake this morning. The...' he broke off as a babble of noise reached them from the hall.

They all heard Isobel Rossington's clear voice saying, 'Well, that certainly puts paid to the chalice question, doesn't it?' And then, sharply, 'Don't be so silly, Steven. Of course you must come with us.'

She entered the sitting room imperiously, still wrapped in her green loden coat with the collar turned up to frame her short iron-grey bob, and Juno trotting close to her heels. They were followed by a sullen Steven, his shoulders hunched in his thick jacket, and behind him came Lucy and David. The estate manager appeared stunned, but Lucy's eyes met Hugh's for a brief moment across the room and then looked away.

'Well!' Isobel said forcefully, turning down her collar and opening her coat. 'I've only been away for a few hours. Just what is going on?' She nodded to the policemen. 'Not again, inspector. While I'm always pleased to see you personally, I can't help wishing these formal calls weren't necessary. Lucy tells us that unfortunate young Hamilton is dead.' She paused and looked round enquiringly at them all.

'I'm afraid so, Mrs Rossington,' Inspector Elliot answered. 'He was found in the lake this morning.'

'Drowned?' she demanded.

'I haven't had the doctor's report yet,' the inspector replied evasively. 'I was just about to go down to the excavation to interview the students, but as you are all back I think it would be better if you could spare me a few minutes now.'

'Of course,' Isobel replied, 'but can we get out of our coats?' She indicated Steven and herself. 'We came straight in here, you see.'

'Please do,' Elliot said as Hugh stepped forward to help her out of her coat, which he put with scant ceremony with his own. 'I'd like to have a word with Mr Carey first anyway. But perhaps you could just introduce me to the people I don't yet know.' He glanced at Steven and David.

'How remiss of me,' Isobel apologised. 'My manners have quite disappeared with the shock. Steven Poole, who is indexing the books my husband collected, and David Weryt, our estate manager.'

The inspector openly assessed both of the young men who

stood in front of him, one sullen and scared, the other half-horri-fied, half-excited. Steven thrust his chin out and stared defiantly at him, his fists clenched in his jacket pockets, while David smiled hesitantly as he held out a tentative hand in greeting.

Inspector Elliot shook it briefly, noting the skinned knuckles and seeing how the young man's face flushed as he remembered them. 'I would like to see you both shortly,' the inspector said, 'so would you wait here.'

Steven's expression grew resentful and he lowered himself into an armchair near the window, where he sat pulling nerv-ously at his lower lip. David thrust his hands behind his back and moved to stand by the fireplace besides Hades, who lay watchfully on the hearth-rug with Juno tucked against his side.

'Are you based in the study again, Elliot?' Hugh asked, adding with a touch of wry humour, 'Perhaps we should make it over to you.'

'For the interim that would certainly be useful,' the inspector said as they left the sitting room and walked down the corridor to the wide hall, which was gloomy in the midday light. 'Would it inconvenience you?'

'No, I don't think so. I can share Lucy's office for anything I need to do over the next few days. Steven is based in here, but he works on his laptop in different rooms as there are books scattered all over the place,' Hugh said as they entered the study at the far end of the house. 'Presumably he can still use this room when you don't need it?'

'Of course. It's useful for talking privately to people, but we shan't keep anything here,' Elliot replied. 'We'll try to inconven-ience you as little as possible.'

'Fine.' Hugh switched on the overhead light and the dull shades of the room vanished as the gilt lettering gleamed on the book spines and the rich red of the brocade curtains sprang to life. His eye was caught by movement beyond the mullioned window in the north front of the house, and he watched a flock of birds skittering across the sky above the overgrown front drive. 'Fieldfares, I think' he said, reaching for the binoculars that hung from a nearby bookcase. 'They arrived early this year. Yes, about forty.' He put the binoculars down and made a note on a nearby pad.

'Sorry about that.' Hugh turned back to the inspector. 'I keep a record of sightings. Take a seat.' He grinned as he saw that his modern ergonomic chair had been replaced by a wing chair behind the desk, which stood at an angle between the north window and the French windows opening onto the eastern terrace. Beyond this a small lawn ran down to a narrow track which connected the front and back drives, and Hugh automatically assessed the blackbirds scurrying busily over the grass now that the frost had disappeared. 'It's quite comfortable,' he assured the inspector, who was eyeing the triangular structure cautiously, 'but use the wing chair if you prefer it.' He seated himself in one of the deep armchairs facing the other man and waited for him to speak.

The inspector seemed in no hurry to begin. He perched on the side of the desk and looked thoughtfully round the room as the sergeant settled himself on one of the upright chairs against the wall near the door. The study was similar in size to the sitting room but looked smaller because the cream walls were lined with shelves full of books. Elliot indicated these with a casual hand. 'Are these what Poole is sorting out?'

'Mainly,' Hugh said, regarding him from narrowed eyes. 'He's looking through all the books in the house, and there are plenty in every room. They've been scattered around according to individual interests, so some of the more valuable ones have been lying on the open shelves. Steven even found a Georgian cookery book tucked away in the kitchen. I believe there are plans afoot for a trial of some of the recipes.' He indicated the locked glass-fronted bookcase behind him. 'As you can see, we're taking slightly more precautions now. The books that I know to be particularly rare have been moved here, and Steven brings in any more that he finds.'

'A wise move,' the inspector commented as he squinted at the books, unable to read the titles embossed on the worn leather covers. 'What have you got?'

'Do you really want to get me started on this?' Hugh enquired in mock surprise. 'I could go on for hours, you know. Why don't you look at them later if you want to?'

'I'd like to,' Elliot replied unabashed. 'I was interested in them last time I came when they were all lying around in heaps, but right now I'm curious about how much they're worth.'

'I see,' Hugh said levelly. 'Well, they haven't been valued yet but, roughly speaking, they're probably jointly worth in the region of ten thousand pounds. But there are a few early editions that are individually much more valuable than the others.' Elliot whistled softly as Hugh leaned over the arm of his chair and pointed. 'That folio there is a copy of Aubrey's *Brief Lives* in mint condition. This large one is Celia Fiennes' *Journeys*. And these on the lower shelf are Clarendon's *History of the Great Rebellion*, his complete works and all first editions.'

He turned back to face the inspector, aware of the sergeant shifting heavily on his seat near the door. 'I know they shouldn't really be here, but they've been lying around for years without any problem. Anyway, Duncan Hamilton had no connection with these. Nor, as far as I know, had he even seen them.'

'Hmm,' the inspector was not diverted. 'Steven Poole. The name is familiar. Why is that?' He shot the question at Hugh, who maintained his composure with ease.

'Your memory has always been pretty good, Elliot,' was all he said, leaning back in his chair.

'Yes. Kingsley Hall, wasn't it?'

Hugh nodded, his hands clasped lightly over the arms of his chair. 'Last year.'

'There's been no trace of the books and the chap they want to question about the theft hasn't been picked up yet,' the inspector said. 'He seems to have disappeared altogether.' He studied Hugh. 'Aren't you concerned about having Poole here?'

'I looked into the matter pretty thoroughly before taking him on,' Hugh said frankly. 'Steven hadn't been able to get a job after the robbery, but there was no indication that he was involved in any way. The whole business has given him a chip on his shoulder, as you'll find out. It's always unfortunate when a crime remains unsolved – anyone connected with the matter stays suspect in the eyes of most people.'

'That's inevitable.'

'Yes, but difficult to cope with,' Hugh said. 'And his personality makes it even more difficult.'

'How about young Weryt?' Inspector Elliot changed his tack. 'What do you know about him?'

'Chapter and verse,' Hugh said succinctly, a smile lightening his face. 'He comes from a farming background in Herefordshire and was the prize student at Cirencester two years ago. A very bright and competent chap. Pleasant too.'

'How did you get him?' Elliot enquired.

'He's enormously keen on organic farming and traditional methods, so we've more or less given him carte blanche to put his ideas into practice.' Hugh met the inspector's eyes with amusement in his own. 'We have an added advantage as the priory land hasn't been intensively farmed. Lack of cash sometimes brings unexpected benefits. Just as well,' he added, 'because job vacancies aren't always easy to fill when the previous incumbent was murdered.'

'Does he get into fights often?' Elliot asked. Hugh raised an eyebrow in surprise. 'You haven't seen his hand?' the inspector queried, and Hugh shook his head. 'Well, he's clearly struck somebody recently.'

Hugh let out an exasperated sigh. 'Damn! I'll bet that's how Steven got his incipient black eye. I have noticed that.'

Elliot picked up a pencil and twirled it between his fingers. 'The markings are fairly obvious. Don't they get on?'

'Not particularly. Steven seems to have got it in for David, and David finds him intolerable,' Hugh said frankly. 'It must have happened after the pub closed last night. They were both there, David with friends and Steven inevitably on his own. Lucy commented at one stage that Steven was lurking by the bar, glowering at David and his party of women.' A thought struck Hugh and he frowned. 'Didn't you meet them when Brett died?' he demanded.

The inspector shook his head. 'I wasn't much involved in that. There seemed to be no need,' he said. 'It was regarded as an accident.'

'Was?' Hugh picked up the tense quickly.

Elliot did not reply directly. 'So Weryt is rather ready with his fists, is he?'

'I'd hardly say that on the basis of one incident,' Hugh responded. 'And Steven can be peculiarly offensive. Other people find him particularly hard to bear too.'

The sergeant's chair creaked as he muffled a snort of laughter, but the inspector was not diverted. 'One incident? I understood that he'd threatened one of your farmers too.'

'What?' Hugh sat up abruptly. 'Where did you hear that?'

The inspector inclined his head towards the sergeant, diligently taking notes in the background. 'Tom was in the Lobster Pot early last night. He overheard a chap complaining about your estate manager.'

Hugh relaxed back into his armchair and said lightly, 'Richard Dollery's an old humbug. They had a disagreement yesterday about a farming matter and David lost his temper. Unfortunate, but understandable. Dollery was probably deliberately winding him up and now he'll play on the incident for weeks.'

'Why did you assume that something had happened to your wife when you saw we were here?' Elliot asked suddenly.

'Yes, I'm afraid that was rather obvious,' Hugh said irritably. 'Lucy has doubts about Brett's death. Nothing definite that she can put a finger on. But,' he continued, aware that the scratching of the sergeant's pen had halted, 'she has what I can only describe as a fine instinct for atmosphere. I suspect that at some time she's noticed something, a nuance or a look, that's stuck in her subconscious.'

'I'd be inclined to agree with you,' the inspector said. 'She didn't mention this when I saw her.'

Hugh shrugged. 'She's adamant that it's just a feeling and is inclined to dismiss it as imagination or strained nerves. If she could identify a concrete fact she'd have told you about it.'

'Of course.' Elliot regarded Hugh thoughtfully. 'So when you saw our man at the door you immediately thought she was right and the murderer had caught up with her.'

'So Hamilton was murdered?' Hugh demanded.

'Yes. I can trust you to keep it to yourself, or at least,' he amended, 'between yourself and Miss Rossington at the moment. It will undoubtedly be common knowledge shortly. Dr Hamilton was hit on the back of the head with the traditional heavy object, irregular in shape and rough edged. We haven't yet found any signs that he was carried to the lake, so we're assuming at the moment that he must have been beside it and knocked in when he was attacked.'

'Wouldn't the coldness of the water have brought him round?' Hugh asked. 'It must be freezing.'

'Possibly, unless he was held down in it.' The inspector's voice was bleak.

'I see,' Hugh said grimly. 'Have you found the weapon?'

'Have you seen how many pieces of wood there are floating on the lake?' Elliot asked flatly.

'Clever,' Hugh commented.

'Do you have any ideas about it?'

Hugh shook his head. 'I'm afraid not. The whole thing seems quite bizarre. Hamilton has only been here since last Friday and seemed an equable sort of chap. He surely can't have upset anyone so badly in that time.' He frowned. 'Are you reconsidering Brett's death?' he asked.

'I think we must,' the inspector said.

'Well, the connection between the two seems to indicate it's something to do with the job. But what, for God's sake?' Hugh demanded. 'It must be pressing, otherwise Duncan wouldn't have been disposed of so quickly. That was taking a hell of a risk.'

'Mrs Rossington mentioned the chalice as she came in,' Elliot intervened, absently tapping the pencil he held against his knee. 'Are you thinking of doing something with it?'

Hugh's eyes held an arrested expression as they met his. 'Yes,' he said slowly. 'We're having, at least we were having, the archaeologists up for seasonal drinks tomorrow and it was suggested that we might show them the chalice.'

'Who suggested it?' Elliot asked quickly, the pencil suddenly still in his fingers.

'Mike Shannon,' Hugh replied. 'But,' he added, 'it would be easy enough to prime him for that.'

'Perhaps,' the inspector conceded. 'Why did he suggest it?'

'Nobody working on the dig has seen it, and it's widely regarded as a very fine example of fourteenth century craftsmanship. Mike feels that it should be more readily accessible to professionals with an interest in the period, and especially those working here where it was discovered.' Hugh added, 'None of us disagrees, of course. In fact, we feel we should have considered much sooner how to arrange for its safe exhibition until we decide whether we have to sell it.'

'Why did Mrs Rossington mention it when she came home?'

'She went into Corrington first thing this morning and called in at the bank to discuss the matter with the manager. I imagine he wasn't encouraging, but I haven't had a chance to hear what he said, as you know.'

'You didn't want to go yourself?'

'No,' Hugh replied. 'Isobel is perfectly capable of dealing with the matter.'

'Of course. I believe you had other arrangements to make anyway,' Elliot said blandly.

A sardonic smile touched Hugh's lips. 'They didn't involve disposing of Hamilton.'

'No, I don't imagine they did. What did they involve?'

'I want to hire a boat so that we can do some sea fishing in the new year,' Hugh explained. 'I had nothing planned for today so it seemed like a good opportunity to go down to the quay and sort it out with old Bob.'

'When did you decide to do that?'

'Over breakfast,' Hugh replied. 'Lucy had some work to finish here and Will wanted to go down to the dig to tell Sue about some new ideas that have just cropped up. Steven joined us at the table.' Hugh broke off and explained, 'He's staying in one of the estate cottages in the village, but he generally has his meals with us.'

'Professor Shannon is staying here too, isn't he?' Inspector Elliot asked. When Hugh nodded silently, a glimmer of amusement showed in the inspector's cool grey eyes. 'That must make meal times lively,' he commented dryly. In the background Sergeant Peters almost failed to smother another grunt of laughter.

'They generally are,' Hugh responded.

'And was today's breakfast any different?' Elliot enquired.

'Not really,' Hugh said. 'Steven was unwilling to participate in any new schemes, and that's certainly his usual attitude. It was over breakfast that I noticed the marks around his eye.' He added, 'I did refrain from commenting. We all did, even Will.'

The inspector put his amusement aside and pursued his line of enquiry. 'When did you go down to the quay?'

'I should think Will and I left the house at about nine o'clock. We went out together onto the back drive, then he set off behind the estate office towards the priory and I walked down the drive to the village. I met three or four people by the gates, including David who was just getting into his Land Rover. He'd already been in to the estate office, but he lives in the lodge beside the gates and had stopped off to collect something on his way

out to make a visit to one of the farms. We chatted for a bit.'
Hugh considered, rubbing his ear pensively as he stared out of
the French windows. 'For about five minutes, I should think.
Then David set off and I walked on down to the quay. I felt at
the time that I was passing virtually the entire population, and
they all wanted to stop and talk about something.' He added
ironically, 'Now I realise how fortunate it is that I saw so many
people. I can give you their names, if that would help.'

'Give them to Sergeant Peters afterwards,' Elliot replied.
'And last night I understand you were in the pub with your wife
and Miss Evesleigh. Did you come straight back here when you
left there?'

Hugh stared at him. 'Yes. Lucy and I left with Anna and
Duncan. She drove off from the pub and we walked home,
parting at the back gates. Duncan went on through the village
to the farm cottage. We walked up the back drive, came in and
didn't leave the house again until this morning. Isobel can vouch
for the time we came in,' he added. 'A bit after eleven, I think.
And we can vouch for each other overnight.'

'Couldn't Dr Hamilton have come back through the grounds
with you?' the inspector asked, twirling his pencil again.

'Of course,' Hugh said.

'Do you know why he didn't?'

'No. There's not much to choose between either route in
terms of distance, but he may have thought the village route
was quicker.'

'Did you see anybody else on your walk back?' Elliot asked.

'No,' Hugh replied, and then his expression sharpened.
'Though we did meet someone outside the gates just after Duncan
sheered off. The wretched woman who's staying with Tilly
Barlow. Shade, that's her name. She has a rather ghoulish appearance, glowing black eyes in a white face, and a general air of
oppression. Maybe Duncan saw her before we did and decided
to get away while he could.' He added, 'She was in the pub earlier with Tilly and I think she'd been waiting to waylay us.'

'For any particular purpose?'

Hugh's mouth twitched. 'She wanted to tell us about the priory and the damage we're doing. To the spirit of the place, not to the stones. She knows all about it, you see, and realises that what we're doing is from ignorance, not malice.' A muffled snort from behind disturbed him and he glanced at the sergeant, whose rubicund face was a shade darker. 'Precisely, Sergeant,' he said sardonically, 'my sentiments exactly.'

'What is it you're ignorant of?' the inspector asked with interest.

Hugh turned back to look at him, an eyebrow raised in mock surprise. 'You surely don't think I understood it. It's something to do with the conjunction of ley lines and the danger of disturbing the past. You know the sort of thing. I believe she's a mystic. Or do I mean a psychic?' He shrugged. 'Anyway, may it stand to my credit that I didn't recommend her to tell Mike all about it.' He added, with laughter in his voice, 'I'm sure she will anyway.'

'I'll keep a look out for her,' Elliot commented. 'So she was in the pub last night, but didn't actually speak to you there. Do you know why not?'

'No. But I can guess,' Hugh said. 'Tilly has, umm, a healthy respect for Mike's temper. I should guess she was dissuading her companion from trying it so publicly. Although,' he mused, 'I imagine Ms Shade is capable of giving as good as she gets.'

'I see,' the inspector responded. 'A battle of the giants.' He tapped his pencil thoughtfully against his leg. 'Miss Evesleigh says that your party was joined by Duncan Hamilton, Mike Shannon and Liz Bexington to talk about her theatre ideas. Who was there when you left?'

'Mike and Liz,' Hugh replied. 'They were still at our table, absorbed in heated discussions about the dig. David and his group had gone out earlier and we caught sight of them at the end of the quay, admiring the moonlight. Steven,' he grimaced, 'was coming up the street behind us. He's staying in the end terrace at the top of the street. He wasn't quite close enough to catch us up, but not quite far enough away to lose us either.' Hugh's expression lightened. 'He may even have fallen alive into the hands of Ms Shade.'

'Heated?' The inspector picked up the first comment, while the sergeant's thick fingers paused over his notebook and he sat up straighter on his hard chair. 'Were they arguing?'

Hugh gave a short laugh. 'Elliot, when didn't they? Not just this group, you understand, but archaeologists in general. About the means of excavating, the priorities, the significance of finds, anything you care to mention really.'

'I see.' Inspector Elliot was, in his turn, amused. 'Are you saying there was nothing out of the ordinary in this conversation?'

'Definitely. They regard debate as part of the job.'

Neither of them noticed the appreciative smile that spread over Sergeant Peters' face as he settled back on his seat.

'Would they all be interested in the chalice?' Elliot asked.

'Yes, even if they couldn't agree about its provenance,' Hugh said. 'Still, they won't be seeing it now. We can hardly go ahead with the party in the circumstances.'

The inspector was silent for a few minutes, his eyes cast down as he twirled the pencil between his fingers. He looked up to meet Hugh's gaze. 'The Kingsley Hall affair was one of a number of similar robberies,' he said. 'Did your researches indicate that?'

'No, they didn't,' Hugh replied slowly.

'Well, there have been four altogether over the last two years, in different counties. All in small country houses where various specialists were involved in some kind of work. Specific items were stolen each time, so the thieves knew exactly what to take. Jewellery, china, embroidery, and books at Kingsley Hall. Nobody has been arrested for any of the thefts, and no individual is linked with all of them, but Scotland Yard is convinced that these robberies are done to order and are organised by one person.'

'And do you think we may be next in line?' Hugh asked soberly. 'There were no deaths connected with the Kingsley Hall robbery. Were there at the others?'

'No. That's the rogue element here. Although deaths have been connected with the thefts, they've always occurred after the event.' The inspector sat up straighter as he explained, 'A number of people wanted for questioning have turned up dead at a later stage. So we have to consider whether they have been deliberately, conveniently, removed. Shot, run over, poisoned. There's no similarity in the way they died, the only connection is our suspicion about their involvement in these robberies.' He frowned as he gazed round the room. 'The books might be an attraction here, if they're well enough known. But the chalice strikes me as the sort of thing that a crooked collector would pay a very great deal for. And there was a fair amount of publicity about its discovery, so it's probably been noted in many quarters.' He looked across at Hugh. 'Do you want me to call in Scotland Yard?' he asked.

Hugh thought for a few seconds and then he shook his head decisively. 'Speaking purely for myself, no, I don't. I have every faith in your capacity to deal with this. With a bit of help from us,' he added with a smile. 'But I would have to consult the family.'

Elliot nodded as he dropped the pencil and got up from his perch on the desk to sit down in the leather wing chair behind it. 'Talk about it as privately as you can. Make absolutely sure nobody from outside can hear you. Not even the professor.' He studied the man opposite him. 'Would you be prepared to go ahead with the party tomorrow and show the chalice?' he asked unexpectedly.

'That's going to look odd, isn't it?' Hugh demanded.

The inspector sighed. 'Yes, I know. We'll have to think of a good reason for doing it.'

'Do you actually want us to produce the chalice?' Hugh

asked, a note of incredulity in his voice.

'I don't know.' Elliot tapped his fingers lightly on the arm of his chair. 'There's over twenty-four hours until you'd need to. We can turn up a lot in that time. Would you prefer not to display it?'

'Obviously I wouldn't want to if there's a risk involved. Apart from its historical value, the chalice is the family's insurance,' Hugh said firmly. 'I must talk to the others. But I don't think we could refuse to help if there's a chance of catching the person behind all this.'

'I can't guarantee that, of course,' the inspector said. 'If we do pick somebody up it's likely to be a front person, a small cog who won't or can't lead us back to the brains behind the operation.'

'That's obviously a chance we'd have to take,' Hugh said. 'Before we discuss it any further, let's get Isobel in and see what happened at the bank.'

The inspector nodded to Sergeant Peters, who rose promptly from his chair and left the room. Silence fell in the study. Inspector Elliot's eyes were running over the books on the shelves around him, while Hugh watched a jaunty robin investigating the cracks between the paving stones on the terrace. The bird looked up as a wren's loud churring alarm rang out, echoed almost immediately by shrill scolding from several blackbirds. They all flew away in a flurry of movement as Hugh glimpsed a sparrowhawk swooping over the rhododendrons.

His attention returned to the room as the sergeant ushered in Isobel Rossington, brisk in her tweed skirt and heather-coloured jumper. Both men stood up and Hugh brought over one of the upright chairs, placing it near his own. She looked from one to the other of them as she sat down. 'You look like conspirators,' she commented. 'What are you up to?'

Hugh laughed as he settled back into his armchair near the French windows. 'Isobel, I hope we won't be that transparent to everybody.'

'So do I,' she agreed. 'It would probably be dangerous.'

The inspector shot a shrewd look at her as he folded himself into the wing chair again. 'Why?' he demanded.

Isobel was fully composed as she returned his gaze, her dark eyes bright and intelligent. 'One death is always too many, Inspector. Two are downright foolhardy. They can't possibly be coincidental.' She considered him gravely. 'Do you know what's going on?'

'No, but we have a theory. That's what we want to discuss with you.'

She folded her hands in her lap, listening as the inspector repeated what he had just told Hugh. When he finished Isobel sat silently for a while, her lips slightly pursed as she absorbed the story. She glanced at Hugh, whose legs were stretched comfortably out in front of him as he watched her over his steepled fingers. 'I don't want to involve Scotland Yard, unless you feel it's necessary,' she said at last.

He smiled at her encouragingly. 'I don't want to either.'

Isobel turned back to the inspector. 'What do you want us to do?' she asked him in her usual forthright manner.

'Carry on with your party as you planned,' Elliot answered promptly, noting the faint frown that appeared on her sallow face.

'Do you mean display the chalice too?' she queried.

'Not necessarily. Just convey the impression that you will.'

Her frown deepened. 'But I'm not sure that we would have been. Mr Chard was very against the idea,' she explained, looking from one to the other. 'The bank manager,' she added for the inspector's benefit.

'I didn't really think he would favour it,' Hugh said. 'Did he say you couldn't take it out?'

'Hugh, you know he wouldn't do that,' Isobel chided. 'After all, it does belong to us. But he very strongly disapproves of the plan. And as he is generally most amenable I'm reluctant to ignore his advice so pointedly. More importantly though,' she added, clasping her hands tightly, 'he pointed out that our insurance won't cover the chalice if we have it here, and the policy may not be valid if other things are stolen while it's on the premises. I suppose,' she commented dryly, 'he thinks it might attract thieves, who'll just take everything they can.'

'That is a sticking point,' Hugh agreed ruefully. 'What do you want to do?'

Isobel turned to the inspector. 'You don't actually want us to show the chalice, do you? Just give the impression that we will be?'

'I wouldn't want to encourage you to risk it,' Elliot said. 'Giving the impression that it's going to be displayed here should be sufficient, as long as you all put on a convincing performance.'

'Well, I can't see any harm in that,' Isobel declared. 'We'll make arrangements to withdraw the chalice from the bank. Maybe we should even actually do it.' She added humorously, 'Naturally Mr Chard wouldn't comment on our actions, but I'm sure his demeanour would be suitably expressive to anybody who might be observing him.'

Hugh raised a quizzical eyebrow. 'No doubt. But we would be taking a great chance with it. Other than the potential dangers here, there are all the problems of transporting it safely. And shouldn't we consult Lucy and Will before deciding?'

'I know the risks are huge,' Isobel agreed. 'If we do actually take it out and bring it home I think we must still reserve the right not to show it if we feel there's any immediate risk.' She paused, then straightened her shoulders. 'Lucy must definitely know what's going on. I think, though, it might be better not to tell Will. He might,' she said with a twinkle in her eyes, 'find it harder to dissemble than we do.'

'That all sounds very reasonable,' Inspector Elliot remarked. 'Whether you do actually take the chalice out or not, I'll have a team of men positioned strategically along your route from Corrington and around the house. We won't take any chances with it, real or otherwise, at any stage.'

Hugh leaned forward. 'How can we still hold the party, though, Isobel,' he demanded, 'in view of Hamilton's death?'

'It is awkward,' she agreed, contemplating him thoughtfully. They all meditated in silence until Isobel's face brightened. 'Lucy originally suggested the drinks to take people's minds off Brett's death,' she said, glancing at the inspector, who was watching her closely. 'I imagine you'll be reopening his case?' Elliot nodded, and Isobel continued, 'Well, we'll carry on with the theme. We'll have the event in memory of him and Duncan Hamilton – and the showing of the chalice will be as a tribute to them both.' She looked at Hugh. 'What do you think?'

'It's just about plausible, I suppose,' he said slowly, casting a questioning look at the inspector. 'And we aren't likely to think of anything better. But,' he added grimly, 'it will be very difficult not to produce the chalice, especially if nothing untoward happens.'

'Well, let's do it then,' Isobel said briskly. 'We have to take some chances in life.' Hugh's rare smile lit his tanned face as he stared at her appreciatively. Isobel acknowledged it with a slight tilt of her head as she continued, 'We really should see what Lucy thinks before we go any further. But we certainly must keep it from Will. He probably wouldn't be able to hide his excitement.'

Inspector Elliot's grey eyes narrowed in amusement. 'That's very likely,' he agreed.

Isobel said, 'Incidentally, Inspector, what's all this I've been hearing about trouble in the church?'

'What!' Hugh straightened abruptly and she looked at him in surprise.

'Liz's painting,' she explained. 'Don't you know what's happened to it?'

'I'm afraid I hadn't got that far,' Elliot said, faintly apologetic as he saw Hugh's reaction.

'What's the problem with it?' Hugh demanded.

'I gather from Miss Bexington that some damage has been done to the wall painting she has just discovered. As I understand it, some of the surface has been lifted badly, damaging the painting underneath,' the inspector explained meticulously. 'Miss Bexington was clearly very upset about it,' he added. 'She wasn't sure whether it was a deliberate piece of destruction, or over-eagerness on the part of a student.'

'Is it just the new discovery that's been harmed?' Hugh asked quickly.

'That's all that Miss Bexington mentioned,' Elliot replied, leaning back in his chair. 'I'm sure she would have told us if anything else had been damaged.'

'It sounds as though it was done last night,' Isobel said. 'Surely that wouldn't have been a student eager to get to work. So how on earth did it happen?'

'What does Mike think?' Hugh asked.

'He seems to think so little of it that he didn't even mention it to me, somewhat to Miss Bexington's disapproval, I believe,' Elliot said dryly.

'He's saying very little at all,' Isobel told them. 'Duncan's death seems to have overwhelmed him. I heard about the painting from Will.' Her voice held a faint amusement as she said, 'He's very cross with Liz, who apparently thought Sue had damaged the wall in an excess of zeal.'

'You appear to have a much better idea of what's been happening here than I do.' Hugh said, and turned to Inspector Elliot. 'Can you tell me the sequence of events as you know them?'

The inspector went briefly through the facts he had gathered as Hugh and Isobel listened carefully to him. When he had finished Hugh said, 'So Liz discovered the damage to the painting before anyone noticed that Duncan was missing.'

'But surely the students must have missed him,' Isobel interposed.

'I believe they did, from what Professor Shannon said, but I'm not sure yet,' Elliot said. 'Perhaps they were covering up his absence for some reason. I shall need to speak to them soon.' He stopped talking at the sound of a gentle knock on the door. The sergeant got ponderously to his feet and opened it to admit Lucy.

She stopped just inside the room and looked at them apologetically. 'I'm sorry to interrupt you, but I thought you might like to know. Mike has rung the university to notify Professor Mersett about Duncan's death, and the professor has said that he'll be coming down immediately. Will it be alright for David to go to the station to meet him at five o'clock?'

'Yes, of course. I'll have a word with him next, so he should have plenty of time,' the inspector said amiably. 'Who exactly is Professor Mersett?'

'He and Mike are colleagues at Oxford. He's responsible for sending down parties of students to gain practical knowledge in the various archaeological techniques,' Lucy replied.

'Can you take a seat for a moment?' Elliot asked, and Sergeant Peters brought up a chair for her, putting it squarely next to Isobel's.

The inspector waited until she sat down under the main light, which brought out the red glints in her chestnut hair. Then he enquired, 'Who appoints the archaeologist in charge of the students?'

'Professor Mersett,' Lucy replied promptly.

'Ah.' Hugh noticed how alert the inspector sounded, although his face remained imperturbable. 'Does he consult with Professor Shannon about the appointment?'

Lucy hesitated fractionally before replying, 'No, I don't think so.' She glanced enquiringly at Hugh, who lifted a shoulder noncommittally.

'I want to speak to Professor Mersett when he comes,' the inspector declared. 'He's being met from the five o'clock train, you said?' Lucy nodded, and Elliot continued, 'So if I come up here at about half-past, he should have just arrived. Is he staying with you?'

'Actually, no, he isn't.' Lucy shook her head as her grandmother turned a disapproving gaze on her. 'Of course Mike offered on our behalf, but, umm, I gather the professor would prefer to stay elsewhere. He doesn't want to bother us.'

There was silence in the room for a moment which Hugh broke with a shout of laughter. 'He's afraid he'll be next!' he said. 'That must have amused Mike.'

'Well,' Lucy said, 'it didn't really. Mike's very subdued. I wonder if he's suffering from shock.'

'That wouldn't be so very surprising,' Elliot said. 'After all, he did get the body out of the lake. Not a pleasant experience for anyone. Did the doctor see him afterwards?'

'I shouldn't think so,' Hugh said. 'Mersett will ginger him up,' he added comfortingly to Lucy, and the inspector turned a penetrating glance on him.

'What about the other man?' Isobel asked suddenly. 'What was his name? You know,' she said to Lucy, 'the man about the wall painting. Isn't he due to put in an appearance too?'

'Dr Archison. Mike spoke to him too and he isn't coming. He said he'd arrange a visit in the new year when things get sorted out. Mike didn't even try to persuade him and really Liz seemed more disappointed about it than he did. I suppose,' Lucy added, 'it's just as well he's coming later, because Mike wants him to see the chalice as well as the wall painting when he's here.'

She looked round at them curiously, affected by the quality of their silence. 'Well?' she demanded. 'Surely you don't think we could go ahead with the party now?'

'Actually, Lucy,' Hugh said, 'we wondered whether it might be possible. We could show the chalice as a mark of respect in memory of Duncan as well as John Brett.'

She stared at him, her hazel eyes growing suspicious. 'Why?' she demanded.

Hugh's lips twisted wryly as he glanced at the inspector. 'I'll explain it to you shortly,' he said. 'Do you want to ask us anything else, Elliot, or would you like to see David now?'

'I'll speak to him next,' the inspector replied, 'but I'll probably want to talk to you again.'

'Fine,' Hugh said, getting to his feet. 'We'll be around.'

The telephone on the desk rang, startling them all. Inspector Elliot picked it up and after listening to the first few words he covered the mouthpiece with his hand. 'Wait just a moment,' he said to the others as they reached the door. There was the continuous hum of a voice coming over the line and the inspector removed his hand from the mouthpiece to reply, 'Yes, I see. What sort of timing should we be looking at? Hmm, yes, interesting. Thanks very much.'

He replaced the receiver and looked across the desk to the others. 'That was the police doctor with the preliminary medical report on Dr Hamilton. He was hit over the head, as we know, and it seems that he had a heart attack, presumably due to the shock of falling into very cold water. His actual death, though, was caused by drowning.'

Sergeant Peters looked at Isobel with concern. Her face had whitened and she swayed slightly on her feet, but before he could do anything she had recovered herself. He put a large hand under her elbow, quietly steering her back to her chair and she sat down gratefully. Lucy's expression was bleak as she turned to her grandmother and put a reassuring hand on her shoulder, while Hugh's mouth set in a thin line in a suddenly formidable face.

The inspector surveyed them. 'There was a very high level of alcohol in his blood. Would you have expected that?'

Hugh's eyes narrowed. 'No. He was drinking beer at the pub, and halves at that.' He glanced enquiringly at his wife. 'I don't think he had more than two while we were there.'

'That's right,' Lucy agreed. 'He joined us with the one he'd just bought, and Liz got another round after that. He certainly didn't seem to have had much before we arrived, either. But the others will be able to tell you how much he drank before we got there.'

Elliot made a brief note on the pad in front of him as Hugh walked across to the window, where he turned to face the room and said, 'So it's possible he saw someone else after he left the pub, and had a great deal to drink with them. Or somebody slipped him a Mickey Finn. I must say, from my very brief acquaintance with him, that the first seems unlikely to me.'

'You see the implications of that, do you?' the inspector queried softly.

Hugh looked at him sombrely. 'Of course. The attack must have been premeditated.'

'What about the time?' Lucy asked. 'When did it happen?'

'Sometime between ten o'clock last night and two o'clock this morning.'

Isobel stared at him in surprise. 'But everyone seemed to think it had just happened,' she exclaimed.

'Mike had his suspicions,' Lucy said quickly.

Hugh looked at her, startled, but the inspector asked, 'How do you know, Miss Rossington? Has he discussed them with you?'

'No,' she replied. 'He really isn't saying much at all, but apparently he told Anna that Duncan seemed to be wearing the clothes he had on last night.'

'Yes, he mentioned that to me as well,' Elliot said. 'Have you ever heard him comment on anything odd in connection with Brett's death?'

Isobel looked at him sharply, but Lucy thought briefly before she shook her head. 'I don't think it ever crossed his mind it wasn't an accident,' she replied. A faint smile flickered across her pointed face. 'A damned fool thing to do, and just what he'd have expected of an idiot like Brett, was the gist of his remarks. Of course he was upset by it, but he was irritated by the apparent stupidity of it too.'

'Apparent?' the inspector queried.

Lucy glanced at Hugh. 'Well...' she began reluctantly.

Hugh interrupted her. 'I've already mentioned your doubts,'

he said as Isobel looked enquiringly from one to the other of them.

'That's all they are, though,' she said as she met Elliot's steady appraisal.

'Don't push it,' he responded. 'Wait and see if anything becomes clearer in your mind, but let me know at once if it does. I suppose Hamilton's death hasn't sparked any memories?'

'No,' she replied, and then looked at him quickly as she absorbed the meaning of his questions. 'Do you think Brett may have been killed too, and by the same person?'

'It's something we'll have to keep in mind,' Elliot said soberly.

'What a risk to take!' Isobel exclaimed in horrified tones. 'Surely it would be crass to kill again so soon when Brett's death was officially seen as an accident.'

'It depends on the reason, and the person,' the inspector replied. 'We could get the situation we have now if the prize is thought to be great enough, and the individual is sufficiently ruthless.'

'They're such inefficient ways of killing,' Hugh commented. The others looked at him in surprise, and he asked, 'If the murderer is so ruthless, why didn't they use a more competent method?'

The inspector stared at him and Sergeant Peters flexed his fingers carefully. It was Lucy who said cautiously, 'Because the murderer is an opportunist.' Her tone strengthened and she became more confident. 'Yes, don't you see? They want these people out of the way, but don't want to do anything too obvious. So they wait for a suitable occasion to arise, perhaps manipulating to make sure that it does. Then they use it instantly.'

She looked round at them as they gazed at her. 'Don't you see?' she asked again.

'Yes,' Inspector Elliot replied grimly, 'that sounds very plausible. Horribly so, in fact.'

Lucy was puzzled and Hugh gave an impatient exclamation. 'Lucy!' he said sharply. 'You've almost certainly put your finger on it, but you can't see the implications.' She stared at him and he went on angrily, 'Other than somebody who is completely irrational, the sort of person you've just described is probably the most dangerous sort of murderer. If somebody gets in their way they'll take the first opportunity to get rid of them, especially now they've managed to do so at least twice. And we don't know who else may be in their way.'

SIX

'I'm that pleased you came down, Lucy,' Molly Leygar said briskly, putting a mug of tea on the large table next to a plate of mince pies. 'Now you help yourself. I only made them this morning and there's plenty. I want to give the students a good send off for the holidays.'

'Thanks, Molly. I've never been able to resist your mince pies,' Lucy said as she picked one up, leaving a drift of icing sugar across the oilcloth that covered the table.

The farmhouse kitchen was filled with the scent of baking, and racks were spread around bearing sausage rolls and jam tarts. At the end of the table Molly lifted a damp cloth off a bowl and took out a lump of pastry. She deftly moulded this into a decorative rim round the lid of the huge watercrust pie in front of her, talking as she worked. 'I could hardly believe Terry when he told me about Dr Hamilton. Well, he was only up here yesterday evening to talk to the students. A pleasant man indeed. It's a great shame.' She looked sharply at the younger woman. 'It seems to me there's a great deal of trouble for you at the priory just now.'

As she took another mince pie Lucy reflected that little ever escaped Molly Leygar. 'Yes, I suppose you hear a lot about it from the students.'

Molly smiled, her red cheeks folding into deep creases. 'Of

course I do. They talk amongst themselves about things when they have their meals, and sometimes they tell me a bit too. They're a nice bunch, you know. I enjoy having them here, and it's good for Philly to have the company of other youngsters.' She took the pie over to the large Aga, resting it on the top as she opened an oven door. When she had put the pie carefully on a shelf inside and closed the door she said in a matter-of-fact way, 'You'll maybe know there was a spot of trouble last night. Not,' she added hastily, 'anything to do with poor Dr Hamilton, of course.'

Lucy looked at her enquiringly as she licked the icing sugar off her fingers. Molly nodded sagely as she sat down opposite her. 'You haven't heard then. Well, it's nothing much, but it upset Philly. I told her she was a silly girl to let it bother her.'

'What happened?' Lucy demanded, restraining her impatience.

'There was a bit of a fight, you see. When they were on their way back from the pub. Between David and that Steven who's doing your books.'

Lucy groaned and clasped her hands around her tea mug. Molly looked at her sympathetically. 'I'm sorry to bother you with it now, but I thought you ought to know. It was nothing much, of course. Young David's a nice lad but he has a quick temper on him. I'm afraid that other one is a nasty piece of work, though. He pesters the girls a bit and they none of them like him.' She glanced down at her work-worn fingers. 'Seemingly he said something to David last night that made him see red and strike out. Our Philly came home with Josie and Sue as soon as the fighting started. Josie was all for leaving them to it. She knows David from home, of course, and she said that he'd be able to handle it. I was a bit worried,' Molly admitted, 'but Sue said it wouldn't amount to anything as Steven's not the fighting sort. I believed her too.'

They exchanged smiles although Lucy's was a little strained. 'He does seem to be rather difficult,' she said glumly. 'I'll have to speak to him.'

'Well, I should wait a bit if I were you,' Molly advised. 'Philly was anxious about them so Sue went back to make sure they were alright, and she said it didn't come to much. They'll probably sort it out between themselves, but I thought you should know what's going on.' Molly pushed her chair back and stood up, straightening her thin body rather wearily. 'And as you're here, could you take the things your grandmother wants? I wasn't sure where they were when she came, but I laid my hands on them easily enough when I looked. I'll just fetch them from the sitting room.'

She turned back from the doorway. 'Why don't you look at the new bathroom while I get them? It's such a good thing we converted the old scullery with all these people in the house. We've locked the entrance from the kitchen, so people only go in from the corridor. You know where it is, the door opposite the dining room.' Molly left the room, walking briskly towards the front of the house while Lucy followed her more slowly, turning left as Molly entered the room on the right. At the end of the corridor Lucy opened the door beyond the kitchen.

The cupboards and shelves that she remembered had been removed from the old scullery, creating a spacious room whose cream-painted walls framed a big new bath. Late afternoon light came through two windows, the smaller to the south, and the larger to the west. Lucy crossed the sanded floorboards and leaned between the fluttering flower-patterned curtains to look out of the small open window, noticing how the hellebores in the sheltered garden had almost reached the windowsill. I suppose, Lucy thought idly, it's warm here behind these thick hedges and sheltered by the stone-walled barns. She gazed over the lower southern hedge into the farmyard, recalling with pleasure the many times she had visited it. Out of the corner of her eye she saw Philly strolling towards the hay barn, one of the farm dogs at her heels, and turned to watch her.

Jack Leygar was tinkering with a tractor near the open

barn door. As Philly approached he straightened up to greet her, and a man moved out of the inner gloom into the fading light. David, Lucy realised with a jolt of surprise. She could not see their faces nor hear what was said, but thought consideringly, Well, I wonder.

She started slightly as Molly Leygar spoke behind her. 'It's draughty with the window open, I'm afraid, but I like to keep the room aired.' She came to stand at the window beside Lucy, leaning out and picking a sprig of rosemary from the large bush nearby. She rolled it absently between her fingers. 'That's the old dovecote David's interested in.'

Lucy followed her gaze and looked at the square stone building near the centre of the farmyard. 'Of course, I remember it,' she said, 'but I didn't realise it was anything special.' She smiled apologetically. 'I don't know much about buildings really.'

'Nor do I,' Molly said frankly. 'I wanted Jack to do something about it, you know, years back. It isn't in a very good state and I've always been afraid it'll fall down. But you know Jack. "That's stood there for hundreds of years and it'll stand for a good few yet. And it'll not be me that takes it down," he said to me. And of course that was that.'

Lucy turned away from the window. 'I should be going,' she said reluctantly.

'You'll stay for another cup of tea, surely?' Molly asked as they walked across the room.

'I'd love to, but I've got to get back. Somebody's coming down from the university and I should be there to meet him.'

'Of course, this must mean a lot of extra work for you,' Molly said sympathetically, entering the kitchen and crossing to the table. 'It was good of you to come and tell me what's happened.' She picked up a brown paper parcel and held it out. 'These are what Isobel was asking for. Tell her I'll look and see if there are any more, but I think they're all there. She's welcome to keep them as long as she wants.'

'Fine. I'll tell her,' Lucy said, taking the package and trying not to betray any sign of her surging curiosity. 'I expect the police will be here to interview you soon, but I'll let you know when we have any news.'

She went out into the cobbled yard. There was no sign now of anybody near the barn, but she could hear muffled voices so she walked over and peered through the open door into the shadowy interior. The voices were coming from behind stacked bales of hay and she followed the sound of them, moving noiselessly over the earthen floor.

David was leaning over a bale, using it as a board to display the estate map he had spread out. 'And see, they'd be invaluable here and here too. You know how difficult it is to operate machinery in those spots, Jack.'

The farmer nodded slowly, his eyes on the map. 'Yes, I do,' he agreed emphatically, 'but I'm not sure about this. It would take some thinking about.'

'Of course,' David said readily, straightening up. 'But I'll bet that's how your grandfather would have worked that land.'

Philly was sitting on the far side of the bale. The girl's head was bent over the map, her short dark curls making a halo about a face which glowed with health. She looked up at David and saw Lucy beyond him.

'Hello!' she called out. 'We didn't hear you come in.'

Lucy smiled as the two men turned round. 'You were all too busy,' she said, indicating the map. 'Hello, Jack. I've just been to see Molly and tell her what's been going on.'

'I've been hearing from David,' Jack said, and the estate manager flushed. 'A bad thing for you all. He seemed a decent chap.'

'He was,' Lucy agreed briefly. 'Don't let me stop you. I just looked in to say hello.' As she turned away she heard the sound of the men's voices as they returned to the discussion. Horses, I'll bet, Lucy thought to herself, remembering something Will had told her. She saw Molly at the kitchen door and waved to her as she crossed the yard, various thoughts buzzing round her brain.

The lane leading towards the priory was gloomy as the bare silhouettes of the oak trees screened the lowering sun. Lucy had only gone a few yards when a sudden idea struck her forcefully. Horses, she mused, need stables. Well, we've got them, and pretty much ready for use too. So much for Hugh's offices, then. Her pace slackened as she considered the implications, thinking practically, so it is Hugh or the manor after all. Well, she realised without surprise, that isn't a difficult choice. It isn't even a choice really.

She heard hasty footsteps behind her and glanced over her shoulder. Philly was hurrying along the lane, obviously hoping to catch up with her, so Lucy stopped and waited. As she drew to a breathless halt beside her Philly's eyes, so like her mother's, looked intently at Lucy.

'Has Mum been telling you about the fight?' she demanded. When Lucy nodded the girl sighed in exasperation. 'I thought she would. It wasn't anything much, you know, and certainly can't have anything to do with Duncan's death. David won't talk about it today, but he isn't even scratched.'

Lucy noticed that Steven's condition had not been mentioned, and listened as the girl carried on after a momentary hesitation. 'It was all so silly. We were coming up the street behind Steven. He'd had too much to drink, ' she said dispassionately, 'but he was getting on pretty well until he met that woman at your gates.'

'What woman?' Lucy demanded, and then remembered. 'Heavens, do you mean Edie Shade?'

'Is that her name?' Philly sounded stunned. 'I don't know her, but she's staying with Tilly Barlow.'

'Yes, that's her,' Lucy said resignedly.

'Well, Steven stopped her and she got rather cross. He is a pest, but I'm surprised...' she broke off abruptly, flushing. 'Anyway,' she hurried on, 'just as we came up she gave him a great shove and he came reeling back, bumping into me. He wouldn't let go and started trying it on. I was startled but I could have coped with him,' she said crossly.

'David got really mad, though, at the things he was saying. He pulled Steven away and told him to push off, but Steven got aggressive and tried to hit him. He couldn't, of course, he could barely stand up on his own, but David told us to go home and he'd see to Steven.' Philly paused and then added, 'Josie was very cross with David. She said we could have handled things better and he was too quick to jump in. But it really wasn't David's fault.' She finished her story and looked at Lucy anxiously.

Lucy smiled at her understandingly. 'You were right, you know. It can't have been anything much because Steven is about this morning, pale but unmarked except for incipient bruising round one eye.'

'Oh good,' Philly exclaimed. 'I knew it was alright because Sue told me. She said it was all over when she went back to check on them. And Steven did have it coming to him. He's such a toad.' She turned away, saying, 'Thanks for listening, Lucy. I thought you ought to know what did happen.'

Lucy watched her go back towards the farm and then started walking down the lane again. All these things I ought to know, she thought ruefully as she passed the granary, a large indistinct shape in the dusk. But, she realised with a nasty shock as she entered the gatehouse, it does mean that David and Steven were both about in the manor grounds during some of the time the police are interested in.

She crossed the priory quadrangles, noticing the students were gathering up their things in a desultory way in the cloisters. She passed under the ruined Prior's Gateway and was walking up the gravel track when an insidious thought pushed its way to the front of her mind. We still don't know what either of them did after the fight. I wonder if anybody else does.

'No, no, my dear. It's very good of you, but I wouldn't want to put you to the trouble.' Professor Mersett retrieved his hat and coat from the rack under the gallery stairs and trod firmly towards the rear door of the hall. 'I shall stay at the village inn.' He glanced penetratingly at Lucy. 'I understand from the young man who collected me from the station that they have accommodation for paying guests. I suppose that is correct?'

'Yes,' Lucy said as she watched the professor putting on his hat and coat. She shoved her hands into the pockets of her jeans as she considered his plan.

He did not wait to hear any more. 'Good, good. He kindly took my bag there and gave me to understand that it was only a short distance to walk. Straight down the drive and turn right towards the quay were his instructions. Quite clear, so I shan't get lost.'

He patted her shoulder in an avuncular fashion. 'You've got enough on your plate without me to bother about as well. This business has got quite out of hand, as I've told the inspector. First Brett and now Duncan Hamilton, one of our finest young archaeologists. We can't have this going on. He must get it sorted out.'

'I'm sure he'll be only too glad to.' Hugh's light voice made the professor jump fractionally and a gleam came into Hugh's eyes as he observed this from halfway down the main stairs. He descended the rest of the steps in a leisurely fashion. 'How are you, Mersett? I'm sorry Lucy can't persuade you to stay with us. We'd feel much happier if you did.'

Professor Mersett's eyes popped as he shook Hugh's hand perfunctorily. 'No, no, very good of you, my dear Carey, but I don't want to get in the way. I'm sure the inn will suit me very well and...' He stopped as he saw the concern written on Hugh's face. 'What is it?'

Hugh studied him with exaggerated anxiety. 'Well, the inn is rather primitive,' he explained.

The professor waved a podgy hand, brushing aside this

comment with relief. 'Oh, if that's all,' he said. 'You forget we archaeologists are used to roughing it. Primitive accommodation won't worry me in the slightest.'

'It isn't just the accommodation,' Hugh began, almost beneath his breath, but Lucy fixed him with a stern eye and he subsided, smiling blandly when the professor looked at him uncertainly.

'You'll want to see Mike,' Lucy said. 'I'm afraid he isn't here at the moment. He went back to the dig to close things down.'

Professor Mersett's full lips tightened. 'No, I don't want to see him tonight. Tomorrow will be time enough. I've spoken to the inspector in charge of the case, which is what I wanted to do.'

Hugh was watching him closely. 'Well, Mersett, if you can stay over tomorrow night too we'd be pleased to see you here for drinks in the evening.'

The older man stared at him in disbelief. 'Drinks? What drinks?' he demanded explosively. 'I haven't come here to go to parties.'

'It isn't a party,' Lucy interposed quietly. 'We'd arranged to have Christmas drinks with the archaeologists, and now we've decided to carry on in memory of both John Brett and Duncan Hamilton.'

The professor drew his stout figure up to its full unimposing height and stared at her pompously. 'I must say, my dear Mrs, er, er, Miss, er...' he floundered.

Hugh said deliberately, 'We should have mentioned that the family are arranging for the chalice to be shown.'

'What! What!' Professor Mersett ejaculated. 'You mean the priory chalice?' A change came over his face. 'Yes, of course that makes a difference. It must be rather difficult to alter those sort of arrangements. Hmm, yes,' he avoided Hugh's eyes, 'yes, I do feel that it is incumbent upon me to represent the university at your little gathering.'

'I'm sure Mike would relieve you of that duty if you found it too onerous,' Hugh offered.

'Professor Shannon is not a fit person to represent the university in any capacity,' the professor snapped, his plump cheeks flushing with anger. 'And so I shall tell him.' He turned to Lucy, his stubby fingers shaking as he pulled his gloves out of his coat pockets. 'I shall be pleased to attend your gathering tomorrow evening, but now I shall be glad to get to the inn. It's been a most upsetting day.'

'Yes, of course,' Lucy agreed. 'We've all found it rather unpleasant.' Hugh smiled meaningfully at her over the professor's oblivious head and she ignored him, although the corners of her mouth twitched. 'I'll come down to show you the way.' She picked up her waxed jacket and crammed a floppy velvet hat onto her chestnut hair.

'No, no, please don't bother,' the professor said hastily.

Lucy smiled engagingly at him. 'It's no bother, Professor. I'll be only too glad to get some fresh air.' She pulled open the heavy oak door and preceded him out into the courtyard, where the darkness was broken by the lights shining out from the uncurtained windows of the estate office in the east wing.

'It would take a firmer man than the professor to gainsay that young lady,' a quiet voice said from behind Hugh as he closed the door. He turned quickly to see Inspector Elliot standing in the shadows of the dimly lit study corridor.

'It would,' Hugh agreed with a fugitive grin. Elliot shifted and as the lighting in the hall fell across his face the humour disappeared from Hugh's expression. 'You don't look as if his presence was altogether beneficial.'

'It wasn't,' Elliot replied evenly. 'Can you spare me a few minutes?'

Hugh nodded. 'In the study?' he queried. 'Or could you do with a drink?'

The inspector grimaced. 'I could certainly do with a drink,' he said with feeling, 'but I think I'd probably better not have one right now. Let's go to the study.'

He turned and led the way back along the corridor in silence. As he opened the door the sergeant was just putting the telephone receiver down. He turned sharply, relaxing when he saw the inspector entering. 'I got through, sir, but there's nobody there who can answer questions. They've promised to get somebody to ring back first thing tomorrow morning.'

Elliot frowned. 'I don't suppose it'll matter much. Thanks, Tom.' He glanced at Hugh. 'Universities seem to operate relaxed hours.'

Hugh's attention quickened, but he replied smoothly, 'The vacations are just starting, Elliot. There won't be many people around.'

The inspector uttered an exclamation of annoyance. 'Of course, I'd quite overlooked that.' He looked across at the sergeant, who was smothering a yawn. 'Go and get yourself a cup of tea if you can, Tom. I want a few words with Mr Carey, and then we'll be off.'

'Go down to the kitchen,' Hugh suggested. 'If there's nobody there you can put the kettle on. The tea canister's right next to it.'

Sergeant Peters left the room gratefully and Hugh sat down in the armchair opposite the desk, where a pool of light shone over the blotter. The main light was not on but the lamps scattered round the room had been lit, casting a subdued glow over the inspector as he prowled around.

Eventually he leaned back against the desk, eyeing Hugh curiously. 'Archaeology seems to be a cut-throat business,' he commented.

'Oh?' Hugh looked surprised.

'Mersett has come steaming down here in such haste because he's convinced that there's a plot against the candidates for the Walbury Chair of Archaeology.'

Hugh stared at him blankly for a second before amusement crossed his tanned face. 'No wonder he wouldn't stay here,' he commented.

'He did seem particularly reluctant, didn't he?' Elliot agreed, with a hint of laughter in his voice. This vanished as he asked, 'Were you aware of the vacancy?'

'The chair of archaeology? Yes, of course. We've heard about it from Duncan and Mike.' Hugh's eyes narrowed. 'And does Mersett have any idea who is behind this plot to remove candidates?'

'Oh yes,' the inspector said. 'That's probably why he won't stay here. He didn't say so in as many words, but he made it very clear that he thinks Professor Shannon would stop at nothing to get the chair for himself.'

Hugh sat back more comfortably in his seat, steepling his fingers together. 'It was clear from Mersett's attitude that he was in a flap. Do you really think his fears are realistic?'

'I keep an open mind,' the inspector replied. 'What do you think?'

'Mike bumping off the opposition because he was afraid they'd beat him?' Hugh smiled sardonically as he tapped his thumbs together. 'No, there are two immediate faults in that construction, Elliot. One, Mike is unlikely to assume that any-body would beat him. Two, if he felt somebody was better than him, which does occasionally happen, he'd feel they had the right to the chair anyway.'

He paused as he considered, and then continued, 'He wouldn't have thought Brett stood a chance, and as far as I can tell he rather respected Hamilton, although he inevitably disa-greed with him on many topics.' Hugh looked at the inspector curiously. 'Are you taking this seriously, Elliot?'

The inspector stared at him. 'You must know that I have to,' he said.

'Yes, of course I do,' Hugh said resignedly, 'but it seems to be a typical academic red herring.'

'Perhaps, but it may leave you with a bit of a crisis.'

'Oh?'

'I gather the professor has come to remove his students from the danger area,' Elliot told him, moving round the desk to seat himself in the wing chair.

Hugh stared at him. 'I imagine he has the right to do so,' he said dryly. 'It will hamper the dig, but he's going to run the risk of looking extremely foolish.'

'I'm sure Professor Shannon will point that out to him.'

Hugh rubbed his forehead with the back of one hand. 'Lord, yes. Let's hope Lucy gets this out of him and finds some way of defusing the situation. At least the Christmas holidays give us a chance to resolve the issue before the egos get too entrenched.' He cocked an eyebrow at the inspector. 'Did you hear Mersett agreeing, against his better judgement, to stay for drinks tomorrow night?'

Inspector Elliot straightened up, interested. 'No. I didn't think he'd be enthusiastic about the plan. I had him down as very socially correct, so I didn't think he would see partying in a death-ridden house as at all the right thing to do. How did you persuade him?'

'No persuasion was necessary. I only had to mention that we'd be showing the chalice and we couldn't have kept him away.'

'I see.' Elliot sounded thoughtful. 'It is a big attraction.'

'Inevitably,' Hugh said. 'Did you find out anything useful from the students or the Leygars?'

'Nothing directly relevant, but some juicy snippets of information from the youngsters. You know the sort of thing.'

'Yes,' Hugh agreed. 'They can give you quite a good picture of what's going on.'

The inspector's grey eyes gleamed with amusement. 'They certainly can. One of those girls, Josie I think it was, is convinced that Miss Bexington nourishes a secret passion for Professor Shannon.' Hugh raised a startled eyebrow, and the inspector continued, 'None of the others said as much, but rather suggestively shied away from the topic.'

'And is Mike supposed to reciprocate this passion?' Hugh

enquired.

'Josie was of the opinion that he hadn't even noticed it,' Elliot replied, grinning. 'She doesn't like Miss Bexington, you know. I got the impression that none of them were very keen on her.'

'Oh? That's interesting,' Hugh commented. 'Mike thinks very highly of her abilities, and although we don't see much of her we've certainly found her pleasant enough.'

'Of course they're very hot under the collar about Sue,' the inspector said, 'but I got the impression that it was more than immediate resentment.'

Hugh sat up. 'Now how the devil...' he broke off and snapped his fingers. 'Will, of course. He was very angry that Liz thought Sue'd damaged the painting.'

'I noticed that he was,' Elliot said. 'But I think the students already knew. I expect they overheard something down there, and put two and two together efficiently. Has the girl said anything about it?'

'No, she hasn't come down yet. What else did you pick up?'

The inspector looked at him impassively. 'Confirmation of your own views.'

'Which ones?' Hugh demanded, regarding him with interest.

'The majority view, expressed succinctly by Josie, who was the most forthcoming, was that Duncan Hamilton was good news and got on pretty well with Professor Shannon. John Brett did not get a decent review.' He grimaced. 'Incidentally, Mike Shannon is held in high regard by the whole crew.'

'Does that surprise you?' Hugh enquired.

'Oddly enough, no it doesn't.' Elliot rubbed the back of his neck wearily. 'They couldn't give me any real help about the damage to the painting, although Josie put forward the interesting idea that Miss Bexington had done it herself to get Sue in trouble with Professor Shannon. She thinks he's shown too much interest in Sue for Miss Bexington's taste.' He looked at Hugh. 'What do you make of that?'

'I haven't seen any signs of this wild passion,' Hugh said, 'but I'll ask Lucy. Even if it exists, it seems highly unlikely that Liz would damage the painting. For heaven's sake, it's her own discovery, and nobody knows the value of it better than she does.'

'True.' The inspector stood up, stretching his back and shoulders. 'I think I'll be off. Tomorrow looks like being another heavy day.'

Hugh rose to his feet as well. 'Come and have that drink before you go.'

'Yes, thanks. I could certainly do with one,' Elliot said.

They left the room together and walked along the corridor, their footsteps on the oak floorboards resounding loudly in the quiet house. They had just reached the hall when they heard a car pulling up in the courtyard. 'Are you expecting anyone?' the inspector asked.

'No,' Hugh replied brusquely. 'I hope to God it isn't reporters already.' He strode to the door and pulled it open, sending a stream of light across the courtyard, which was now completely dark as David had left the estate office. Car doors slammed and rapid footsteps brought Lucy and Anna into the beam of light.

'Brr,' Lucy said as she came into the hall, 'it's turned really cold. I was glad of the lift when Anna picked me up at the gates.' She touched Hugh's hand with her own icy fingers. 'See. I shouldn't be surprised if we had some snow tonight.'

'That will seal Professor Mersett's pleasure,' Anna chipped in merrily, kissing Hugh lightly on the cheek. 'Oh, hello, Inspector. I don't expect you'll enjoy it much either.'

He smiled at her as she peeled her scarlet duffle coat off and shook out her long curls, wafting a faint trace of floral scent around the hall. Hugh spoke to Lucy as she hung up her waxed jacket and tossed her hat onto the shelf above the coat rack. 'How did you get on with Mersett?'

Lucy wrinkled her nose. 'Not brilliantly.' She shivered. 'Let's go in by the fire and I'll tell you all about it.' She looked at the inspector enquiringly. 'Are you interested too?'

'Of course,' he said, and fell into step with Anna as they followed Lucy to the sitting room.

'Where's my friend the sergeant?' she enquired. 'Have you sent him home already?'

'Gossiping over a pot of tea with Gina, I should think,' he replied.

'They're cousins, aren't they?' she asked.

He glanced sideways at her, a little taken aback, as they entered the sitting room. 'Yes, they are.' He hesitated, and then said frankly, 'I'm surprised that you know.'

She looked into his cool grey eyes with laughter in her own. 'Oh, alas for my image. I know all sorts of things like that. I sometimes remember them too, which surprises me as much as everyone else.'

She settled herself comfortably in her favourite armchair by the fire, and he lowered his length into the one opposite her. Lucy was already standing in front of the log fire warming her hands. She turned towards the room and sank down onto the hearth-rug, folding her legs underneath her, as Hugh came into the room with a tray of glasses and a large pewter jug from which steam swirled gently upwards.

'Mulled wine,' Hugh said, as the spicy aroma infiltrated the room. 'Gina had this warming for us.' He glanced at the inspector. 'There's ordinary wine or beer, if you prefer, Elliot.'

'This will be fine,' the inspector replied. 'I hear a lot from Tom about the mull at the Lobster Pot, but I've never had a chance to try it.'

'You should,' Anna said, her blue eyes sparkling as she accepted the glass Hugh gave her. 'It's one of the seasonal highlights locally.'

'I hope it gets Professor Mersett through the evening,' Lucy commented. 'I tried to explain to him about the mummery, but he didn't really understand what I meant.' She pulled a wry face. 'He's come across lots of wild local celebrations in the course of his work, you see, so he's quite used to them.'

Hugh laughed as he handed her a glass and passed one to the inspector. 'Well, he's in a prime position to get some interesting revelations about local customs and habits tonight then.'

'Why on earth is he staying at the inn?' Anna demanded, tucking her feet up on the chair as she sipped the wine cautiously.

Lucy twirled her glass in her fingers. She looked up, then hesitated, glancing at Hugh as he sat down. She made up her mind swiftly and spoke initially to the inspector. 'I expect he's already told you, but I gathered that he thought he might be the next victim if he stayed here.'

Anna choked on her wine. Tears sprang to her eyes, so the inspector thoughtfully removed her glass and helpfully patted her on the back until the paroxysm had passed. 'Why should he be?' she demanded as soon as she could speak.

'Well,' Lucy chose her words carefully, 'he seems to think the common factor is that both men were candidates for this new chair of archaeology at the university.'

Anna spluttered with laughter. 'What on earth is he like? I must come up and meet him tomorrow.' She became aware of an undercurrent in the room, and looked round piercingly. 'Who are the other candidates?' she demanded.

'Well, Professor Mersett, and Mike, and I think Duncan said Dr Archison is. He's the painting expert,' she explained to Anna, 'who was coming to look at Liz's discoveries. And I think there's some woman in the running, too.' Lucy glanced enquiringly at Hugh, who nodded in agreement.

'And this Mersett man thinks Mike is removing the opposition,' Anna declared in an unsteady voice. 'Heavens, will we ever be able to tease him safely again?'

'Yes,' Lucy said slowly, 'that was the gist of what he was saying, but he didn't seem to see the full implications.' They all stared at her, and she looked surprised. 'Well, don't you see? It's a possible motive, however implausible, and although he's busy fingering Mike as the principal player, the motive applies equally well to himself.'

'Surely he wouldn't be stupid enough to mention the motive if he were behind it all?' Anna asked in astonishment.

'It would be a good blind,' Hugh answered, 'if Mersett is more, er, complex than he appears.'

'But he wasn't here when either Duncan or the other one, what's his name, died, was he?' Anna demanded.

'Not as far as we know,' Hugh said, 'but his movements are undoubtedly being checked.' He cocked an eyebrow at the inspector, who smiled slightly.

'If he did appear here unexpectedly,' Lucy added, 'who else would be accepted so easily by either John Brett or Duncan?'

'Well, I haven't met him, of course,' Anna conceded gracefully, 'but he's beginning to sound subtly possible.' She broke off as Lucy's gamine smile lit her face. 'Or maybe not. But surely more possible than Mike. He enjoys his arguments too much to kill his opponents. Or I hope so,' she added with a dramatic shiver.

'Professor Shannon has some eloquent supporters among the ladies,' the inspector said with deliberation.

'Oh?' Anna sat up, interested. 'You surprise me, Inspector.'

He met her eyes, mock astonishment in his own. 'Really?' He sounded unconvinced. 'Wouldn't you expect his colleagues to support him?'

Anna's eyes narrowed. 'Which ones?' she enquired sweetly. 'I thought they were dropping like flies.'

'Miss Bexington, for instance,' the inspector offered, and saw Anna's gaze flicker.

She shrugged elegantly. 'Oh, that's different. Hugh, darling, do you think I could have another drink?' She held out her glass and he took it without comment, his eyes scanning her face and then passing on to consider at Lucy, who was carefully studying the rug she was sitting on.

'Different?' the inspector persisted quietly. 'In what way?'

Anna shrugged again, deliberately vague. 'Oh, I don't know precisely, just different.' Hugh handed her the refilled glass and stood beside her, looking down as she bent her head to gaze at the wine.

'There's a rumour going the rounds, you know,' he said quietly, 'that Liz is infatuated with Mike. Had you heard that?'

Both women looked up at him quickly. 'No,' Anna said, 'I hadn't.' Lucy shook her head when he glanced at her.

'But it doesn't surprise either of you, does it?' he asked, and felt a pang of exasperation as neither of them answered. 'Do you think she is?' he demanded.

Lucy met his eyes squarely. 'Interested, yes, perhaps,' she replied guardedly. 'Why? Does it matter?'

'I don't expect so. Why do you think so? I haven't seen any sign of it.' Hugh began to feel irritated as he saw the two women exchange glances.

'I don't know.' Lucy spread her hands apologetically.

'Woman's intuition!' Hugh said sarcastically, and turned to Anna. 'You think so too, don't you?'

'Yes,' she said reluctantly, 'just the odd look here and there, you know. And,' she added with satisfaction, 'she doesn't like me because I needle him so much.'

Hugh stared at her with arrested interest, but she was sipping her wine with great attention. 'What a damnable complication, if you're right,' he said, just as Hades bounded into the room and rushed over to snuffle around his feet.

Will appeared in the doorway, his thin face rosy with cold. 'It's snowing!' he declared. His thick dark hair was spangled with flakes that were melting as he looked round. 'Where is everyone?'

'Well,' Hugh began, 'if there aren't enough of us here...'

'No,' Will broke in exasperatedly. 'I expect Mike's still down in the finds room, but Gran's not here and neither is Sue.'

Anna pushed Hades away from her armchair. 'Get off, Hades, you're all wet. Your Gran is having dinner with my father, Will.' She smiled at Lucy. 'Daddy must have rung her when he heard about this and she's gone over to gossip with him. That's partly why I'm here. I thought you might feed me on a reciprocal basis.'

'Yes, I remember her mentioning it, now,' Lucy admitted, keeping Hades' head out of her lap with difficulty, 'but I wasn't really paying attention at the time.' She looked across at her brother. 'Sue was still asleep when Gina last looked in on her, but I expect she'll be awake soon.'

'I'll go and see,' Will said, turning on his heel.

'Will, just a minute,' Hugh called after him. 'Are you sure Mike's still down at the dig?'

'No,' Will said, turning in the doorway, 'but he was when I left a while ago. I went into the village for a bit.' He glanced at Lucy with a grin. 'I was in the shop when you went past with that chap, jawing away for all he was worth. Didn't you notice the audience at the window? All the shopping was suspended until you were out of sight. Was that Professor Mersett?' Lucy nodded, and Will said frankly, 'Well, I think I'll steer clear of him. I'd heard he was a pompous git.'

'Oh?' Hugh asked. 'Where did you hear that?'

Will's face became tinged with pink. 'Well, all the students say so. They think he's a bore.'

'What are they saying in the village, Will?' Anna interposed curiously.

'Not much, really. They've heard, of course, so they're not talking about anything else, but they didn't say anything interesting. Still, it'll make the mumming go with an extra swing, won't it?' He smiled wickedly. 'Professor Mersett's going to get a shock.'

'I told him about it,' Lucy said defensively, 'but he doesn't think it will bother him.'

Will snorted with laughter. 'I might go down and see just how he's enjoying it.'

Inspector Elliot broke into the conversation. 'Is it usual

for Professor Shannon to stay down at the dig after dark?' he enquired, glancing from Hugh to Lucy.

'He does sometimes,' Lucy said, brushing a strand of hair away from her face as she looked up at the inspector.

'I don't know what he's actually working on, but he's been in the finds room for ages,' Will remarked. 'After you'd gone Terry asked him if they should carry on with their jobs, and Mike said he thought it would be better than doing nothing. I think he and Liz rearranged the students' work, so that they weren't doing anything too important. Then Mike disappeared into the finds room and didn't come out again, even when the others finished and went off. Liz kept going in to him, but the rest of us didn't see him at all.' He glared round at them impatiently. 'Does it matter? Can I go and see Sue now?'

Hugh glanced at Elliot and then nodded, so Will left with alacrity and was soon heard running up the west stairs. The inspector put down his glass and got to his feet reluctantly, but before he could speak they heard the courtyard door open and then close quietly. Hades' head shot up as he listened intently for a second, and then he leaped up and raced out of the room to give the new arrival an exuberant welcome.

Mike appeared in the sitting-room doorway with Hades at his heels. His eyes were tired and strained and he ran his hand wearily through his red hair as he looked dispassionately around the room. His glance passed unseeingly over Anna and Lucy, hesitated for a moment on the inspector, and then moved to rest on Hugh.

'Is there any more news?' he asked in an unusually flat voice. Anna sat up and studied him unobtrusively, a frown pulling her delicately arched eyebrows together.

Hugh shook his head, appraising his friend penetratingly. 'I'm afraid not, but Elliot has got the matter well in hand.'

Mike looked incuriously at the inspector, and again pushed his hand through his hair. 'I've been trying to work it out,' he said slowly, his eyes returning to Hugh, 'but I can't make any sense of it.' He frowned. 'I can't seem to think at all,' he said fretfully. 'Liz has been in and out of the office with things she could have sorted out herself, and every time she came in I seemed to lose any thread of thought I'd got.'

Anna got to her feet and came to his side in one swift elegant movement. 'You're cold, Mike,' she said, touching one of his hands lightly. 'Come and sit by the fire.'

He gazed blankly at her, but when she put her hand on his arm he went with her unresistingly and let her push him down into the armchair. She glanced over at Lucy, who was getting to her feet. 'A mug of good strong tea, I think, don't you? I'm sure Sue could do with one too.'

Mike's protest was cut short. 'Sue?' he said doubtfully. 'I'd forgotten about Sue.' He looked at Anna anxiously. 'Is she alright?'

'She's fine,' Anna replied calmly. 'She's been resting and I expect she'll be down shortly for something to eat. Will's just gone up to see if she's awake yet. The sleep will have done her a world of good, you'll see. That's what you need, too.'

'Sleep.' He stared at her, a hint of anger in his expression. 'I can't sleep now. There's too much to sort out.'

'Of course you must get some sleep,' Anna said severely. 'I expect the doctor left Sue pills to help her get some rest, and you can have one of those.'

She glared at Hugh as he began to expostulate, and turned her attention back to Mike when he protested, 'I'm not taking any muck like that.'

She noticed with relief that some of his usual vigour sounded in his voice. 'You will if you want to be any use tomorrow,' she said tartly. 'There'll be plenty to do, and Professor Mersett to see as well.'

'Mersett,' he repeated, frowning. 'Of course.'

Lucy came back from the kitchen and handed Anna a large mug of tea. 'Gina has just made a fresh pot, so there's plenty.' Anna pressed it into Mike's grasp and he clasped his hands gratefully around the warmth of the mug. 'She sent these too,' Lucy added, putting down a plate on the table beside Mike. 'Ham sandwiches. And she's got a meal ready too. Meat loaf.'

He took a great gulp of tea, flinching as the hot liquid passed his lips, and looked across at Lucy as she settled herself on a chair near Hugh. 'Has Mersett come yet?'

'Yes,' she replied quietly.

'Where is he then?' Mike asked, picking up a sandwich and taking a big bite out of it. He stared around the room as if he had overlooked the professor, tucked away tidily in a corner.

'He's staying down at the inn,' Lucy said. 'You remember, he thought it would be better.'

'Oh yes,' Mike said vaguely, leaning his head back against his chair.

'Drink up your tea, Mike,' Anna urged him gently, 'and go up to bed for a while.'

'I'm not taking any muck to make me sleep,' he told Anna with a spurt of defiance.

'You'll do as you're told without any fuss,' she said. 'In my opinion you're suffering from shock, and you should have been in bed before now. I'll get the doctor out to you if you won't do as I suggest, and you'll probably find he'll keep you in bed tomorrow too.' She glared at him belligerently, oblivious to the stunned amazement in the room.

'Oh, alright, alright,' Mike said, to everyone's surprise. 'Such a fuss.' He sat up abruptly. 'Sue isn't going back, is she?'

'Back?' Lucy began doubtfully.

Anna broke in. 'No, she's staying here for the night, so that Lucy can keep an eye on her. Isn't that right, Lucy?'

'Yes,' Lucy agreed. 'Josie brought up her things from the farm earlier this afternoon.'

'Good. I don't want her to go back,' Mike said.

'Why not, Professor?' the inspector asked.

Mike stared up at him blankly. 'I don't know,' he said wearily. 'I just want her to stay here.'

Anna threw a reproving look at the inspector, but a gentle cough from the doorway drew the attention of everyone in the room.

Sergeant Peters looked around apologetically, meeting the inspector's eyes momentarily. 'I'm sorry to interrupt, but Gina felt the professor might like to have his meal now, as he missed his lunch. She's got it all ready and wondered where he'd like to eat it.'

'In the kitchen with her, I think,' Lucy said, getting up again. 'We'll come too. It'll save her any further bother.' She looked at the inspector. 'Will you join us?'

'Thank you, but we must go. I expect we'll be back pretty early in the morning.'

Lucy took Mike by the arm and led him towards the kitchen, escorted attentively by Hades. Anna turned abruptly on the remaining men. 'What on earth have you been doing?' she demanded angrily. 'He's in a bad state of shock and you shouldn't have left him like that.'

Hugh warded her off in mock fear. 'Peace, Anna. We didn't know.' He glanced at the inspector. 'I certainly didn't realise it had hit him so badly, but I haven't seen him for a few hours.'

The inspector corroborated this. 'Yes, he was obviously shocked this morning, but he's got noticeably worse since then.'

'Well, whatever Liz thought she was playing at...' Anna broke off as she heard the clatter of footsteps on the west stairs.

Will burst into the room, followed closely by Sue, whose hair was still sleep-rumpled. Her eyes were alert behind her narrow spectacles though, and she had obviously recovered from the morning's shocks.

Will uttered an exclamation of relief when he saw the policemen. 'Oh good! I'm glad you're still here. I've told Sue about the painting,' he added with a touch of defiance, ignoring the look of disapproval that crossed Hugh's face, 'and she wants to talk to you.'

The inspector smiled. 'Come and sit down then, Sue. Are

you feeling better?'

She looked at him doubtfully as she sat down in the arm-chair opposite him, while Will leaned supportively against its back. 'Yes, thank you. Look,' she bent forward in her eagerness to speak, 'Will told me that the new picture has been damaged, and that Liz,' her grey eyes darkened stormily, 'thinks I did it.'

She was indignant and continued eagerly, 'Well, I didn't. I haven't touched it and I can prove it too. As far as I know it was alright when we left last night.' She glanced interroga-tively at Inspector Elliot, who nodded in agreement. 'Well then, I went straight back to the farmhouse for a meal, and was with the others for all but the odd few minutes here and there until I went down to the pub with Josie and Philly Leygar. We went back together after closing time, and I had a bath, then went straight to bed in the room I share with Josie.'

She paused for breath, and then went on, 'Dr Hamilton had asked me to go into Coombhaven to collect his manuscript for him this morning before I started work. He'd left his car in the yard for me, so I went straight after breakfast. I expect some-body saw me go. Anyway,' she finished breathlessly, 'if you ask the others, they'll tell you it's true.'

'I already have, Sue,' Elliot assured her, 'and they did. It's only fair to tell you,' he added, 'that it was just an initial thought on Miss Bexington's part, and she soon came to see that you couldn't have been involved.'

Sue stared at him scornfully but did not say anything.

'Do you have any idea how the damage could have been done, or why?' he asked her.

She frowned, her body suddenly taut. 'I hadn't thought about that,' she admitted, adjusting her spectacles with one finger. 'But I can't see why any of us would do it deliberately, and I don't believe anyone else would have dared touch it.' She drew in her breath with a surprised hiss, glancing quickly at the inspector and then away again.

'What is it?' he demanded.

'No.' She bit her lip. 'It's too silly.'

'Tell me anyway,' he persisted.

She shrugged. 'Alright, but it sounds so tit-for-tattish.' She lifted her chin and deliberately met his eyes. 'I can't see that anybody but Liz would normally touch that painting. Isn't it possible that she did the damage herself and then was afraid to say?'

Stunned silence fell over the room, and Sue's frown deepened. She spoke again before anybody could answer. 'I must say, it does seem unlikely because she's so good at her work. But why on earth should somebody damage it deliberately?' She sat up abruptly. 'What does the professor think?' she demanded. 'He doesn't think I did it, does he?'

'Professor Mersett?' The inspector was purposely obtuse. 'I don't know what he thinks about it.'

'Not him,' Sue said impatiently. 'Professor Shannon, of course.'

'No, I'm sure he doesn't,' Anna interposed. 'But you can have a word with him yourself shortly. He's been worried about you so it will do him good to see you.' The girl was staring at her, puzzled, and Anna indicated the others with an expressive gesture. 'None of this lot recognised that he was in a state of shock, rather like yourself, so he's been left to worry himself all day and he's a bit weary now.'

Concern filled Sue's pale face, but Anna smiled reassuringly at her. 'He just needs a good night's sleep, that's all. When he sees how much better you are it'll be one worry off his mind.'

'Come to the kitchen and see him now, Sue,' Will urged. She hesitated, looking uncertainly at the inspector.

'Yes, I should go. It sounds as though your meal is ready,' Elliot encouraged her. 'And, Sue, you did very well today, you know.'

She glanced at him as she got to her feet and gave him a wavering smile. Anna and Will went out of the room with her, leaving Hugh to escort the policemen to the hall door.

Mike looked up as the trio entered the kitchen and got hurriedly to his feet, his bench screeching protestingly against the flagstones as he pushed it back from the table. 'Sue!' he exclaimed with some of his usual energy. He strode up to her, almost tripping over Hades, and took her hands, regarding her anxiously. Anna had to conceal an urge to laugh as she realised that Sue was gazing just as worriedly at him. 'Sue,' he repeated. 'Are you alright?'

'Professor,' she spoke simultaneously, 'I didn't touch the painting.'

He shook his head irritably. 'I never thought you did, girl. Anyway, the damage doesn't seem to be as bad as it first appeared.' He drew Sue to the bench and pressed her down onto it. Lucy looked at him sharply and opened her mouth, then closed it again when Anna shook her head slightly as they seated themselves on the other side of the table.

Will sat down next to Sue, exclaiming, 'Great, meat loaf. Gina knows how much I like it.' His nose wrinkled as Hades settled at his feet. 'It even makes cabbage bearable.' With his enthusiastic encouragement Sue piled her plate with food and they both began to eat in silence.

'Sue,' Mike said after a while, 'you're staying here tonight.'

The girl looked up at him in surprise and then glanced at Lucy, who murmured, 'You'll be more comfortable here.'

Mike ignored this. 'Listen, Sue, until this is sorted out I don't want you to go out on your own.'

Will dropped his fork as he sat up alertly. 'Gosh!' he exclaimed with a thrilled note in his voice. 'Do you mean Sue may be in danger too?'

'I don't know, Will,' Mike said. 'I don't know what's going on yet, but I'd feel happier if Sue always had some company. Even if it's only you.'

Will began to protest but Mike turned back to the girl, whose pale face had become tinged with pink. 'Please be careful, Sue.'

She nodded speechlessly and met Will's eyes, speculation obviously rife in both their minds.

Lucy interpreted their thoughts effortlessly. 'And remember we're making a team effort of this,' she said warningly. 'Pooling of thoughts and no solo expeditions,' she glanced meaningfully at her brother and he blushed.

'Let's see what ideas we have about it tomorrow,' Anna said, getting to her feet, her own meal half-eaten. 'Mike, you've finished, so you should go to bed.'

He jerked his head up. 'Now just a minute...'

She paid no attention to this, but turned to Sue asking, 'Did Dr Bishop give you some spare sleeping pills?'

'He said he would,' the girl replied.

'Can I have one for Mike?' Anna asked. 'Just to make sure he gets to sleep?'

'Yes, of course. Shall I come and get it?' Sue stopped. 'How silly, I don't know where they are.'

'They're beside your bed,' Lucy said, smiling. 'Anna, you'll see them. In the spare room next to Will's.'

Mike had subsided, glowering round the table, and Anna went over to him. 'Come on, Mike. Do you want me to help you?'

He looked at her in horror, getting to his feet hurriedly. 'For God's sake, woman, I'm not incapable of putting myself to bed. Just get me that damned pill and leave me in peace.'

'I'll see you take it, though,' she said sweetly as they left the room and began to climb the west stairs.

'You've got a nasty suspicious mind,' he grumbled.

She smiled mischievously. 'It must be the company I keep,' she retorted.

He stamped into his room and poured himself a glass of water from a carafe by the bedside, standing ostentatiously in the doorway with it until Anna came back with a small white pill. She held it out on the palm of her hand and he took it without a word, putting it into his mouth with deliberation and gulping down some water.

He pulled a disgusted face and Anna gurgled with laughter. 'Mike, don't be such a fool. You couldn't possibly have tasted it.' He snorted and turned away. 'Goodnight,' she called after him as he began to close the bedroom door, and was rewarded with an indeterminate grunt.

She hesitated for a moment and then went back along the upper corridor into Sue's room, where she drew the curtains and straightened the bed. When that was done she turned out the light and went to wander quietly around the gallery, glancing at her watch from time to time.

She stopped in front of one of the portraits and gazed at it thoughtfully. The thin dark painted face stared back at her, conveying an impression of amused understanding. He was a slight wiry man in doublet and hose, leaning negligently against a sea-wall with a tall-masted galleon beyond him, and she noted the features he had passed on to Will. Suddenly she met Harry Rossington's painted eyes with laughter in her own.

She glanced at her watch again, realising with surprise how long she had been standing there. She walked quietly back to the door of Mike's room and tapped on it gently. There was no reply, so she turned the handle and cautiously pushed the door open.

The windows were pale oblongs in the darkness of the room and flurries of snow pattered gently against the glass. Anna walked slowly over to the bed and looked down at the man who lay there. He had pulled the sheet and blankets over himself but the bedspread was pushed down to the end of the bed. In sleep his face had relaxed and looked strangely vulnerable. She was surprised to feel an urge to smooth back the disordered hair, and contented herself with pulling the cover up over his shoulders. She looked at him for a further second and then walked to the windows to draw the curtains before leaving the room, closing the door quietly behind her.

SEVEN

Lucy stirred the cereal in her bowl and asked, without looking up, 'Hugh, have you arranged to see Withern again?'

Hugh glanced up with a wary expression from the newspaper he was scanning. 'No, I haven't. Why?'

'Well,' Lucy's face was hidden by a curtain of hair as she fiddled with her spoon, filling it carefully, 'is the Talmage man coming back?'

'He's sending an outline of his plans for the priory conversions first,' Hugh replied cautiously. 'Then we'll see what we think of them, before we decide what to do.' He studied her bent head. 'There hasn't been time, somehow, for us to discuss them. Do you want to hear what he suggested?'

'Yes, that would be interesting, but not right now.' She looked at him quickly and added resolutely, 'When he does come again, I'd like to see Withern too.'

Hugh laid down the newspaper, staring across the table at her, and she hurried on with a touch of anxiety, 'At least, I would if it seems okay for your publishing company. Would it still be too isolated?'

'It isn't ideal,' he replied, rather dazed, 'but I could manage.' His eyes became brightly alert. 'Do you mean...'

He broke off as Will erupted into the dining room, saying loudly, 'That snow's not going to last, you know. What a pain! I was hoping to do some tobogganing this winter.'

'There's plenty of time yet,' Hugh replied, gathering his thoughts with an effort, his eyes still on Lucy as Will went to the end of the table, sitting down near the tray laden with tea and coffee pots.

Lucy laid down her spoon, feeling strangely relieved. She shook back her chestnut hair and met Hugh's gaze with a light-hearted smile. 'When are you going to transcribe the Dudley letters?'

'Hmm, I don't know.' His mind was still abstracted. 'Why? Is there some urgency?'

'No, not really. But I'd like to show them to Anna before she returns to Paris.'

'That's soon after Christmas, isn't it?'

Lucy agreed, and Hugh said, 'I'll have started them, but I certainly won't have got far by then. Perhaps you'd better show her the originals. Some of them are fairly easy to read. I've locked them in the desk drawer, so let me know when you want them and I'll give you the key.'

'Pooh, that stuff!' Will said scornfully. 'Just the sort of thing Steven would find. Now I think…' He broke off at the sound of footsteps in the corridor and looked round with a guilty expression which changed to relief as Sue came rather shyly into the room.

'Good morning,' she said, her thin body held stiffly in her patched jeans and blue sweatshirt. She had wound a patterned scarf into a rope to hold back her tow-coloured hair, so that her blue and green spectacles seemed very prominent on her pale face. 'I hope I'm not terribly late. I don't usually oversleep.'

Hugh pulled out the chair beside him and said reassuringly, 'Don't worry, there's no set time for breakfast in this house. Isobel, for instance, had hers at the crack of dawn, and the rest of us have only just started. Gina just provides the wherewithal in here when she's busy in the kitchen and wants us out of her way.' Hugh indicated the cereal boxes littering the table, and the loaf by the toaster on the bow-fronted walnut sideboard. 'We help ourselves. Frequently,' he added, 'in some cases.'

'Anyway, Mike isn't down yet and Steven is always late,' Will said, taking no notice of Hugh's jibe. 'There's coffee and tea on the tray here, Sue. What would you like?'

'Coffee, please,' Sue said as she went over to the sideboard. She slotted a couple of slices of bread into the toaster and glanced out of the window. Snow lay lightly over the ground and emphasised the rounded shapes of the lavender and santolina bushes that edged the narrow bed of roses that separated the front garden from the wide gravelled turning circle. The sky was lined with white clouds in thick ridged sheets, but here and there patches of blue showed through with the promise of a fine day. Good for working, Sue thought, turning back as her toast popped up. She put it onto a plate and turned to the table, asking, 'Is Professor Shannon alright?'

'Fine,' Mike replied, coming briskly into the room, followed by a jubilant Hades. 'Although I nearly fell over this damned dog. He was lying outside my door like a hearth-rug.' He scowled in mock anger at Hades, who wagged his long tail ecstatically.

Will looked at his dog approvingly. 'He's intelligent, isn't he? I expect he was making sure you weren't disturbed.' Mike snorted scornfully as he jerked out a chair beside Will and sat down heavily on it.

Will ignored him and leaned forward to look speculatively at Sue, who had seated herself between Hugh and Mike. 'Maybe I should set him to guard you,' he said thoughtfully. Sue stopped spreading butter on her toast to grin at him companionably as she accepted the cup of coffee he passed down to her.

Mike was pouring a stream of creamy milk over the mound of cereal in his bowl and did not look up as he commented, 'It might keep him out of the way, but he'll be distracted by the first stick he sees.'

Hades was sitting upright on the rug in the window bay

watching activities around the table, and his ears pricked up hopefully as Mike spoke. When there was no sign of action he lowered them again and turned to stare out of the window, gazing with intense longing at the hunched rabbits nibbling the grass beneath the trees on either side of the neglected main drive.

Lucy sipped her coffee and studied Mike unobtrusively across the table. She was relieved to see that he looked his usual energetic self as he shovelled up his food. His red hair looked as though he had forgotten to comb it, but his square face was clean-shaven and tinged with healthy colour and his blue eyes were clear.

He confirmed her views almost immediately, pausing after a few mouthfuls of cereal to look down the table to Hugh, who was again peacefully glancing through his newspaper. 'Do you know what time Mersett is coming up?'

Hugh lowered his paper resignedly and replied, 'No, but it may well be rather late. I don't imagine he had a quiet night.'

'Why's that?' Mike demanded suspiciously.

'The mummers' revels were centred on the Lobster Pot last night,' Hugh replied, with a twisted grin.

Mike stared at him, a reluctant smile touching his own lips. 'From your expression I gather they're fairly riotous.' He paused, then added, 'In fact, now you mention it I remember hearing about them down there. They sounded rather rough and ready to me.'

'They are,' Will assured him. 'They do the play early in the evening. You know, St George with the Saracen and Father Christmas and all that on the quay, and then they go round the village and end up back at the pub where they have mock battles.'

Mike was regarding him intently as he absently buttered the slice of toast Sue passed to him. 'That's interesting. I hadn't heard that much about them before, but they sound like a medi-aeval survival. The names and events get garbled over the years.'

He looked at Lucy, licking excess butter from his fingers. 'How long have the villagers been doing this?'

'I'm not really sure,' Lucy replied doubtfully. 'I think the revels were an earlier tradition that was revived in the nineteenth century. I suppose Steven might have more information on them.'

Mike banged the table in exasperation, making the delicate cups rattle in their saucers. 'Why on earth didn't any of you tell me about them before?' he asked angrily. 'It would have been interesting to see what happens.'

'I'm sorry,' Lucy said contritely. 'We take them very much for granted, so it never occurred to me that they might be anything special.'

'Well, what does happen in these battles?' Mike demanded, spreading a deep layer of marmalade over his toast.

Will glowered across the table at his sister. 'I don't know,' he said grumpily. 'I've never been there at the end.'

Lucy's gamine smile lit her face as she confronted Will's scowl. 'Well, I expect you'll both soon be able to hear a first-hand account from Professor Mersett. I don't think he'll have been able to avoid them.'

Mike snorted with laughter and almost choked on the mouthful of toast he had just taken. Sue patted him helpfully on the back and when he recovered from his spluttering he demanded, 'Why the devil is he staying there anyway? I thought I'd offered him a room here.'

'Well, to be honest, Mike, I think he was afraid to stay in the house,' Lucy explained.

'Afraid?' Mike repeated as he brushed toast crumbs from the front of his brightly-checked woollen shirt. He stared at her in astonishment. 'What's he got to be afraid of? He's surely not involved in anything that's going on here.'

'He thinks he could be,' Lucy said, 'because the only connecting link he can see between the two deaths is their candidature for the chair of archaeology.'

Mike's hand froze halfway to his mouth with the last corner of his toast. 'Silly old fool! What about me? Nobody's tried to nobble me yet,' he said amiably, and pushed the rest of his toast into his mouth. He chewed it thoughtfully and then looked round the table, considering each of them in turn.

'And who,' Mike asked as he met Hugh's eyes, 'does Mersett think is behind the removal of candidates?'

Hugh lifted an eyebrow. 'Can't you work it out?'

'Of course I can. Silly old fool,' he repeated without heat. 'Does he think I've nothing better to do than go around bumping off the opposition. Brett wouldn't have stood a chance of the chair, and Hamilton,' Mike paused, a look of regret briefly crossing his face, 'Hamilton was worth competing against. Anyway,' he added, ignoring Steven who had sidled unobtrusively into the room and taken his place next to Lucy, 'I'd certainly have started with Mersett, pompous windbag, if I'd been tempted to remove anyone.' He became aware of Sue, who was gazing at him wide-eyed. 'Lord,' Mike said ruefully, running a distracted hand through his hair, 'I'd forgotten you were here, Sue. That was probably indiscreet. Professionally, you understand,' he glanced round sardonically, 'not criminally. So be a good girl and forget what you hear me say while you're here. It's an enormous strain being discreet on site,' he admitted frankly, getting up and moving down to the toaster, 'and I can't manage it here as well.'

Lucy bit her lip, looking away from Hugh and catching the sly expression on Steven's face as he looked across the table at Mike, dislike gleaming out of his narrowed eyes.

'Don't worry, Professor,' Sue said earnestly. 'I shan't say anything. We all know he's a pompous windbag anyway, and we've heard you say so before.'

Mike groaned as he cut two thick slices of bread. 'How long's he going to be here?'

A thought struck him as he jammed the bread into the toaster. 'Why did he come down so rapidly? Surely this business has given him plenty to sort out at the university?' Mike demanded. He struck his head theatrically with the heel of his hand. 'No, don't tell me. How stupid I'm being. Of course he came to present his theory to the inspector and get police protection for himself. Surely nothing else would bring him into the danger zone.'

'Excuse me,' Gina's voice made itself heard as Mike paused and he started at the sound of it. She stood in the doorway, her flowered pinafore bright against the dimness of the corridor. 'Lucy, a man's arrived wanting to see you or Hugh. He's waiting in the hall.'

Lucy frowned and glanced at Hugh. 'Are you expecting anyone?'

He shook his head. 'Gina, he isn't a reporter, is he? There isn't anything about Duncan's death in the papers this morning,' Hugh indicated the pile he had been working through, 'but I don't expect it'll be long before they hear the news.'

Will stiffened and looked excitedly down the table at Sue, but Gina shook her head. 'Oh no,' she said confidently. 'I wouldn't let one of them in. He's the man who was here yesterday, that David fetched from the station.' She hesitated before adding, 'He's in a bit of a way, poor man. I hear they had rather a night of it down at the Pot.'

Mike snorted in delight. 'I'll fetch him in, shall I?' he asked, ignoring the whiff of burning bread.

'No.' Lucy got swiftly to her feet. 'You stay here and sort out your toast. I think it's done. I'll bring him in.'

She left the room with Gina and the others waited in silence, hearing her speaking in the hall and being overridden by an agitated male voice that carried clearly. 'It was horrendous, quite horrendous. I'd no idea that they would be anything like that. The damned, I beg your pardon, wretched actors in those cumbersome costumes just came up and surrounded me, dancing round and round like maniacs. I couldn't get away for the whole evening, and it snowed most of the time too. And then the battles.' His voice trembled as he remembered. 'I was right in the middle of them, they wouldn't let me out. I'm bruised black and blue. It's a wonder I wasn't injured.'

Lucy asked something quietly and he replied testily, 'No, no, I believe nobody was hurt. A very great surprise too. And,' they could hear him gobbling with rage as he approached, 'as if that wasn't enough, I was accosted by some mad woman on my way here this morning.' He appeared in the dining-room doorway with Lucy at his shoulder and came to an abrupt halt, his stout figure quivering with anger as he stared around the room.

'Ah, Mersett,' Mike looked up from the charred bread he had just dug out of the toaster and regarded his empurpled face with interest. 'A mad woman? What did she want?'

Professor Mersett glared at him, quite forgetting the larger issues he had come down to discuss as he stomped into the room and sank down onto the chair Lucy indicated next to Steven. 'To tell me my business, as far as I could make out,' he said bitingly, ignoring Steven's curious stare. 'The impudent harpy told me to think about what was happening here and not to interfere with things I don't understand.' His heavy cheeks became even more suffused with colour. 'She advised me to leave while I still could, the...' he spluttered to a halt, just repressing the description trembling on his tongue.

Lucy put up a hand to conceal the smile that she could not repress as she resumed her seat. Out of the corner of her eye she noticed that Steven was scowling as he hunched over his coffee cup.

Will demanded, 'Who was she?' He added eagerly, 'Maybe she's the killer.'

'A fragrant thought,' Hugh drawled. 'I rather fancy Ms Shade in the role.'

'Do you know her?' Will asked in surprise.

'I imagine she's the dotty woman staying with Tilly,' Hugh replied. 'Tall and thick-set with very short dark hair.' He raised a questioning eyebrow at Professor Mersett.

The professor grunted as he leaned forward, his elbows on the table. 'Yes. Who is she?'

'I have very narrowly avoided the pleasure of meeting her myself,' Hugh said lightly. 'I gather she's a psychic, or something along those lines. She disapproves in her, ummm, professional capacity of the excavations at the priory.'

'Damned woman,' Mike said dismissively, sitting down again at the table. 'She hasn't said anything to me.'

'I expect Tilly restrains her,' Lucy said, her hazel eyes sparkling with amusement. 'She's terrified of you.'

A sudden silence fell across the room and Professor Mersett sat back slowly in his chair. Mike's gaze settled on his face and the professor glared at him.

Mike said provocatively, 'Maybe she saw you at the mummery last night and took you for a like-minded soul. What was it like?'

Professor Mersett swelled with anger and said sharply, 'An atrocious mangling of historical issues. It just provides the local riffraff with an opportunity to run riot. I'm surprised it's allowed.' He transferred his glare to Hugh.

'Well,' Hugh responded, 'I believe this type of play has evolved down the centuries as a mishmash of traditions, and so that does give ours a touch of authenticity. They were presumably always an opportunity to work off high spirits.'

'High spirits!' The professor was outraged and struggled to find words to express himself adequately.

'You really must come and stay here tonight,' Lucy intervened. 'The revels go on now until Christmas Eve.'

He stared at her, horrified. 'Well,' he temporised, 'it's very kind of you...'

Mike interrupted the professor's dragging speech. 'Nobody is likely to regard your application for the chair of archaeology seriously, Mersett, so you should be quite safe. On that front at least. I can't guarantee Ms Shade's actions, of course.' He buried his face in his coffee cup.

The professor's richly coloured face set in rigid lines. He stared icily at Mike. 'If it weren't for the chalice, Professor Shannon, I shouldn't dream of staying here a minute longer than is necessary to withdraw the students from the dig. As it is, I...' He got no further.

'The chalice? What about the chalice?' Mike demanded. He looked down the table at Hugh. 'Surely you're not going ahead with this evening's drinks?'

'We discussed it yesterday,' Hugh said, 'and felt that it was a suitable way of paying tribute to John Brett and Duncan Hamilton.'

'Tribute?' Mike made the idea sound bizarre. 'What the hell has that got to do with anything? For God's sake, Hugh, haven't there been enough deaths? I...' he broke off, startled, as everyone around the table jumped nervously at a loud bang.

'I'm so sorry,' Lucy said contritely. 'The lid slipped through my fingers.' She bent down to pick it up from the floor and replaced it carefully over the butter on its stainless steel dish. 'Look, Mike, why don't you go off and argue with Hugh somewhere else so that the professor can have some breakfast in peace? You'll be able to have a discussion with him afterwards.' She glanced at the professor as she spoke. 'I'm sure you could do with something to eat, couldn't you?'

'Well,' he looked appreciatively at the array of food, 'I must admit that I am feeling rather hungry. I didn't stay to eat at that place before I left this morning.' He shuddered.

Mike pushed his chair back abruptly, causing Hades to leap up eagerly from his post in the window bay. Hugh got to his feet in a more leisurely fashion as Mike admonished the big dog, 'Sit down, you beast. Stay!'

'Will,' his sister said, 'would you ask Gina to make some fresh tea. Or would you prefer coffee, professor?'

'No, no, tea will be fine. So much better for the system than coffee, you know.'

Steven put his coffee cup down loudly and got to his feet,

muttering under his breath. Professor Mersett frowned disapprovingly as he watched him leave the room. His glance, ranging round the table, fell on Sue. 'Ah, Sue, my dear girl, I hear it was you...'

Will came back as he spoke and interrupted him without compunction. 'Are you ready, Sue?' he demanded. Hades ambled over and hovered hopefully at his master's side.

'Ready for what?' Lucy asked quickly.

'Well,' Will grinned, 'Mike doesn't want Sue to go back to the dig just yet, so I thought it would be a good chance to hunt through the attics to see what we can find. There may be something for Anna's theatricals.'

Lucy studied her brother for a minute, amused appreciation rippling across her face. 'That's a good idea. I may even join you later, even if it's only to dig out the Christmas baubles. Bert's bringing up some holly and a few of his fir swags this morning and once they're here I must start the decorating.' She glanced at Sue. 'It's probably very dusty up there in the areas we don't normally use.'

Sue was unconcerned. 'That won't matter. I don't expect I'll get any dirtier than if I were working on the dig.'

'No, of course not. Still, it might be worth taking some dusters up with you.'

'Okay,' Will said carelessly. 'I'd better leave Hades down here. The attics are rather crowded. Come on then, Sue.' She got to her feet with alacrity and they left the room together, obviously keen to get started on their search. Hades still trailed hopefully behind them, but his long tail began to droop.

'Hmm,' the professor said a trifle thickly as he masticated some cereal, 'the experience doesn't seem to have done that young woman any harm.'

'She was in a bad state of shock yesterday,' Lucy explained as she went over to the toaster, 'and Mike wants her to take it easy today so she'll be staying around the house.'

Gina came in with the fresh pot of tea and strode around the table to put it on the tray, which she moved closer to Professor Mersett. 'Thanks, Gina,' Lucy said gratefully. 'It sounds as though Hades will be staying with you while Will searches the attics. He may actually be searching for dusters first in the kitchen.'

Gina looked over her shoulder as she returned to the doorway. 'I've already given them to him,' she said. 'He wouldn't have had a clue where to find them.'

Professor Mersett poured himself a cup of tea and studied Lucy shrewdly as she passed him a plateful of toast. 'It's very wise to keep the girl here,' he said as he buttered a piece. 'It's possible I may have been a bit hasty, but it's all been a very great shock. The university can't afford this sort of publicity.'

He ate a prolonged meal, talking himself back into his usual complacency. When he was at last ready to speak to his colleague Lucy felt worn out with the effort of maintaining her end of the conversation. She thankfully left the professor finishing off his third round of toast and went to find Mike.

Hugh was alone in the study with a piece of unfolded parchment in front of him, reading through the scrawled lines of writing on it. He looked up blankly when Lucy put her head around the door. 'No,' he gathered his thoughts with an effort when she enquired about Mike's whereabouts, 'he isn't here. He wanted to get down to the dig.' Lucy withdrew quietly, noting that Hugh was absorbed in the sixteenth century without any qualms about the present one.

The rest of the house was deserted, apart from Gina in the kitchen. When Lucy looked in she was just fetching a bowl of meat from the fridge, with Hades lying on the stone floor by the far door watching her with interest. There was a pile of apples and heaps of dried fruit on one of the counters beside a chopping board and Lucy wondered what they were going to have for dinner.

She returned to the dining room, where the professor had risen and was standing, hands clasped behind his back, gazing out of the window. 'It looks as though Mike must have gone to the dig, Professor. Would you like me to take you down there?'

He turned and waved a pudgy hand graciously. 'No, no, my dear. Don't trouble yourself any further. I know my way.' He hesitated fractionally before saying, 'I would like to take up your offer of a bed for the night, if it isn't inconvenient. I feel I ought,' he ended with great dignity, 'to stay to see the chalice.'

'Of course it isn't inconvenient,' Lucy said. She added mendaciously, 'We're very glad that you can stay.'

'Thank you,' he said. 'Now, if you'll excuse me, I'd better find Professor Shannon and see what we can sort out.'

Lucy returned to the kitchen with a sense of relief and found that her grandmother had joined Gina and the two women were chatting companionably as they chopped vegetables. Isobel looked up with a smile. 'We're having curry for dinner. Gina's adapted one of my recipes from India.' She broke off as she studied her granddaughter. 'You're looking harassed, Lucy.'

Lucy brushed a strand of hair away from her face rather wearily. 'I'm feeling it.' She uttered a sudden exclamation. 'In fact I'm quite addled. Molly Leygar gave me a parcel for you yesterday afternoon. I left it on the table in the sitting room. She said to tell you she thinks they're all there and you can keep them as long as you like. And,' Lucy finished meticulously, 'if she does find any more she'll let you know.'

'Thank you, dear,' Isobel said. 'Are you going to help here or do you have something else to do?'

Lucy stared at her and her grandmother indicated the pile of apples waiting to be peeled. Lucy made a small exasperated sound and picked up the knife.

Even Will felt daunted as he dropped Gina's pile of dusters onto a cluttered table. He and Sue stood in the large attic and gazed around at the accumulated jumble of centuries. 'Gosh! It doesn't look as though anything was ever thrown away,' he said disapprovingly, poking at a pile of old papers with one foot.

'Well, they probably always thought things might come in useful sometime,' Sue murmured, bending over a heap of wooden toys. 'Look at these puppets, Will. See how cleverly they've been painted.'

'The strings are all tangled up,' Will pointed out unnecessarily as Sue's deft fingers struggled with the knots.

She glanced up at him humorously. 'So they are,' she said as she settled down on the floor, oblivious of the thick layer of dust on the oak boards.

Will watched her for a while and then wandered off, lifting the lids of chests and peering into their interiors. He disappeared behind a large mahogany tallboy and soon all Sue could hear was the occasional bang and thud as he shifted heavy objects, and sometimes a cry of pain as he tripped over something. She looked at the tallboy disparagingly, concluding that it had been banished because of its utilitarian ugliness, and returned to the tangle of strings that she was unravelling.

'Sue, come and see these!' Will's excited voice startled her, but she laid the puppets out neatly on the floor before scrambling to her feet in a swirl of dust. She brushed her jeans down with a cursory hand, wincing as the blood rushed back into her feet, and picked her way through the jumble around the tallboy. Her heart leaped suddenly into her mouth as she was confronted by a row of shrouded figures. She smiled inwardly, mocking her fright, as she realised that they were dresses covered in dust sheets, hanging neatly on a rail.

'Sue!' Will summoned her again so she resisted the urge to peer under the sheets.

'Where are you?' she called, and his face popped up above a stack of boxes that screened him like a rampart. 'Okay, I see you now.'

She worked her way past a dappled rocking-horse, stranded immovably among multifarious other toys, and edged around the boxes. Will had taken one of the longer boxes down and tried out a set of rusty keys in the lock. Rather to his surprise, one of them had opened the box and he had lifted the lid to reveal a pair of gleaming rapiers.

Sue stood still and stared entranced at them as Will gingerly picked one out of its velvet bed, peering at the gilded handrest curiously. 'Look, do you see how cleverly it's carved. And see, here, this is our crest.' He looked at the weapon in some awe. 'Just think, it must have belonged to one of my ancestors. I wonder if he used it.'

'I should think so,' Sue said practically. 'Even if it was only for practice. But duelling was very common in the eighteenth century so it's possibly been used in anger. Do be careful, Will,' she added sharply, as he assumed a duelling stance and presented his rapier. 'Shall we see what's in the other boxes?'

By the time Will heard his sister calling him from the attic doorway he and Sue had managed to open three more boxes with the keys. They were gloating over a pair of pistols with delicately engraved butts, a set of daggers with jewelled handles and another pair of rapiers.

'Hang on, Lucy,' Will called back. 'I'll come and get you. Wait until you see what we've found.' He squirmed round the obstructions, barking his shins frequently in his haste.

'Oh, hello, Anna. What a good job you've come,' Will said, to Anna's well-concealed astonishment. 'You'll be interested too. Coffee, smashing. And chocolate biscuits. Gosh, I'm hungry!' he added, glancing at his watch. 'I didn't realise it was so late. Look, leave it all here for a minute while I show you our best find.'

Lucy stared at him in surprise as she put the tray on a nearby chest. He had already turned back towards the centre of the room and she met Anna's amused eyes as they followed him behind the tallboy.

Will forged ahead to the rampart of boxes but Anna paused by the rail and pulled one of the dust sheets carefully aside just a fraction, revealing a glimpse of a richly embroidered silk dress.

'Lucy, just look at this,' she exclaimed in delight.

'Anna, come on,' Will said impatiently. 'You must see these first.'

Reluctantly Anna replaced the sheet and followed Will and Lucy. Sue was sitting on a chest examining one of the blades and looked up as the others appeared. 'Hello,' she said, smiling. 'Will's made quite a find.' She indicated the open boxes laid out on the floor in front of her. 'Will,' she beckoned him to her side, 'look, there's something engraved on the blade.'

He peered closely, doubtfully, and she moved the blade slightly so that the dim light from one of the casement windows shone on it. 'Yes,' he said cautiously. 'I can just see some writing, I think. Is it writing?'

'I think so,' Sue replied. 'Sometimes the swordsmith would write some appropriate words like 'The Fire-eater of Treviso', and sometimes he would engrave the owner's motto. I can't read this though. I'm not even sure what language it is, but I think it's Italian.'

'Do you know how old they are?' Anna asked, balancing one of the pistols carefully in her hand as she admired the pearl inlay on the butt.

'Not really, but I should think between two and three hundred years.' Sue looked at Will. 'You can probably find out exactly when they were made and who for, you know. There may well even be letters or accounts in here somewhere.' She waved her free arm broadly around the attic.

'I'd like to do that.' Will was enthusiastic as he threw a quick look around the room. He turned to Anna as she replaced the pistol in its silk-lined box. 'We could use them in your theatricals, couldn't we?'

'They'd look marvellous,' Anna agreed. She added regretfully, 'But they're probably too valuable, and,' she gingerly tested the edge of one of the blades, 'too dangerous.'

Will's face clouded with disappointment and she said hastily, 'The best solution may be to have identical copies made. After all, you wouldn't want to risk damaging these, would you?'

'No, I suppose not,' Will said grudgingly.

'Have you found anything else?' Lucy demanded, gazing around the room. 'I'd forgotten just how much stuff there is up here.'

Will shook his head. 'Not really. Just junk. Sue's been messing around with some puppets.'

Lucy was unstacking a pile of chairs she had spotted. 'Anna, will you look at these? I'm sure they're Sheraton. See how delicate they are.'

'You're probably right,' Anna said, looking at them without much interest. 'Do come back with me and look at that dress. If we could copy things like that too the theatricals would be spectacular.'

She picked her way past the rocking-horse and nearly tripped over a large drum, which resounded hollowly as her foot collided with it. Anna barely noticed, her eyes on the rail in front of her. As she reached it she hesitated in front of the row of shrouded shapes. Taking a deep breath she slowly lifted the sheet to reveal the ruby-coloured silk dress she had already caught sight of. She glanced at her friend's chestnut hair. 'Well, you couldn't take that colour, but I'd wear it.'

Lucy had pulled back another sheet, 'You're welcome to it, Anna. I'm having this one.' A white brocade gown with a full skirt drooped on the hanger, sparkling as light touched the crystals sewn onto the material.

'Just look at the embroidery,' Anna murmured and glanced at Lucy, who was enthralled with the dress. 'It would probably have been worn over panniers and its owner would have powdered her hair, but it would suit you perfectly. If we can find the accessories,' she glanced at the boxes scattered about, 'these clothes would be even more impressive.' Her face lit up with excitement. 'Why don't we have a costume party?'

'That would be fun,' Lucy agreed. 'Just once, before they're copied for your theatricals.' She stopped, flashing an apologetic smile at Anna. 'I'm sorry, we're all calling them your theatricals.'

Anna was unshrouding a ruched green satin cloak, and looked round at Lucy, who was still admiring the brocade. 'Well, you know,' she said slowly, 'I've started to think of them as mine. I'd like to see what I can do, if you and Hugh will let me.'

Lucy tore her gaze from the white dress to stare at her in surprise. 'Anna, are you sure? It really does sound like a fantastic idea, but it would surely be a big project. And we couldn't pay you anything for doing it,' she ended apologetically.

'I know, don't worry,' Anna said lightly. 'But this would be a fantastic professional experience for me. And I've earned enough to tide me over for a bit. Perhaps we could arrange a salary based on the profits or something like that.'

Lucy frowned. 'That doesn't seem very fair. I mean, suppose that they don't make any profit?'

Anna shrugged elegantly, lifting the cloak from the hanger and draping it in casual folds about her shoulders, taking care to keep it well clear of the dusty floor. 'Then I don't earn anything. But I'd still have the experience. We should see after the first performance whether there's anything in the idea. Anyway, I believe there is and I couldn't bear to see somebody else fiddling with it. Will you let me try, Lucy?'

'Well, if you really want to, Anna, I'm sure there's nobody we'd rather have to do them,' Lucy said frankly. 'And we do all seem to be taking it for granted the theatricals are going ahead.'

Anna removed the cloak and replaced it carefully on the hanger, saying, 'I suppose we shouldn't really go through any more of these clothes up here as it's so dusty. Let's take them downstairs and do it properly as soon as we can.' She sat down on a nearby box and tossed her long curling hair back over her shoulder. 'I've thought about the theatricals quite a lot, you know. There are loads of people I can ask to help with the first production on a payment by results basis, so that it may not cost all that much to mount. And if it works we could pay them properly for future productions.'

She glanced at Lucy, who was watching her with open amusement in her hazel eyes. 'I know, I know, but isn't it fascinating?' Anna's enthusiasm was unmistakable but she added practically, 'We'll need somebody to run the day-to-day things. I wouldn't enjoy that very much, even if I had time to do it. Do you really think Philly could manage that sort of thing?'

'I'm sure she could,' Lucy replied. 'She's taken over some of the farm management from Jack, who's very proud of her ability. But I think she'll be glad to have something else to do that brings her in contact with more people. We can discuss it with her after Christmas and see what she says.'

She hesitated, glancing over beyond the rocking-horse, but a murmur of voices there reassured her. 'What about Edouard?' she asked quietly.

'Edouard?' Anna queried blankly. 'Oh, I see. Well,' she looked at her friend ruefully, 'I'd forgotten about him. And if I can't miss this opportunity on his account, I can't want to be with him enough to marry him. No,' she said more strongly, 'I don't want to marry him.' Unaccountably, colour stained her cheeks as she met Lucy's questioning look.

'And what about all those other offers of parts you could play?' Lucy persisted.

Anna lifted an elegant shoulder. 'You know I wasn't taken with any of them. Anyway there'll always be other chances later.' She leaned forward. 'Lucy, I am quite serious. I know what I want, I usually do,' her brilliant smile dazzled Lucy, 'and I want very badly to do this.'

'When would you plan to put on the first production?' Lucy asked, moving a heap of albums off a faded crimson velvet chair. As she sat down in it the springs groaned protestingly and a puff of dust spurted out of the seat.

'I'm not sure,' Anna said thoughtfully. 'I couldn't reasonably expect to get away from *The Queen's Necklace* before Easter.

But I can get in touch with a lot of people while I'm there, and perhaps pass on some names for Philly to contact. That would mean the earliest we could manage a production would be late next summer. There'll be a lot of research to do though.' She glanced at Lucy enquiringly. 'I don't suppose Steven would be any use, would he?'

'I shouldn't think so,' Lucy said. 'As he's so obviously not keen about the idea there's no point in bothering with him. I wondered if it was something else that Philly could do, at least to begin with.'

Anna looked doubtful. 'Would she know what to do? And won't it take a lot of her time?'

'I don't think she'd need any specialist knowledge. If we point her towards the right books she only has to pick out things that might have concerned the priory, and then you or somebody else can build the scenes around them. That shouldn't take a lot of time,' Lucy said encouragingly.

'Yes, but what might have affected the priory won't always be obvious,' Anna demurred.

'True, but if Philly has any interest in history I think she'd quickly get the idea. And,' Lucy added, struck by a sudden thought, 'I expect Hugh could guide her a bit.'

'I suppose it won't hurt to try,' Anna agreed dubiously. 'But let's see what she thinks about the idea first. Then we can see what she comes up with before we make the arrangement too definite.'

'Okay, that's reasonable.' Lucy caught herself up with a deprecating smile. 'We're planning already, Anna. Let's wait until we can discuss it with the others. We'd better get on with finding the dress accessories while we're here. What do you think they'll be? Hats and gloves, that sort of thing?'

'Yes. And tippets, veils, shawls, anything like that.'

They searched silently for a while, bringing boxes out from under piles of papers, toys and miscellaneous bric-a-brac. At first they found glassware and china, each piece carefully cocooned in individual wrappings, and a Victorian writing desk filled with letters which Lucy put on one side to investigate later. At last Anna uttered an exclamation of satisfaction and drew a long pink feather boa from the box she had just opened. She shook it out and draped it round her shoulders, mincing a few steps across the floor. Lucy sat back on her heels, watching as Anna's posturing conjured up a picture of the 1920s woman who had originally worn it.

Anna pulled it off, saying regretfully, 'Lovely, but much later than our dresses. I wonder what else there is.' She bent over the box again, pushing the boa to one side of it, and began to rummage through the layers of material.

Lucy returned to the small walnut chest that she had just dragged out from beneath a pile of rugs. She stroked the polished wood gently and tried the lid, which lifted easily. Inside were layers and layers of tissue paper. She lifted the top ones cautiously, drawing in her breath with surprise at what lay beneath. 'Anna, come and see this,' she said softly.

Anna came quickly to her side and peered over her shoulder. 'How exquisite,' she exclaimed. 'Don't touch it, Lucy,' she added urgently. 'We're both too mucky to risk it. It would be fatal to leave marks on it now. Do you see how tiny the stitches are?' She peered more closely at the embroidered panel.

'Yes, and just look at the detail in the flowers. You can identify them instantly. See,' Lucy pointed, 'violets, primroses, wild daffodils, bluebells, wood sorrel, celandines, stitchwort, speedwell, and here at the back there's blackthorn in bloom and hazel catkins. It's a spring scene.' She stared eagerly at the contents of the little chest. 'I wonder how many more there are.'

'Lucy,' Anna began warningly, putting a hand on her arm.

Lucy slanted a smile at her. 'I know, but I'm itching to look. Won't Gran be fascinated?'

'Definitely,' Anna agreed. 'Is Isobel up to something, Lucy?' she asked unexpectedly. 'Daddy seems to have been searching the house since she visited him. He won't say what he's looking for, so I don't it expect he'll find it.' Lucy was looking puzzled and Anna hurried on, 'She wasn't best pleased to see me in Coombhaven this morning either.'

'Oh? I didn't know she'd been there,' Lucy said, recalling vividly how general Isobel had kept the conversation in the kitchen earlier that morning.

'Well, I was there unusually early so she wouldn't have expected to see me. Daddy doesn't have any hot chocolate and I do love the kind with orange zest, so I'd just popped in to the deli to get some,' Anna confessed. 'Isobel was coming out of Walden's Yard when I saw her bump into David.' A smile touched her lips. 'He was looking rather hunted and wasn't watching where he was going. In fact, he seemed to be rather anxious to avoid one of your farmers. You know, that old chap who was always so grumpy whenever we went riding across his land. Anyway, your grandmother dropped some of the papers she was carrying and I went over to help her pick them up, but she wouldn't let me or David stop. She positively hustled us away.' She looked at her friend. 'Hadn't you better find out what she's doing?'

Before Lucy could answer a hesitant voice called, 'Lucy, are you in here?'

They stared at each other in surprise, and Lucy glanced round the tallboy to see Liz standing uncertainly in the doorway, her brown hair escaping as usual from its chignon to straggle about her face. 'Hello, Liz, we're here.' Lucy moved towards her round the jumble of furniture and boxes. 'Come over. You'll be interested in what we've found.'

Behind the rocking-horse Sue and Will glanced at each other and Will put his finger to his lips with a grin. They sat very still, waiting to see if they were called.

'Lucy,' Liz broke off as she caught her foot in a holed rug. 'Heavens,' she said, regaining her balance, 'you have to be careful where you go in here.' She glanced at the puppets that Sue had laid out on the floor and picked her way more cautiously round the tallboy. 'Your grandmother asked me to tell you that the Christmas greenery has been delivered.' A mild humour sounded in her voice as she added, 'When I arrived there was a squat little gnome of a man in the hall surrounded by holly and fir.'

'That'll be Bert,' Lucy said. 'General purveyor of anything in the evergreen line for Christmas. For the rest of the year he comes up from the village to help us with the garden.' She cast a wistful look around the attic, her eyes lingering on the piles of unopened boxes. 'I suppose I'd better go and get on with the decorating. But look,' she gestured at the embroidered panel in the chest. 'Isn't it lovely?'

'It's beautiful,' Liz said, catching her breath. 'Do you know who made it?'

'No,' Lucy replied, 'but I'm taking the chest downstairs so that I can look through it thoroughly. There may be a name or some information about the work somewhere. I hope there are going to be four seasonal panels in it.' She replaced the layers of tissue paper and closed the lid.

'That would be lovely,' Liz agreed, looking about the attic with interest. 'Heavens, you could have all sorts of things tucked away here. Do you know what there is?'

Lucy smiled ruefully as she picked up one of the dusters Will had discarded and rubbed it lightly over the chest. 'No, I'm afraid we don't, but it's going to be interesting to find out. You must see what Sue and Will have already found.' She mentioned their names deliberately, conscious of their frozen presence nearby.

Liz's matt skin flushed, but her soft voice was even when she spoke. 'What is it?'

'Come with me and see,' Lucy said.

Liz followed her carefully, pausing beside the rack of dresses, her eyes widening in appreciation. Anna had begun to replace the dustsheets and smiled at her understandingly. 'I know. Aren't they gorgeous? There may be accessories to go with them as well. We're going to look at them properly downstairs some-time soon, so you should come and see them then.'

'Yes, we'll let you know when we do,' Lucy said. 'But come and look at Will's discovery now.' As she spoke she led the way round the rocking-horse and pointed at the rampart, which had now been lowered considerably and supported open boxes dis-playing a variety of weapons.

'Heavens!' Liz exclaimed. 'What a bloodthirsty lot they must have been.'

Will looked up from the box that he was trying to open and stared at her in disgust, while Sue rose stiffly to her feet and the two women faced each other with some awkwardness. Liz said with an effort, 'Sue, Mike thought you would be in the house so I came up to see you. I'm sorry,' she said resolutely, the colour in her face deepening, 'that I thought you were involved with the damage to the painting.' Sue opened her mouth to speak, but Liz continued firmly, 'I was very upset when I saw it, but it was wrong of me to think you were responsible.'

'Don't worry, Liz.' Sue had relaxed. 'I'd probably have felt the same in your shoes.'

Liz looked at her sharply, and went on, 'Mike wants you to have company all the time, so we've discussed how you can carry on working. He's happy for you to come down to the priory if Will or I walk with you between the house and church. Would you like to do that?'

'Yes, I would,' Sue said eagerly. 'What's happening down there? Is everybody else carrying on?'

'Oh yes,' Liz said. 'It's all a bit subdued, of course, but when Professor Mersett suggested that the students should be with-drawn he provoked a near-riot.'

'I should think he's had enough of those,' Will muttered under his breath.

A smile touched Sue's lips, but she asked anxiously, 'He can't make us go, can he?'

'No, I don't think so,' Liz assured her. 'I don't think he really wants to now.' She added, 'He avoided making a decision on the matter himself by asking the students what they wanted to do. Mike didn't have to say anything either, which was just as well.' She looked across at Will, who was staring exasperatedly at the box he had been attempting to open. 'Can you use these in Anna's plays?' She indicated the weapons on show around him as she spoke.

Will brightened momentarily, then looked gloomy again. 'That's just what I thought,' he said, 'but Anna thinks we'd have to use replicas.'

'Yes, I suppose you would,' Liz agreed. 'I suppose these would be rather dangerous.' She glanced at her watch. 'It's almost lunch-time,' she said to Sue, and Will sat up sharply. 'Why don't you come down afterwards for a bit?'

'Alright,' Sue said. 'Will can come with me, can't you, Will?'

'Sure,' he replied, 'me and Hades'll look after you.' He pushed the box crossly. 'Anyway, I can't get this open. None of the keys seem to fit.'

'I expect one's got lost,' Sue said philosophically as they began to pick their way back through the jumble. 'It's surprising really that we've been able to open the others.'

As they passed the clothes rack Lucy turned to Liz and asked, 'Won't you stay and have some lunch with us?'

'Thanks,' Liz answered gratefully, 'but the professors are going off to the pub for lunch and it might be better if I join them.'

Anna glanced up from the box of accessories she was rummaging through and gave an exaggerated shudder. 'Rather you than me,' she said. 'Look, do you think these match this cloak?' She held three bedraggled ostrich feathers against the green cloak and Lucy and Liz studied them carefully.

'Well,' Liz began doubtfully, 'it's a bit difficult to tell. The feathers were obviously green, but they've faded so much that it's hard to know what shade they were.'

'Would they have been worn together anyway?' Lucy asked.

'I think so,' Anna said. 'In the hair as a theatre-going ensemble, or something along those lines.'

'Will these give you ideas for your plays?' Liz enquired curiously.

'Yes, I'm sure they will,' Anna said. 'And Will's armoury might too.'

'Are you going to write the plots yourself?'

'Maybe. It depends on whether I can find somebody else who can do it better,' Anna said frankly as she put the feathers back in the box and closed it up.

'Is Steven going to do the research? I met him as I was coming in and he seemed quite elated.' Liz looked apologetic as Anna turned round in surprise from reshrouding the green cloak. 'I'm asking loads of questions, but Steven drove off in such a hurry I didn't have time to find out how it's going.'

'Well, he certainly won't be doing anything,' Anna said bluntly, 'as he thinks the whole idea's a load of rubbish.'

Lucy was frowning. 'What a nuisance. I suppose he's going into Coombhaven too. If only he'd said so at breakfast he could have got me some more cds for my computer.'

'I expect he was sulking,' Anna said brutally, moving reluctantly away from the clothes rack and picking up the box of embroideries to pass to Lucy. 'Here, don't forget to take these with you.'

Liz looked at Anna in surprise. 'I had no idea he was so difficult,' she said. 'I thought it was...' she broke off in confusion.

Anna's dark blue eyes gleamed mischievously as she considered her. 'Just Mike,' she finished, and Liz smiled unwillingly and blushed. 'Well, I wouldn't condemn anybody on Mike's recommendation,' Anna commented. 'But in Steven's case he has, possibly uniquely, got a great deal to support his views.'

'Do get a move on,' Will said impatiently from behind them. 'Who cares about Steven. At least he won't be at lunch.'

On this generally pleasing thought they made their way carefully across the attic and down the stairs.

EIGHT

Lucy was curled like a cat on the plump cushions of the window seat as she watched her grandmother. Isobel Rossington stood just inside the door and surveyed the drawing room approvingly. A fir swag glittering with silver stars hung over the stone mantelpiece, while a roaring fire in the hearth sent shadows flickering over the cream walls. A stoneware vase stood on a small table against the wall, filled with shaggy chrysanthemums in tawny and ruby shades. The russet curtains framing the nearby window were open, so that behind Lucy the glass created dancing lights against the darkness outside. 'Gran,' she said softly, 'what are you up to?'

Isobel turned to look at her, raising her strongly marked eyebrows. 'Did Anna mention seeing me in town this morning?' she asked. Lucy nodded, her thick chestnut hair swinging around her face. 'I thought she would,' Isobel said, sounding resigned. 'I haven't talked to you about it before because I wanted to be sure myself. And partly I suppose,' she looked penetratingly at her granddaughter, 'because it might have impinged on your own dilemma.'

'Mentioned what?' Lucy enquired evenly.

'My future plans,' Isobel replied. 'It's time for me to move on, and I shall.' Her eyes began to twinkle as an expression of blank astonishment appeared on Lucy's face. 'There are still things I want to do, you know. I'm very interested in some of the old embroideries I saw in Florence and I'm sure I could reproduce the designs, or something similar, quite easily. And there are so many exquisite pieces lying around unappreciated in this country that I'd like to find and copy. That's what Molly Leygar sent up to me, her grandmother's work, which was put away in the attic years ago. I'm thinking of going into business, you see,' she said calmly.

Lucy stared speechlessly at her grandmother, whose dark eyes were alight with enthusiasm. 'I'll probably buy a flat in Florence, so I'd be near Veronica and Martin,' Isobel continued. 'It's a lovely city and I like the Italian way of life. I'll spend the winter months there doing some research and let the flat out during the summer.'

'Will you come back here then?' Lucy asked, sliding off the window seat and moving across to the long central table.

'Possibly.' Isobel pursed her lips. 'I haven't decided yet, but I think I'd prefer to get a cottage in Coombhaven. It would be much more convenient for the things I want to do, and I'll still be close enough to see plenty of you all. That's why I was in Walden's Yard this morning. I wanted to see what sort of property Payne's have on the market.' She glanced at Lucy, who was fiddling with the fir cones in the bowl in the middle of the table, her back towards her grandmother. 'Don't say anything to the others yet, Lucy. I'd rather tell them myself when I'm ready.'

The carriage clock on the stone mantelpiece chimed the half-hour and Isobel said, 'We must talk more later, but I ought to see how Gina's getting on now.' She walked briskly over to the door, opened it and then stood back to let Anna through.

'I don't know that I should really be here,' Anna said as she came into the room on a cloud of scented air, holding a tray with a couple of platters full of small pastries. Her high-heeled shoes beat a light tattoo as she crossed the polished oak boards, falling suddenly silent as they encountered the rug in the middle of the room. She stopped by the long table with its crisp linen cloth, brightened here and there by the sprays of vivid berried holly in copper jugs that gleamed in the light of the table lamps. The surface was already laden with biscuits, tarts, pasties, crisps and nuts so Anna said, 'There doesn't seem to be much room for anything else. Where do you want these? They're those lovely curry puffs your grandmother makes. Gina's keeping some back for later.'

'Oh, put them anywhere. Hang on, I'll just make some space,' Lucy replied, making an effort to collect her scattered thoughts. 'Of course we want you here, Anna. You're part of the family. Nobody's likely to question your presence anyway, but now we can use your theatricals as the reason if we need to.' She studied the table and then pushed a few dishes closer together at either end of the table.

Anna held the tray steady until Lucy had removed the plates and added them to the buffet, then she propped it against a chair and looked round cautiously. She went over to the door and closed it, placing her back against it as she turned to face the room. 'Lucy, are you really going to put the chalice on display?' she demanded.

Lucy had observed this display of stealth and now her lips quirked in amusement. 'Why do you doubt it?'

Anna looked at her with an unusually serious expression, her dark blue eyes shadowed with concern. 'Well, it seems to me that the idea is a sprat to catch a mackerel,' she said bluntly. 'I'm not quite sure about the mackerel, but I guess it's got something to do with Duncan's death. And if that's true then it would be risky to bring the chalice here.'

Lucy regarded her with respect. 'Got it in one, Anna. We didn't intend to show it but the police are no further forward and neither are we.' She hesitated, then said quickly, 'There's no definite link between the chalice and Duncan's death, but we've decided to chance carrying on with our original plan in the hope that something, or someone, will be flushed out of the woodwork.'

'Lucy, are you sure?' Anna asked. 'It's a huge risk to take.'

'I know,' Lucy said. 'But two men we knew are dead. If displaying the chalice can help to catch the killer we don't feel we have any choice. There hasn't been time to have a copy made, but,' she added with intense feeling, 'if it survives tonight we're going to have one done immediately.'

Anna looked at her thoughtfully as she walked back into the room and sat down near the table. 'Yes, of course you're right,' she said slowly, 'but I'm glad I didn't have to make the decision. Does Mike know what's going on?'

Lucy frowned as she realigned a couple of dishes. 'I'm not sure. He hasn't said anything, which is unusual. He didn't know until this morning that we were still having the drinks, and he wasn't very happy about it then. I gather from Hugh that he pretty much washed his hands of the matter. I don't know if he's thought about it any more.'

'Where is Hugh?' Anna asked. 'Surely he's not still working?'

'He's fetching it,' Lucy replied succinctly.

'Lord, Lucy, how can you be so calm!' Anna exclaimed. 'Is he coming back with it on his own?'

'Under massive, but hopefully discreet, police surveillance.' Lucy cocked her head slightly. 'I thought I heard a car drawing up a few minutes ago.' She glanced at the clock on the mantelpiece. 'He should be back about now.'

The courtyard door slammed and Hugh shouted from the hall, 'Lucy, where are you?'

Lucy looked at Anna in alarm and hurried to the door of the drawing room. 'Hugh, I'm here. What is it?' she called anxiously.

Hugh strode furiously down the corridor, his arms full of evening newspapers. 'Come in here,' he said abruptly, entering the drawing room and kicking the door shut behind them.

'Where is it?' Lucy demanded as Anna stood by the table watching Hugh fearfully.

'What? Oh, it's under this lot. There hasn't been any problem with it.' He lowered his armful onto one of the chairs and drew a stout wooden box out from underneath the newspapers, looking round for somewhere to put it.

'Here, give it to me. There's loads of space for it because we're using so many dishes.' Lucy took it from him and placed it carefully in the carved and pilloried sideboard, locking the door and handing the key to Hugh.

He shoved it into his trouser pocket and picked up one of the newspapers, thrusting it towards her. 'Just look at this!'

Lucy took it and rapidly scanned the page that it was open at. She stopped halfway down at the article that Hugh obviously meant, her eyes widening in surprise. Anna came to her side and peered at the page too, immediately spotting the headline 'Murder Mystery'. 'Good Lord!' she exclaimed. 'They've got onto it pretty quickly.'

'Haven't they just.' Hugh bit the words off forcefully and both the women looked up at him in surprise. 'Read it carefully,' he instructed them tersely and they bent their heads over it again.

Lucy looked up first. 'Who was it?' she asked simply.

Anna's expression was puzzled, but it cleared as she reached the relevant line. '"We understand from our informant",' she quoted. 'So it seems we have a traitor in our midst.'

Lucy's hazel eyes had darkened and she regarded Hugh sombrely. 'Is there anything about it in the other papers?' she asked.

'No,' Hugh replied curtly. 'It's only in the evening papers – the nationals as well as the locals.'

'So it must be information they were given today,' Lucy said. 'Nobody's likely to have rung from here or the farm in case they were overheard, so it's presumably somebody who went into town.' Hugh regarded her as she thought about the logistics. 'Do you know who did it?' she demanded.

'Don't you?' he countered, and she nodded reluctantly, her

lips setting firmly.

Anna glared at them both in exasperation. 'Well, I don't,' she said crossly. 'I know Gran Rossington was in town, but it obviously wasn't her.' She caught her breath. 'David? Surely not. Why on earth should he?' Her glare deepened as she looked from one to the other of them. 'Come on, tell me who it was,' she demanded.

Lucy's pointed face was tight with anger as she looked at her. 'Who is it getting at, Anna?'

'Mike, obviously,' she replied. Her eyes widened in astonishment. 'You can't mean Professor Mersett?'

Hugh laughed involuntarily. 'What a fragrant idea. I hadn't thought about him. No, he isn't petty or vindictive enough for this.'

'He's too intelligent as well. I should say Mike could have a case for libel,' Lucy said, scanning the article again.

'Who gave them the information?' Anna clenched her hands as she enunciated the words with deliberate emphasis.

'Steven,' Lucy said, glancing at Hugh, who inclined his head in agreement.

Anna stared at her. 'I know he doesn't like Mike,' she exclaimed, 'but this is wicked. Does he really hate him so much?' she asked in disbelief.

'He's got a chip on his shoulder,' Hugh replied shortly, 'and he feels Mike picks on him. No doubt he felt this was a way of getting even.'

'Is it going to affect this evening?' Lucy asked.

Hugh leaned against one of the chairs, watching her as he answered, 'We don't think so.' He smiled at her enquiring look. 'I stormed into the police station after I'd picked up the papers. Of course it's headline news outside the newsagents, so I couldn't miss it.' His mouth twisted wryly. 'It was quite convenient in its way, as it gave me the chance to go over the arrangements for the evening again. Elliot was very interested in the leak, but not too concerned. There usually is at least one, and, after all, plain malice is not police business.' Hugh looked at his wife encouragingly. 'If you read that poisonous junk again you'll see there's no mention of the chalice. And the other papers have turned out similar garbage.'

Anna took the paper from Lucy, and read out slowly, 'A second archaeologist died yesterday in mysterious circumstances on excavations at an old priory in the West Country. Dr Duncan Hamilton's body was found in the lake at Rossington Manor and the local police regard his death as suspicious. They are presumed to have reopened the investigations into the death of Dr Hamilton's predecessor, Dr John Brett, who strangely fell to his death from a nearby cliff two weeks ago.

'Both Dr Hamilton and Dr Brett were strong contenders for the Walbury Chair of Archaeology at Oxford, as is the leader of the excavations, Professor Michael Shannon. We understand from our informant that Professor Shannon was on poor terms with both of his rivals, and that they found him belligerent and impossible to work with. It is believed that the university is initiating its own investigation into the matter, and that there is a strong possibility that the excavations will be stopped by Professor Mersett, who appeared at the site with exemplary speed to represent the university.'

Anna looked up with an expression of distaste on her face as she passed the newspaper back to Lucy. 'It's really just spite, isn't it? Hugh's right, there's nothing that will put your plan in jeopardy.'

Hugh raised an eyebrow as he regarded her with interest. 'Oh, so you've cottoned on, have you?' he asked mildly.

'Of course,' she retorted. 'I'm surprised Mike hasn't.'

'Well, he may have done by now,' Hugh replied. 'He was too annoyed this morning to think about it very clearly. After a bit of ranting he washed his hands of the affair and rampaged off to the priory.'

'What are we going to do about this, Hugh?' Lucy demanded, tapping the newspaper lightly. 'Are you going to speak to Steven or shall I? He can't stay here now.'

Hugh grimaced. 'Well, he won't be any great loss. He's perfectly capable in his job, but his manner makes him almost impossible to work with.' He sighed in exasperation. 'I don't imagine it all stems from the trouble at Kingsley Hall either. I'll speak to him but not, I think, until tomorrow.'

'Hugh,' Anna spoke uncertainly as the idea formed in her mind, 'don't you think it might be useful to do it now?'

'Why?' he demanded.

'If you're producing the chalice as a temptation,' she said, 'won't any kind of scene with Steven seem to be a distraction from the murderer?'

Lucy pondered this, tossing the newspaper onto a nearby chair as she looked across at Hugh. 'It's a good point.'

'Yes, it is' he agreed thoughtfully. 'Particularly as our plan seems to be transparent enough for Anna to see through. Others might have done the same.'

'I do know you all well,' Anna pointed out. 'It might not be so obvious to outsiders.'

'Hmm,' Hugh said. 'But you are right, a confrontation with Steven might provide cover for somebody else. But do we want him to leave before this evening is over?'

'Why not?' Lucy asked. 'It would be quite a relief to everybody.'

'The police may want him to stay here, or at least in the area, for a while longer,' Hugh replied.

There was no chance for further discussion as the door opened suddenly and Steven walked into the room. 'Lucy,' he began without any preamble, his tone tinged with annoyance, 'your grandmother wants to know if you want ice for the drinks.' He broke off as he saw Anna. 'Hello there,' he said more brightly, 'I didn't know you were going to be here. Are you staying for the evening?'

Anna smiled sweetly at him. 'Yes, I wouldn't want to miss it.'

He looked at her in surprise. 'It'll be frightfully dull, you know,' he began rudely. 'All trowels and trenches...' He broke off as his gaze fell on the newspapers and he flushed darkly red.

'Lucy, I'll go and tell your grandmother that you do want ice, shall I?' Anna asked. When Lucy nodded she walked quickly over to the door, her heels tapping out a staccato beat in the silence.

As Anna shut the door quietly behind her Steven looked at it resentfully. 'She's in a hurry,' he muttered crossly, pulling at his shirt cuff with his gaze averted from the others.

Hugh picked up the newspaper Lucy had dropped and held it out to Steven. 'Have you seen this?' he enquired.

Steven glanced at the newspaper, but made no move to take it. 'No,' he said sullenly, 'I haven't.'

'I thought you'd be interested,' Hugh replied, letting his arm drop back to his side.

'Why should I be?' Steven demanded belligerently.

'They've used the information you gave them very quickly,' Hugh said bluntly. 'Perhaps you didn't expect that.'

'Me?' Steven's indignation sounded forced and he could not meet Hugh's eyes. Lucy moved back to the window seat, perching on the edge of the cushions and observing Steven carefully. His eyes shifted and met her own briefly before falling away. 'I don't know what you're talking about,' he declared unconvincingly, 'but I suppose I should expect to be blamed for everything.' His voice took on a self-pitying whine.

'Why?' Hugh asked, trying not to feel too contemptuous.

'Everybody always blames me. They always do,' Steven said bitterly, 'and now you are too.'

'Are you telling me you aren't responsible for this?' Hugh demanded, tapping the newspaper article with his forefinger.

'You wouldn't believe me if I did, would you?' Steven countered dully.

'You hoped you wouldn't be suspected when you went to Coombhaven to ring them, though, didn't you?' Lucy asked quietly.

Steven's face drained of colour. 'I suppose some busybody saw me and couldn't keep quiet,' he blurted out. 'Well, I don't care. He had it coming to him anyway, and I was going to make sure I wasn't fingered for this as well.'

Hugh's eyebrows rose and he stared at Steven, before looking at Lucy, whose face was inscrutable.

'It's no use trying to say that I wouldn't have been,' Steven rambled on, his voice getting louder as he worked himself into a frenzy. 'None of you like me, and you needn't think I care. I can't stand any of you with your airs and graces, thinking you're all somebody. I'm just here to be patronised and given all the duff jobs to do. Well, I'm not as dim as you think. I could see that you were all getting together to put the blame on me, and I wasn't going to have it. I wouldn't be surprised if you were all in it, if there was a way to make money.'

Lucy sat stunned, aghast by the hysterical outpouring of vitriol, but Hugh spoke sharply, 'That's enough, Steven.'

Steven's stream of abuse and self-vindication stopped abruptly and he stared at Hugh, tears starting to his eyes. 'I'm sorry,' he muttered. 'I didn't mean it. I can't seem to help it.'

'That is rather obvious,' Hugh said.

Steven stared at his feet. 'It's alright, I'll go. You won't want me to stay now.'

'You have made it rather difficult for us to say we do,' Hugh agreed dryly. 'But I'm afraid you won't be able to leave just yet.'

Steven raised his head. 'Why not?' he asked in confusion.

'For one thing, we don't want to turn you out on the spot. And for another, I believe you should notify your departure to the police.' He saw the sudden fright in Steven's eyes and said, 'Don't be so stupid, man. It's purely a matter of the correct behaviour when the police are investigating a crime. It would apply to any of us if we wanted to leave here right now.' He sighed in exasperation. 'If you could bring yourself to look beyond your fears for your own skin, you'd see we're all pretty much in the same boat.'

Steven's voice was heavy with disbelief. 'You weren't at Kingsley Hall. They've got no reason to be suspicious of you.'

'I know enough of police procedure,' Hugh said, 'to be fully aware that they have to consider all of us as potential suspects until they have a line to follow.'

'Have they got one?' Steven asked eagerly.

Hugh shrugged. 'I expect we'll find out when they want us to know. In the meantime, I suggest that we discuss this matter again tomorrow morning. Let's try to put it out of our minds for this evening, so that we can get the drinks party over. It's going to be hard enough as it is.'

Steven's expression was blank, but his face reddened even more. 'Yes,' he said slowly, 'I suppose it is.' His eyes moved between Hugh and Lucy. 'I am sorry, you know,' he muttered. A thought struck him and his fingers pulled nervously at his lower lip. 'But Professor Shannon's bound to be furious when he finds out.' The note of anxiety in his voice did not escape either of them.

'Probably,' Hugh said impatiently. 'Can you blame him? But he's got enough on his mind at the moment, so he's unlikely to care very much about this.' Lucy glanced at him and he continued, 'I'll have a word with him, so that it doesn't catch him by surprise.'

Steven's head was bent as he fidgeted with his shirt cuff again. 'I suppose,' he said with difficulty, 'I should apologise to him.'

Hugh and Lucy were silent and he looked up pleadingly. 'He makes me feel small.' The words burst out. 'And I'm afraid of him.'

'He can be difficult,' Hugh said. 'But he's pretty much the same with everyone, Steven. He hasn't picked on you individually, and he certainly wouldn't over the Kingsley Hall business. He probably doesn't even remember about it most of the time.'

Steven gritted his teeth. 'I'll speak to him. I'll do it now.' He glanced at the newspaper. 'Can I take it with me?'

Hugh held it out, but Lucy came forward to his side, asking, 'Wouldn't you rather wait until he comes back to the house?'

Steven shook his head with grim determination. 'No. I won't be able to do it if I wait that long.' He looked at them desperately, 'I don't even know if I'll be able to say anything when I do see him.'

Lucy touched his arm gently. 'Just remember, if you can weather the sound and fury he always blows himself out.'

Steven swallowed hard and essayed a wavering smile. 'Thanks. I'll try.' His hand closed on the newspaper as he turned on his heel and left the room.

Lucy went back to the window seat and sank down on the cushions, feeling quite drained. Hugh came to stand beside her. 'What a hell of a situation,' he said with considerable feeling. He put his arm round her shoulders and she rested her head gratefully against him.

'You know,' she said softly, 'I've never liked him better than when he went out to apologise. What a shame.'

Hugh's arm tightened. 'Yes, I know. Look, let's skip it now. I ought to change.' He glanced at his watch as he spoke, then looked at her and smiled. 'I'm cutting it rather fine. Still, you'll be here if I'm not ready. That dress looks very good. Where did you find it?'

Lucy smiled at him impishly, standing up and twirling so that he could appreciate the finer points of the golden jersey dress that flared around her legs as she moved. 'I found the material in that little shop in Coombhaven, and Jenny Totton made it up for me. Isn't she clever?' She pulled a face. 'It was really for Christmas, but I thought it would give me courage for tonight. Oh,' she suddenly remembered, 'I haven't had time to tell you what we found in the attic.'

'Tell me later, Lucy. I really must get changed.' Hugh began to walk towards the door as he spoke. 'Or can you come up and talk to me?'

She looked at the carriage clock on the mantelpiece and said regretfully, 'I ought not to. There are still a couple of things to do. But, Hugh, I must just tell you quickly…' He paused with his hand on the door knob and looked at her enquiringly. 'Will found quite a few boxes of weapons in the attic. You know, swords and pistols, and some daggers. He found keys nearby that opened all except for one of the boxes, but oddly the key for that one is nowhere around. Of course he's dying to get into it and wants to break the box open, but I thought you'd better see it first. He's probably lying in wait for you,' she finished, 'so be warned.'

'Thanks,' Hugh said. 'As long as he isn't lurking about with one of the daggers I shan't mind.'

He closed the door behind him and Lucy turned round to survey the room again. The darkness outside seemed to have crept in, so the pools of light cast by the table lamps seemed brighter than ever. The warmth of the glow from the leaping flames on the hearth gave her a feeling of primeval gratitude. She raised her chin, causing her dangling earrings to chime faintly, and moved to the door to switch on the main light. The drawing room was immediately flooded with brightness from the candles on the overhead chandelier, and Lucy's intuitive awareness of lurking danger receded.

The door opened a crack behind her and Anna's dark head appeared cautiously around it. 'Oh good,' she said with relief, pulling the door wide and entering the room. 'I heard Hugh go upstairs but I wasn't sure if Steven was still here. Was it awful?' she asked sympathetically.

'Pretty dreadful,' Lucy said, glancing over her shoulder as she walked down the room, her dress rippling around her and red highlights gleaming in her hair. 'But he's gone down to apologise to Mike, which did surprise me.'

'Heavens! This is going to be a lively party, isn't it?'

'Not one of our better ones, I fear,' Lucy replied as she added a couple of logs to the fire and stood back, brushing her hands together as she turned round. 'I'm glad you're looking festive, too.' She regarded Anna's flamboyant dress with approval. 'That should stun them.'

One of Anna's hands smoothed down the dress that fitted her shapely figure perfectly. It was a bright crimson, her favourite colour, splashed with exotically coloured flowers. 'I'm very fond of it,' she said, appraising Lucy's dress as she spoke. 'You'll create quite an impression yourself. That suits you very well.' She gave a small unexpected gurgle of laughter. 'We're both overdressed, aren't we? But isn't it good for morale?'

The front door bell clanged loudly and Lucy met Anna's eyes. 'And so it begins,' she said, straightening her shoulders and lifting her chin. 'I wonder who's arriving so promptly?'

'Do you have to let them in?' Anna asked.

'No, Gina's doing that. She offered to stay on for the evening, and she's always invaluable. We've had to leave the front door on the latch anyway. You know how difficult it can be to open, and not everyone remembers to come through the courtyard.'

The drawing-room door opened and Isobel Rossington came in with Liz, whose long brown hair, both the younger women noticed immediately, was tightly confined in a neat chignon, fixed with a festive diamanté clasp.

Lucy went forward to greet her. 'Hello, Liz. I'm glad you were able to come.'

'I couldn't miss it,' Liz said frankly. 'The thought of your party has been like a beacon in the gloom down at the priory. Nobody on the dig is talking about anything except the chalice. You won't have any absentees,' she said with a smile. 'At least,' she added, the smile fading and her matt skin flushing, 'Mike did ask me to make his apologies. He's got involved in some work and would like to finish it, so he may be rather late.'

Lucy's surprise showed as she stood back to allow Gina to pass her with a large flagon of steaming mulled wine, which she placed beside a battalion of glasses under the flowers on the smaller table. 'Would you like some?' she asked Liz, gesturing to the flagon.

Liz nodded gratefully, but Anna ignored this byplay, a look of total disbelief on her face. 'I suppose,' she said without restraint, 'he's still feeling moody and disapproving.'

Liz shot her a quick look and then relaxed. 'Well, I don't think he entirely agrees with this,' she said tactfully, 'but I'm sure he has every intention of looking in later on if he can.'

Isobel said, 'We understand his feelings, of course, but I do hope he'll be able to display the chalice. It was originally his idea to show it, and it would be a shame if he should now miss talking about it.'

'Was it?' Liz asked, surprised, accepting a glass of mulled wine from Lucy with a murmur of thanks. 'That was good of him. I think,' she added deprecatingly, 'we've probably all shown a great interest in it.' Anna regarded her curiously as she accepted her own glass from Lucy, and thought that she had never seen Liz look so animated and relaxed. Her blue dress suited her, while the diamanté earrings and brooch which matched her hair clasp seemed to have lit a sparkle in her eyes.

Liz sipped her wine and glanced round the room, passing over the plates of food on the long main table to rest approvingly on the fire burning on the stone hearth and the large bunch of tawny and ruby chrysanthemums on the table against the wall. 'It all looks very seasonal,' she said.

The front door bell rang again as Lucy passed Isobel a glass of wine and Gina was soon ushering in a group of students. Lucy cast a quick eye over them, noting that they were all there, and moved forward with her grandmother to meet them.

'How was lunch with the professors?' Anna asked.

'Reasonably amicably,' Liz said. 'A lot of huffing and puffing, but no real pyrotechnics. I don't think I've ever seen them get on so easily.' Puzzlement touched her placid face for a second, then disappeared. 'Anyway, it makes life more straightforward. Which is just as well.'

Anna looked at her enquiringly, and she explained. 'Mike had visitors who upset him this afternoon. He's been in the finds room most of the time and a couple of women from the village went up to see him. I recognised one of them when they came out.' Her lips twitched. 'It wasn't really amusing, but they came rocketing down the stairs in the gatehouse and we could all hear Mike urging them on their way from the tower room.'

'Was it Tilly Barlow?' Anna asked, suppressing an inclination to laugh.

'I don't know their names,' Liz replied, and took a sip of her wine. 'The one I recognised lives in that cottage on the way down to the harbour with all the gnomes cluttering up the front garden.'

'Yes, that's Tilly,' Anna said resignedly. 'I expect the other woman was this mystic she's got staying with her. She looks rather frightening, but I'm sure Mike was more than capable of dealing with her. Heavens,' she added regretfully, 'I'm sorry I wasn't there to see it.'

'It was rather frightening at the time.' Liz shivered. 'The other woman looked absolutely furious when she came out.' She took another sip of wine and changed the subject. 'Did you find anything else in the attic?'

Anna pulled a dismal face. 'No,' she said. 'We didn't go back after lunch. Will went into town with David. I suspect they both had to do some belated Christmas shopping. And Lucy had to get things ready for this evening, so I helped her decorate the house. I always enjoy doing that, and Bert's greenery is so fresh that you get that lovely pine scent from it.' She looked approvingly at the swag over the fireplace.

Liz followed her gaze. 'It does look good,' she agreed. 'But I was hoping you'd have got the dresses down to look at.'

'It was supreme self-denial on my part,' Anna replied blithely, 'but I hope we'll have another chance before Christmas. I can hardly wait to get my hands on them.'

'It did look as though an extensive search would be interesting,' Liz said. 'All sorts of things got tucked away in attics in a place like this. Do let me know what you find.'

'I'm surprised Will didn't go back,' Sue said, joining them with a glass of wine in one hand and a plate full of pastries in the other. 'But I saw him come back with David just as it got dark. It looked as though he'd been shopping,' she added incredulously.

Anna's beautifully painted lips curved upwards. 'I was just explaining to Liz that Christmas has become rather pressing for some of the males in the household, including Will.'

Sue grinned as she perched her plate carefully on the sideboard. She glanced at her colleagues clustering around the main table and said ruefully, 'I'm afraid the same goes for most of us, males and females. Josie is the only one of us who's at all organised. She's even got her presents wrapped up and her cards written.' She added insouciantly, 'I haven't done much about it yet.'

She took one of the curry puffs from her plate and bit into it, eating it neatly as she looked round the room. Licking the crumbs delicately from her lips she said, 'Mmm, these are delicious.'

'I know,' Anna agreed. 'They always are. They're one of Mrs Rossington's specialities from her time in India.'

'I didn't know she'd been in India.' Liz's eyes lit up with interest. 'Was she there very long?'

'Several years,' Anna replied vaguely. 'I'm not precisely sure how long. It was ages ago though.'

'I must have a word with her about temple paintings. I've always been fascinated by them,' Liz said eagerly, glancing around to locate Isobel. She smiled apologetically at them and began to weave her way through the students towards Isobel, who was listening with great interest to Josie's impassioned conversation.

Sue watched her go and then turned to Anna. 'I don't think I'll ever be that dedicated,' she said unexpectedly. 'Liz is completely absorbed by the things she's interested in.'

Anna looked at her sharply, hearing a strange note in the

girl's voice, but Will came up to them at that moment. 'You just won't believe this!' he began explosively.

'Coombhaven shops have sold out of Christmas presents,' Anna inserted swiftly.

He stared at her obtusely, while David, just behind him, caught the comment and grinned.

'No. That's all sorted.' Will waved a hand dismissively. 'Hugh said we could force that box. You know,' he explained impatiently as both women looked at him blankly, 'that one in the attic that doesn't have a key. He did it with a chisel just before everyone arrived. The box should have held a pair of daggers, but one of them's missing. Isn't that a pain? What do you imagine happened to it?'

'Perhaps it was lost,' David suggested. 'After all, if they were used it's quite likely.'

Will gave a spurt of laughter. 'In somebody's back, you mean?'

Anna's cheeks seemed to lose a little of their delicate rose colour. 'Don't, Will,' she said abruptly.

'Oh Lord,' Sue said, her attention distracted. 'I didn't realise he was coming.' They followed her gaze and saw Professor Mersett standing near the doorway, talking amiably to Lucy. He had clearly made a concession to the festive nature of the evening, while remembering its ostensible purpose. His dark suit was brightened with a green tie, tastefully dotted with red, and a matching handkerchief.

'I must get something to eat,' Anna said, as Sue picked up a pasty from her plate.

'I should,' Sue responded. 'There won't be much left once he gets started.'

Anna noticed that the students had placed themselves strategically in twos and threes by the main table and were eating earnestly. They had all made some sartorial efforts for the evening. The women almost uniformly wore thick cotton skirts, but were more individual in their choice of jumpers. The men were generally in denims, but some sported a tie. Tinsel adorned most of them, as ribbons in the women's hair and tucked into the button holes of the men's shirts or forming ruffs round the necks of their jumpers.

Anna edged her way through to the table to pick up a plate. She started with the curry puffs, aware that they would disappear first, and as she moved sideways to reach the sausage rolls she bumped into Terry's lanky figure, nearly dropping her plate.

He straightened it deftly. 'Steady! You don't want to lose those. I've heard they're quite something, so I've come to try a few myself.' He eyed the three she had on her plate. 'It looks as though you already know about them.'

She flashed a conspiratorial smile at him. 'I do. That's why I'm making sure of sufficient supplies.'

'Good idea,' he said, helping himself generously. 'What else shouldn't I miss?'

'It's all good, but the cranberry tarts are special too.'

'Cranberry, huh? Look, can't I come round with you?' He glanced meaningfully at the professor, who was sipping his red wine and surveying the room genially. 'We'd better get going. He has an appetite like a horse.'

When they could not fit any more food onto their plates they withdrew to the window where Anna sat down on the cushions, stretching her legs out in front of her as they began to make inroads in their supplies. She listened with one ear to Terry, who seemed quite content with monosyllabic contributions to his commentary, and looked round, noting that Professor Mersett seemed more skilled at fitting quantities of food onto a plate than either of them.

Hugh had entered the room unobtrusively, adding a dandified touch to the gathering with his embroidered waistcoat and velvet bow tie, which she regarded with approval. He was in the middle of a throng of students, where Gavin was obviously telling a story that amused them. A careful dresser, Anna judged as she assessed the well-pressed dark jeans and the oversized red shirt that contrasted strikingly with his black face. Josie was at his elbow, her spiky hair creating an unusual halo effect around her chubby features. Her round chin jutted out, and Anna received the distinct impression of suppressed anger. Now I wonder what that's all about, Anna thought.

Professor Mersett gravitated to Liz's side and joined in her conversation with Isobel Rossington. Lucy was taking the opportunity to move away from his vicinity, Anna noticed with amusement. She frowned suddenly and looked quickly round the room again. She had not noticed Steven come in but he was over by the fireplace, looking rather strained as he talked to David. The estate manager was resting an arm against the mantelpiece, casually surveying the room. His broad-shouldered figure straightened as Sue approached.

Anna's frown deepened. Mike still had not come. Really, it is too silly of him, she thought crossly, to persist with this attitude. Quite unlike him, too. A pang of doubt stabbed her and fear swirled in her stomach. She put her plate down abruptly on the nearest table and, with a charmingly rueful smile for Terry, she picked her way across to Lucy, who was looking at the empty platter where the curry puffs had been.

'Lucy,' Anna said urgently, surreptitiously peering round to make sure nobody was too close to them, 'I'm worried about Mike. He's probably just being bloody-minded, but I'm going down to the priory to see what he's doing.'

Lucy looked at her quickly. 'Isn't he here yet? We'll be showing the chalice soon.' Her eyes narrowed as she glanced swiftly round the room. 'That is odd. Take care, then, Anna.'

She tried not to watch Anna as she made her way to the door, and stared instead at the plates in front of her. 'Will,' Lucy called, spotting out of the corner of her eye that her brother was approaching the table. 'The curry puffs have gone. Can you see if Gina has any more?' She proffered the empty platter, pushing it against his chest, and he stared at her in surprise.

'But...'

'Hush,' she said rapidly. 'Anna's going down to look for Mike. Go with her, but don't tell anyone.'

Will's thin face reddened with suppressed excitement. 'Okay,' he said loudly, taking the platter. 'I'll see whether Gina's got some left.'

The panelled hall was quiet after the hubbub of voices in the drawing room. Anna rummaged through the shoes near the coat rack, sighing with relief when she found a pair of Lucy's soft leather ankle boots. She pulled off her own high-heeled embroidered silk shoes and threw them carelessly down with the others, before easing her feet awkwardly into Lucy's boots. She snatched her yellow woollen coat from the rack under the stairs but as she turned away she paused. Reaching her hand up to the shelf above the coat rack she felt through the jumble that cluttered it, muttering crossly under her breath until her hand closed round the rubber torch she was seeking. At the sound of footsteps coming down the corridor towards the hall she turned swiftly, thrusting the torch into one of the deep coat pockets. 'Will,' she said sharply, 'you startled me.'

'Lucy told me where you're going. She said I'm to come with you,' he told her, putting the platter he carried down on the mule chest with a sharp bang. He hesitated and picked it up again. 'Perhaps I'd better give this to Gina and ask her to take more curry puffs in, so nobody wonders what I'm doing.'

'Catch me up then. I'll go round the usual way in case Mike's already set off,' Anna said, opening the courtyard door and letting a draught of chilly air steal into the room to set the Christmas cards clacking as they swayed on the strands of string looped across the walls. 'You come the front way,' she commanded. 'If we get as far as the priory without meeting him we'll try the gatehouse first.'

The night seemed very dark when she closed the door of the house behind her and Anna had to resist the urge to turn on the torch immediately. The moon had grown fuller, glowing through streamers of cloud that drifted gently across the sky. It lit the scene brightly enough as Anna made her way round the estate office and her eyes adjusted to the night light. A few patches of snow still glittered in sheltered spots, making the hunched mass of bushes by the brook seem less threatening as she turned onto the track to the priory. Anyway, she reassured herself as she strode between the rhododendrons, the police must surely be about somewhere, even if I can't see them.

She reached the Prior's Gateway before she heard hurrying footsteps on the gravel behind her. She glanced over her shoulder as Will reached her, with Hades at his heels.

'Gosh,' he panted, 'you're in a hurry. What d'you think's wrong? Lucy didn't tell me.'

'I don't know, Will,' Anna replied, keeping her voice low. 'I just want to make sure that Mike is alright.'

'But...' Will began to expostulate.

She silenced him quickly. 'Look, Will, I don't think we should make too much noise. Just keep close to me and let's hope we find that he's only sulking.'

Will opened his mouth and shut it again, resigning himself with difficulty to uninformed silence as he stretched his stride to keep up with Anna.

They reached the cloister garth and crossed it rapidly, carefully avoiding the trenches. Will glanced round, noticing involuntarily the shadows that lay eerily under the arches and in the depths of the arcades. He remembered with a twinge of fear the last night expedition he had made here. Anna was ahead of him as they passed into the entrance courtyard. She paused so abruptly that he bumped into her before he could stop himself.

'Sorry,' he whispered.

'Look,' she hissed, 'the office light's on.'

A faint gleam shone through the small panes of the first floor window, barely impinging on the darkness of the courtyard.

'He's probably still working then,' Will said prosaically.

'I don't like it, Will, I really don't.' Anna muttered shakily. She bit her lip and said urgently, 'Come on, but do be quiet.'

He followed her, with Hades close beside him, under the gatehouse arch. The ancient studded door at the base of the tower swung silently open when Anna turned the handle, and she stepped cautiously into the porter's room. Boxes and ropes were piled up in one corner, with a heap of papers next to some stakes on a wooden trestle table against the wall. A dark rectangle on the opposite wall showed where the stairway went up to the office. Anna crossed the room carefully and peered up the short flight of stairs. They were in darkness and only a faint glimmer showed under the door of the finds room above. Anna hesitated, but felt uneasily that she could not press the light switch to illuminate the stairs. She fingered the torch in her pocket but finally began to climb the stairs in the dark, feeling her way carefully up the narrow worn treads, conscious of Will's quick breathing behind her and the scrabbling of Hades' claws on the stone.

When Anna reached the top step she turned the door handle, keeping well back as she slowly pushed the heavy door open, praying that Mike would shout at her. There was no sound and she peered fearfully into the dimly lit room, gripping the edge of the door so tightly that her knuckles whitened.

The room was filled with opaque shadows, and dark shapes loomed haphazardly along the tables around the edges. The only source of light was streaming down from a lamp on the desk in the far corner, falling full onto Mike's hunched figure.

'Oh God!' Anna exclaimed, pushing the door wide open and running across the room. She bent anxiously over the still figure, calling his name imperatively. Mike was seated in his chair but had fallen forward across the desk in front of him, his head resting on a paper covered with his scrawling script, his pen fallen from a slack hand to roll across an open journal.

Will was on his other side. 'Maybe he's asleep, Anna,' he said hopefully. 'Try shaking him.'

'No,' Anna said forcefully. 'Be careful, I don't think he's asleep.'

Will's eyes widened. 'He isn't...' He could not bring himself to finish the sentence, staring fearfully at Anna's white face.

She stretched out a hand resolutely and gripped one of Mike's limp wrists. At first she could only hear the thudding of her own heart, but suddenly she became aware of Mike's pulse beating slowly but strongly. The relief made her feel unexpectedly weak and she had a momentary struggle to overcome a swimming sensation in her head.

'No, he isn't dead,' Anna told Will, her voice strangely calm as she dropped Mike's wrist. 'But he mustn't lie like this. Help me lift him off the desk.'

It was quite a struggle to raise Mike's weight, but between them they at last pushed him into the chair where he lay unconscious against its back. His breathing was shallow and hurried, his face drained of blood and strangely putty-coloured.

'He's been poisoned or drugged, I think,' Anna said grimly, lifting one of Mike's eyelids to peer at his glazed blue eye. She let the lid slide closed and stared at Mike in despair. 'God, what shall we do?'

'Shall I get him something to drink?' Will stretched his hand out towards the glass on the desk.

'No! Don't touch it, Will!' Anna shouted at him. He stopped in alarm with his hand outstretched. 'I'm sorry,' she apologised, 'but it probably contains whatever he's taken, and it may have fingerprints on it.' She gritted her teeth. 'Look, Will, you'll have to go and get help. We need a doctor, and an ambulance too.'

'And the police,' Will added quickly.

'They're already here.' Anna saw how surprised he looked and explained swiftly, 'They hope the murderer may try to steal the chalice this evening, so the house is staked out. I don't know where they are, but they must be in the grounds.'

'Gosh! Well, I can find them then,' Will said, his eyes wide with excitement.

Anna shook her head. 'There's no time for that. Besides,' she added, 'the murderer may be out there. Get to the house and tell Hugh or Lucy. I'll stay here and try to bring Mike round.' She stared at Mike desperately, clutching his shoulders and shaking him vigorously as she spoke, acutely aware that she was making no change to his state.

'But, Anna, will you be safe?' Will asked anxiously from the doorway.

'Yes, yes. Just go!' she ordered without glancing up from Mike's figure.

'Look, I'll leave Hades with you.' Will took the big dog's collar and pulled him over to the corner near the door. 'Stay, Hades, stay,' he commanded firmly and turned away from the reproachful gleam in the dog's bright eyes. Hades' paws twitched at the sound of his master running down the stairs, but he sighed deeply and sat obediently on the spot where Will had left him.

Anna moved swiftly across to the window and stood at the edge of it, peering through the distorted panes of glass. She heaved a sigh of relief when she saw Will running across the courtyard. As soon as he was out of sight she turned back to the room, looking round it in despair.

Apart from the desk in the far corner, trestle tables lined the walls. These were cluttered with finds from the excavation, mainly rows of pieced-together pots and bowls. Several fragments of pottery were laid out across another table, which almost filled the centre of the room, only leaving a narrow space to move around it. Anna groaned and then her heart leaped as she saw a tap and sink in the corner where Hades lay, almost hidden by the door which Will had left open. She studied the collection of earthenware pitchers that stood on the nearest trestle table, and was relieved to find one that was intact, other than a few chips on its lip. She was aware as she walked quickly to the sink that it was probably one of Mike's prized artefacts but her only concern now was that it should still hold water.

She filled it under the tap and found to her intense relief that the clay had remained impervious, although water leaked from tiny holes. She carried it carefully back to the desk and without any compunction lifted the jug and emptied the water over Mike's oblivious head.

The water plastered his red hair to his skull and ran in rivulets onto his shoulders, but he did not stir. Anna banged the pitcher carelessly back onto the trestle table and began to slap his face angrily.

'Mike! Mike!' she shouted at him. 'Come on! You can't die like this.'

She had not heard footsteps on the stairs but suddenly became aware of a figure in the shadows outside the door. She looked up and breathed a sigh of relief. 'Thank God you've come!'

Anna broke off as the figure came into the doorway and she saw the ornate tip of a dagger handle protruding from a coat pocket, winking and gleaming in the light.

NINE

Will ran as fast as he could along the track beyond the Prior's Gateway, gravel crunching noisily under his feet. He hesitated at the bridge over the brook, peering into the thick shadows around the rhododendron thickets. The clouds had cleared from the night sky, and moon and starlight created a scene of stark black shapes around pools of unworldly light. Will stared at the bushes and trees until his eyes watered, but he could not see any sign of the hidden police presence. A longing swept over him to shout out and see if one of the shadows moved, but he remembered Anna's caution and felt he could not just yell into the night. Nothing moved around him but Will suddenly felt afraid and caught his breath sharply. A large pale form swooped down with a wild screech in front of him and Will took to his heels as the owl swept upwards again.

He ran on to the house, whose white Jacobean façade glowed brightly as he approached it, grateful that for once he could go through the front door. It stood ajar so Will bounded up the porch steps and pushed it fully open, almost falling across the threshold into the hall, grateful for the warmth and security he felt within the panelled walls. The lighting was soft and subdued, but the half-seen shapes around the room were familiar and comforting, full of rich colours, while tiny glitter stars twinkled as the Christmas cards swayed on their draped strings. Will discarded any idea of stealth as he hurried across the hall, his footsteps ringing out on the polished oak boards between the rugs. He ran down the corridor to the drawing room and threw open the door to stand panting before the crowd of people.

The party had gathered in a group around Hugh, their eyes fixed on the chalice he was holding up. It gleamed richly in the overhead light and as Hugh turned it slowly round in his hands the jewels which encrusted the golden surface flashed with red and green fire. Professor Mersett was holding forth, his voice booming out, 'And as you can see, this example of craftsman-ship demonstrates...' His audience was silent and attentive, although very few of the students appeared to be listening to him. Most of them gazed transfixed at the shining gold and jewels, admiration and awe and plain cupidity touching their countenances. Josie's chubby face was intent under her spiky black hair, and she seemed barely aware that Gavin was mur-muring in her ear.

Isobel sat in a chair near the window, her hands folded neatly in her lap as she watched the performance. Lucy and David stood nearby, beside the table whose surface was now littered with crumb-ridden plates and empty glasses. Out of the seasonal display only the gleaming jugs of berried holly still held their original colour and pristine appearance. David looked rather bored as he leaned an arm on the mantelpiece, staring at the fire. Beside him Lucy's dress rippled with waves of light as she bent to place a log on the flames. The small noise it made as it settled on the hearth distracted Josie. As she glanced round Lucy looked up to meet her gaze, and saw over her shoulder to the doorway. The smile on Lucy's lips froze as she spotted Will and the look on his face. She hurried down the room, pushing past students on the edge of the group to reach her brother.

'What is it?' she demanded urgently, ignoring the heads that turned in her wake.

'It's Mike. He's been poisoned!' Will gasped, struggling to

catch his breath. 'Anna's stayed with him in the gatehouse. She wants a doctor and an ambulance at once.'

He tried to speak quietly but the urgency in his voice attracted even more attention from the students. The ripple of movement at the edge of the group spread inwards as more people became aware of the disturbance and drew their gaze away from the chalice.

Lucy left the room without a backwards glance, heading rapidly to the study next door to use the telephone. Hugh lowered the chalice as he watched her go. Most of the students had their backs to him now, staring curiously at Will's thin flushed face. Even Professor Mersett came to a halt, his mouth still open in mid-flow as he looked indignantly down the room to see who or what had proved more interesting than his discourse. Hugh stepped forward, holding the stem of the chalice lightly so that it swung beside him as he moved, a glittering swirl of fire and flame that seemed to have leaped from the hearth to attach itself to his hand. He raised an eyebrow in a query as he drew closer to Will and met the youth's dark eyes.

Will abandoned any instinct of caution that still lingered in his mind. 'Lucy's gone to ring for a doctor. Somebody's tried to poison Mike,' he said bluntly, his hands clenching into fists.

A collective gasp of horror rose from the students, drowning Professor Mersett's spluttering, 'What? What?' His stout figure seemed to be rooted to the spot, his full lips quivering with shock. Liz paled and put out a hand to steady herself against the back of a chair. The professor visibly pulled himself together. He took her by the elbow and virtually thrust her onto the chair.

Hugh's grasp on the chalice tightened as he said sharply into the microphone concealed in his bow tie, 'Elliot! Trouble. In the drawing room.'

The students nearest to Hugh stepped back involuntarily, gaping and uncertain. He walked quickly round the table to the window, brushing past Isobel who had risen to her feet. The casement was fractionally ajar, and Hugh used one hand to push it fully open as several figures materialised outside. The inspector's eyes went immediately to the chalice that Hugh held in his other hand.

Hugh shook his head. 'It's not the chalice. Mike's been poisoned. Lucy's ringing for the doctor.'

'Where is he?' the inspector demanded.

'In the gatehouse,' Will replied from behind Hugh.

'Inspector,' Lucy called urgently from the study window. Hugh leaned over the drawing-room sill and just caught sight of her face. 'The bookcase has been forced and a number of books have gone.'

Hugh drew in his breath quickly. 'Look, Elliot, I'm going to lock this back in the sideboard. Can you spare somebody to guard it? I must go down to the gatehouse.'

'Anna's there on her own, although I left Hades with her,' Will interposed urgently behind him. 'She said there were police in the grounds, but I didn't see any.'

Hugh glanced at him, frowning, before turning back to the inspector. 'Did you catch that?'

'Yes. I'll send a man down there at once. We'd better sort out what's happening here before we take any other action. I'll come in.'

Hugh strode to the sideboard, ignoring the students scuttling out of his way to hover anxiously about the room. Professor Mersett loomed up, his chest puffed out like a pouter pigeon as he demanded crossly, 'Just what's going on, Carey?'

'There's no time to explain right now,' Hugh said, without looking up from the chalice he was carefully fitting back into its box. He locked it away in the sideboard as Inspector Elliot entered the room, flanked by Sergeant Peters and two young constables. At a nod from the inspector one of the constables took up his post at the end of the sideboard, where he had a clear view of the door and the window, as well as the occupants of the room. He stared impassively at them as they milled around uncertainly, muttering urgent questions and comments to each other.

Isobel Rossington moved forward from the inconspicuous stand she had taken by the open door and Hugh spoke briefly to her as he thrust the key of the sideboard in his trouser pocket. 'Isobel, would you stay by the sideboard too. Perhaps, Professor, you'd stand with her. This may be a distraction to draw us away from the chalice. Don't let anything or anybody move you away from this spot until I or Elliot get back.'

He did not wait for a reply and did not even hear Professor Mersett's querulous questions as he took his place beside Isobel. Hugh looked round the room and caught sight of Steven spasmodically biting his lip as he stood white and frightened by the table.

'Ah, Steven, just the person,' Hugh said. 'You'll probably know what's gone as well as we would. Come and advise us.'

Steven gulped and looked as though he might protest. He clearly thought better of it at once and moved forward reluctantly, but without a word, his gaze fixed on Hugh's face.

Hugh's eyes swept round the room again, this time pinpointing David, who had edged quietly round the group until he was within call. The young estate manager was now wholly alert, his broad shoulders squared purposefully. Hugh stepped over to him and said quietly, 'Keep a general eye on things, David. Don't let anyone leave the room alone, although I expect the police will take care of that.' David nodded, his jaw set grimly, and Hugh led the policemen out of the room with Steven glumly bringing up the rear.

'Doctor Bishop's going straight to the gatehouse,' Lucy informed them as soon as they entered the study, where the main light shone down on her chestnut hair as she crouched in front of the glass-fronted bookcase. 'He wasn't very pleased,' she added wryly, 'but I said we'd see him there.' She indicated the bookcase. 'Look, this has been forced quite roughly. One of the doors swung open as I passed it.'

Hugh studied the books, a frown creasing his forehead. 'It looks to me as though a random selection has been taken. See, Steven, the Clarendon volumes have been left, and they're extremely valuable.'

Steven crouched down to scan the shelves more closely, the fear fading from his eyes as he looked. A puzzled expression crossed his face. 'Yes, I think you're right.' He hesitated fractionally before saying nervously, 'In fact, it looks as though it's mainly the lighter books that have gone.'

Lucy put her hand on Hugh's arm. 'Is it a diversion?' she asked uneasily.

He turned towards her, his eyes narrowed. Suddenly they widened and his body stiffened as he moved abruptly, causing Lucy's hand to drop. Brushing past the inspector who was standing behind them, Hugh rapidly crossed the space to the front of the desk, making one of the red brocade curtains waver as his shoulder caught it. He uttered a forceful expletive, quickly pulling his handkerchief out of his trouser pocket to wrap round the handle of the top right-hand drawer before he pulled it out. It slid out smoothly and was quite empty.

Hugh stared down at it, his lips tightened into a thin line. 'This lock's been expertly forced,' he said as the others crowded round him.

'The letters, Hugh?' Lucy asked. He nodded, while Steven sucked in his breath in a low hiss.

'What letters?' demanded Elliot. 'Were they valuable?'

'Very probably,' Hugh said grimly. 'Certainly our clever friend thinks so. It's a collection of letters that Steven found recently, which I've just brought home from showing to experts in Oxford. They seemed to have been written by Elizabeth Tudor's favourite, Robert Dudley, to Harry Rossington with lots of juicy court gossip. The two men had been friends from their youth, and there is faint evidence that Dudley may have been a visitor here at least once when Harry was grandifying his new property. I left a few of them in Oxford for more specialist testing to determine their authenticity. But,' he said, 'the bulk of them were in this drawer before the party started. I checked them myself when the visitors began arriving.'

The inspector's eyes were intent as he watched Hugh. 'How many people know about them?' he asked sharply.

Hugh shrugged. 'I couldn't tell you,' he said frankly. 'I've spoken to a few people about them and I expect the others have too.' He noticed Steven's ready flush appear again. 'And no doubt word has gone round from Oxford as well. It's potentially a very exciting find.'

'Hugh,' Lucy broke in, looking from him to the inspector, 'shouldn't we go down to the gatehouse? This can surely wait, but Mike can't.'

Inspector Elliot glanced at her. 'Yes, you're quite right. The professor must be our first priority.' He beckoned the second police constable, who came to stand at the end of the desk. 'Giddens will make sure nothing else is disturbed in this room. Do you want to leave anyone here too?'

Hugh spoke without hesitation. 'Steven, would you stay?'

'If you want me to,' he said awkwardly.

Hugh was turning away when a thought struck him. 'I'd forgotten, Steven, you must have seen Mike last. How was he then?'

Steven's colour faded patchily, leaving blotches on his white face. 'But I didn't,' he blurted out. 'I didn't see him, I mean.'

Hugh and Lucy looked at him in obvious surprise, and perspiration broke out on Steven's forehead. He thrust his shaking hands into his pockets. 'I saw Liz when I got there,' he said, almost stammering in his haste. 'She was just coming out of the church and she said it wouldn't be a good idea to disturb him then as he'd had a bad afternoon. She said he probably wouldn't come to the party this evening so I'd do better to see him tomorrow. Ask her,' he ended with pathetic eagerness, 'she'll tell you.'

The inspector was listening impatiently. 'Later,' he said,

turning to Hugh and Lucy. 'It's more important right now for us to get down there. Tom,' he looked at Sergeant Peters who was waiting stolidly by the door, 'get the team out to go over this room thoroughly. Get another man in and leave him next door to make absolutely sure nobody goes away. Then leave them to it and join us down at the gatehouse as soon as you can.'

The sergeant absorbed his instructions without a blink, but as the inspector turned away he asked, 'Do you want me to leave men in the grounds, sir?'

'Yes, I think it would be wise to keep some out there,' Elliot replied. 'I'm not convinced that we know the killer's full agenda, so we can't be sure what we're up against yet. Tell them to detain anyone they come across.'

He left the study with Hugh and Lucy, almost colliding with Will as he rushed out of the drawing room to meet them. His face was tight with anxiety and he spoke to them in a low voice, conscious of others listening from the room.

'Are you sure she's missing?' the inspector demanded.

Will nodded miserably. 'I've only spoken to Gran about it,' he said in a subdued voice, 'and she last saw her looking at the chalice, just after Hugh brought it out. She may have told somebody else where she was going,' he added hopefully. 'I haven't asked any of the others.'

Lucy uttered an exclamation of horrified understanding. 'The dagger!' The inspector turned to her uncomprehendingly, noting the look of shock in her eyes. 'She was in the attic today when we discovered some old weapons. Swords and pistols, things like that. We later found a dagger was missing from one of the boxes.'

Will gaped at her, but Elliot drummed the fingers of one hand against his leg. 'I don't like the sound of this. A lot of the pieces of this jigsaw are falling onto the table, but I still can't see the pattern.' His face seemed as imperturbable as ever, but a hint of unease touched his voice. 'I'll get Tom to organise a search in the grounds but I think you'd better get down to the gatehouse with one of the constables from outside. I'll join you shortly.'

'What on earth's happened to Mike?' Sue demanded from the doorway of the finds room. She took one step into the room, out of the shadows at the top of the stairs and into the light. The dark coat she wore hung loosely over her long cotton skirt and swung with her movement so that the pocket and its contents were hidden by the broad cuff of her sleeve.

For a second Anna doubted what she had just seen as she stared transfixed at Sue, whose face looked stricken. Hades had got to his feet in the corner where Will had left him and was wagging his long tail tentatively. The student's gaze was fixed on Mike so she did not notice the big dog, who hesitated, puzzled, and then subsided, laying his head on his paws and watching the women.

Sue's eyes widened behind the narrow frame of her spectacles as she took in the appearance of the unconscious man lying back in the chair, with water dripping steadily from his shoulders to form puddles on the stone floor. 'What are you doing to him?' she demanded. 'Is he ill?'

Anna drew a deep breath, realising that if she followed Sue's lead she might have a slight chance to save herself and Mike. 'I don't know,' she said frantically, trying desperately as she spoke to calculate how long Will had been gone. She summoned all her resources to play the most important role of her life and allowed her mobile features to express the fear she was quite genuinely feeling. 'Thank heavens you're here, Sue,' she said. 'I didn't like to leave him, but somebody needs to go for help.'

'I suppose they do,' Sue replied, not moving from her position just within the doorway as she turned an unblinking stare onto Anna. 'But what's wrong? Has he had a heart attack or what?'

'I don't think so.' Anna was afraid that the thudding of her own heart would be heard across the room. 'It looks as though he may have taken something.'

'What!' Sue exclaimed in dismay, and her gaze flickered to Mike. Her concern sounded genuine and Anna's thoughts wavered, doubt creeping in for a second until she recalled firmly what she had seen in Sue's pocket.

Sue moved unexpectedly, skirting the central work table to reach the desk before Anna had time to react. The girl stood beside Mike, looking down at his pale wet face, before she lifted her head and fixed her eyes on Anna over his comatose body. She said almost fearfully, 'You don't think it's because of Dr Hamilton, do you? No, surely not.' Her gaze remained steady but her voice wobbled. Again doubt wriggled in Anna's mind as she wondered whether she should be admiring a born actress or castigating herself for unworthy suspicions.

Sue hurried on anxiously, 'He was quite alright earlier. I came in to see him before the party and he asked me to deliver a parcel for him. He seemed so concerned about it that I thought I'd better come and tell him I hadn't had a chance to do it yet. I wasn't sure he was still here so I've left it downstairs.' Her forehead wrinkled in concern. 'Heavens, I wonder what it is. I hope…' Her voice tailed off and she shook her head. 'This is impossible. Are you sure he's drugged?'

Before Anna could stop her Sue leaned forward and lifted one of Mike's eyelids, without removing the supple leather gloves from her hands. As she bent over him her sleeve uncovered her pocket and the tip of the dagger handle banged against the arm of the chair. It was only a tiny sound, but in the quiet room it sounded like a clap of thunder. Sue let Mike's eyelid slip back as she glanced down at her pocket and saw the glittering shape. She straightened slowly, a peculiarly unpleasant smile touching her lips as her eyes met Anna's.

Anna made a valiant effort to divert the danger. 'Heavens, is that one of Will's daggers? What a good idea, Sue. I wish I'd thought of it myself. I'd have felt a lot safer.'

Sue eyed her thoughtfully and the smile widened as she drew the dagger slowly out of her pocket, keeping her eyes on Anna. 'Yes.' She balanced it in her hand as she said softly, 'I thought it might come in useful.'

'I'm beginning to think they should be standard issue at the priory,' Anna said with a shudder, which was not entirely feigned. 'Will you feel safer taking it with you to get help, or could you bear to leave it with me? We really must do something, you know.'

'Yes,' Sue agreed in an even tone, 'we must.' She looked quickly over her shoulder as Hades shifted in his corner. He raised his head at Sue's movement, obviously considering whether to approach her. Anna's heart leaped hopefully, only to sink again a second later as the big dog lowered his head back onto his paws and resumed his study of the protagonists.

'I see you brought your own protection,' Sue said, her face alight with laughter. She took a swift step round the chair towards Anna, who was caught off guard and stepped back instinctively.

Sue stopped. 'Yes, you're good,' she said, a note of admiration in her voice, 'but not good enough. You were cautious about me as soon as I arrived. Why? Did you see this?' She lifted the dagger, shifting her grasp to grip the hilt more firmly. 'Or did you already suspect something?'

Anna let her weight rest on the trestle table as she leaned back with both hands pressed against the edge. 'I don't really know,' she said, relieved that her voice sounded so steady. 'Of course the dagger made me wary. But even then I wasn't sure that I was jumping to the right conclusion.'

'But you are now.' It was a statement.

Anna did not even think of contradicting it or trying to bluff. 'Of course,' she replied flatly, appalled by the gradual change that had come over Sue, whose eyes held a look of distinct malevolence. Anna's mind raced. Shall I mention Will? No, not if I can help it, she decided. That might precipitate matters, so it's probably better to keep her talking if I can. Someone must come soon, she thought, keeping her courage high as she tried to ignore the insidious niggling fear that they might not be in time. Infusing her voice with as much interest as she could muster, she asked, 'Has it been you all along?'

Sue's lips parted slightly to show her gleaming teeth. 'Oh yes, all along,' she replied complacently. 'And it's been me in lots of other places for the last two years. After all, who really notices a student? And it's been so easy. Until now.' She frowned, in thought rather than concern. 'But then,' Sue said softly as the frown disappeared and the unpleasant smile returned, 'you can be turned to good account.'

Anna decided she preferred the frown. She was gripping the trestle table so tightly that her hands were beginning to go numb so she carefully unclenched them. There must be something I can use as a weapon, she thought frantically, trying to cast her mind over what she had seen. Her fingers crept out, trying to feel something, anything.

'Two years?' Anna repeated, her blue eyes widening in surprise. She forced a touch of admiration into her expression. 'Surely it wasn't you at, umm, wherever Steven was? I heard something valuable was taken from there.'

Sue's smile became a smirk. 'Of course it was. That was one of my early jobs. I met him there, but it was child's play to persuade him not to mention it. You might think we were accomplices, you see, and then I'd have to report something suspicious about him that I'd spotted. He's in such a feeble state about it,' she said derisively, 'that it was simple to scare him off. Anyway, if he'd been a problem I could easily have got rid of him.' She fingered the blade of the dagger. 'You didn't really think it was him, did you? He hasn't got the brains, or the guts.' She dismissed him scornfully. 'I didn't think even the police would believe it if I set him up, so I didn't bother.'

A germ of an idea sprouted in Anna's mind. 'How on earth did you do it?' Anna asked, genuinely interested. 'The police seem to be completely baffled.'

Sue considered the other woman, but the urge to display her cleverness overcame her caution. After all, she thought complacently, Anna isn't going to repeat anything she hears. Anna read the thought in the eyes that watched her so closely and restrained a primordial urge to scream and run.

'I went on every dig I could,' Sue told her in a spurt of speech. 'The ever-willing student, you see, that's me,' she added mockingly, relaxing marginally as she spoke and rubbing her thumb casually over the hilt of the dagger. 'It gave me a chance to suss out possibilities, and then I had to find out who collected the items that I could make available. It was easy enough to work out which collectors to approach, and it wasn't long before I was beginning to get orders,' she said proudly. 'I arranged for somebody to pick them up and somebody else to hand them over, so there was never any link with me. There were always experts of one kind or another working at the sites, and I preferred to arrange things so that the goods were connected with their work. It's very appealing to provide links for the police to consider.' She grinned engagingly. 'I always managed to leave a doubt in their minds. It's great fun.'

Anna was horrified and inadvertently let it show on her face. Sue's grin faded. 'You're just like them,' she said, dislike filling her words. 'So smug. Well, I know how to dent that smugness.'

She began to edge round the chair where Mike still lay supine. Anna backed away along the trestle table, anxious not to be boxed into the corner, but agonisingly aware that she was leaving Mike exposed to any action Sue might take. Surely, Anna thought desperately, I'm the threat now and she won't bother with him. For every slow deliberate step that Sue took towards her Anna slid a corresponding pace away, aware that she would soon have to try to escape down the narrow space around the central work table.

'Surely it was dangerous to use intermediaries?' she asked, grasping at a straw. 'They could make the link with you, couldn't they?'

Sue stopped abruptly and stared at her. 'Dangerous? That's the fun of it, don't you see? Anyway, it's never dangerous for me. They can't harm me.'

Anna did not like the look in Sue's eyes as she said this. 'Why not?' she asked, swallowing hard against a sudden obstruction in her throat.

'I don't leave them around to tell tales. It's easier that way,' Sue said, sounding quite matter-of-fact.

'Is that why you killed John Brett and Duncan Hamilton?' Anna asked.

Sue snorted with suppressed amusement. 'There was nothing for them to tell. No, I decided it was time to finger somebody as the mastermind, rather than just leave delicate hints. The police have been very slow on the uptake and it's been getting rather boring. I wanted to make sure the police were well interested in this project. Anyway,' she said frankly as a spark danced uncannily in her eyes, 'I liked killing them.'

Anna's legs felt weak and she leaned carefully back against the trestle table to support herself. Her mouth was dry and she had to force her next words out. 'But who are you trying to blame?' she asked, sounding as confused as she felt, and wondering what on earth was keeping Hugh and the others so long. 'Mike? But you've tried to kill him too.'

Sue looked at her in contempt. 'You think you're so clever, don't you? And yet you can't see what's right under your nose. Mike's killed himself, you know. Out of remorse,' she sniggered, 'at betraying his friends. They'll swallow that, the fools. He was the ringleader, of course, wanting the money. They all do, if not for themselves, they want it for their work. So when Brett and Hamilton began to suspect him, he had to get rid of them. He was too deeply involved in it by then to refuse to do this job, even though it meant ruining his friends. But he felt the net tightening round him and couldn't bear the disgrace, or the loss of the Walbury chair.' She looked delighted. 'There are lots of motives. They can take their pick. I did think of pinning it on Liz,' she added wistfully. 'Seeing her mooning around after him,' Sue gestured at the still figure in the chair behind her, 'made the idea almost irresistible. I don't like her,' she confided to Anna. 'She patronises me. Her and her paintings. It would've been easy to set it up too, but she doesn't have enough brains to make it plausible.'

Anna felt a hysterical desire to laugh as she realised that Sue considered Mike was bright enough to have carried out her crimes, but it faded rapidly as Sue moved again. Matching her steps and still holding onto the table lightly, Anna's hand brushed the pitcher. She asked curiously, 'But how did you kill Duncan? John Brett must have been easy. You just pushed him off the cliff, didn't you?'

'It's always easy if you've got the wits and the guts,' Sue sneered. 'I just make the most of my opportunities, that's all. Brett was in a state over his marriage that day, and when I saw him go off I knew where he was going. He always walked the same stretch of cliffs. I met him there accidentally,' she stressed the word with a smile in her voice, 'and of course all he wanted to do was talk about his problems and how unreasonable his wife was being. I walked with him for a while listening to his whining, and when we came to the narrow bit of path I baulked at it, so he nobly rushed ahead to show me it wasn't a problem. I crept along nervously at his heels and when we reached the worst bit I insisted on walking right behind him and just took the chance to push him over.'

She described it as if it were the most natural thing in the world, and Anna was rather afraid that it might be for her. Sue's face clouded. 'He managed to grip the edge as he went over, though,' she said peevishly, 'so I had to prise him loose.' Her eyes gleamed. 'You should have seen his face. He just couldn't believe it.'

She began to laugh softly and Anna felt her skin crawl. She kept her face composed with a huge effort as her thoughts raced wildly. Where on earth are the others? Has something happened to Will? Her blood chilled and she glanced at Hades, lying quietly in his corner watching them with bright eyes.

All I can do is keep her talking, Anna realised with despair, and pray that somebody comes soon. 'But surely,' she managed to sound puzzled as she tried to encourage Sue's revelations, 'Duncan must have been more difficult?'

The inhuman laughing stopped abruptly. 'Difficult? Of course not.' She stared scornfully at Anna. 'Steven gave me the opportunity I needed when he started fighting with David that evening on the way home from the pub. We left them to it but Philly was fussing about David so I went back from the farmhouse to check on them. They'd run out of steam when their audience left so I took the chance to call at Duncan's cottage, and tell him I was afraid something was going to happen at the priory that evening. He was already bothered about all the little incidents that he'd heard about, so I knew that he'd want to go out and see what was going on.' Sue's face was rounded with complacency, but then she frowned. 'It was funny, though, the painting being damaged. Almost,' she smiled unpleasantly, 'as if somebody was helping me.'

She shrugged dismissively. 'But I don't need any help. While Duncan went out to the back of his cottage to check a noise I'd heard, I slipped a large dose of vodka in his drink. I knew he had a bottle. I was in the shop when Mrs Hamble was talking about how much alcohol he'd bought.' A flash of amusement crossed her face. 'He'd probably got it for the party, but I planned to emphasise the story if I needed to. And I bought him another bottle of vodka when I collected his manuscript – and could easily say he'd asked me to get it.' Her eyes glittered with pleasure. 'He didn't notice a thing when he returned to the room, and just knocked his drink back while we talked. We definitely didn't want to arouse any suspicion if there was something going on,' the nasty smile touched her lips again, 'and I certainly wasn't going to let him go out on his own, so we arranged to meet later that night by the lake.' She sighed theatrically. 'It was all so easy. I just went back to the farmhouse and chatted to the others until they went to bed. I had a late bath, slipped out of the bathroom window and went down to the lake where I spotted him waiting. I'd already chosen a good piece of wood and put it ready, so all I had to do was pick it up before I approached him. The alcohol had really hit him and the fool just couldn't understand why he was so groggy,' she giggled. 'He was unsteady and his reactions were slow, so when I got him to come to the edge of the lake and hit him he went in without any struggle. I thought I'd have to hold him down, but he didn't even try to get up. I waited until I was sure he was dead and then I went back to the farmhouse, through the window into the bathroom. I went to bed soon afterwards with a particularly good alibi as I passed Philly, who'd come down to make a drink in the kitchen.'

Sue looked mockingly at Anna, who was unable to keep the shocked aversion out of her expressive face. 'It was easy,' Sue said complacently. 'Luck is always on my side. But just in case, I made sure I found him in the morning so any marks on the ground or my clothes would be accounted for.'

Anna was appalled at the simplicity of it all. 'And now you've poisoned Mike,' she said forcefully. 'How did you get him to take something from you?'

'Why shouldn't he?' Sue replied. 'He wasn't suspicious of me, so I just gave him a large whisky with a sedative overdose in it. I always carry supplies with me, they're so useful to have to hand, and this time I just dissolved all I had and mixed them in with a small amount of Jack Leygar's whisky. I was sure the alcohol would improve the effect of the sedatives, and I wasn't sure I'd be able to supply it here. But it was simple,' she said arrogantly. 'I was so concerned about him, you see, that I called in before I left and insisted that he have something to drink. I spilled whisky from his bottle when I poured it into his glass, so I dried it off with my hanky when I put it down on his desk. No fingerprints except his will be found on it. He didn't really want it, but he knocked it back to please me. You don't like that, do you?' she asked shrewdly. 'You fancy him yourself. That's why Liz doesn't like you.'

Her eyes glowed as she stared at Anna. 'That's going to be useful. Funny really that it should be you. I thought it was Lucy who might be a problem.'

'Lucy?' Anna looked completely puzzled. 'How does she come into it?'

Sue's tone was irritable as she said, 'She was at the stile when I came back down the cliff path after dealing with Brett.' She frowned. 'I was careless, I didn't realise she was there until Hades came up to me. Fortunately a sea mist had come down unexpectedly and she decided to turn back. For a while I thought she'd come to get Hades, who was keen to stay with me.' She laughed, a chilly unamused sound. 'I always make friends with dogs. Then they never object to me if I'm wandering around their territory. It generally pays off, but for an instant I thought it was going to misfire that time. In the end I just ignored Hades and he went back to Lucy, so I only had to wait until she'd returned to the house with him. I didn't think she'd seen me, but I wasn't sure.'

Anna blood ran cold as she thought of Lucy's narrow escape. 'Why did you come back here tonight?' she asked abruptly. She was curious in spite of the increasing danger, but anxiously wondered how much longer she could spin out the conversation. She glanced at Mike fearfully, thinking that she heard a slight alteration in his hurried breathing, but he still lay motionless in the chair beside the desk.

Sue put her hand into her other pocket and drew out a small leather-bound book. 'Conclusive evidence,' she said with pleasure, holding it up so that Anna could see it before she put it down on the work table. 'The fools thought the chalice was the target. And so it will be when I get a chance. But he'd arranged for the theft of the letters they're keeping so quiet about, involving me innocently to deliver them to his accomplice on the drive. But he made his first real error, he couldn't bear to leave the books behind or to give this one away. I know he's fond of it, he told me so himself in front of the others when I asked. Those friends of his will probably remember it too. Clever, don't you think? And I'll make sure it has his fingerprints on it.'

Anna was gazing at her incredulously when Mike's shallow breathing faltered and he groaned. The sound distracted both women, but Anna recovered first and turned to grab the pitcher. She swung round to face Sue, whose figure was now between her and Mike, concealing the unconscious man.

'It won't make any difference, you know,' Sue said complacently. 'A few broken pots can be explained quite easily. You smashed them in a frenzy when you realised what he'd done. Then you killed yourself. Such a shame nobody realised how much you cared about him.'

'Nobody will believe that.' Anna was defiant, ignoring the doubt niggling in her mind. Sue's version did sound plausible. And all her previous scenarios had been accepted without question. 'How will you explain where I got the dagger from?' she asked, rallying her thoughts and noting out of the corner of her eye that Hades had risen to his feet and was watching the two women uncertainly. 'I suppose that's what you plan to use.'

'Well,' Sue hesitated, then her voice regained its confidence, 'I suppose you must have abstracted it this morning. I'll make sure I remember when you had the opportunity.'

Anna spread her arms wide so that her yellow woollen coat flared out around her, bumping the rubber torch against her hip. A new hope sprang up in her mind as she demanded, 'And where would I put it?'

Sue's eyes narrowed as she stared at her suspiciously. 'Why not in one of those big pockets?' she asked.

'Because the handle would show, wouldn't it, just as it did in your pocket?'

Sue shrugged. 'So? Who'd have noticed?'

'Will,' Anna spat out triumphantly. 'He came down here with me, and he's the last person to have missed any sign of the dagger.'

Sue stared at her, her mind grappling with this. 'Will,' she repeated slowly, glancing round the room as if she expected him to be lurking in the shadows. Hades' ears pricked up alertly at the sound of his master's name, but Sue's eyes began to gleam as she saw the implications. She turned back to Anna, her hand tightening on the dagger.

Anna recognised the danger immediately and responded instinctively while Sue's attention was still distracted. She raised the heavy pitcher and lobbed it as hard as she could, praying that her aim would be good. Sue saw it coming and ducked, but it still caught her heavily on the shoulder, knocking her off-balance and loosening her grip on the dagger, which dropped with a clang to the floor as the jug shattered around it. She recovered almost immediately and bent over to pick up the weapon, but Anna sprang forward and struck her wrist heavily with the rubber torch. The two women faced each other, Sue grasping her injured wrist with her other hand and Anna gripping the torch firmly, waiting for her adversary's next move.

Inspector Elliot did not see the figure at the foot of the tower and reacted sharply when Will stepped out of the shadows by the porter's door. 'Sssh,' the youth hissed warningly, raising a finger to his lips as the inspector lowered his arm. 'They're on the stairs outside the finds room. Sue's in there with Anna. She's got a dagger.' His voice wavered and he turned sharply at the sound of a light step on the stairs.

Lucy crossed the porter's room swiftly and stood beside her brother. 'Thank God you're here. It's getting hairy in there. Do you think there's a chance of distracting Sue? Or should we just try to rush in and overwhelm her?'

'Is she threatening Miss Evesleigh?' Elliot asked quickly.

'Yes,' Lucy said. 'Anna's been stringing her along so we've heard the whole story, but she's almost run out of things to ask.' She twined her fingers tightly together as she looked at the inspector. 'Anna doesn't know we're here. I'm worried she'll try to do something on her own. She must know there isn't much time left.'

'Do you know whereabouts in the room they are?' the inspector demanded.

'We haven't risked looking into the room, but it sounds as though they're both on the far side,' Lucy replied.

'That's where Mike is,' Will said quickly. 'At the desk in the corner.'

'Is there any chance he'll come round?' the inspector asked, without much hope.

Will shook his head decisively. 'No. He's dead to the world.' He flinched as he heard the words he had used.

'Then we'd better take a chance on rushing her,' the inspector decided with distaste.

'Or,' said Lucy, 'I could go in and try and distract her, even if it's only for a moment.'

The inspector studied her and then nodded. 'Very well. We'll be close behind you.'

Lucy went cautiously back up the stairs, pausing at the top to raise her finger warningly to her lips as Hugh and the police constables turned in the darkness to look at her. She pointed down the stairs, which the inspector was climbing cautiously, with Will behind him. As Hugh peered past her she slipped round the door into the room, neatly evading the hand he put out as he realised her intention.

'Anna,' she began as she appeared in the dimly lit interior. Both the women near the desk swung round, startled. 'Will...'

'Look out, Lucy!' Anna shouted as Sue stepped back, kicking the dagger along the floor with one foot and bending swiftly to pick it up. Anna sprang forward, raising her torch, but Sue was faster. She moved, not towards Lucy, but to the recumbent figure in the chair.

She wrapped the fingers of one hand in Mike's wet hair, pulling his head back to hold the point of the dagger to his exposed throat with her other hand. She looked triumphantly from Lucy to Anna, smiling. Her smile broadened as she saw the reinforcements coming through the door, pausing just inside the threshold.

'Stay where I can see you,' she commanded in a steady tone. 'Ah, Inspector, I'm glad you're here.' Elliot stepped forward from the others and approached the central work table, but Sue said sharply, 'No, stay where you are. Come any further and he loses what chance he has.' She increased the pressure on the dagger she held as the inspector came to a halt, and a slight sluggish trickle of blood began to run down Mike's neck.

Sue noticed with pleasure that Anna's lips were tightly compressed and said pointedly, 'He'll bleed a lot more if you don't do what I say. And if you don't do it quickly he'll be dead anyway.' She looked down at him dispassionately. 'I'd say you've just got a chance if you get to work on him immediately.' Her eyes turned to the inspector. 'I want out,' she said bluntly, 'and if you want him, alive,' she nodded down at Mike, 'you'll make sure I get out.'

Elliot met her stare squarely. 'You know I can't do that,' he replied. 'I'd need higher authority to arrange something this important. By the time I've got it you'll have lost your bargaining counter.'

She shrugged nonchalantly. 'Your choice, then. I haven't got a lot to lose, after all. I was only doing what he told me.'

Anna drew in her breath with a hiss, but Hugh spoke first. 'That isn't what we heard you say just now,' he said deliberately.

Sue's eyes narrowed and she glanced with sudden hatred at Anna, her hand tightening on the dagger so that the flow of blood down Mike's throat increased.

'What the devil's going on here?' A loud grumpy voice

distracted them all. Anna took immediate advantage of the opportunity, to the open-mouthed surprise of the doctor standing dumbfounded in the doorway. She leaped forward with the torch raised and hit Sue hard on the side of the head, so that her spectacles fell to the floor. The student staggered and Anna hit her again, while Hades joined the fray, barking wildly, and bit Sue in the leg.

Elliot caught Anna's hand as she raised the torch again. 'That's enough. It's alright now. You've done it.'

One of the police constables had seized Sue's right hand and pulled the dagger out of it, kicking it far aside under the trestle table. The other constable went swiftly to his aid as she fought wildly, kicking out at Hades who was darting round her legs nipping every time he got the chance. Will rushed to pull his dog away and the constables managed to pinion her arms behind her back while the inspector clipped handcuffs around her wrists. She stood silently, her chest heaving and her eyes looking malevolently round at them.

Dr Bishop had edged past the work table during the struggle and was making a quick examination of Mike's still body. His face was impassive, his eyes hidden by his bushy eyebrows as he bent over his patient, raising Mike's eyelids, taking his pulse and listening to his heart. Anna joined him, shaking all over, but she controlled herself with difficulty until he straightened up and looked at her. 'Do you know what he took?' he demanded.

'She,' Anna nodded towards Sue, who glared back at her, 'said she gave him a sedative overdose in whisky.'

The doctor frowned. 'How long ago?'

'Between five and six o'clock, I should think,' Anna said after making a quick calculation.

'Hmm,' he drew up an injection and inserted it deftly into Mike's arm. 'Be a good girl and go down to guide the ambulance crew.'

Anna made a gesture of impatience. 'Me? Can't...'

'I'll go,' Lucy offered quickly.

Doctor Bishop glanced at her as she stood behind her friend. 'Better both go,' he said brusquely. 'Company's a good thing right now.'

'But,' Anna began to protest and was summarily cut off as he roared at her, 'Don't argue with me, young lady. Get on and do as I say if you want to help him.' He relented slightly as she gazed fearfully at the man in the chair. 'Nothing will change before you get back. And,' he added with a flicker of humour, 'you've already done your best here.'

Lucy touched her arm gently. Anna turned and followed her out of the room silently, passing by the imprisoned Sue without a glance.

Dr Bishop met the inspector's eyes as the two women ran down the stairs. He shook his head. 'There's a chance,' he said wearily in his gruff voice, 'but a mighty slim one if I'm honest. It's been a long time.'

Hugh's face was grim. 'Can we do anything for him now?'

'Pray,' the doctor replied bluntly. 'The less we move him before the ambulance gets here the better.'

He looked at the girl, held firmly between the two policemen, and shook his head again. She met his gaze defiantly and then her eyes faltered as she caught sight of Will. He had hold of Hades' collar and stood miserably beyond the doctor, gazing at her in horror.

'It was such a thrill, Will,' she said, attempting to stretch out a hand towards him. 'They thought they were so clever, but I fooled them all.' She stared at him, wanting him to agree, to understand, and then she saw the tears trickling unheeded down his white face, while Hades pressed close to his legs. Her eyes fell for the first time and her brows drew together.

A bustle at the foot of the stairs disturbed them, heralding heavy footsteps on the stairs. Sergeant Peters poked his head around the door. 'Sir, we're here, and the ambulance is coming down the drive.' He glanced round the crowded room, his eyes widening. 'Cranley has picked up another woman outside.

Swearing at him like a trooper, she was, when we appeared. He'd caught sight of her near the lodge and followed her up here. He didn't intervene until she tried to light a fire in the cloisters.'

'Who is she?' the inspector demanded.

Sergeant Peters shrugged. 'Won't say, sir. A nasty piece of work, though.'

'Do you want me to come down and see if I know her?' Hugh asked.

'Yes,' Elliot said gratefully, 'that would be a good idea.' He turned to the sergeant. 'Take over here, Tom. Get her down to the station, and,' he added as the sergeant took hold of Sue's arm, 'watch her.'

TEN

'I suppose it had to be the good jug,' Mike said in a resigned voice as he sprawled with his hands behind his head and his feet up on the squashy sofa in the manor's sitting room. 'It was the only complete one we found. There were plenty of other things you could have thrown at her.'

Anna turned from the table, where she was flicking through the pages of a heap of newspapers, and glared down at him. 'You ungrateful pig! I really don't know why I bothered to save you. It would have been a lot easier just to have left you to die.' Her voice faltered and she looked away from him as tears sprang unexpectedly into her eyes.

Mike leaned sideways on the sofa, reaching out to take one of her hands, clenched into fists by her side. Anna wrenched it away sharply and stalked over to the French windows where she gripped one of the thick blue curtains and stared out unseeingly. Snow had been falling heavily for some time and already the terrace was coated in white, while swirling curtains of large flakes obscured the lawn and the trees beyond the side drive. Against the monochrome backdrop her long dark hair lay like a cape around the red jumper she wore over narrow tartan trousers.

'Anna, I'm sorry,' Mike said contritely, swinging his legs to the floor and sitting up. 'Of course, I don't mind the jug. You could have smashed the whole damned collection for all I care.' He grinned broadly. 'At least you hit her with it, so it wasn't completely wasted.'

Anna sniffed and surreptitiously took a lace-edged handkerchief out of her pocket to wipe her eyes. She blew her nose defiantly and Mike said, 'Anna, look, I was just trying to be funny. Please come back here. I didn't mean to upset you.'

'Huh!' Anna sounded disbelieving as she kept her face towards the window. Behind her the sofa creaked and she swung round. 'Mike!' she declared angrily. 'You know you're not supposed to get up.' She walked stiffly back across the room to the table. 'Alright, let's forget it,' she said frostily, her blue eyes shadowed and her smooth cheeks lacking their normal rosy tint. 'But,' she added as he studied her face, 'don't try to be funny again. I can't cope with your humour at the moment.'

Mike leaned forward and took her hand after a slight struggle, drawing her down to sit reluctantly beside him. 'For God's sake, Anna,' he exclaimed in exasperation as she contemplated the floor, 'stop being so difficult. I'm really grateful. Really and truly. Thank God for that self-defence course. We seem to benefit from it all the time.'

She lifted her head and looked indignantly at him. He frowned as he ran his free hand through his hair, demanding crossly, 'What do I have to say for you to believe me?' He yanked her towards him, catching her by surprise. They glowered at each other as he said roughly, 'Thank you for saving my life.' He kissed her hard and then pulled away abruptly, staring at her in horror. 'That damn drug must still be affecting me,' he growled, his face reddening.

Anna hit him on the shoulder with a clenched fist. 'Mike!' She leaped to her feet, flushed with rage, but the words that sprang to her lips were never uttered as she became aware of the opening door.

'Oh, I'm sorry,' Lucy stammered, halting disconcerted just inside the doorway. 'I didn't know, at least, I mean...' She stopped, aware that she was babbling. Hugh pushed her gently into the room as he glanced from Anna to Mike, his eyebrows raised, and amusement deepened in his eyes.

'Well, you could have timed it worse, I suppose,' Mike said grudgingly. 'At least we've been spared a display of judo.'

Anna's blush deepened. She inadvertently met Lucy's eyes and giggled. 'I know, I know,' she spluttered, and suddenly the two of them were laughing.

Mike stared at them in outrage as they sank weakly onto chairs near the table. 'I'm glad to see you're both in such good form,' he said sarcastically. 'Do you want something in particular?' he asked Hugh. 'I'm supposed to be resting quietly, but nobody seems to recognise the fact.'

Hugh was regarding the women tolerantly as they mopped at their streaming eyes. He turned towards the sofa and dropped another newspaper on Mike's lap. 'I thought you'd like to see this one. It only gives a brief account of the evening, but it's got a couple of good photos. They must have acquired one of Anna's publicity shots. Yours,' he grinned, 'is rather more basic.'

He strolled over to add another log to the steadily burning wood on the hearth before he sat down in an armchair near the fireplace. 'Elliot has just rung to say he's on his way up here. Apparently he's got a lot to tell us, and we thought you and Anna would like to hear what he has to say.'

Mike was glowering at the newspaper in his hands, his expression mirroring the one in his photographic image. He looked up, his face hardening. 'Yes, of course I would.' He glanced quickly at Anna, who face was recovering its usual vivacity and colour. 'I still can't believe any of it,' he said, shaking his head. 'Why on earth did Sue do it?'

'The sheer pleasure of being able to, from what we heard her telling Anna. She seemed very proud of her achievements,' Hugh said. He added dryly, 'I imagine that her defence will try to make out a case for diminished responsibility.'

The laughter drained from the faces of the women at the table as they heard this. Lucy lifted her head, brushing back her curtain of chestnut hair, and Anna swivelled on her seat to face Hugh.

'Do you think she's mad?' Mike asked Hugh doubtfully.

Hugh shrugged. 'I think she has a very acute mind, which she chose to turn to criminal activities. It seems to me that she lacks a conscience, an acceptance, if you like, of general values of right and wrong.'

Anna shivered, remembering that egotistical voice in the gatehouse on Thursday evening. 'She talked about killing people as if it was a logical solution to a problem,' she said flatly.

'We were lucky,' Hugh commented, 'in more ways than one. The Dudley letters were found with the books, hidden among the papers on the table in the porter's room. She could quite easily have disposed of them before coming back to finish incriminating Mike, but it seems that she worked totally alone this time.'

'It's incredible how easily she fooled us all,' Mike sounded irritable as he yanked at the neck of his jumper.

'I know,' Lucy said. 'I'm afraid Will is taking it rather hard. He got on very well with Sue.'

'He'll get over it,' Isobel Rossington said briskly as she entered the sitting room, with Juno tripping daintily at her heels. Lucy hastily pushed the newspapers on the central table to one side so that Isobel could put down the tray she was carrying. A tantalising aroma arose from the jug as she began to pour coffee into delicate patterned cups.

Gina appeared in the doorway holding another laden tray. 'Where would you like this one, Isobel?'

'You'd better put it here,' Isobel replied as Juno settled herself comfortably underneath the table. 'There'll be plenty of room if Lucy takes the papers off the table. We seem to have all the Saturday editions,' she added, glancing quickly at the pile.

'Hugh had to go into Corrington to get them,' Lucy said

as she got up from her seat, gathering the newspapers together and moving a few steps to deposit them in an untidy pile on the sideboard. 'Mrs Hamble had completely sold out in the village shop.'

Gina moved lithely across the room, her flowered pinafore flying out around her long legs. 'I've made everyone's favourites,' she announced, holding the tray as Lucy unloaded plates of cakes and biscuits.

'Thanks Gina,' Anna said as she got to her feet and took the pile of individual plates to pass around. 'Fancy remembering how much I like those ginger shortbreads. There was nothing that good in Paris.'

Mike regarded the blueberry muffins appreciatively as Gina picked up the empty tray and left the room. 'Mmm, I think I'm getting my appetite back.'

'I hadn't noticed you'd lost it,' Anna said mockingly as she picked up a couple of plates of cakes.

Mike lifted his gaze from the table and looked across at her as she offered them to Hugh. 'I meant the food,' he said meaningfully, and enjoyed the flush that stained her cheeks as her eyes met his furiously.

Mrs Rossington observed them with a knowing eye, raising one of her strongly marked eyebrows as she glanced at Lucy. 'Well, Mike, you've got competition,' she said ambiguously, passing him the dish of muffins. 'The inspector was parking in the courtyard as I left the kitchen, so I asked Will to bring him along here.'

As she spoke Hades came bouncing into the sitting room, heralding his master and the inspector, whose hair was glistened with melting flakes of snow. Mike hastily took a muffin and dropped it onto his plate as Isobel put the dish safely back on the table, just as the black dog came over eagerly to investigate.

Elliot glanced round the room, appreciating the pine bough above the fireplace and the strings of cards looped around the walls. The stoneware vase had been brought from the drawing room to stand on the sideboard, where the tawny and ruby shades of the shaggy chrysanthemums glowed against the polished wood and mingled their earthy scent with the smell of burning logs.

The inspector crossed to the sofa to shake Mike's free hand. 'Well, Professor,' he stood back and considered the other man. 'Will told me you were here. I'm glad to see you looking so much better. You had us worried on Thursday night, but once we'd got you to the hospital the consultant said you had a constitution of iron.'

'That wasn't all he said,' Will muttered, not quite beneath his breath, pausing by the coffee table to reach out for a coconut macaroon.

'I bet it wasn't,' Mike said, grinning at him as the youth moved to take up his stance on the hearthrug, while Hades exchanged greetings with Juno before sniffing hopefully around the table. He explained to the inspector, 'The doctors wanted me to stay in for longer but it was bl...flaming awful in there. There wasn't any reason why I shouldn't come back here, so I discharged myself last night.'

'And you didn't want to miss anything,' Lucy said, passing a cup of coffee to her brother as Hades sat down beside Elliot, pressing himself against the inspector's immaculate grey trousers.

'Well,' Mike responded indignantly, 'of course I didn't. I'd already missed quite enough.' He scowled. 'When I think...'

'Don't,' Anna said quickly as she resumed her seat near the table. 'Don't think about it.'

The inspector had been tickling Hades behind the ears. He straightened now and the big dog looked at him reproachfully before he wandered with deliberate slowness over to the fireplace to throw himself heavily across Will's feet. Elliot lifted an upright chair into a position on the far side of the coffee table so that he could see the whole room. He sat down and stretched out his long legs as he studied Anna. 'You did very well, Miss

Evesleigh,' he said as she met his gaze. 'The outcome could have been rather different if you hadn't acted as you did.'

All Anna's happy colour had receded and her face was pale again. 'I can't bear to think of what might have happened,' she muttered, lowering her blue eyes to stare at her hands.

'Now don't be stupid,' Mike commanded. 'It didn't, so don't fret.'

'And that's mainly thanks to Miss Evesleigh,' the inspector interposed with respect. 'Sue's got some noticeable bruises, you know. I'm glad we don't have to account for them ourselves.'

'Did the jug do that much damage?' Mike asked with surprised interest.

'I hit her with the torch as well,' Anna said crossly. 'More than once, I think.' She caught sight of Will's white face as he bent down to fondle the big dog who lay at his feet, his curly head on his paws and his eyes gleaming as he gazed at his master. 'I had to stop her,' she explained slowly, 'but oddly enough I don't think she understood that what she was doing was, oh, what's the word...' She looked round hopefully.

'Criminal?' suggested Hugh.

'Wrong?'

'Unprincipled?'

'No, no.' She waved her hand impatiently. 'Sue knew that alright, but it's almost as if she thought she'd find like-minded people who'd appreciate what she'd done.' Anna looked at Will uncertainly. 'I think it was only when she saw how horrified you were that she had an inkling of how her actions would place her completely beyond the pale.'

'Indefensible,' Hugh interposed quietly.

'Yes,' Anna agreed gratefully, 'that's the word I wanted.'

Will had straightened up and was listening with interest. His expression was a little brighter as he walked across to the table to take the last macaroon.

'Whatever her thoughts may have been,' the inspector said bluntly, 'to our certain knowledge she tried to murder Professor

Shannon, successfully killed two other men here and disposed of we don't yet know how many more elsewhere. Not to mention masterminding various specialist thefts during the last two years.'

'It will be a load off Steven's mind,' Mrs Rossington said, placing a cup of coffee on the table near the inspector's elbow and pushing the dishes closer to him. 'He seems a different man this morning. I suppose there were others left under suspicion too?'

'Yes,' Elliot said. 'She seemed to have a knack for doing that. One she enjoyed indulging. There will be a lot of people feeling a great deal of relief soon.' He smiled ruefully. 'The police really did suspect most of them too, you know, but couldn't take any action because of the lack of sufficient evidence.' He sipped his coffee, glancing over the cup at Hugh. 'I was very concerned to find young Poole ensconced here, although I couldn't really believe he had the brains to carry out any of the jobs.'

Anna shivered, reminded again of Thursday night. 'Sue said you wouldn't believe he could do it,' she said quietly. 'Mike fitted her bill better.'

The inspector put his cup down and continued, 'She was obviously suspicious about your intentions when you still brought out the chalice that evening, so she went right down to the lake to make her way round to the gatehouse. That's why none of my men in the grounds saw her. They were all concentrated near the tracks.' He looked at Mike. 'We think she might have been pushed into acting rather faster than she'd planned. Our preliminary enquiries have thrown up an interesting name. Dr Archison visited one of the excavations she worked on, at a house that was later robbed...'

Mike snorted with laughter. 'Archison!' he interrupted. 'You're not going to tell me they were in cahoots. It's impossible. Wait until you've met the man. He wouldn't have the gumption.'

Elliot's face remained imperturbable, although his lips

twitched. 'She isn't likely to have had a permanent collaborator. But it is possible she was afraid Dr Archison might recognise her, even though she changes her hair style and colour whenever she moves on. She didn't need the spectacles she wore either, but they altered her appearance quite considerably.'

Hugh uttered a sharp exclamation and they turned to look at him in surprise. 'Anthony Talmage thought he'd seen a familiar face, you know, when we were looking round the priory on Tuesday.' He explained, seeing the puzzled expression on the inspector's face, 'Anthony's an architect who specialises in historic building conversions. He's looking at some options for us. It's very likely that he's worked at one of the other houses that was robbed when Sue was around.'

'Oddly enough,' Lucy said slowly, 'I think the only person who was at all suspicious of her was Liz, who had an inkling that she wasn't quite what she seemed to be.'

'You're probably right,' Hugh agreed. 'I imagine Sue knew it too and tried to poison people's minds against her. If you think back, it was Sue who managed to insert little jibes at her, often planting them in Josie's mind so that she repeated them. They shared a room at the farm, so it was quite easy. You both had a lucky escape, you know.'

He met and held Lucy's eyes. 'If she had really thought you'd seen her on the cliffs she would have got rid of you. I doubt that even her fondness for Will would have overcome her instinct.' His lips twisted. 'And that business with Liz and the wall painting in the church really played into Sue's hands. Her reputation as a promising student certainly wasn't wrong. She's a very clever young woman, but what a waste of her quite genuine talents.'

'She'd have been a damn good archaeologist,' Mike said morosely. 'A shame that wasn't enough for her. And,' he added furiously, 'we still don't know who was responsible for the damage to the painting.'

'Who was the other woman?' Anna demanded suddenly.

'The one you found in the courtyard that night.'

The inspector smiled approvingly across the table at her. 'Ah, yes. Now that's interesting.' His glance flickered around the enquiring faces that were turned towards him. 'You haven't mentioned it then?' he asked Hugh.

Hugh shook his head. 'Only to Lucy. I thought,' he said blandly, 'you might enjoy the effect.'

A spark of humour shone in Elliot's cool grey eyes. 'Well,' he looked at Mike, 'Mr Carey identified her as the woman who is staying with Tilly Barlow in the village. Her name is Edie Shade.'

Colour surged up into Mike's face. 'That psychic woman?' he demanded curtly.

'Yes,' the inspector replied. 'We've questioned her and Tilly Barlow about any complicity with Sue.'

Lucy gasped. 'Surely you don't think Tilly's involved in it?'

'Not really,' Elliot said levelly, 'but she's been on the fringes of trouble here before, so we can't ignore the possibility. I think we'll find again that she knew or guessed what was going on. I'm sure it was the Shade woman who was behind all the petty incidents at the priory.'

'Did she damage the painting?' Mike demanded, his fists clenched on his knees as he leaned forward.

'I think so, but whether we can prove it is another matter.'

'Why?' Mike asked angrily.

'We haven't got any evidence,' the inspector replied succinctly. 'And she isn't the sort to admit anything. We've got her on a charge of trespass and attempted criminal damage at the moment, but that won't take us far. Although,' he added, 'Steven apparently saw her walking away from the gatehouse on Tuesday at about lunchtime, when he was returning from the village. He mentioned it to her that evening and she reacted rather violently, but I don't think he realised the implications at the time.'

Hugh rubbed his ear thoughtfully as he looked at Mike.

'Wouldn't the damage done to the painting have been rather messy? Liz always seems to be covered with dust and bits of plaster when she's working there.'

'Of course she is. The plaster crumbles however carefully she operates,' Mike agreed impatiently, and then his eyes widened. 'You mean...'

'Yes.' Hugh turned to the inspector. 'If this woman is responsible for the damage in the church, surely you'd find traces of plaster on her clothes.'

A satisfied expression spread over Elliot's countenance as he considered this. 'It's a long shot,' he said, 'but worth trying, even if it only puts the wind up her.' He looked faintly apologetic as his gaze met Hugh's. 'She's the type who gets my goat. You know, anything she wants is right and anybody in her way is wrong.'

'Heavens,' Lucy groaned. 'Tilly will never forgive us if you're going to turn up at her cottage demanding this woman's clothes. I ran into her on my way to the shop this morning. She was lying in wait to tell me that Edie was quite innocent and that it was a vendetta against her. It took me ages to get away.'

'Did she realise she's a suspect too?' Anna asked curiously.

Lucy's gamine smile lit her face. 'She didn't seem to. I'm sure she'd have mentioned it.'

'I can't really believe she knew what was going on,' Anna commented. 'I shouldn't think Edie would let Tilly in on anything. I know I wouldn't.'

Will smiled at this. 'Why did Edie do all those things, though?' he asked, puzzled.

'Well,' Elliot said slowly, 'I think we'll find that she wanted to stop the dig. From the few comments she's condescended to make to us, she obviously regards it as a form of sacrilege.'

'Mad, quite mad,' Mike said as he leaned back on the sofa. 'Speaking of which, where's Mersett?'

'He stayed to make sure you were going to be alright,' Hugh replied. 'He was very concerned, you know.'

Mike threw back his head and laughed loudly. 'Still afraid he was going to be next?' he asked when he could speak.

'No,' Hugh said. 'That was sorted out by then. Once we'd got the all clear on you he took himself back to Oxford to fill them in on what's been happening. David drove him into Exeter to catch the early train yesterday.'

Lucy said quietly, 'The whole thing has shaken him very much, you know. I don't think we'll see him down here again for a while.'

Hades lifted his head curiously as the door opened and Gina breezed into the room, balancing another tray. 'I thought you'd just about be ready for this,' she said cheerfully as she crossed the room to put the tray down on the sideboard. 'I'll clear this lot away too, if you've all finished,' she added, glancing at the coffee table.

'Oh, definitely,' Lucy said, stacking the empty dishes, plates and cups onto the other tray. 'Will, it'll be lunch soon,' she admonished her brother as he hastily collected the macaroon crumbs with his finger.

'Lunch will be at one,' Gina declared as she picked up the tray of china. 'Pheasant casserole. There's plenty for everyone,' she added as she left the room.

Hugh closed the door behind her and walked over to the sideboard. 'Very nice,' he said, regarding the bottles of champagne in surprise.

'Would you open them please, Hugh. I bought them for a celebration,' Isobel said. 'This whole business has been very distressing for us all. Such a waste of life and intelligence. But it's time we put it behind us. We have lots to be grateful for. Mike's survival of course, but also the opportunities we've all got for interesting and happy times.' As the first champagne cork popped she glanced at her granddaughter and slightly closed one eye in a companionable wink. 'So,' she accepted a finely engraved glass as she spoke, 'let's drink to the future and the success of all our plans.'

Lucy passed the glasses round to the others and raised hers silently to Hugh as everyone repeated Isobel's toast.

also by MARY TANT

Coming soon, the third mystery in the Rossington series

Friends…and a Foe

Life looks promising for Lucy Rossington and her family.
There is no way they could guess that in just a few days
their happiness might be shattered for ever.

Old friends rejoin the family circle – one of them brings
in their wake a secret that somebody would kill to keep.
How could the Rossingtons know that this secret will
cost them dearly?

Publication Spring 2009   ISBN 978–1–903152–22–5

Now in paperback

The Rossington Inheritance

Lucy Rossington has put a promising career on hold,
so that she can keep the family home going for her
young brother Will – not an easy task, when home is
an Elizabethan manor that the family have lived in for
generations.

When the taint of avarice and deceit from the past
seems to stain the present, it becomes essential to know
who she can trust, not only for her own happiness, but
also for the safety of her family and friends. Will she find
out in time?

Publication Spring 2008   ISBN 978–1–903152–21–8